Pinchh111

Suncoast Society

Tymber Dalton

SIREN SENSATIONS

Siren Publishing, Inc.
www.SirenPublishing.com

A SIREN PUBLISHING BOOK
IMPRINT: Siren Sensations

PINCH ME
Copyright © 2014 by Tymber Dalton

ISBN: 978-1-62740-774-8

First Printing: February 2014

Cover design by Harris Channing
All cover art and logo copyright © 2014 by Siren Publishing, Inc.

ALL RIGHTS RESERVED: This literary work may not be reproduced or transmitted in any form or by any means, including electronic or photographic reproduction, in whole or in part, without express written permission.

All characters and events in this book are fictitious. Any resemblance to actual persons living or dead is strictly coincidental.

Printed in the U.S.A.

PUBLISHER
Siren Publishing, Inc.
www.SirenPublishing.com

DEDICATION

To my Hubby, the love of my life, who makes it possible for me to pursue my dreams. And to Sir, who's taught me more than I ever thought possible. Cheese!

This one's also for Scudder, who was the inspiration for Doogie. We'll always love you, Buddy-butt. You'll always be part of our pack. Wait for us at the Rainbow Bridge with the others and say hi to them for us. We'll see you all again one day.

AUTHOR'S NOTE

While the books in the Suncoast Society series are standalone works, the recommended reading order to avoid spoilers is as follows:

1. *Safe Harbor*
2. *Cardinal's Rule*
3. *Domme by Default*
4. *The Reluctant Dom*
5. *The Denim Dom*
6. *Pinch Me*

Tony is also a minor character in *Domme by Default* and *The Reluctant Dom*. Tony and Shayla are featured in *The Denim Dom*. Tony also makes a vanilla appearance in *Two Geeks and Their Girl*. Sully, Mac, and Clarisse's story is told in *Safe Harbor*. Seth and Leah are the focus of *The Reluctant Dom*. Tilly and her men are featured in *Cardinal's Rule*.

PINCH ME

Suncoast Society

TYMBER DALTON
Copyright © 2014

Chapter One

Pain dragged her from the comfort of blissful, velvety dark unconsciousness. She didn't dare move, not even to open her eyes. Muted, distorted sounds wound their way to her brain seemingly from down a long hall. Her throat hurt, inside and out, painful and scratchy.

Something moved next to her, startling her. Before she could think she turned her head. Fireworks of pain blossomed behind her eyes.

Fade to black…

* * * *

"Is she awake?"

The nurse glanced up from her charts to the man who had stepped into the room. "Not yet."

Rob looked past the monitors, the IVs, the respirator standing silent sentry next to the bed. At first, he had a hard time remembering if it was Monday or Tuesday.

He glanced at his phone.

Nope, Tuesday.

For the first three days, Laura had been intubated, the respirator breathing for her. The neurologists thought it best to keep her in an induced coma to allow the brain swelling to subside.

"She still might not wake up for a while." The nurse tried to sound kind, but she was a professional, had seen too much. Knew the odds. She also knew Rob could handle the truth.

Paramedics were all too familiar with the effects of trauma.

"I know." But Laura had startled when he bent down next to her earlier. She was *there*. The monitors proved it. They had all gone off, recording her sudden agitation.

He leaned over the bed again and gently stroked the unconscious woman's cheek. "*Please*, baby girl," he whispered. "Come back to me. I love you."

"I'm afraid visiting hours are well past over," the nurse gently said. "You know I would normally let you stay, but I'm putting my foot down. You look horrible. You need to go home and get some real sleep. You're going to collapse if you keep this up. That won't do Laura any good. I promise we'll call you immediately if there's any change."

Rob kissed Laura's cheek and left, nodding to the deputy standing guard outside her ICU room before turning toward the elevators. It was after nine in the evening. Despite the late hour, on the way home he stopped by the sheriff's office on the off chance Det. Thomas was in.

He wasn't. There was nothing else Rob could do but go home and wait.

And that was all he'd done for the past four days.

He was sick of waiting. He couldn't help Laura, and the police had yet to catch the sadistic fuck who'd attacked her last Friday.

* * * *

Glimmers teased her mind—a dog's tail impatiently flicking, a loud splash and muffled sounds like she was underwater, the gentle caress of a man's touch and his tender words, the feel and sound of a hand smacking against bare flesh—

Her eyes snapped open and she couldn't stop the scream. It came out sounding more like a croak. She tried to sit up, bringing new bursts of agony from all over her body as well as renewed screams, of pain instead of fear this time.

An older woman dressed in white ran in, shouting something she didn't understand. Every movement brought new pain, and now she heard alarms going off.

A man. Where was the man who'd hurt her?

Where am I?

She should know this.

Another nurse and a man wearing blue scrubs ran in. He wasn't *the* man, but she shrieked and thrashed, hitting at him, pulling away from him in instinctive, primal terror.

The first nurse wrapped an arm around her and she finally collapsed against her, crying.

She was awake, she hurt like hell, she didn't know where she was, and worse...

She didn't know *who* she was.

* * * *

When Det. William Thomas' cell phone rang at 4:00 a.m. Wednesday morning and jolted him from sleep, he suspected it wouldn't be good news.

He grabbed it on the second ring. "Thomas."

"Det. Thomas? This is Dr. Singh from Charlotte County Regional Medical Center. Laura Spaulding woke up twenty minutes ago. You instructed us to call you."

Now he was more awake. It wasn't as bad as he thought it might be. "Can she talk?"

"She's still crying. She won't let go of one of the nurses. Male staff can't get within twenty feet of her. She nearly took my eye out when I tried to examine her."

He scrubbed his face with his hand and sat up on the edge of the bed. "When can I question her?"

"You should wait a couple of hours. Maybe until later in the morning. Hopefully we can get her calm and stabilized by then. We'd rather avoid sedating her considering she just awoke from a coma."

"Okay. I'll be there in a little while and wait for you to clear it. Nobody, and I mean *nobody*, except medical staff and my deputies, gets in to see her until I get to talk to her."

"Not even Rob?"

"Is he there?"

"No. The nurses ordered him home last night to sleep."

"Has anyone called him yet?"

"He's my next call."

"Hold off. I'll call him myself in a few minutes. I'll make sure a female deputy gets sent over."

"He won't like it, but okay."

Thomas hung up and dialed dispatch to get a female deputy sent over to the hospital. His second call was to Rob Carlton, Laura's fiancé.

"I'll be right over."

"No, you won't. She's upset and combative and they don't want to sedate her again. Meet me there at six."

An ominous moment of silence followed. "She's my fiancée."

"Yes, and she's also the victim of a violent crime. You want us to catch the animal who did this to her, then you need to not go barreling in there and scaring her."

"I can talk to her, calm her."

"Maybe, maybe not. But if you love her, you'll wait. And if you don't wait, I'll call over and make sure they take you into custody if you try to get into that room." He felt for the guy, he really did. However, Rob had to get it through his head that being emotional right now wasn't in Laura's best interest.

He waited for Rob to speak next.

"All right. Fine. I'll be in the ICU waiting room." Rob hung up on him.

As Thomas got up and headed for the shower, he knew he needed to get over to the hospital even sooner. Rob wasn't the kind of guy who would tolerate being kept from the woman he loved very long. The last thing he wanted was to have the guy arrested.

* * * *

When she finally calmed down, the nurse asked her if she wanted a drink of water. She nodded, and another nurse brought it. Her throat still hurt, the cold water setting off a coughing spell that made her ribs and stomach explode with agony.

She felt like passing out, but held on until the pain abated a little.

The second nurse took the cup from her while the first propped her up with some pillows. It took her three tries to get her swollen tongue to actually form coherent words.

"…name."

The woman smiled. "I'm Nancy Russell. I'm the ICU nursing supervisor tonight."

She shook her head.

Nancy Russell looked at the other woman. "That's Linda Kelly. She's your other nurse."

She shook her head again, licked her lips, and tried again. It hurt so much to talk, she had to make it count this time. "*My* name."

Nancy and Linda looked at each other. Nancy nodded toward the door. "Tell Dr. Singh we probably need someone from neuro. Stat."

Chapter Two

Thomas looked over the report one more time before leaving for the hospital.

Laura Spaulding, thirty-two, single but engaged. Last Friday evening, March third, the neighbor couple next to her condo heard something around 11:00 p.m. and the wife called 911.

The husband went over and knocked, then rushed in through the unlocked door when he heard the struggle, scaring the attacker off. The attacker—presumably a male based on the neighbor's description, even though he didn't see his face—ran through the back door. All they knew was an approximate height, and that the man's hair was a lighter shade than her fiancé's, and his build slimmer.

When the responding officers arrived they found Laura on the living room floor, unconscious. The neighbor had removed a rope that the attacker had wrapped around her neck. She'd been beaten nearly unrecognizable, choked, kicked, but not raped.

Probably only because her neighbor, Tom Edwards, had intervened. Very brutal. Potentially fatal, if not for the interruption.

She remained unconscious over four days. Mild cranial swelling, but it subsided on its own without surgery and it was too soon to tell how much, if any, brain damage had occurred. Cracked ribs. Lacerations, severe bruising. Whoever did this had it in for her in a bad way. It appeared to be more than just a random attack.

This looked like a rage-filled vendetta.

Her fiancé, Rob Carlton, had immediately been ruled out as a suspect. A county paramedic, at the time of the attack he'd been working a bad multi-car wreck on I-75, on the other side of the county, with at least ten other firemen and three Florida state troopers, not to mention several deputies, as witnesses. He'd also been caught in videos made by three cruiser dash cams on the scene, so there was no possibility anyone had lied to cover for him.

He was innocent.

Rob had spent the first forty-eight hours camped out either at her bedside in the ICU, or in the nurse's lounge, curled up in a chair.

Thomas never met Rob before this, but deputies who had all universally said he seemed to be a nice guy, devoted to Laura. They'd been together for two years, engaged for six months.

The condo on her other side was vacant, the snowbird owners already back in Ohio for the summer. Two of the condos in the other building were also vacated by their snowbird owners, and the third was occupied by an elderly couple in their eighties, who'd been awakened by a deputy knocking on their door that night.

They were immediately ruled out as suspects, considering the husband needed a walker to get around and the wife had bad arthritis.

He'd also ruled out her coworkers and employees. No one had motive to hurt her, and everyone had alibis. The universal reaction to the attack was shock and anger, with more than one person expressing an interest in helping to save the state of Florida the expense of a trial when the perpetrator was caught.

One man, Steve Moss, an old family friend of Laura's as well as a coworker, had offered Thomas the use of a wood chipper to take care of the attacker.

Thomas wondered if he'd be forced to deal with prosecuting a vigilante by the time this case was over.

Searches of her laptop, phone, iPad, and office computers also revealed nothing that would lead to a suspect.

Rob was already pacing in the ICU waiting room when Thomas arrived. In silence, they made their way past carts of breakfast trays to the ICU unit main desk. Laura's door was closed, the shades drawn. A female deputy sat outside in a chair by the door.

The officer, Corporal Dayton, stood when they approached.

"How is she?" Thomas asked.

Dayton shook her head. "Still freaked out. I hate to say this, sir, but you can't go in there without me. She's terrified of men. It took the nurses twenty minutes to talk her into letting a male doctor examine her with me in the room."

"Has she talked?"

"Only to ask a few questions. Her name, where she is, who we are." She looked at Rob. "I'm sorry, Rob, but she apparently doesn't remember anything."

* * * *

A chill settled over Rob as he stared at Dayton. He'd crossed paths with her many times during the course of his duties. "You mean Laura doesn't remember the attack?"

Dayton shook her head. "Anything. I heard the doctors say she has total amnesia. She didn't know her own name. The staff had to tell her." She nodded toward a doctor in blue scrubs and a white coat walking down the hall in their direction. In his hand he carried a chart.

Rob had gotten to know Dr. Singh quite well over the past few days. He was young, but good, based on his reputation.

"How is she?" Rob asked him.

Dr. Singh looked grim. "Fragile. Right now she appears to have total amnesia. We don't know if it's related to the physical or emotional trauma of the attack." He glanced at the deputy. "And thank you for sending a female deputy. That helped."

"Can I go talk to Laura?" Thomas asked.

Singh pursed his lips. "One at a time. I reserve the right to end it if she reacts badly. She's overwhelmed right now."

"Rob, you'd better wait out here," Thomas said.

Helpless anger rolled through him. "She's *my* fiancée!"

"Look," Thomas said. "All you're going to do is scare her. I know that's hard to hear. I *have* to talk to her. The guy who did this is still out there. I'll see how she is and we'll go from there." He hit below the belt. "If you love her, you'll listen to me."

"How *dare* you—"

"If we're going to catch who did this, I *need* to talk to her."

"He's right, Rob," the doctor agreed. "Let him talk to her."

Heartsick, Rob walked over to the nurses' station and leaned against it for support. "All right." He wasn't used to not being in charge.

Not when it came to Laura.

She was his life, his love.

His heart and soul.

His submissive, and soon to be his slave, once they got married.

Thomas nodded to the deputy. She slowly opened the door and went in ahead of him.

Dr. Singh put his arm around Rob's shoulders. "Are you okay?"

Rob shook his head. "I thought the end of this nightmare would be when she woke up."

"You have to focus on her and her needs. You can't get upset in front of her. She needs as much stability and strength as she can get right now. I don't want to sound callous, but if you can't hold it together, you need to stay out here. She's scared and confused and the last thing she needs is someone stirring things up."

Rob looked at him. That was a cruel irony. He spent his life focused on Laura and her needs, caring for her. His entire world revolved around her.

Not that he could ever tell any of these people about that aspect of their relationship. "She's my life. How do I go in there acting like everything's hunky-dory, when y'all are telling me she doesn't even know who I am?"

"I'm not saying you pretend everything's fine. I'm saying you have to be strong and stable right now. She needs to know that you're someone she can trust."

"I *am*."

"She doesn't remember that. Right now, she's terrified of men. She nearly took my head off when she came to." He pointed at his cheek.

Rob noticed a fresh, deep scratch on the doctor's face. "She did *that*?" He couldn't imagine his Laura attacking anyone.

Not *his* Laura.

He nodded. "She was freaked out. She woke up disoriented and combative. Fortunately, Nancy and the other nurses were able to get her calmed down so we didn't have to sedate and restrain her. She was screaming and swinging like she was fighting someone."

"From the attack?"

"I'm no psychiatrist, but I'd guess yes. Once she fully woke up she calmed down a little. Having a female uniformed deputy in there with her helped. But right now she's still very fragile."

* * * *

"Laura?" Corporal Dayton stuck her head through the door.

Laura looked up from her bowl of chicken broth. Her hand went up to her throat. She realized she'd been doing that a lot, like a reflexive gesture, but she didn't understand why.

It almost felt as if something was missing, something comforting.

"Det. Thomas is here to talk with you. I'm going to come in with him. He has to ask you some questions, okay?"

Laura looked at Nurse Russell, who sat in a chair next to her bed. She patted Laura on the hand. "It's okay, honey. I'll stay, too."

Laura gingerly nodded, pain and fear still in control of her body.

Dayton brought Thomas in and he stood by the door. "Hi, Laura. I'm Det. Thomas from the Charlotte County Sheriff's Office." He held up his badge holder so she could see it. "I need to talk with you for a few minutes. About what happened. Okay?"

Laura stiffened, but nodded, even though it hurt her neck to move her head much.

He took a few steps closer and pulled a notebook and pen from his back pocket. "Do you know what day it is?"

"It's Wednesday." She hesitated. "The nurses told me. I didn't know."

"Do you know what happened to you?"

"I only know what they told me. I don't remember anything. They said I was attacked."

Thomas slowly moved a chair over and sat a few feet from the end of her bed. Laura relaxed a little when it was obvious he wasn't getting any closer.

"Do you know where you live?"

She shook her head.

"Do you know where you are?"

"A hospital."

"Do you know which one?"

"In Pt. Charlotte. They told me that, too."

He looked at his notes. "Last Friday night, five days ago, around eleven o'clock, someone attacked you at your condo. Do you remember anything?"

She slowly shook her head. "Did he rape me?"

"No. Whoever it was didn't have time. You said 'he'? Do you remember it was a man?"

Laura thought about it. "Not really." She closed her eyes and let her mind drift, grasping at tenuous thoughts that escaped her. "All I remember is thinking it was a man."

"Do you have any idea what he looked like?"

Her eyes stayed closed. Eventually, she shook her head again.

"Okay. That's enough for now. I'm going to have a deputy stay by your door for as long as you're here. It sometimes might have to be a man though, okay?"

Her eyes opened, considering. She looked at Nurse Russell, who smiled and nodded. Finally, Laura nodded.

* * * *

Thomas looked at Nurse Russell, then back to Laura. "Do you remember anything about your family?" he asked.

She glanced at her left hand, where a pale, narrow strip of flesh circled the finger where she usually wore her engagement ring. When she was brought in, an ER nurse had given it to Rob for safe keeping.

"Am I married?" she asked.

A wave of sadness swept through Thomas. As a widower, he couldn't imagine having someone who was still alive but didn't even know you. "No, you're engaged."

Laura stiffened. "Did he—"

"No," he quickly reassured her. "We already know for certain he wasn't the one who did this. He's a paramedic. He was working an accident when this happened." He paused. "He's very worried about you and he'd like to see you. May I send him in?"

He watched as Laura studied her hands. She didn't work her fingers together or rub her thumb over her ring finger like someone recently missing a ring.

She seemingly had no memory of Rob at all. If she was faking it, she was faking it very well.

Unfortunately, he doubted she was faking it.

"Okay," she finally said.

He nodded. "If you remember anything, please tell the staff immediately, all right? They'll call me and I'll come to talk with you again."

She slowly nodded. He'd seen his fair share of domestic violence victims, victims of assault.

Laura Spaulding looked like a walking ghost.

Thomas stood to go when she stopped him. "Detective?"

He turned. "Yes?"

"What's his name?"

Chapter Three

Rob stood in the doorway. He hated himself for thinking it was almost worse seeing Laura conscious. The purple bruises and swollen cheekbones looked out of place on someone sitting up and awake.

At least when she was unconscious, he knew she couldn't feel the horrible beating she'd suffered. The bandage on her forehead had been removed, exposing the twelve stitches closing the ugly gash. Her upper lip still looked puffy and had been split open. The bruises around her neck were starting to fade from deep purple to an ugly brown that looked even worse.

She used to take pride in bruises he left on her ass from a play session. But this…

He successfully fought back the rising bile in his stomach. "Hi, honey. Laura."

She looked at Nurse Russell, who still sat by her bed. The nurse smiled and nodded to her, apparently trying to reassure her he was safe.

Laura stared at him. He wanted to hold her in his arms and stroke her long auburn hair, comfort her, tell her how much he loved her. The walk across the room felt like the longest of his life. Laura's blue-grey gaze nervously followed him the entire way until he stopped at the foot of her bed. She still hadn't said anything.

He swallowed hard and tried to maintain his composure. "The doctors told me you're having trouble with your memory because of the—because of what happened. Do you recognize me?"

* * * *

Laura was getting pretty good at shaking and nodding her head without causing too much agony, as long as she did it slowly and deliberately. Quick, sudden movements caused her the most pain.

The man *looked* familiar, but there was no name to go with the face in her mind's black void. Rugged, but kind. Light brown hair, soft brown eyes. Kind eyes.

Familiar eyes.

He wasn't built like a brick outhouse, but he looked like he could easily scoop her into his arms and sweep her away. He wore a casual uniform, a navy T-shirt tucked into black slacks with cargo pockets.

Fireman?

No. Paramedic. That's what the detective had said.

Safety and warmth were the first feelings to come to mind. Kindness, sincerity, tenderness.

Peace.

Love.

Trust.

Her hand went to her throat again, fingers fluttering helplessly, searching for something not there.

She sensed some sort of a connection with him but he was still a stranger. Det. Thomas had said his name was Rob.

It *felt* right, but she had no memories attached to it, just those random emotions.

Her memory consisted of a huge abyss where unconnected thoughts and feelings swirled just out of touch like some sort of maniacal carnival ride. There were things in her mind she knew how to do—she could read, and she knew what some of the equipment in her hospital room was used for.

Images floated past her conscious, but weren't tangible enough for her to grasp and slide home into their proper place.

She felt she had a past with this man, sensed he was an important part of her life. Yet while some of the feelings were there, the knowledge was not.

Overlaying all of this, fear.

Fear of whoever did this to her, fear that they might come back…

Fear she might never recover who she was and what that would mean for her future.

* * * *

Rob wanted to kiss her, comfort her. He felt around in his pocket and pulled out her engagement ring, a diamond solitaire he'd saved six months to buy. They already had the wedding bands picked out, hers a ring with diamonds and rubies that slipped around her solitaire and highlighted it.

In another pocket he carried her leather play collar, the one she normally wore when they were alone. He knew he couldn't just whip it out and show her now, but he'd carried it with him, a talisman.

A comfort.

A prayer, even though he wasn't religious, that she would come back to him so they could forge the life together that they'd envisioned.

Still missing, and likely taken by her attacker, the silver necklace with the heart-shaped charm on it, her day collar, although he hadn't called it such when reporting it to the investigators.

She always wore it, even in the shower, unless she had her play collar on. Only when out diving did she take it off.

He moved closer and held the ring out to her. She followed his hand with her eyes, but made no move to take the ring.

"They gave it to me in the ER," he eventually said. "You never take it off. The only time you did, you were going to wash Doogie and you couldn't remember where you put it. You called me in a panic and we looked for an hour before we finally found it. You swore you'd never take it off again."

At the mention of her black Lab, she reacted a little. "Doogie?"

"He's your puppy." He stopped. "Well, that's not exactly correct. He's five months old, and he's as big as a moose. You still call him your puppy."

Her brow furrowed. "They didn't tell me about a dog. Where is he? Is he okay? Was he hurt?"

"He's okay. He wasn't there. I picked him up from the vet yesterday. You'd dropped him off to be neutered Friday morning. We were supposed to pick him up Saturday morning." Rob still held the ring out to her.

She reached for it, drawing back quickly once she had it. Turning the ring over in her hands, she finally slipped it on her left ring finger and stared at it.

"Does it bring anything back?" he asked hopefully.

Laura didn't take her eyes off it. "I don't know. I have snippets, like pieces of sentences, little pictures that are gone before I can put a name or place to them. How long have we been together?"

He struggled to keep his voice steady. She didn't even *sound* like the same woman. Her voice sounded different, and not just from being strangled. The whole cadence of her speech had changed.

"We've known each other a little over two years, dated most of that. I proposed to you last Thanksgiving."

Another nurse came in with a wheelchair. "They're ready for her in radiology."

Nurse Russell stood. "Okay." She turned to Rob. "I'm sorry, but you'll have to leave now. Neurology wants to evaluate her. We'll probably be moving her, depending on the MRI results, to a private room later today."

Rob tried to get Laura to meet his gaze and she couldn't—or wouldn't. "Can I come back later, Laura?"

She finally looked up, as if getting used to her own name. "Oh, yes. I guess so. If they say it's okay."

He paused, wanted to say something else, then turned to go before he started crying in front of her.

"Thank you, Rob," Laura said as he reached the door.

He turned and smiled before leaving. He found Thomas and Dr. Singh waiting for him in the hall.

"Well?" Thomas asked. "Anything?"

He walked over to the nurses' station and once again held on for support. It felt like his soul had been ripped from his body. "She doesn't know me at all. It's like she's never seen me before in her life."

Rob couldn't bear looking at Thomas' expression of pity. He turned to Dr. Singh. "When can I come back to see her?"

"Wait until this afternoon," Dr. Singh told him. "Let her have a chance to absorb everything. She's overwhelmed right now, and the neurologist needs to evaluate her."

"Will she get her memory back? Is this temporary?"

"We don't know. I'm sorry, but I don't have a better answer for you right now."

"Is there anything I can do?"

"Bring photo albums, pictures, mementos she might have a strong attachment to. They might trigger something."

Rob's hand drifted down to touch the play collar through his slacks. He slowly nodded before turning to Thomas again. "They finished with her place?" He'd been allowed to walk through Laura's condo with Thomas only once, the next day, to help them verify if anything else had been taken besides Laura's necklace.

Thomas nodded. "They're finished with it." He cleared his throat. "I'm sorry, Rob. About this morning. I just needed to talk to her first."

He looked at the detective. "You're not a fraction as sorry as that fucker will be if I find him before you do."

Chapter Four

When Nancy Russell's shift ended, Laura relaxed a little after the nurse took the time to introduce her daytime counterpart before leaving Laura in her care for the MRI series.

The nurse stayed with Laura throughout her MRI, while the deputy sat in the control room with the technicians. When they'd first mentioned leaving Laura in there alone, she'd started to panic until a nursing supervisor okayed it.

Laura found the machine loud and confining, and she wondered if she'd ever been in one before.

It doesn't feel familiar.

They had placed her head in a brace to hold it still for the MRI series. She closed her eyes and asked them to turn up the music to help drown out the hammering sound a little. It was a soft rock station, and during one of the commercial breaks she found herself humming along with their station jingle.

Her eyes popped open. Another spark, just not enough to kindle a large flame of memory.

Pt. Charlotte. They'd told her that before, but now it *felt* more real. She struggled for a state.

Florida. That was right. That's where she was.

But I don't live in this town, do I? She closed her eyes and listened intently to all the commercials. When an air conditioning company commercial played and listed their service areas, she realized she recognized some of the locales they mentioned.

Sarasota, Venice, North Port. A few flickers of recognition, but more shadows than anything.

Finally, an advertisement for a Ford dealer.

Englewood!

An image of a neatly kept condo complex popped into her head.
Mine?

The noise in the machine subsided for a moment while they adjusted it. The radiology technician asked how she was doing.

"I'm okay," she replied, not sure if she was.

It struck her that with each little nugget of returning memory, it only served to emphasize just how much she *didn't* remember.

Back in her room a short while later, the neurologist stopped by to see her. The deputy sat in the room with her while the doctor gave Laura a battery of tests and asked her numerous questions that seemed to have little to do with her situation.

Finally, frustrated, Laura dug in her heels.

"*When* am I going to get my memory back?"

The doctor sat. "I don't know. It's impossible for me to say if it's due to the physical or the emotional trauma of the attack, or maybe both. Sometimes memories come back rapidly and completely. Sometimes long-term memories return while recent ones are lost. The sooner you regain your memory, the better a chance you have at getting it all back."

"What are my options?"

"For now you need to heal from your physical injuries. There's a medicine that's sometimes used to help bring back memories, but I'm not about to prescribe it. Or you could try therapeutic hypnosis, although again, I can't tell you if it'll work or not. I'll refer you to a psychiatrist."

She bristled, although she didn't know why. "I'm *not* crazy. I was attacked."

He shook his head. "I didn't say you are. But as a neurologist, my area of expertise is the physical condition of your brain. It's up to a psychiatrist to look inside it. If your memory doesn't return quickly and completely, they may want to try several different options before resorting to drastic measures. Even if you regain your long-term memory, you might not regain those from right around the time of the attack. You seem to be retaining new memories. It appears only previous memories are impacted."

"*Those* are the ones I need right now." Laura found herself quickly losing patience and had half a mind to tell him off.

Then it struck her that she didn't know if she was normally a patient person or not.

"You're fortunate to be alive," he continued. "I know it's frustrating, but you have to focus on healing your body first. We'll monitor your progress and follow up after discharge. I really wish you'd consider seeing a psychiatrist. Attacks like this often bring on post-traumatic stress disorder, and that can also hinder how quickly your memories return."

When the doctor and deputy left her alone, Laura collapsed against her pillows, the emotional drain almost as painful as her physical injuries.

She reached up and brushed a strand of hair from her face and realized for the first time that she had long, brown hair. Mindful of her sore ribs, she carefully sat up again and swung her legs over the edge of the bed.

Her nurse came in and caught her. "Where do you think you're going?" She moved to stop Laura from getting up.

They'd removed her catheter that morning and brought in a potty for her, but she was done with that. "I'm going to the bathroom." She pointed at the potty. "I refuse to use that thing. I have a little dignity even if I don't have my marbles."

The nurse took her arm and steadied Laura as she slowly walked into the bathroom.

A battered, unknown face returned Laura's gaze from the mirror. The bluish-grey eyes were all she sensed a kinship with. Her long, auburn hair hung in stringy clumps from not being washed in several days, and the stitches in her forehead appeared huge. Her nose was swollen, but they told her it somehow had miraculously escaped being broken in the attack. The black eyes looked like ugly purple moons on her high cheekbones.

When she reached up and touched her cheek, the woman in the mirror did the same.

This woman was a total stranger to her in nearly every way.

"Would you like to take a shower?" the nurse asked. "The doctor said we can take your IV out since you kept your breakfast down. We have to leave the Hep-Lock in, though, just in case. I can get an aide in here to help you."

"That would be great, thank you."

It was more a sponge bath than anything, because Laura's cracked ribs made it hard for her to move. At least the aide helped her get her hair washed with water and shampoo and not just the waterless cap thingy they'd wanted her to use.

Freshening up raised her spirits a little.

Once she was back in bed, she asked if she could have a TV. Within an hour though, they'd moved her to a private room one floor up, her deputy bodyguard in tow.

She'd almost forgotten about Rob in the process, but they assured her they'd give him her updated room information.

Laura and the deputy sat and watched TV. She asked him questions, fascinated by familiar yet totally foreign images on the screen. She imagined it was like reading a textbook in school about a country you'd learned about but never visited.

I wonder if I've ever been out of the country.

Occasionally there was another blip, a fraction of a thought that struck home and fitted itself in her mind like a puzzle piece, usually triggered by local commercials. Despite being totally useless in a practical sense, every step was one closer.

* * * *

Rob's stomach tightly knotted as he made the half-hour drive from the hospital in Pt. Charlotte back to Englewood, to Laura's. The condo complex was small, only six units, split into two one-story triplexes with a shared green space in the middle that both buildings backed up against.

He swallowed hard as he stared at the lock. He'd had new locks installed and hesitated before he inserted the key in the knob, unlocking it, then the deadbolt.

Slowly, he let the door swing open, revealing the entryway. The theory was Laura had willingly opened the door for her attacker. Maybe she'd known him, maybe she hadn't. There were no marks on the outside of the door to indicate it being forced open, and it had been unlocked when her neighbor rushed in and scared off the attacker.

Tom himself appeared, sticking his head out his front door and then walking over when he recognized Rob. "How's she doing?"

Rob nodded. "She's awake."

"That's good!" He eyed Rob, then added, "Isn't it?"

A sad heaviness settled over him as he pondered the words he had to say but didn't want to accept. "She awoke from the coma with amnesia.

Complete."

The man's eyes widened. "Oh. I'm so sorry. Do they know if she'll get her memory back?"

"They don't know. I'm here to get some things for her. Clothes, and pictures. Photo albums. They said maybe it'll help."

Tom patted him on the shoulder. "Please give her our best. We wanted to visit but didn't want to intrude."

"Thanks." He swallowed back the lump in his throat. "And thank you for saving her."

Tom's gaze dropped. The older man looked a little embarrassed. "I wasn't sure at first if I should go over." He wouldn't meet Rob's gaze. "We've heard…you know. Sometimes."

Rob felt his face heat. "Sorry," he mumbled. "We didn't know you could hear us."

"No, it's okay." He finally smiled a little. "We were young once, too. It was when she kept screaming and yelling for help we realized it wasn't just…you know, the two of you playing around. She never screams like that with you. She sounded terrified."

Rob tried to process that, feeling sick in the depths of his gut.

Tom didn't seem to know where to go from there. He just patted Rob on the shoulder again and retreated toward his door.

He turned before going in. "Please let us know if there's anything we can do. Or when we can come visit her."

"Thanks. I will."

Rob turned back to the doorway as Tom Edwards' door gently shut.

Damn.

They'd thought the walls were thick enough the neighbors couldn't hear them playing. They did most of their heavier play at the club or during private parties, or at his house, where it was completely private. But sometimes he tossed her over his knee and spanked her with his bare hand.

The thought that it could have contributed to her dying had the neighbors ignored the noises and chalked it up to kinky sex nearly made him sick.

He closed his eyes as he stood there, hoping for some sort of impossible, psychic glimpse into the events. Laura wasn't an overly trusting woman. But the safety chain still hung by the door, unbroken, so she apparently hadn't hooked it when she answered. She would have looked through the peephole, first, too. She always did that.

Who was it?

It took a monumental effort for Rob to force his legs to carry him inside. He found himself unable to ignore the large ruddy stain on the carpet runner near the front door. Streaks of dried blood also smeared the entryway wall where Laura had fought back against her attacker.

They'd removed traces of blood and tissue from under her nails, so she'd gotten her licks in. The attacker didn't go away unscathed, something Rob felt more than a little bit of pride over. She was a fighter. The samples were being processed in hopes of a DNA match from a past crime giving them a suspect's name.

Thomas had told him they had word out with all local doctors and hospitals to keep an eye out for anyone looking for treatment for deep scratches or bite marks.

So far, nothing.

He closed his eyes yet again and tried to put his rage and guilt aside, picturing instead how terrified she must have been. If he hadn't been working, he would have been there with her. She likely would have spent the evening naked, collared, and kneeling on the floor next to him by the couch, if she wasn't curled up in his lap.

He walked over to the couch and sat in his usual spot, closing his eyes again.

In his mind's eye, he envisioned himself stroking her hair, a blissful peace enveloping both of them as they each unwound from their day and let the stress of work evaporate.

Alone together, the outside world always disappeared. He felt like he could spend forever just like that with her, his hand cupping her chin and staring into her eyes. Eyes a beautiful shade of blue-grey, like the Gulf under an overcast sky.

How, without a word, he could sit back and smile at her and she'd dive for his zipper, finally getting the silent permission she'd longed for to go down on him.

Despite the circumstances, his cock hardened as he mentally relived one of the countless times spent with her like that. The warm press of her cheek against his thigh as she sucked his cock between her lips and slowly laved her tongue over it.

The way it felt twining his fingers in her hair before wrapping it around his fist and gently holding her in place. Not that she needed holding. He suspected if he'd let her, she'd spend hours going down on him.

And she was good at it, too. Not that he'd had a ton of other partners, but none had ever been as good in that way. None had ever felt as compatible as she did.

She knew when and where to lick, loved to run her tongue up and down his shaft and over his balls. Loved to deep throat him, and always made a delicious, purring moan that vibrated all the way through his dick when she sensed him close to coming.

The way she always let out a happy chuckle as she swallowed every drop of cum he pumped out of his balls…

His eyes snapped open, his aching cock going from hard to wilted when his gaze landed on the bloodstains again.

Shoving himself up and off the couch, he got to work. He spent the morning there, gathering photo albums and some of Laura's favorite loafing clothes, as she called them.

He also cleared out their stash of sex toys, including leather cuffs, a flogger, and other things. He didn't know if the cops had found them or not. But when he brought Laura home, they'd also have vanilla friends helping out and he didn't want to risk them stumbling over the items, either. It might give someone the wrong idea about their relationship.

Well, the right idea, but he'd found that a lot of people who didn't understand the BDSM lifestyle were frequently judgmental about it.

Packing up those items proved to be almost more than he could take. He quickly finished what he needed to do and left, slamming the door shut behind him and locking it. He'd fully intended to clean up the bloodstains and other damage, but even he had his limits.

There's no way I can bring her back to that. I'm going to need help cleaning the place up.

Rob stopped by his house long enough to walk Doogie and gather more items he hoped would trigger something, anything. All morning he'd fought back tears while sorting through both her things and their life together, pictures of trips and reminders of better times.

He pulled her leather play collar from his pocket and rubbed his fingers over it, hooked a finger through the D-ring on the front, the way he would if she was wearing it. To pull her in and give her a kiss, or to lead her to bed.

He angrily brushed the back of his hand across his eyes to wipe away his tears. It was bad enough that he could do little to help her, and worse that she couldn't remember him.

Wrapping his head around that still proved impossible.

At the end of the driveway Rob threw his Explorer into park and checked the mail.

The mailman had left a package for him in one of the lockable boxes he shared with his neighbors.

Their wedding invitations had arrived from the printer.

His knees buckled. The day they picked them out was still firmly fixed in his mind. How they'd joked maybe they should add "collaring" to the announcement as well, since she wanted him to formally collar her as his slave in front of their friends.

While he stared at the box of announcements, his cell rang. He answered it without looking at the screen. "Carlton."

"Hey, Rob. It's Tony."

He closed his eyes. Tony Daniels had been his first call after trying to reach Laura's brother following the attack. Tony and another friend, Seth Erikkson, had shown up at the hospital in those initial darkest hours to wait with him, when they weren't even sure if Laura would pull through or not.

"Hey."

"How you holding up?"

"Not good, man." Rob filled his friend in. Tony was one of the first people he'd met when he'd entered the lifestyle, and had been the one to introduce him and Laura. They had a close-knit group of friends who'd met through the lifestyle, but had become like adopted family outside of it.

Tony and Seth had helped with getting information out about Laura's condition to their lifestyle friends, including spreading the word to stay away from the hospital until Rob gave the okay to visit.

In retrospect, he was even more glad he'd done that. Laura would be too overwhelmed by all the people, now strangers to her, who wanted to visit.

There was a moment of silence. "She doesn't remember *anything*?" Tony asked. "Or do you mean about the attack?"

Rob sucked in a ragged breath. "Anything. They said it's too soon to tell if it's temporary or permanent."

"Can I bring Shayla over to see her tonight, or do I need to make her wait? She's beside herself worried about her. I'm not trying to sound like a shit." Tony sighed. "She won't stop crying, Rob. Can I at least bring her, even if I need to sit outside? I'm good with that if need be."

Rob wanted to say no, but hesitated. *Then again, maybe another familiar face will be good for her.* It would definitely be good for him. "Yeah, how about six? Both of you."

"Can we bring you and her dinner from Sigalo's?"

His stomach rumbled at the name of his favorite restaurant. "Shayla knows her favorites. I'll take anything."

"Maybe a little gastronomical prompting will help her memory."

"Can't hurt." They ate there nearly every Saturday night with Tony, Shayla, and their other friends.

Except last Saturday.

Last Saturday, Rob had been praying she'd make it through another night.

"See you then," Tony said.

"Thanks, man." Rob stared at the phone for a moment after ending the call. Their little social group, which they'd dubbed the Suncoast Society because of the munch they'd met through, had been through thick and thin with each other. For some of their members, including Laura, they'd been closer than family.

And they never hesitated to rush to a friend's side to help or provide support.

Maybe it was selfish of him, but he needed his adopted family's support, and he didn't have any close biological family to turn to.

He usually wasn't one to wear his emotions on his sleeve, except in front of Laura.

But he wasn't ashamed to admit he needed Tony's strong and steady presence for a little while. And maybe Shayla would help jostle something in Laura's memory. The two women were closer than sisters.

He put the box of invitations on the passenger seat and headed for the hospital.

Chapter Five

When Rob returned to the hospital, he felt a slight lift in his spirits to learn Laura had already been moved to a private room.

That was quickly dashed when her doctor informed him her memory hadn't returned.

Rob found her sitting up in bed, watching cable news with the deputy and the barely eaten remnants of her lunch still sitting on her bed tray. The deputy nodded to him and left to sit in the hall, closing the door behind him.

"Hi, Laura."

She didn't look away from the TV, where she stared at it, frowning over a commercial for a local landscaping firm out of Venice. "Hi." The engagement ring sat on the bedside table next to her.

Rob tried not to show his pain. The last thing Laura needed now was to deal with his emotions. He wanted her to focus on getting her memory back.

He pulled a chair up next to her bed and showed her the albums. "I brought some stuff for us to look at. The doctors said maybe it would help."

Then she pulled her attention from the TV. "Can we talk first?"

"Sure."

"How did we meet?"

He paused, not sure how to handle this hot potato. "Through mutual friends," he said, their usual answer to someone vanilla who asked that same question.

He thought she might ask him for more details, but then she started asking about other things and the questions came one right after another.

Where she was from? Florida. Where was her family? Her parents were dead, killed in a car accident a little over a year earlier, and he hadn't been able to contact her brother, Bill, in Montana. What did she do for a living? She owned a dive shop and charter business, and wrote freelance articles for fishing and scuba diving magazines and websites.

Why, who, what, where—it nearly wore him out until he put it into perspective that she was, essentially, hearing these things for the first time.

Laura finally paused and lay back in bed, closing her eyes.

"I also brought you some clothes. Your clothes," he said. "I thought it might make you a little more comfortable." He opened the duffle bag for her. She reached in and sorted through them, finally selecting a T-shirt and pair of sweat pants.

When he offered her his arm to help her sit up she hesitated at first, then tentatively let him assist her out of bed. He helped her to the bathroom, standing back while she locked the door behind her. She obviously wasn't comfortable having him so close.

He wasn't used to this from her, someone he'd shared his life and bed with for two years.

Someone who, until a few days ago, had called him Sir.

Someone who had trusted him with her life and safety when they played very edgy scenes.

Someone who had never hesitated—before—to turn herself over to him completely and without reservation.

Once again he had to force himself to remember he was a stranger to her.

She took several minutes to change and when she emerged, he helped her back to bed. The Laura he knew was physically there, but the tangible emotional gulf felt miles deep and infinitely wide.

Laura reached for the photo albums. The first were from her childhood. Rob thought maybe the older memories would return faster, based on what the doctors had told him.

He watched while she slowly flipped through the pages, occasionally asking him for a name or place. Some he knew, some he didn't. Once they got to the albums with pictures of them as a couple, he told her the stories, trying to relive them for her as best he could. He also had a ton of pictures on his phone, but until he could sanitize the photo album and remove the ones of her in bondage, or her proudly sticking her ass out so he could take pictures of her bruises, he'd hold off showing them to her.

They were halfway through one album when she smiled at a picture of them on a fishing boat. Rob held a large amberjack. Laura used two hands to hoist an impressive grouper.

"Do you remember that day?" he asked.

Laura closed her eyes, deep in concentration. "Something about a ledge."

Rob didn't give her any information, made her search for it.

"Maybe a...croaker?" She looked at him, her brow furrowed. He nodded.

Her finger traced the picture. "We were scuba diving?"

"Yes."

"I know how to do that?"

He forced the smile. "You're an instructor."

"Oh, yeah. You said that, didn't you. Sorry."

"No, it's okay. I know you're overwhelmed."

That earned him a sad smile. "*That's* an understatement."

She stared at the photo for a few more minutes without speaking. The obvious intensity of her effort was mind boggling. "Something about a lobster." After several more minutes she finally shook her head. "That's all I remember."

He tried to hide his disappointment. She'd been so close to getting it. "We were spearfishing in the Gulf. You shot the grouper, and he went under a ledge, making the loud croaking noise they do when they're wounded or scared. While you were digging it out, I shot that amberjack and had my hands full. You yelled into your regulator and I turned and you had a hold of the grouper, but a large lobster had backed out of the hole and you didn't have any hands to grab it."

"Was that good?"

He laughed. "Well, it would have been if we could have got it. Lobsters aren't common this far north in the Gulf. It was lobster season, and we had lobster stamps on our fishing licenses. But he got away, baby girl."

She flinched and looked at him with a suspicious glare.

"What's wrong?"

"Baby girl?"

That was one of his pet names for her, had been for years. She was his "baby girl," even though they didn't do age play, and he could call her that regardless of who was around. In front of vanillas, she'd teasingly call him Fireman instead of Sir. Or Hose Jockey, depending on her mood and whether she was trying to get him into bed. She had a hellacious sense of humor.

But alone, she always called him Sir.

"That doesn't bring anything back?" he softly asked, hoping his voice didn't tremble. He tried to remember Singh's warning, that he had to stay strong for her.

"Not really." She wrinkled her nose again. "You really called me that? I liked it?"

"Yeah." He hoped he could choke out the statement without breaking down. "If you don't feel comfortable with that now, I won't."

She slowly nodded. "Thanks." She returned her attention to the album.

He felt another piece of his tattered soul ripped from him. But if she didn't want him calling her that now, he wouldn't.

No matter how much it hurt.

* * * *

Laura finally shook her head as she stared at the picture again. She was going to ask him more questions when someone knocked on her door.

The deputy entered. "You have another visitor." An older woman with short blonde hair walked in. It was obvious she made an effort not to react to Laura's battered face.

"Hi, honey. How are you feeling?"

"Laura," Rob said, "this is Carol Langhbine. She's an old friend of yours. She was in some of the pictures I showed you."

Laura looked at her, feeling something as new memories swirled in the darkness without fully surfacing, but she wasn't sure if they were true memories, or just things she'd seen in the pictures. "Hi. Nice to meet you."

* * * *

Rob somehow managed not to swear when Carol entered the room. He'd specifically told her and Steve both not to come to the hospital yet.

Then he spied the tears in Carol's eyes.

"Excuse us for just a minute, Laura. I need to talk to Carol outside." He hustled her out of the room and into the hallway.

Carol's voice barely rose above a tearful whisper. "Oh my god, Rob. She looks horrible!"

Rob had kept both her and their friend Steve away from the hospital while Laura was unconscious. There was nothing they could do for her, and he knew Laura—the old Laura—wouldn't want them seeing her like that.

"That's why I warned you not to visit until I told you to." He struggled to contain his irritation. He'd wanted a chance to sit down with Carol and Steve and fully brief them before having them come in.

Tony and Shayla were different. He knew he could count on them to maintain a strong façade in front of Laura.

And especially to not say anything about their BDSM activities.

Carol, however, was practically family, even though she had no clue about the private aspects of their relationship.

"She doesn't remember anything."

Carol looked at him. "Nothing?"

Rob shook his head. "Everything's a blank. Even me."

"Oh my god." She dug a tissue out of her purse and tried to clean herself up. "What can I do?"

"Just put on a smile and come in there with me and talk to her. She needs information and support right now." He glanced at the clock over the nurses' station. "And let's keep the visit short so you don't overwhelm her."

He wanted Carol out of there well before Tony and Shayla arrived so he didn't have to deal with Carol's hurt feelings about him inviting others to see Laura before her.

Carol sniffled and nodded. "Okay."

He waited while she went to the bathroom and washed her face. They returned to Laura's room and Rob pulled a chair next to the other side of the bed.

Carol had been best friends with Laura's mother since Laura was five. They returned to the old family photo albums, where Carol was able to fill in names and places Rob couldn't.

Eventually, Laura asked, "Who would want to do this to me? Who had a motive?"

Rob and Carol looked at each other across the bed. Carol found her voice first, something for which Rob felt extremely thankful.

"We don't know, honey. The police are working on it."

"I just keep thinking I must have been some sort of horrible person for something like this to happen to me…"

That's when Laura's reserve melted and her tears flowed. Rob tentatively put an arm around her, and when she leaned against him, he slipped the other around her and gently held her.

"Laura, whoever did this was a monster. You're not to blame."

That proved no consolation. She cried long enough for him to consider ringing the nurse for a sedative. When she finally calmed down he handed her a tissue and Carol brought her a cup of water.

He snuck a glance at the time. It was later than he'd realized, after five thirty already. "Carol, they'll be bringing her dinner soon and she needs to rest. Why don't you let me walk you out?"

Carol nodded, leaning in to give Laura one last hug. "I'll come see you tomorrow."

He waited until he got Carol out the door and down the hall toward the elevator. "I think you'd better wait to hear from me before you visit again."

"What? Why?"

He tried to soften the blow as much as possible. "Because she's overwhelmed. You saw her. And right now, frankly, I need some alone time with her, okay?" That was partly the truth. "Please?"

She looked sad, but nodded. "How long until we can see her again?"

"Soon." He hugged her. "You know how she was…is. If she had her memories she'd be holed up at home refusing to see anyone looking like that." His Laura wasn't vain, but she hated being around other people when she didn't feel good.

And she despised what she considered "pity." There was no way in hell she would have allowed anyone but Rob and Shayla and Tony to see her that soon.

Which was another point. He also wanted to make sure he could get their closest lifestyle friends in to see her. They'd bared more than just their bodies in front of each other in the course of play, but their souls as well. He needed Laura to spend as much time around them as possible in hopes it would jog her memories.

Down in the parking lot, Carol lost her composure.

"Rob, will she get her memory back?"

"I don't know. I sure hope so."

"What if she doesn't?"

He didn't want to think about that. "We have to wait and see. It's all we can do."

By the time he'd returned to Laura's room they'd brought her dinner tray. She stared at it, looking disgusted.

"What's wrong, sweetie?"

He hoped that endearment, at least, would be all right.

Apparently it was because she didn't flinch. She did, however, shake her head. "Blech."

That was, he happily noted, directed at the food on her plate and not him.

He smiled. She wasn't a picky eater, but she definitely had her preferences. "I have a little surprise for you. Some really close friends of ours are bringing dinner for us soon. Your favorite meal."

A skeptical eyebrow arched. The familiar gesture nearly made him cry.

"Really?"

"Really."

She replaced the cover over the plate. "Can't be worse than this slop."

"Tony and Shayla know your favorites. It's an Italian restaurant several of us eat at every week."

* * * *

Laura's stomach grumbled. "That actually sounds good. I couldn't finish lunch. It was horrible. Bland."

"Did they say you can eat a normal diet?"

She nodded. "I had oatmeal, and then eggs this morning, after I kept the broth down. It hurts to chew is all."

Rob gave her another sad smile. She wondered if he always looked so sad or if it was due to the circumstances. "I didn't even think to ask if they were keeping you on a restricted diet when I talked to Tony earlier."

"Who are they?" she asked. "The people coming to visit." The older woman, Carol, she jostled a few memories, but they felt like old ones. Very faded, disjointed, like she was a kid when they happened.

At least, she hoped they were true memories and not just wishful thinking on her part as they'd gone through photos together.

"Tony and Shayla Daniels."

"How did I meet them?"

"You've known them for several years. They're the friends who introduced us. You and Shayla are extremely close. Best friends."

She felt like maybe he was holding something back but it didn't feel bad, or like he was lying.

She wasn't sure how she knew that, or if it was simply more mental gymnastics courtesy of her battered brain.

She opted to let it go for now.

"Why haven't more people come to see me?" She feared the answer.

"Oh, sweetie. I've told people to stay away for now. You were in the ICU, and now…" He didn't finish.

He didn't have to.

"Because I can't remember them anyway," she quietly said.

He let out a sigh as he nodded. "I didn't want you to get overwhelmed. And…" She forced herself not to flinch away from him as he reached out and gently stroked her cheek with the back of his fingers. "I knew you wouldn't want a lot of people seeing you like this."

"You're seeing me like this." She felt an instinctive urge to tip her face toward his hand, to nuzzle against it.

Familiar.

She closed her eyes and hoped more came to her but it didn't.

For now, she'd settle for that little beacon of goodness in the middle of the inky sea that still comprised most of her memories.

"That's because I love you," he said. "You're my life. Good luck trying to keep me from your side."

"What about the couple bringing dinner? Would I want them seeing me like this?"

"They're like family to us. You wouldn't care what condition they saw you in."

The door opened again and the deputy popped his head in. "Rob, there's a couple here to see Laura."

"Send them in." He stood to greet them. Laura clutched at the sheet and waited for them to get all the way in.

They did feel familiar.

More importantly, like Carol earlier, they felt safe.

Tony Daniels stood a little taller than Rob and had green eyes, dark brown hair, and a friendly smile surrounded by a neatly trimmed moustache and goatee. Even though he had his hands full of take-out bags, he accepted an awkward one-armed hug from Rob. His wife, Shayla, had hazel eyes and wore her brown hair down past her shoulders.

She also noticed Shayla wore a gold necklace with a heart-shaped charm on it. Something about the look of it pulled a wistful pang from deep in Laura's heart. Her hand flew to her throat again, fingers helplessly fluttering against the empty real estate there.

I need to remember to ask Rob about that.

Tony put the bags down on the bed tray. "We come bearing food," he joked.

"Thank you," Laura said. "Rob told me you were bringing dinner."

Shayla hesitantly walked around the bed to the other side. She looked like she was on the verge of tears. "May I hug you?" she softly asked Laura.

Laura pulled back the sheet and turned to sit on the edge of the bed. Shayla tentatively wrapped her arms around her as Laura did the same.

She heard Shayla sniffle. "I love you so much, sister," she whispered in her ear. "I don't know what I would have done if I'd lost you."

A wave of emotion Laura couldn't process swept through her. She let out a sob of her own as she tightly clutched Shayla and they cried together.

* * * *

Alarmed, Rob started toward the women. Tony stepped in his path and gave a terse shake of his head. He motioned for Rob to follow him out into the hall.

When the door closed behind them, Rob whispered, "Why are we out here?"

"Give them a couple of minutes alone together," he said, peeking through a crack in the blinds. "It'll do them both some good. Even if it doesn't jostle Laura's memory, she's obviously reacting to Shay." He eyed Rob. "And Shayla was about to go crazy with grief, so she needs to let it out."

Rob tried to look through the same space in the blinds as the women remained motionless, obviously still crying.

Shayla and Laura rarely went a day without talking on the phone. The reason Rob and Laura had an unlimited text plan was due to the tens of thousands of texts the women exchanged every month.

Laura was nearly as close to Leah, Tilly, Loren, and Clarisse, but Shayla and Laura were closer than sisters. When Laura first entered the lifestyle, Shayla had immediately scooped Laura under her wing, both her and Tony offering Laura mentorship and protection from douchetards.

On FetLife, they had each other listed as sisters on their profiles.

That did nothing to soothe the ugly jealously trying to ooze its way through Rob's soul. Laura hadn't had such a visceral reaction to *him*.

Then the ugly jealousy tried to spawn a whole lot of dark, nasty eggs of doubt.

Tony put his hand out and caught Rob's arm. He waited until Rob finally looked at him. "Women relate differently than we do, okay?" he quietly said. "It's not a personal statement against you. And she's known Shayla a few months longer than she's known you. Try not to read too much into it."

Rob slumped against the wall. Tony was spooky like that in his ability to read and relate to people. It was one of the reasons people liked him so much, and why his classes in communication and negotiation in the lifestyle were so popular.

"What if she never remembers me?"

Tony's expression softened. "She will. Just give her time." He stared through the window again. "The way she looked at you before all this? You are her heart and soul. You will be again. Love like that doesn't just disappear."

"I hope you're right."

After a few minutes, Tony nodded. "Okay, let's see if that did any good for either or both of them."

* * * *

Laura hated that she couldn't coax any concrete memories from the abyss to go with the overwhelming emotions swamping her.

The only thing she knew for certain was she did love this woman, and that she was a safe person to confide in.

"I can't remember anything," Laura tearfully whispered. "I can't remember Rob or you or your husband or anything."

Shayla stroked her hair. "I know. Rob told us. It's okay. We're here for you. You're not alone."

After a few minutes the men returned. Rob walked over to her while Shayla stepped into the bathroom to blow her nose and wash her face.

"Are you okay?" Rob asked.

She nodded. "Yeah." She looked up when he didn't say anything else. He didn't have to voice his question. "No new memories. But," she quickly added when disappointment flowed across his face, "it's like when I met you. I feel something, I just don't have the memories."

Before he could step away, she wrapped her arms around him and pulled him close. After hesitating, he draped his arms around her and buried his face in her hair.

As she closed her eyes and deeply inhaled, she pictured a laundry room, where she stood holding her face pressed against a shirt she had to put in the wash, one of his, maybe.

She pulled herself from the vision. "It's a yellow jug," she softly said, surprising herself.

"What?"

She didn't want to look up or let go, afraid to break whatever tenuous connection she had with the delicately sprouting memory. "The laundry soap. It's in a yellow jug."

"Yeah," he said.

Tony spoke from across the room. "I once read that the sense of smell is very powerful in anchoring and triggering memories."

She pressed her face more tightly against Rob's stomach, against the firm abs that no doubt lurked beneath the fabric, and deeply inhaled again.

Warm, slightly musky, and...

"Coconut?" she asked, mostly to herself. "Coconut body wash."

She felt him exhale sharply, as if someone had punched him in the gut. "Yeah. Your favorite."

After a few more minutes, she released him and wiped at her face. "Sorry. That's all."

He caught her hands and gently kissed them. "Hey, it's a start."

Bitter disappointment coursed through her. "It's not very much."

"Don't be hard on yourself," Tony cautioned. "Don't push yourself. They'll come back when they come back."

"If." She looked at him. He was setting the food out on the rolling bed tray table.

He shrugged. "What comes back will come back. We'll help you make new memories, if that's what it takes. Somehow, I don't think that'll be necessary. You're a strong woman. Your body is trying to heal right now. I can't imagine you not getting your memories back."

Shayla returned from the bathroom, her face freshly scrubbed and devoid of makeup. Laura realized Shayla hadn't been wearing any makeup when she arrived.

In a flash, the words were out of Laura's mouth before she knew she was saying them. "Tony, why don't you let her wear makeup?"

The three of them froze, staring at her. Tony recovered first. "What?"

Laura turned on the bed to face him. She didn't miss how Shayla was now totally focused on Tony. "You don't let her wear makeup?" It was more a question than a statement.

Tony's gaze darted to Shayla before returning to her. "That's not true."

"But she has to ask?"

He set down the food container he'd been in the process of opening. "Rob?"

Rob looked clueless.

Tony sighed. "Shayla and I have a very close relationship," he carefully said. "She asks me my opinion. My opinion is she's beautiful without makeup. If she wants to wear makeup, that's her choice."

Shayla rapidly nodded.

Laura processed that while Tony continued setting out the food. His answer didn't feel exactly like the truth. Then she got a strong whiff of the dinner and her eyes dropped closed again as she deeply inhaled, her previous train of thought completely and aromatically derailed.

"Eggplant parm," she practically sighed, the picture of a restaurant's dining room coming into view in her mind's eye. "Sigalo's." She realized what she'd said. "Is that right? It just popped into my head." She looked at them.

Maybe Tony is right about the sense of smell triggering stuff.

Everyone nodded. "That's right," Rob said. "It's your favorite."

Tony handed her a container. "And a batch of their famous garlic knots," he said, holding up another container. He opened it for her, revealing it was crammed full of the bread.

"Oooh!" She grabbed three and jammed one into her mouth, letting out a soft moan as she carefully chewed. Her jaw still hurt like a bitch, but she would willingly endure the pain so as not to have to eat hospital food. "That is sooo good."

She didn't miss how the other three intently watched her as she chewed. "Are you going to eat or let it go cold?"

Shayla kicked off her shoes and settled, cross-legged, on the end of the bed, facing Laura and using the other side of the bed table for her food. "I'll make you a batch of my dark chocolate Buckeyes and bring them in tomorrow," she said. "They're one of your favorites."

That sounded familiar to Laura, but no memory accompanied it. "What are they?"

"A peanut butter mix covered with dark chocolate," Rob said. "You love them."

"Am I allergic to anything?" She didn't know why that thought emerged out of left field, but something about peanut allergies had suddenly sprang to mind.

"No," Rob assured her. "You get seasonal allergies sometimes, and sometimes to dust, but nothing serious."

"Oh." She dug into her eggplant parm and closed her eyes as she chewed. "This is amazing," she softly said, her previous thoughts about Shayla and makeup completely set aside in the face of the best meal she'd ever eaten in her life.

That she could remember up until this point, at least.

"I'm surprised I don't weigh three hundred pounds," she said after savoring another bite.

Rob smiled, but it looked sad. "You're out scuba diving many weekends. Or teaching in a pool. Taking care of the boats, hauling scuba tanks, jogging, swimming—you're pretty active. This is the least active you've ever been since I've known you."

"I don't relax?"

"Sometimes. Not willingly."

She looked at him as she forked another bite into her mouth and carefully chewed. "Do they have pictures of Italy on the walls? Paintings? No, wait…" She closed her eyes. "Murals." She opened her eyes again to look at everyone.

They nodded. "You love their murals," Rob confirmed.

She stared at the food, the tears taking her by surprise. "Why can I remember stupid stuff like laundry soap and restaurant walls and not anything about people?"

The men flanked her on either side while Shayla reached across the bed tray and held her hands. "We're here for you, sweetie," Shayla assured her. "Tony's right. Don't try to force things. That might make it harder. Go easy on yourself, okay? We'll be here every step of the way with you."

"We promise," Rob said.

"Yep," Tony echoed.

* * * *

Laura took her time eating, savoring every bite. It didn't matter how many times she'd supposedly eaten this dish before. She appreciated every nuance of flavor.

She wished Shayla could spend the night with her there at the hospital. More guilt she wouldn't readily admit to Rob, but she suspected she'd spent many long hours with the woman, baring secrets and their souls together.

Rationally, she understood she shouldn't feel that way. The doctors had gone out of their way to explain her memory might return in odd spurts, or all at once, or not at all.

But that she'd had this reaction to Shayla and not Rob unsettled her. It didn't shake her trust in Rob, but it did make her wonder if Rob didn't know all the secrets of her soul…before.

It also made her wonder how much she'd confided in Rob…

Before.

And if things in their relationship had really been good…

Before.

…or maybe they'd been better for Rob than her, and she'd never said anything.

She'd have to wait until she could talk to Shayla in private. She suspected the woman likely held many of those clues.

They stayed until after ten o'clock. She started yawning, and Shayla was actually the one who called it a night despite Laura wanting her—all of them—to stay.

Tony and Shayla both hugged her, with Laura eliciting a promise from the other woman to return the next morning to stay with her. Then they left, giving Laura and Rob a little privacy.

She held out her hands to Rob, a little thrill running through her when he stepped into her embrace. She once again buried her face against his stomach and breathed in deeply, hoping for another insight.

Nothing.

She sighed, then remembered her question.

"Did I used to wear a necklace or something?"

She felt his body tense a little. "Why?"

"It feels like I'm missing one. I keep finding myself reaching up to my neck, like I'm used to playing with it."

She didn't mind it when he kissed the top of her head. "Yes. Apparently your attacker stole it."

"Oh." She felt a keen sense of loss, even though she had no memory of it. Of its own volition, one hand went to the base of her throat. "What did it look like?"

"A lot like the one Shayla wears," Rob mumbled into her hair. "I got it for you because you loved hers so much. I promise I'm going to get you another one, sweetheart. I *will* get you another one."

Her eyes squeezed closed. "He took everything from me. And that, too. How much more, Rob? How much more did he steal from us?"

His embrace felt like a safe harbor in which she could hide from the swirling vortex of a storm she found herself trapped in. "He can't take our love, Laura. That's ours, and ours alone."

The idle thought crossed her mind that she wished she knew whether she was a religious person or not, and if she found comfort in prayer.

* * * *

Rob wanted to spend the night there with her and knew he couldn't. He had to go home and take care of Doogie, for starters.

And she needed time alone to process the day.

As he drove through the darkness his mind drifted. To the last time they'd made love.

He never imagined as he'd held her wrists pinned over her head, her legs wrapped around his hips as he slowly thrust, patiently waiting for her to come first, that it might be the last time in a long time.

Their bodies fit perfectly together. As if made to be together. Despite his profession he never dreamed a future without her was something he might have to contemplate this soon.

He could still envision the unfocused look in her eyes, the way her lower lip caught under her teeth, hear her soft gasps at the bottom of every stroke as his cock filled her and he bumped against her clit.

The way she felt when she came, her cries of pleasure as he hurried to catch up and join her.

Nothing had ever felt as right in his life as loving her. Making love to her.

Owning her.

And now…

Now their entire future was a huge, murky *if* instead of the certainty he'd known not even a week before.

And seeing her battered face, even if she did get her memory back, could he ever bring himself to lay a hand on her again? Even when, before, she would sometimes playfully beg for her daily spanking? When, before, she would tease him if he didn't leave bruises on her ass after a scene?

Doogie eagerly awaited his return. He walked the dog before stripping and stepping into the shower in an attempt to relax.

Closing his eyes, he turned his face into the stinging spray. Even here held countless memories. Of pushing her up against the wall and fucking her brains out while she begged for more. Or fisting her hair while she gave him a blow job.

Everywhere lay memories of not only her and their love, but of their dynamic. The plastic storage bins of toys and implements under the bed, and his rolling black suitcase in the closet that held rope and implements and other toys and went with them to the club. The tube of lube on the bathroom counter for when he decided to fuck her ass in the shower.

The bottle of soap under the bathroom sink they used to clean their toys.

The matching black leather leash and collar in the bedside table that had never been around Doogie's neck, and yet were well used. Along with several wooden spoons and bamboo spatulas that would never be used in the kitchen.

Not for cooking, at least.

I just want her back. However I can have her, I just want her back.

Chapter Six

The next morning, Laura woke shortly after six, before rounds started, and managed to get out of bed and make it to the bathroom without assistance. Idle thoughts played through her mind. One of them, she wondered if she was normally a morning person or a night owl.

Once dressed in clothes Rob had brought for her the day before, she stood staring out her window at the parking lot. Apparently her room faced north. It looked like the sun was coming up to her right, and this side of the building remained cast in shadows.

When she closed her eyes, a mental image of early mornings spent on a boat, on open water, came to mind. Trying to catch the slippery tail end of those memories is what occupied her thoughts when she heard a knock on her door.

She turned as the deputy assigned to morning guard duty stuck her head in. "The hospital chaplain is here and wanted to know if you'd like him to come in."

She nodded. "Okay."

"Do you want me to come in with him?"

Laura shook her head. "No. I think I'll be all right, but thank you." It hadn't taken Laura long to process that uniformed deputies were safe. And to look for name tags on anyone wearing medical uniforms or scrubs. As long as a man fit in those two categories, she forced herself to stay calm.

And Rob. And, after last night, Tony.

Chaplain Ben Pelletier was an older man, with a kind and gentle face mirrored on the official hospital ID he wore clipped to his shirt pocket. Laura felt at ease right away as he sat in a chair next to her bed.

"I know it's early, but they said you were awake so I figured I'd stop by. Nancy Russell suggested maybe I should come talk to you. See if you wanted a friendly ear."

"I have to be honest with you, Father. I don't know what religion I was, if any."

He laughed. "I'm not a priest. You can call me Ben, or Pastor Ben, if it makes you feel better. I think my wife wouldn't like it if I was a priest."

He got her laughing, which hurt her ribs but felt good to her soul. He stayed, talking with her all during morning rounds and breakfast, chatting, exuding gentle patience while she quizzed him about local places and events, hoping anything would jog her memory.

Eventually, he turned serious. "I'm also a counselor, if you feel you need to talk to someone. It's not uncommon for people who've been through serious trauma to develop post-traumatic stress disorder. Sometimes it doesn't show up right away. In your case, you've got other things to focus on right now. It could catch you by surprise."

"All I care about is getting my memory back." She thought about Rob, about Carol, about the pictures they'd both shown her.

About Tony and Shayla.

She sensed Rob held something back, but didn't know what. That feeling conflicted with the innate sense of trust she had when she thought about him.

"And what if it doesn't come back?" he asked. "That's a possibility, and one you should consider. In that case, you really should talk to someone about it."

She frowned. "I *will* get my memory back. Most of it, at least. I know I will." Although she didn't know, not for sure.

Yet a stubborn tenacity rolled through her. Not getting her life back wasn't an acceptable option to her.

"If nothing else, you might want to go for Rob's sake." Her surprise must have shown, because he smiled. "I know him from here at the hospital. He's a good man. Very devoted to you. If you have any doubts about him—"

"I don't." Now that she said it, she realized she felt it. Truly felt it.

Still, little niggling things. Not about her love and trust for Rob, but…something.

Nothing that she felt like verbalizing to the chaplain, at least.

Shortly after breakfast, Rob walked in the door. "Hi," the pastor said. "I'll get out of your hair. We were just having a chat." He reached out and gently squeezed Laura's hand. "Would you like me to come back tomorrow?"

She nodded. "That's fine." He was nice to talk to, and unlike the medical staff, he apparently had the freedom to sit and relax with her. She didn't feel like he was rushed, or like she was holding him up from other duties.

"Then I'll see you tomorrow." He shook hands with Rob as he left.

Rob turned to her. The hesitantly hopeful look on his face made her extend her arms to him from where she sat on the edge of the bed.

Stepping into her embrace, she felt him relax a little. "Are you okay?" she asked.

He let out a barking laugh before looking down at her. "Sweetheart, you're the one in here. I'll be fine."

"I'm sorry."

He gently cupped her chin in his palms. "Please don't ever apologize to me for this. You didn't do anything wrong."

"I feel like I'm putting you through hell."

"I'd go through it a thousand times to have you with me. Besides, it's *not* your fault."

There was another knock on the door. The deputy opened it. "Shayla Daniels is here to see you."

Laura felt an emotional surge roll through her. She jumped up off the bed, ignoring painful protests from all the still-sore spots in her body. "Yes!"

* * * *

Rob watched as Laura rushed over to Shayla and engulfed her in a hug.

I wish she was that happy to see me.

He immediately hated himself for the thought.

I think I need to spend some time talking with Tony. He didn't want Laura to get even a hint of some of the thoughts that had crossed his mind. He was smart enough to know they were from his own insecurities, not because of her.

Shayla carried a small plastic storage tub in her hands and walked over to set it on the tray table. She popped the lid off, revealing it was full of dark-chocolate-covered peanut butter candies. "Buckeyes," she said. "Go ahead."

He didn't miss how Laura glanced at him first, almost as if seeking his approval. He smiled and nodded. She reached in and picked one, then took a tentative bite.

Her face lit up. "Oh. My. God. This is great!" She shoved the rest into her mouth and reached for two more.

Shayla smiled, her eyes looking a little too bright. "You always loved them. *Love* them," she corrected herself.

Laura stopped chewing, her gaze dropping to the floor. "No, it's okay," she softly said. "I guess I did kind of die, in a way."

"No, you didn't," Rob firmly said.

"Didn't I?" She finally raised her gaze to look at Shayla before it landed on him. "I feel like I did. I feel like I was just born, in a lot of ways. I don't even know what my favorite color is—"

"Blue," Rob and Shayla said.

She stared at the remains of the candy in her hand as if seeing it for the first time before she put the rest into her mouth and chewed. "That, and the fact that I love eggplant parmesan and Buckeyes won't help the police figure out who did this," she softly said. She popped another one into her mouth.

Rob ached for her. It warred on every level of his soul with the hatred he felt for whoever had done this to her.

To both of them.

* * * *

Rob and Shayla spent the rest of the morning with Laura, talking, going through pictures, sometimes more than once. He even went down to the cafeteria to get lunch for him and Shayla and brought it back to the room. Around three, he had to leave to walk Doogie. Shayla volunteered to stay with Laura.

They both looked at her, as if wanting to know if it was okay. She'd had her head buried in one of the older photo albums again, slowly staring at each picture, trying to coax the stubborn memories to step forward.

She finally realized they were waiting on her. "Oh. Sure. That's okay."

She hated how sad Rob looked. He telegraphed his emotions through his body language, through the expression on his face. She hated even more that she knew it was because of her, of what had happened to her. At least she felt more at ease around him today. The more time she spent with him, the more she knew yes, she had loved him, and he loved her.

She just couldn't fricking remember it.

Setting the album aside, she reached for him, letting out a soft sigh when he stepped into her embrace while she sat on the edge of the hospital bed. She closed her eyes and once again pressed her face against his shirt. Today, he'd dressed in jeans and a blue, collared, short-sleeved shirt, not his paramedic uniform.

"Shayla has my number if you need me."

Laura nodded. "I'll be fine."

She'd even put the ring back on, more to keep it from disappearing than anything, but she still didn't have any tangible memories to rely on.

He kissed the top of her head and moved to step back, but she held on and looked up. After a moment he leaned in and kissed her forehead, lingering a few seconds before straightening again.

She released him.

"I'll be back in a couple of hours," he said. "Do you want me to bring you dinner?"

"Please!"

That won her another smile. "I'll keep it easy and get us a pizza. Shayla, will you be staying?"

"If it's okay?"

He gave her a brief, friendly hug. Laura could see it was far more platonic than the hugs he'd given her so far, no wistful lingering to his motions. "Of course it's okay," he told her. "If it's okay with Laura."

She nodded.

When Rob left, Laura felt more than a little pang to see him go, but she was looking forward to the alone time with Shayla.

"You won't get in trouble for taking the day off, will you?"

"Oh, no. I have vacation time built up. When…" She faltered and looked like she nearly burst into tears before forcing a smile. "When Rob called us, I immediately put work on notice that I might need to take time off. They're okay with it."

"That's nice of them." She popped another candy into her mouth.

"These are sooo good."

Shayla sat in a chair next to the bed. "The past couple of years, we've made them together at the holidays. Us and Leah, Loren, Tilly, and Clarisse. We get together at Leah and Seth's. They've got a big kitchen. We do a massive bake-a-thon for all our holiday stuff on one Saturday or Sunday. We each have our own favorite recipe, in addition to other stuff we make."

"What do I make?"

Her eyes widened. "Oh. My. God. I should have made those last night!" She clapped a hand to her mouth and looked like she was a breath away from crying again. "I wasn't thinking. I'm sorry!"

She really didn't want Shayla to start crying. If she did, Laura knew she would be right behind her. "It's okay. These are great."

"You always make shortbread cookies. You have a recipe that was your mom's. You said you used to help her make them every Christmas when you were a little girl."

Laura felt the hitch in her breath. "I can't even remember my parents. Rob said he can't get in touch with my brother."

Shayla nodded. "He's a bush pilot in Montana. It's not uncommon for him to be out of touch for a week or two at a time if he's out in the back country."

"Am I close to him?"

Shayla shrugged. "Pretty close, I guess. You've talked about him before, give us updates when you hear from him. He's older than you by a couple of years. You've never said you guys were on bad terms. You and Rob talked about going out to visit him later this summer, to visit Yellowstone."

"Yellowstone? That's…" She closed her eyes and concentrated. "That's a big park, right?"

"Very. He lives near there."

Hazy images swam into her mind, along with the memory of the smell of…

"Sulfur?" She opened her eyes and looked at Shayla.

Shayla wore a puzzled expression. "What?"

"Sulfur. The smell of sulfur. Or…something."

"Oh. Yeah, you said you can smell it all over the park because of the thermal features. I've never been there, though."

Laura looked at the stack of photo albums sitting on another chair. "I don't remember seeing pictures of that."

"You've got them all on your computer, I think. You have a few gorgeous pictures you had blown up and framed at the condo."

"Oh." The surge of memory faded as quickly as it had arrived. "Darn. So how did you meet Tony?"

Did Shayla's eyes suddenly widen? "Oh. Uh, during an interview when I first started at the magazine. One of my first assignments."

"What about?"

Now Shayla definitely wore a deer-in-the-headlights look. "Ah, he runs a data center." She rummaged around in her purse for a moment. "Hey, I loaded pictures on my phone of you and the gang to look at."

Laura got the feeling there was more to it than that, but was soon distracted by Shayla walking over with her phone and swiping through pictures with her.

Somewhere deep inside, Laura felt familiarity when looking at the first picture. It was her and Shayla with four other women. They were sitting at a table in a restaurant and all holding up glasses at whoever was taking the picture. "Leah, Loren, Tilly, and Clarisse," she said. "The waiter took it for us. This was just a few weeks ago. Our first all together since Clarisse had the baby."

"Baby?"

"Yeah. Her second with, uh, here's another from the same day." Shayla quickly swiped to the next picture. They looked like they were standing in front of a giant shark hanging upside down. "That's in Tarpon Springs."

"Fake shark?" she asked, squinting a little to see.

"Oh, yeah." Shayla laughed. "Over at the Sponge Docks. Clarisse lives there. In Tarpon Springs, I mean. Not at the docks."

"With her husband?"

"Yes." Shayla swiped to another picture before Laura could ask why she sounded so nervous.

Little flashes of memory sparked here and there in Laura's brain as they looked through them all, odd, random snapshots briefly coming into mental view before disappearing again. Laura didn't know if they were true memories or not, but it totally distracted her from asking more about Clarisse and her family.

She realized that thought scared her even more than not getting her memory back at all. "What if what I remember isn't what happened, but what I think happened, or what other people tell me?" she asked Shayla.

Her friend looked sad. "I don't have an answer for you. I'm sorry."

Laura's gaze returned to the phone. "I wonder if anyone will."

* * * *

Rob went home and walked Doogie first. Then he headed by the dive shop. He wanted to make sure Carol didn't decide to just randomly drop by the hospital again without asking first. He'd hoped yesterday's talk had ensured that, but it never hurt.

Steve stood behind the counter, ringing up a customer. He wore a grim look on his usually cheerful face. He looked up as soon as Rob walked in and hurried to complete the transaction.

Once the customer had left, he rounded the counter. "All right. Enough with the bullshit. I want to see her."

He took a deep breath and held his hands up, trying to placate him. "Did you talk to Carol?"

The older man frowned. "Yeah, but if she could go see her, why can't I?"

Rob treaded carefully. "Carol stopped by without asking first. You know how Laura is. She's been beaten to a pulp and trying to come to terms with the fact that she has no memory. Do you want to see her for your benefit or hers?"

Steve recoiled as if slapped. "How dare you—"

"How dare *you*? Look, I love you like family, but what if she gets her memory back today and chews me a fucking new one for letting Carol see her like that, huh? Yeah, you've known her nearly her whole life. You tell me what she'd want."

He took a step back and stared at the floor, his face going red, jaw working. Finally, he looked back at Rob. "When can we see her then? And why aren't you there now?"

Rob took a deep, relieved breath. He kept his tone calm and apologetic. "I'm going to talk to her today about that. And I had to walk Doogie. I was already there a few hours this morning. You have no idea how many people want to come visit her. If I let everyone descend on her at once, it could set back her recovery from the stress, okay? I need to do it in stages, manageable bites, so we don't overwhelm her. That's what the doctors said. Okay?"

Rob reached out and touched the man's arm. "I promise, you'll get to see her soon."

"Why can't we talk to her on the phone?"

"Because she doesn't know you. I'm not even talking to her on the phone."

Steve leaned against the counter and shook his head. "I just...I can't believe it. Does she remember anything?"

"She almost had a memory about that trip when we found the lobster. The picture triggered something."

"Then we should get her in here soon."

"I know. I agree. But she needs to be in the hospital right now for another couple of days. She's still in a lot of pain from her injuries, and she looks like hell." He choked back his own emotions. "He beat the crap out of her, Steve," he admitted. "He nearly killed her. And to be honest? I feel better having her in the hospital right now. As long as she's there, they'll keep a deputy at her door. Once she's out of there I can't protect her every second of the day."

"You know damn well I'll help."

"I know. But what if who did this is a customer? What if he walks in here and shoots her?"

Steve's face darkened. "That detective was already in here. Went through records a few times. I gave him everything he asked for. Class rosters, charter manifests, receipts, everything."

"And that's a start."

After a few silent moments, it looked like all the anger seeped out of the older man. "What aren't you telling me?"

Rob knew he needed to give the man a little more info to keep him happy. "I told Laura's friend, Shayla, she could visit her. She came last night with her husband, and she's there with her right now. I don't want Carol to know that. I don't want her feelings hurt."

Steve slowly nodded. "She's really close to Shayla."

"I thought if there was a single person other than me who could trigger something, it might be Shayla."

Steve let out a resigned sigh. "You're right. No, I won't tell Carol." He met Rob's gaze. "If I could get my hands on that fucker…" He didn't finish.

Rob squeezed Steve's shoulder. "You and me, both. Believe me."

* * * *

As he climbed into his Explorer, Rob spotted a duffel bag on the floor behind the passenger seat. He dragged it into his lap and unzipped it.

Royal blue rope.

He fingered it. He didn't have to unpack the rope to know that under it lay several carabiners, other clips, a ball gag, and a blindfold.

Angrily, he zipped it up and tossed it into the backseat before starting the engine. His mind drifted as he drove.

Two? No, three weeks earlier. He'd packed that bag for a small private party at Tony and Shayla's.

Seth and Leah, Loren and Ross, and Tilly and her men had also been there. Rob was scheduled to work that Saturday and wouldn't be at dinner or the club, so they'd set it up for him.

Because they were friends and loved him and Laura both.

Laura still went out to Sigalo's on Saturday night with the rest of the gang, and then spent a little time socializing later at the club.

But that night, in Tony's private playroom, Rob had tied Laura in a chest harness before binding her, helpless, to a bench.

Her soft cries still rang in his ears as he'd inserted a vibrator into her pussy before using another piece of rope to secure it in place.

And turned it on, forbidding her from coming under threat of five cane strokes, part of the sadistic fun knowing she wouldn't be able to hold back and that she was more than willing to sacrifice five strokes for the orgasms.

How she'd moaned when he stepped in front of her and unzipped his jeans, her eager mouth wide and willing while a fine sheen of sweat coated her skin.

How he'd grabbed her head firmly. "Have you come yet?"

She shook her head, mouth still wide open and ready.

Sadistic glee filled him. This was a routine they'd gone through countless times before, one she loved despite the resulting cane strokes.

Loved him taking charge and owning her, loved knowing he would follow through.

How she moaned, the sound vibrating through his cock, deep into his balls, as he fucked her mouth and her warm lips and tongue stroked him.

How she moaned again, harder, louder, with a mix of dismay and gleeful anticipation when he reached down and twisted her nipples.

How she moaned even more deeply when that finished her off and the orgasm washed over her, arching her against her restraints as she sucked him harder.

"There's your five, baby girl," he'd told her, loving how she moaned again, sucking him harder, more deeply, writhing against the ropes as she fucked her hips against the air and the bench as the vibrator hummed inside her.

It only made him want to fuck her more and harder, but instead, he withdrew before she could make him come. She whined in disappointment, but he wouldn't be denied. He carefully tucked his protesting cock back into his jeans and walked around behind her.

First, he prepared a butt plug and, even as the vibrator continued humming inside her, he slowly and carefully inserted it, making her cry out as another series of orgasms washed through her.

And then…

Then, the Hitachi.

How he held it pressed firmly against her clit, still turned off, as with his other hand he brushed the cane against her ass.

"Time to pay up, baby girl. Ask me for it."

She struggled to speak through the effects of the vibrator and butt plug on her brain. "Please give me my five, Sir!"

"Good girl." He clicked on the Hitachi, on high, and took the first swing across her ass with the cane.

She screamed, in pleasure and pain, as she came again.

He drew it out, knowing how she loved it, the short-circuiting of her brain as he combined each painful cane stroke with the overwhelming pleasure of the Hitachi.

When she'd taken all five strokes, he turned off the Hitachi and set it and the cane down before returning to her head.

She still shivered, the other vibrator inside her not letting her completely stop orgasming.

He unzipped his jeans again and she opened her lips without prompting.

"Such a good girl." He stroked her hair as he fucked her mouth, going faster but careful not to gag her, his own groan joining with hers as his balls tightened, then emptied, and she swallowed every drop of cum he fed her.

How later, on Tony's couch, Laura had blissfully curled up in a blanket, her head in his lap while he talked with their friends.

How they'd gone home and she'd fallen asleep in his arms.

He barely missed rear-ending a car in front of him, jamming on the brakes and forcing his brain back to the present.

What kind of monster am I to think about stuff like that now?

When she looked horrible and had barely begun to heal from the attack?

Now was not the time for those kinds of thoughts.

And if she didn't get her memory back, he was all too aware of how those thoughts might be all he had left of their former dynamic.

Chapter Seven

When Rob returned to the hospital a little before six that evening, he found Laura and Shayla both sitting on the bed, cross-legged, side by side. Shayla had her iPhone in hand and was showing something to Laura.

They both looked up when he walked in. The nearly identical expressions on their faces made his heart ache. He and Tony had frequently joked with each other that the two women truly were twins from different mothers. Not just their mannerisms and how they talked, they even looked a lot alike.

"What're you looking at?" he asked.

"Shayla was showing me the website for the shop and some of the articles I wrote."

Why didn't I think of that? He set the pizza boxes on the bed tray table. He'd grabbed three extra large pies, more than enough to feed them and the deputy on duty, with plenty left over to give to the nursing staff. He knew from experience they didn't always get a chance to get a good meal. "Anything?"

Laura shrugged. "A little. I looked at pictures on the shop's website. Shayla said I built the website?"

He didn't miss how it was a question, not a statement. "You did. You taught yourself how to do it."

"Oh." She cocked her head as if she didn't believe him, either. "Really?"

He smiled. "Really. You're quite good at it."

"Oh." She wrinkled her nose as she sniffed at the pizzas. "That smells good."

He felt the shift in her focus as surely as he could feel a shift in the winds on the open Gulf. Laura was now fully focused on the pizzas.

Part of him hoped that was just a side effect of the memory loss. His

Laura would remain almost maniacally focused on one thing for hours on end. It was what made her a great writer, as well as a good teacher.

He moved the plastic bag containing the handful of paper plates, roll of paper towels, and several bottles of water he'd grabbed from the house after walking Doogie. Opening the top box, he said, "Extra cheese, mushrooms, black olives. One of your favorites."

She peeked in. "The others?"

"One with the works, for me, and one with ham and pepperoni."

Within a few minutes, the three of them, joined by the deputy, were all eating.

Laura wore a thoughtful expression. "Are you all right?" Rob asked.

She slowly nodded.

"Is the pizza okay?"

She nodded again. "I like it."

"What's wrong?"

She shrugged as she stared down at her plate after a quick glance at Shayla. "It's like I told her. I don't know if what I'm feeling is because I liked it, or because I've been told I've liked it. Does that make sense?"

* * * *

Laura looked back up at him, relieved when he nodded.

"I get it, honey. Believe me, we all hope your memory returns so that's no longer a doubt you have to deal with."

She felt a little guilty that Shayla had spent all day there with her. But after dinner, when it seemed like Shayla was trying to figure out how to say good night, Laura didn't want her to leave.

"It's okay," Shayla assured her. "I'll be back tomorrow morning. I promise."

"And I have to work a half shift tomorrow," Rob said. "So that works out well. When I get off work at eight tomorrow night, I'll come here. You won't be alone."

Laura nodded, sniffling away the tears that tried to break through. It annoyed her that she didn't know if she was normally a tough person, or emotional and weepy.

Right now, her nerves felt as raw as some of the sore spots on her body.

Add to that the guilt over not feeling the same kind of desperation over when Rob left.

At least Shayla had alleviated some of Laura's fears. According to Shayla, Laura had been madly and deeply in love with Rob…before.

That damned word again.

Boy, how she despised it.

Yet…

There was something. Like a missing link everyone else was privy to except her. She didn't know if it was related to the attack or something else. Like a subtext she didn't have the ability to understand. She didn't feel like she was being lied to, exactly. She just…

It would drive her nuts if she let it. She decided to drop it for the time being.

Finally, after another series of hugs and good-byes and promises she'd return in the morning, Shayla went home, leaving Laura alone with Rob.

He looked like he wasn't sure what he should do with himself.

Frankly, it relieved her.

She sat cross-legged on the bed and looked at him. "I'm sorry this feels weird."

He leaned forward in his chair and took her hands in his. "Please," he gently said, "sweetheart, stop apologizing. You haven't done anything wrong."

She stared into his eyes. Sweet, soft brown eyes she'd no doubt spent plenty of hours staring into before. Here and there, tiny little flecks of amber and green caught the light. His light brown hair hadn't started going grey at the temples yet, although the occasional stray grey hair peeked through here and there.

He had a kind face, too. Paired with the feelings of love and safety she got every time she was around him, it made her want to fall into his arms and hide forever.

Except part of her still felt afraid to do that. The gaping maw in her mind kept her isolated on the other side of the chasm, staring over it at him from the other side.

"Was I a really fearful person?" she softly asked.

He tilted his head. "No, sweetie. Why?"

"I feel scared. About everything."

"Do I scare you?"

She needed to think about her answer. "You don't scare me," she carefully said. "The situation scares me. Shayla told me how much I loved you before all this. I'm scared that what if I screw something up and you don't love the new me?"

"Aw, babe." He stood and slowly encircled her in his arms, waiting for her to lean into his chest before he held her close. "I will *always* love you," he whispered into her hair. "No matter what happens. *Never* forget that. I held your hand and begged you to wake up and come back to me and you did. I will never walk away from you. *Ever*."

She let out a deep, relieved breath she hadn't realized she'd been holding. "Okay."

He kissed the top of her head. "Okay."

* * * *

It was after eight when she started yawning and couldn't stop. She knew sleep wouldn't come soon, but something told her she'd reached her daily limit on close, personal interactions. She already felt emotional enough as it was, as if she'd overloaded and couldn't absorb any more information.

She needed a break.

He brushed the back of his hand over her cheek. "You look wiped out. Do you want me to see if they'll let me stay in here with you? I can run home and walk Doogie and come back."

"That's okay." She offered him a smile. "I'll be all right. You need to get some sleep."

That seemed to help soften the blow. And when she let him hug her before he left, she sensed his reluctance to let go of her.

"Oh, here." He pulled an index card from his pocket and put it by the phone. "Those are my phone numbers, and Shayla and Tony, and Carol, and a few others." His brow furrowed. "Although I just realized some of the people you…" He sighed, his shoulders slumping. "I guess some of them you don't remember yet."

She hugged him again, slipping her arms around his waist. "Thank you," she whispered against his chest.

The feeling of safety returned as he wrapped his arms around her and held her. She could easily spend all night just like this, standing there anchored to him physically, if not mentally.

Once he'd left, Laura invited the deputy guarding her to watch TV with her. They spent more time talking than watching, with Laura quizzing him on local details.

"Do you know Rob?" she thought to ask.

"Carlton? I don't know him personally. I've crossed paths with him a few times during work. Everything I've heard about him is that he's a nice guy, though."

"Did I know you…before?" She hated that word. It had quickly become the quantifier by which her life was now gauged.

He shook his head. "No. I've never met you before now."

She let out a sigh as she turned to the TV again. "That makes two of us."

* * * *

Det. Thomas scrubbed a hand over his face as he stared at the printouts on his desk.

Fuck.

He knew beyond a shadow of a doubt Rob Carlton had nothing to do with Laura Spaulding's attack.

Unfortunately, the records of the text messages pulled from her phone account had just added a wrinkle to his case. One that, if it got leaked, could make life very difficult for the man.

Could even cost Rob his job.

It was half past eight when he picked up the phone and called him. "It's Det. Thomas," he said when Rob answered. "I need to speak with you tonight about Laura's case."

"Did you catch the fucker?"

Thomas stared at the printouts. "No. But I need to talk with you in person."

"I'm on my way home from the hospital. I'll be there in a few minutes."

"That's fine." He grabbed a pen. "Give me your address again so I don't have to look it up." He quickly wrote it down. "I'll be there in about thirty minutes."

He ended the call and stared at the sheets of paper fanned out in front of him.

Her cell text records for the past two months didn't give him any obvious leads about who attacked her. The majority of the messages were between Laura and Rob, and between Laura and her friend, Shayla Daniels.

Messages that led him to believe Rob and Laura had a BDSM-type relationship.

While his first and gut instinct had been to suspect the crime was a random attack, this added a new twist to the case. Whoever attacked her had done so viciously…

Sadistically.

Maybe he needed to look into personal connections they had in the local BDSM scene. He knew there was a group out of Sarasota, and another there in Charlotte County, both very active. Their members apparently kept their events under-the-table, took great cares to cloak their activities from blipping law enforcement radar in either jurisdiction.

With fictional books about BDSM now topping worldwide bestseller charts, as with any phenomenon he expected more people to be attracted to it and network with people already involved in it.

It wouldn't be beyond the realm of the improbable for a violent offender to join them and seek out victims.

Thomas arrived at Rob Carlton's house a minute shy of his predicted time. Rob held back a huge, young-looking black Lab when he welcomed the detective into his home.

"He's a handsome dog." Thomas held out his hand for the dog to sniff.

Rob let out a snort. "Thanks. He's a moose. He's barely six months old."

"Holy crap." He stared at the dog. "He's going to be huge."

"Tell me about it." He finally released the dog's collar once he'd settled down. "You sounded pretty serious on the phone," Rob said. "What's going on?"

Thomas held out the sheaf of papers to Rob. He watched Rob's face flash from enraged to a schooled neutrality as he realized what they were.

Rob looked up at him. "What do you want me to say? I didn't hurt her. You know that."

"Hold on. That's not what I'm saying. Before I go blundering around and possibly costing you your job if this gets out, is there anything else you need to tell me about your relationship with Laura? Anything that might help me figure out who did this to her?"

Rob slumped down onto the arm of the sofa as he leafed through the papers again. "We're a Dominant-submissive couple, okay? She wanted me to officially collar her as my slave when we get married. Got married."

Rob stared off into space for a moment before shaking his head. "Fuck," he softly said. "I don't know if we're even getting married now. I don't even know how to *talk* about it. Do I still talk like it's going to happen? How the *fuck* do I deal with this?"

"One day at a time."

"I love her." Rob held up the papers, anger contorting his features. "You can see that, can't you? How much I love her? How much she loved me?"

He nodded. "It's pretty obvious."

"Is she even going to want me?"

Thomas sat in a chair opposite the couch. "If she doesn't get her memory back?"

Rob nodded.

"Nothing?"

Rob shook his head and returned the papers to Thomas. "I was there most of today. Nothing yet."

"I'm not a psychic or a psychiatrist. Although in my not-so-humble opinion, the two are sometimes so closely linked it's hard to tell the difference." He rubbed a hand over his face. Stubble rasped against his palm. "Okay, so back to this." Thomas indicated the papers. "Have you told her about this?"

He let out a snort. "No. She doesn't remember me. I…" His voice choked. "I called her 'baby girl' yesterday and she…" He shook his head. "It was her favorite pet name. I can't even call her that now."

"Anyone you know into this BDSM stuff that might want to hurt her?"

He let out another snort. "You mean besides me?" Rob's voice held a bitter tone.

"I mean nonconsensually. Isn't that what this is all about?"

Rob slid from the arm of the couch onto the seat. "We're a close-knit group. We have a lot of really great friends who I don't want to drag through the dirt. Some of them have a lot to lose if they're outed. I can't believe any of them would ever hurt her. I can give you her FetLife username and password, if you want it, to go through her account. I'm guessing your geeks didn't go through her computer very carefully, huh?"

He ignored the jab. "You have it back already?"

"I'll get her laptop." He stood and disappeared to the back of the house, returning a moment later with the laptop and a charger. He set it up on the table and Thomas walked over to stand behind him while he powered it up and logged into it. He brought up the browser and opened her FetLife account before standing and pointing at the screen.

"There. Knock yourself out. And yes, I already went through it just in case there was anything that might help. Her email, too. Nothing. Although your guys did that, too, and said they didn't find anything."

"Yeah." Thomas slid into the chair and, with Rob guiding him, went through her private messages back to a few months earlier. "Did she have any other email accounts that you know of?"

"No. Just personal and for the shop, and they both filter to her iPhone."

"Any other sites she's a member of?"

He let out a snort. "How many? She's a writer. She's a member of a ton of different sites, from fishing, to diving, to writing, and even some dog and Labrador retriever sites now because of him." He pointed at the dog, who was calmly lying on the floor and staring at them. "And she follows I don't know how many blogs."

He'd have to hold off on that. This was an immediate lead he had to follow through with. His gut told him whoever did this, she'd had up close contact with, not randomly on the Internet. And everything else he'd found out from both their computer techs and Rob told him Laura was super cautious about never giving out personal information online to others. The only contact info people had were her email or the shop's info.

Unfortunately, as Rob had said, her FetLife account contained nothing other than banal, everyday chatter. "What if she deleted a message?"

Rob showed him how to access the archive. Nothing. She had no pending friend requests, either.

"Would she have had any issues and not told you about them?"

"I seriously doubt it. I don't control who she can and can't friend. She doesn't need my permission to friend anyone, but anytime she has a creeper hit on her on the site, she immediately blocks them and tells me about it so I can block them, too."

"Any way to see who's been blocked?"

Rob shook his head. "It's not a feature they have yet. You can block people, but unless you hit their profile and see that you've blocked them, you have no master list to look at. Maybe if you email the site administrators."

Thomas wasn't sure he wanted to go down that path yet without evidence pointing that direction. It would likely mean getting a court order, meaning he'd have to put Rob's private life under the microscope. He wasn't willing to do that.

Yet.

"Who else would she talk to?" he asked.

"She's close to Shayla, Leah, Loren, and Tilly. In fact, Shayla spent most of the day with her today, including when I had to come home to walk Doogie. They're all in the Sarasota area. She's also friends with Clarisse, but she lives up in Tarpon Springs. We're a sort of close-knit group."

"Last names?"

He shook his head and crossed his arms over his chest. "I'm not outing my friends."

Thomas fought the urge to order him to hand over the names and decided to take the more tactful path. "Can you call them for me and arrange a meeting to talk with me? Here, if that would make them feel better."

He nodded. "When?"

"The sooner, the better."

"I have to work tomorrow."

"Then tonight."

"Clarisse and her husbands have a toddler and an infant. I doubt she or her men will be willing or able to drive down here tonight. That's like two hours, one way."

He mentally swore and decided to not question the plural Rob had used for the woman's spouses. "Then call them for me now and see if they'll talk to me without you around. I'm not the enemy here. I'm trying to run an investigation. I don't want to go dragging a bunch of good people through a public mud bath, but I suspect this guy will attack again, if he hasn't already attacked in the past."

He didn't have concrete evidence because they were still awaiting DNA results. But if his hunch was right, Laura's attacker might be connected to other crimes in Florida and elsewhere.

Rob nodded and pulled out his cell phone.

Thomas listened as Rob made the first call, to someone named Tony, who apparently proposed a different solution after Rob explained things. Rob pulled the phone away from his ear and offered it to Thomas. "He wants to talk to you."

Thomas took the phone. "Det. William Thomas."

The man's quiet confidence didn't come off as abrasive to the experienced investigator. "My name's Tony. For now, that's all I'll share without a court order. I told Rob I'll arrange for us all to get together to talk with you tomorrow night in private up here in Sarasota. None of us want to stonewall you, but you have to understand, some of us have jobs and families to protect."

"I get that. But I have an investigation to run, and if you all cooperate with me, it'll be easier on all of us. The sooner I can rule you all out, the sooner I can look elsewhere."

"And believe me, we all love Laura and want to do everything we can to catch the bastard that did this to her. You'll get our cooperation. One of our friends is a former cop. I'm sure he'll agree we need to do everything we can to help."

Thomas felt a little of his tension ease. He'd been worried he'd meet some weird, kinky code of silence, and have to end up getting court orders for more phone records.

Not something he wanted to do. "Then we're on the same page, Tony." He gave Tony all his contact info and Tony promised to call him by nine the next morning to give him the details.

He returned the phone to Rob, who talked with the man for a few more minutes before ending the call. He turned to Thomas. "Okay?"

"Yeah."

Rob chewed on his lip. "They really are good people. Good friends. More like family. We band together to help each other when something bad happens."

"Where have they been the past several days?" Thomas regretted saying it the moment it left his mouth when Rob's expression turned angry.

"Because I know Laura better than anyone and knew she wouldn't have wanted people seeing her like this. And then she woke up not knowing anyone. All our friends know that Laura has amnesia. They've been giving me all the support they can, but we don't want to flood the hospital with a ton of people Laura doesn't know. We all agreed that because none of our vanilla friends or family know what's going on, it was better for them to wait to hear from me before coming to visit her."

That made a lot of sense. "I'm sorry. I understand."

"No," Rob exploded, "I don't think you do! She's my life, my heart. My future. She's the other half of me. And she doesn't even fucking know who I am, much less how much we loved each other before this happened!"

Thomas flexed his shoulders to ease the tension in his neck and buy him a few seconds to calm his own temper. Then he snatched the sheaf of papers from the table.

"I'm a widower, Rob," he softly said. "She went in for routine gallbladder surgery, had a stroke on the table, and spent four weeks in a coma before she died."

He headed for the door. "At least you can count your lucky stars you have a second chance. Some of us don't get that. I didn't even get a chance to tell her one more time how much I loved her."

He didn't need to turn and look to see the shock on Rob's face. It was painted in his voice. "I'm sorry. I didn't know."

He stopped at the door. "Well, now you do." He yanked it open, mindful not to let the dog out. "If I don't hear from your friend Tony by nine o'clock tomorrow morning, warn him to immediately expect a bundle of search warrants to pull the phone records of everyone who has a phone number on here." He shook the papers at Rob before leaving and slamming the door behind him.

Dammit. He headed for his car and didn't even bother buckling his seatbelt until he'd hit the end of the long drive and turned onto the street. He hadn't meant to lose his temper with the man, but it'd been a long damn day to start with.

It didn't help that he had a bad feeling in his gut that whoever attacked Laura might be tied in with several unsolved murders in Florida and around the country.

And if that was the case, he suspected Laura would still be in the guy's sights.

The sooner he could track the monster down, the sooner she, and others, would be out of danger.

Chapter Eight

Friday morning, Laura again awoke early, this time just as the sun was breaking its sleep over the eastern horizon. She'd spent a restless night having vivid dreams she wondered might actually be memories, between waking up when nurses came to check her vital signs.

Several of those dreams she spent on a boat, heading out on the open water with the sun rising at her back and the greyish-purple horizon ahead of her to the west.

She managed to take a shower without help, that little victory raising her spirits somewhat until she got another look at her battered face in the mirror.

Who are you?

She desperately wanted to know.

Needed to know.

Fuzzy little bits of stray memories had started filtering back, but still nothing concrete she could hold on to. And nothing recent. She had no active memories of any substance concerning Rob, or Shayla, for that matter. Just her emotions about them.

Trying to avoid the mirror, Laura dressed and returned to her bed in time for the doctors to arrive for morning rounds. The neurologist in charge of her treatment, now that she was awake and otherwise healing, ran her through a brief series of questions and movements while talking with a gaggle of residents tagging along.

"Any idea when my memory might come back?" She knew it couldn't hurt to ask even if she already suspected the answer.

He offered her a smile. "Unfortunately, no. I want to run at least one more MRI before we discharge you, though. I'm thinking we'll shoot for letting you go home on Monday, as long as everything else seems okay."

She nodded but didn't reply. Part of her wanted to get out of there.

Part of her felt terrified to leave the safely guarded confines of the hospital. Other than Rob and Shayla, the outside world was still full of strangers she had no clue how to identify, much less whether they were friend or foe.

She didn't even know where she lived.

A few minutes after the doctor left, her bedside phone rang, startling her out of her thoughts. She stared at it for a moment before tentatively reaching out to answer it.

"Hello?"

"Hi, sweetheart. It's me. Um, Rob."

Her fingers curled around the receiver. He sounded a little tentative himself. "Hi."

"I just wanted to check in this morning and see how you're doing."

She felt a wistful pang she hoped boded well for rebuilding her relationship with him. "Thanks. Are you still coming by tonight?"

"Yes," he quickly said. "Absolutely. And if anything happens, I already put the captain on notice that I might have to cut out."

"I don't want you to get in trouble."

"I won't." She got the feeling he wanted to say something else. After a moment, he did. "No more memories?"

She thought about the dreams she'd had. "No. Nothing yet."

"Okay."

She couldn't bear his sad tone. "I miss you."

He suddenly sounded choked up. "I miss you, too, sweetheart. I'll be there tonight as soon as I get off work. Carol's walking Doogie for me, so he'll be okay."

"The doctor said this morning they want to do another MRI on me. They might release me Monday."

That seemed to buoy his spirits. "That's great! I'll make sure I tell the captain so I can be there Monday for you."

After they said their good-byes she stared at the phone. She'd need to ask Rob about her cell phone, what happened to it, or if he could bring it to her. Maybe something on it might help trigger some memories.

At this point, she'd willingly try anything.

Pastor Ben stopped by a few minutes later.

"So how are you today?" he asked.

She shrugged. "Still no memories. Nothing that really matters, anyway."

"I'm not one to harp on a subject, but I would be professionally remiss if I didn't mention again that I think you should consult with a psychiatrist. It might help." He watched her when she didn't object. "I can call my friend, Dr. Simpson. She has privileges here. Have her come here to see you for a consult. Her office is only two blocks away."

With not just the pastor, but the doctors also pressing the issue, Laura finally caved. "Fine," she quietly said.

"It doesn't mean you're 'crazy,'" he firmly insisted.

She let out a frustrated sigh as she pulled her hair away from her face. "That's what you people keep telling me."

"You don't sound convinced."

"I don't know what I am at this point. But I guess if it's possible it'll help me get my memory back I should try it no matter what my feelings are on the subject."

"No idea why you feel the way you do about it?"

"No." She let out a ragged laugh. "Maybe I was already seeing one."

"Did you ask your fiancé?"

She hadn't thought about asking Rob. "No," she admitted.

I should ask Shayla. If anyone would know, it would be her.

"Well, I'll call her as soon as I leave and see if she can stop by to see you today."

They were still talking twenty minutes later when Laura's breakfast arrived, almost immediately followed by Shayla.

Laura got up and hugged the woman, nearly making her drop the plastic food containers she was carrying.

"Sorry, I didn't mean to interrupt," Shayla said after getting the containers safely stacked on the bed tray.

Pastor Ben stood. "It's quite all right. Laura, I'll call Dr. Simpson for you and notify the nurses about it."

"Thank you." After he left, Laura eyed the containers. "What is all this?"

Shayla smiled. "I'm glad I got here when I did. I brought you breakfast." She peeled the lid off one of the containers. "Spinach, swiss, and mushroom omelet. One of your favorites." She handed Laura a fork. "Who was that guy?"

Laura climbed back into bed and took a bite of the omelet. It tasted as good as it looked and smelled. "Pastor Ben. He's also a pastoral counselor. He's going to call a psychiatrist for me." She looked at Shayla. "Did I see a counselor or psychiatrist? Or have anything against them?"

Shayla took the chair the pastor had occupied. "No. Why?"

She shrugged as she forked another bite into her mouth. "I just have this…I don't know. Visceral reaction to the idea of seeing someone. A psychiatrist. I mean the doctors talked about it, too. Said it might help, so I guess I should."

Shayla looked thoughtful. "You've never said anything about it to me. I would think if you were going to tell anyone, it'd be me or Rob."

"Hey, am I religious?" She studied her friend.

Shayla let out a snort. "No. Definitely not. You're not anti-religious, or an atheist, or anything like that. You're just…not."

"Oh."

"Why? Did Pastor Ben make you want to take it up?"

"No, not that. Just didn't know if there was something I was missing out on. Or if I should be asking some higher power for help."

Shayla wore a smirk.

"What?"

The other woman shook her head. "No, the only pleas to a deity I ever heard come out of your mouth had nothing to do with religion." Then Shayla's eyes widened as a sudden look Laura could only describe as horror crossed the woman's face.

"What is it?"

A deep red filled Shayla's cheeks. "Sorry. Nothing." She stood and rushed into the bathroom, shutting the door behind her.

What the hell?

She set the food container on the bed tray and pulled herself back out of bed. It was getting a little easier to move around the more she did it. Walking over to the bathroom door, she knocked. "Shayla?"

Inside, she heard the toilet flush. "Just a minute."

"Are you all right?"

"I'm fine."

She was waiting by the door when Shayla emerged. "What did you mean?"

Laura didn't need to have her memories to know the smile now pasted on the woman's face was forced. "Just...you know. Girl talk. Sorry. I shouldn't have said it like that. Is the omelet all right?"

Laura's stomach growled in protest at being interrupted. "It's delicious. Thank you."

Whatever had hit Shayla seemed to be receding as she noticeably relaxed. "Let's get you back into bed." Laura let her gently take her arm and help her.

Their eyes met. "What aren't you telling me?"

Shayla pressed her lips together until they formed a thin line. "You and Rob love each other," she eventually said. "And you had a great relationship before...before this. I don't want you hearing the things I have to say and it influences you one way or another about Rob."

"Why? Are there things I shouldn't know about him?"

"No, it's nothing like that." She studied her fingernails for a moment. "I started thinking about it last night. You and I told each other everything." A little laugh escaped her. "*Everything*. And Rob and Tony both know that. And they don't have a problem with it. But knowing it and suddenly having another woman telling your fiancée stuff you did, it might not make him very comfortable."

She finally raised her gaze to Laura's. "I'd feel better if you and Rob try to find your more...private memories together. Does that make sense?"

Oddly enough, it did. Laura nodded. "I just want to know everything. I want it all back. I want my life back. I want my memories back."

Shayla gently gripped Laura's hands. "I promise, if they don't come back after a while, well, then I will. And meanwhile, I'll tell you anything I know that happened that you told me that's not...well..."

"Sexual?"

Shayla smiled as she nodded. "Right. Or stuff that I was there for." Her smile faded. "I promise you," she softly said, "there's nothing bad. Not that I know of, and we were close enough that if there was bad stuff, I'd know about it."

A thought occurred to her. "Did I have any exes? Anyone who might want to do this to me?"

"No. No one that I know of. You dated a couple of guys before you met Rob."

Suddenly, this felt very important. "Why did I break up with them?"

"Well, one guy cheated on you. Another took a job in New York and you didn't want a long-distance relationship. And another guy, you only dated him a few weeks before you realized you just didn't have a lot in common with him. But I knew him. He met someone else and ended up marrying her over a year ago. They're expecting a baby."

Laura's hope faded. "Amicable break-ups?"

"Yes. Well, except for Cheater McSleazy. You were ready to kill him, but he left without a peep. And that was years ago. Why?"

She reached for her omelet. "It was just a hope that maybe there might be a clue to who did this."

"I don't know anyone who'd want to do this to you."

Laura stared at her omelet and made herself take another bite even though her appetite faded with her hope. "I wish I did. I wish I could *remember* if I did."

* * * *

At 8:55 a.m., Det. Thomas' desk phone rang. He'd been in the middle of going through several reports he'd been emailed overnight from other law enforcement agencies about unsolved cases with striking similarities to Laura Spaulding's attack.

"Thomas."

"Detective, this is Tony Daniels. We spoke briefly last night."

His full attention shifted from the reports to the caller. "Rob Carlton's friend?"

"Yes. Everyone will be available to meet with you at nine o'clock tonight at my house."

He rifled through a pile of papers on his desk for a pen. "Address?"

It was off Bee Ridge in Sarasota, east of I-75.

"No need for court orders, then, I take it?" Daniels asked.

Thomas closed his eyes and pinched the bridge of his nose. He'd awoken with a migraine threatening, with no signs of it going away anytime soon. "Look, as long as everyone cooperates with me, I don't have any desire to drag anyone through the mud."

"Believe me, we want the asshole who did this to her caught as badly as you do. Unfortunately, none of us know anything that will be of help. You don't think one of the first thoughts we had was maybe someone from the lifestyle had it out for her?"

He leaned back in his chair. "You let me be the judge of the value of the information, Mr. Daniels."

"We will. The only person who might not be there right on time is my wife, Shayla, and that's because she's at the hospital with Laura while Rob's at work."

Maybe he'd have to pay Laura another visit that morning or afternoon. "I take it she's close to Laura?" He already knew that much from the text messages.

"They're best friends. But if you do go talk to her at the hospital, keep in mind Rob isn't telling Laura anything about their BDSM dynamic, or about any of us being into it, either. So please do everyone a favor and not mention that in front of Laura."

He didn't want to lose his patience with the guy, but between stress and the migraine, he was heading in that direction. "I'll respect your intelligence, Mr. Daniels, if you'll respect mine. If you'll drop the adversarial attitude we'll all get along just fine. I'll be there at nine." He hung up before the other man could respond, his head throbbing.

Despite putting a rush on it, they still hadn't received the DNA results back from the FDLE labs yet. He glanced at the email he'd been reading, the PDF copy of a file about a case in Georgia. Seven months earlier, a college coed home for the weekend had been viciously beaten, raped, and strangled.

And the knot on the rope looked like the knot on the rope put around Laura's neck by her attacker. Not that it was a concrete clue, just one of many. That victim, twenty-year-old Alicia Smith, hadn't merely been beaten, but kicked, bitten, and brutalized so badly that her parents had been unable to identify her by her face.

It had been a small butterfly tattoo on the inside of her right ankle, a memorial to a friend killed in a car accident the year before, that had provided their positive ID.

No suspects. No sign of forced entry. Her parents discovered her body when they returned home from an overnight trip to Savannah the next morning.

Nothing stolen from the home, but a bracelet she normally wore was missing. Unfortunately, neither parent could positively remember if she'd been wearing it when she arrived home from her dorm, and it hadn't been found among her possessions there, either. Her roommate remembered seeing her wearing it earlier in the week, but had left for her home Friday afternoon before Alicia and didn't know if she'd been wearing it.

The case was at a standstill. No history of drug use on the part of the victim, she wasn't in a relationship, and the roommate and the roommate's boyfriend had concrete alibis and no motive.

DNA results hadn't matched up with any samples currently on file from inmates in any criminal database. It was, however, linked to three other unsolved crimes scattered across the US with similar patterns.

As Thomas rubbed at the bridge of his nose and stared at the crime scene photos included with the report, he suspected he was about to become far better acquainted with Alicia Smith's case, and the others.

* * * *

Rob hated that he couldn't spend the day with Laura, but knew Shayla would call him immediately if any issues cropped up.

The morning started out busy, with an accident and then a call about a heart attack.

Unfortunately for him, the rest of the morning slowed down, leaving plenty of time for thinking while doing busy work like inventory and cleaning the rig.

He'd looked through some old pictures last night, one standing out in his mind. For Tony and Shayla's private "Kinkmas" party that past December, Rob had turned Laura into his own Christmas tree. Complete with decorations hung from nipple clamps, wrist cuffs, collar, and hip harness, and a strand of battery-operated lights wrapped around her while she struggled not to climax from the vibrating egg held inside her by the harness. The picture showed her decked out with a playful, sexy grin on her face.

Fun times.

He closed his eyes and relived the night. They'd arrived early so they could help Tony and Shayla get things ready. Once it was time for the others to arrive, he'd ordered Laura to strip.

And the fun began.

She'd spent the evening in a perpetual state of horniness, the vibrating egg tormenting her but not strong enough to get her off. He'd taken great sadistic pleasure in periodically removing the nipple clamps, to let the blood flow back into them. Then he'd play with them, rolling them between his fingers and driving up her need even more before reapplying the clamps.

Two hours later, she'd been begging him for a scene, knowing full well pleasure would come at a cost.

He'd started out by undecorating her, except for her cuffs and play collar, and removing the egg before strapping her down to a bench. Next came the bare-handed spanking, warming her ass and making his cock ache with desire. He'd spent the evening hard, and this made him throb even more.

Others were already playing but Rob's full attention totally focused on Laura. As if the entire world faded away, he watched every breath she took, listened to every sound she made. He caressed her flesh, tracing her sweet curves and enjoying the way she arched against his hand.

He grabbed a fistful of her hair and pulled her head up. "Tell me what you want, baby."

"I want Sir to play with me and make me come."

He leaned in closer. "That means you take the pain to get the pleasure."

"Yes, Sir."

"Do you want to take it?"

"Yes, Sir." It came out a happy sigh.

He tenderly kissed her forehead. "Such a good girl," he murmured in her ear.

He went to his implement bag and pulled out a leather slapper that he knew she liked. It delivered just enough sting to give the desired effect.

With his left hand on her ass and the implement in his right, he gave her a light slap as a warning. Then he started in earnest, working up and down her ass and thighs, across her shoulders and the back of her arms, even between her legs, lightly slapping her pussy.

When he reached between her legs he found her juices practically dripping from her. After slowly fucking her with his fingers, he walked around and pulled her head up again by her hair.

"Open."

She did, sucking his fingers without hesitation. He judged from her glazed expression that she'd already gone deep into subspace.

"Such a good girl."

He blindfolded her and buckled her favorite rubber ball gag around her head before delving into the implement bag again. This time, he pulled out several items. The first, an etched acrylic paddle that he used with a little more force than he had the slapper. By the time he finished with it a couple of minutes later, Laura's ass and thighs were pink and she'd started squirming against her bonds.

Next, the riding crop. This drew muffled yelps from her as welts began appearing across her flesh. Followed by a wooden paddle that had her sobbing after just a few strokes.

He gave her a little bit of a respite and switched to a braided leather flogger. More harsh than one of his suede mop floggers, it was still a breather for her, as well as a build up to the finale.

He readied the Hitachi vibrator. Holding it in his left hand, he pressed it to her clit as he laid a cane across her ass with the right. "Time for fun, baby girl." He switched on the vibrator as he took a stroke with the cane.

She screamed from pain as much as she did pleasure, the climax drawing her body into an arcing flex of muscles. He spaced out the cane strokes, never pulling the vibrator away as he did. Her moans drilled through him, amplifying the way his cock throbbed inside his jeans, wanting nothing more than to be buried inside her.

After the tenth stroke, he put down the cane and switched off the vibrator. Laura collapsed, limp and panting, onto the bench.

"Oh, you think you're done, do you?"

Even through the ball gag he heard her laugh as she shook her head.

"You know what it means, right?" This was something he'd learned from Tony, something that cracked him up every time he watched his friend do it to Shayla.

Laura nodded, her body now heaving with laughter.

"What's it mean, baby girl?"

Although muffled by the gag, he heard her say, "Just one more."

"Very good." He unzipped, pulled out his cock, and then grabbed the Hitachi. He sank his cock deep inside her cunt, pausing and letting out a sigh of pleasure.

Then he switched on the Hitachi again and reached around her, pressing it to her clit once more.

The effect, as always, felt electrifying. Laura had once joked he'd succeeded in rewiring her brain to respond to the sound of the vibrator. She came almost immediately, her body once again arching against her restraints, the walls of her pussy squeezing his cock.

Only through sheer force of will did he hold back and not start fucking her, waiting while she undulated against the vibrator, thrusting herself deep onto his cock. He took his time, enjoyed watching her lost in the depths of her orgasm. Once he sensed her growing close to the end of her endurance he began thrusting, hard, knowing he'd come fast.

She matched him thrust for thrust. As he felt his balls draw up, his climax close, Laura came one more time. He fucked her harder, faster, feeling her pussy quivering around his cock just as he exploded and filled her with his cum.

He shut the vibrator off and braced himself on the bench to catch his breath. Laura lay there, a happy smile on her face even with the ball gag in her mouth.

"One more?" he teased.

She laughed and shook her head. "No thank you, Sir. I'm good."

He startled at the sound of the station's alarm going off, signaling an incoming call and yanking him out of his memory.

Springing into action, he tried to push the thoughts from his mind and get into work mode. Still, he took a moment to reach into his pocket and finger Laura's play collar.

Chapter Nine

Shayla had also brought the promised shortbread cookies, as well as white chocolate chip macadamia nut cookies, and banana nut bread.

The poor woman must have been up all night baking, in addition to making the fresh omelet for her.

"You didn't need to go through all this trouble."

"It's okay. I wanted to." She shrugged. "If it helps, it's worth it."

The shortbread cookies were actually little squares, less than an inch big each. "You told us your mom used to make lots of shapes, but your favorites were rolling out large swaths of dough and then cutting them with a pizza cutter."

Shayla reached in and took a handful of the cookies despite her full stomach from breakfast.

With a silent prayer, she popped one into her mouth and closed her eyes as she slowly chewed.

Sweet, buttery, and just the right hint of salt. The cookie practically dissolved in her mouth…

And she stood in a bright, sunny kitchen as a girl. Warm, sweet aromas filled the air. She perched on top of a chair next to a counter, a pizza roller in her hand as she carefully made straight cuts in the dough.

"Doing good, Laur," a woman said.

She looked up at the older woman's face, a woman in the photo albums.

Her mother.

She smiled down at Laura. "You're getting so good at making these, honey."

And then Laura felt ripped out of her body as the scene changed. She stood under a hot sun, sobbing as Rob kept a firm, steadying arm around her shoulders. Next to her, a man she knew was her brother, Bill, had an arm around her waist and his fingers laced through hers.

In front of them, two caskets were being lowered into the ground as the gathered crowd somberly watched.

And she remembered.

She remembered thinking about making cookies with her mom while standing at their graveside.

How she'd never get another chance to do that with her. Or to go fishing again with her dad.

Her eyes flew open and she was staring into Shayla's alarmed face.

"Honey, what's wrong?"

"Their funeral," she sobbed. "Mom and Dad, I remember their funeral."

Shayla wrapped her arms around Laura as she sobbed against her shoulder. "I'm so sorry."

"No, thank you." She couldn't stop crying. She didn't care that it was the first firm memory that fitted itself back into its proper place in her mind.

It was solid.

It was real.

That it hurt as badly as it did told her it was the truth. It wasn't just an idle thought or a false memory planted by something someone said.

And it was hers. Something she could hold on to and hopefully build upon to bring back more. "Thank you," she whispered. "Thank you for giving them back to me."

* * * *

It was a bittersweet victory. Laura immediately began pouring through the older photo albums again, focusing on any pictures of her parents, or of her at the approximate age of the cookie-making memory. She discovered as she looked through them, now some memories of the events had returned, as if they'd never left.

It seemed that regaining the traumatic loss of her parents, which Laura discovered also included remembering receiving the news of their death and most of that time period, of dealing with the loss and grief and funeral preparations, triggered something in her brain.

It didn't, however, include everything. She still couldn't remember how she met Rob, or where. And more current memories were still a blank.

By lunchtime her small victory had turned into frustration. Shayla ran out to bring them back subs for lunch, and they sat watching the local noon news.

"Can you call those other people for me and ask if they can visit?"

"Which ones?" Shayla asked.

Laura struggled to recall names she'd heard Rob and Shayla mention. "Leah? And her husband."

"Seth. Leah and Seth Erikkson."

"Right. Them. There were more though, weren't there? Tilly?"

Shayla once again had that deer-in-the-headlights look. "Yes, but I think Rob's right that we shouldn't overwhelm you right now," she quickly said. "I'll call Leah and see when they can come visit. Besides, they live the closest to the hospital. Everyone else is either up in Sarasota, or clear up in Tarpon Springs."

Laura bumped up against a blank wall, frustrating her. "Where are those?"

Shayla looked up from her phone. "Where's what?"

The tears fought a valiant battle to break through, but Laura beat them back into submission. "Sarasota. And Tarpon Springs. I heard about Sarasota on the TV. But where are they?"

The look of sympathy on Shayla's face almost finished Laura off again, but somehow, she held on and didn't cry.

"Here." Shayla tapped into her phone and then held it so Laura could see. A map was displayed on it. "We're right here," she said as she pinched the screen and zoomed in. "There's where the hospital is, in Pt. Charlotte." She flicked the screen with her finger, panning it to the north. "Here's Sarasota." She pinched again, zooming in farther. "Here's my house."

Once again, she zoomed out and pointed. "Tarpon Springs is way up here. North of St. Petersburg." More zooming in, south of where Shayla lived, but north of the hospital. "Here's where Leah and Seth live."

Laura found the geography lesson helpful, but it didn't trigger any more memories. "Where do I live?" she quietly asked.

Without replying, Laura zoomed in more and showed her. "Englewood. There's where your condo complex is." She panned a little to the west and south. "There's the house." A little more panning, onto a peninsula on the other side of Charlotte Harbor from Pt. Charlotte. "And there's where your shop is."

Nothing.

From elation to frustration, the ebbs and flows of emotion wore at her energy levels. After lunch, she lay back to watch TV with Shayla and found herself dozing off.

She awoke to Shayla gently touching her shoulder. "Laura? The psychiatrist is here to see you."

She rubbed her eyes and sat up. An older, matronly woman with a warm smile stood just inside the closed door. "Hi. I'm Dr. Katherine Simpson. Pastor Ben Pelletier suggested I come see you."

"Do you want me to wait outside?" Shayla asked.

"No, please stay." She waved Dr. Simpson in as Shayla pulled another chair over to Laura's bedside.

The psychiatrist began by going over Laura's recent ordeal, taking notes as they talked and putting her at ease. Dr. Simpson agreed recovering the memory of her parents' funeral was a good step.

"It's also encouraging that you had a chain of memories recovered as a result, especially interconnected like that."

"But you can't tell me if or when they'll all come back."

"I'm afraid not." They talked for over an hour before Dr. Simpson gently confronted Laura. "You realize there is a lot more at stake here than just recovering your memories, don't you?"

"What do you mean? What could be more important than getting my life back? Well, other than catching the guy who did this to me."

"You might never regain your memories of the attack. However, as Ben told you, there is every real possibility of developing post-traumatic stress disorder. It can manifest itself in very odd and unexpected ways."

"If it does, it does. Frankly, I don't care if I get it or not if I can get my memories back."

"You might find yourself very jumpy, startling easy. You might have panic attacks. You might have bad dreams."

"I haven't had any bad ones yet. Just what I told you. And I don't know if they're dreams or memories."

"Well, you should pay attention to your dreams. They may hold answers."

"Calling Dr. Freud." Laura laughed. "I'm sorry. I don't know where that came from."

The doctor smiled. "That's okay. Believe me, next to lawyers, shrinks hear a lot of jokes."

"I bet you do. What else can I do to help bring back my memories?"

"You need to keep talking to people. Talk about pictures, feelings, whatever hints of memories that come back. And I suggest, if you're open to it, seeing a hypnotherapist."

Laura looked at Shayla. "We've been doing a lot of that. Talking. And photo albums."

"That's good. Exactly what you should be doing."

"It was the shortbread cookies this morning that triggered all those memories," Laura said.

The doctor smiled. "It doesn't matter what triggered them, if it helped."

"If it'll help, I'll try anything. One of my doctors mentioned using medicine?"

"Yes, but that's not something I want to mess with except as a last resort." She stood. "And there's a hypnotherapist who works in my office. She's very good, if you decide to go that route."

"Thank you."

She handed Laura a card. "I'll tell my office to make sure they fit you in as soon as possible when you call for an appointment."

Laura looked at the card. The address might as well have been in Greek to her for all the recognition she had. "Thanks. I might go home Monday."

"I'm going to talk to your doctor first, but I'll leave a prescription for some anti-anxiety medicine for you in case you need it. Nothing strong, just something that if you start feeling too overwhelmed, you can take it to help calm you."

When Laura was alone with Shayla again, she felt exhaustion wash over her. "I want my life back," she said, her head on the pillows. "I want whatever was normal for me. I'd give anything to have it back. I don't even care if I thought it was crummy." She turned to Shayla. "I didn't think my life was crummy, did I?"

"No, you didn't. You were very happy."

Somehow, that almost made it worse.

* * * *

Rob showed up a little after eight that evening, just as he'd promised. Laura wasn't happy to see Shayla go, but she did want the alone time with Rob. And Shayla promised to return—once again bearing an omelet—first thing in the morning.

Once Laura was alone with Rob, she closed her eyes and happily pressed her face against his chest as she filled him in on her day.

"That's great that you remembered the funeral. Well, you know what I mean."

She smiled, but didn't want to lose her contact with him. "I know what you meant. Dr. Simpson said it was good because it was a connected chain of memories."

He gently stroked her back, mindful of her sore ribs. "Little by little, you'll get it back. I know you will."

"But what if I don't?"

"You will."

She wished she felt as confident as Rob sounded.

* * * *

Thomas didn't expect to have any trouble with Rob's friends, but he still left word with dispatch where he was going before he drove north to Sarasota Friday evening. Fortunately, the worst of his headache had popped after lunch, leaving him with a nagging ache that he could ignore and live with.

Tony and Shayla Daniels lived in a rural neighborhood of larger, expensive houses sitting in the middle of lots ranging from one to ten acres. Many of the properties also had barns, with horses or cows milling in the pastures around them.

Daniels didn't have either, but several cars were parked in the driveway of his house. When he walked up, a man opened the front door.

"Det. Thomas?"

He held out his hand. "Mr. Daniels?"

"Tony." They shook. "Look, I'm sorry we got off on the wrong foot this morning. This has been hard on all of us."

"Thank you. I appreciate that."

Tony led him into the living room, where several women and men were gathered. Other than unusual necklaces or bracelets on several of the women and two of the men, any of them could have been upper-middle-class people indistinguishable from any other average citizen.

Tony started the introductions. "This is Det. Thomas. Can I get you anything to drink? Tea, water, coffee?"

"No, thanks. I'm good." He looked at the assembled group after Tony had introduced everyone to him. "As I told both Rob and Tony, I'm not here to out anyone. I don't care what you all do in your bedrooms, or who you do it with as long as they're consenting adults. All I'm interested in is any information that might possibly lead to us figuring out who this guy is."

One of the men, Sullivan Nicoletto, raised his hand. "Has FDLE got back to you with the DNA results yet?"

That must be the former cop. "Not yet."

"Do you want to speak to everyone together, or individually?" Tony asked.

"Since you've already had time to compare notes, I guess it really doesn't matter." He turned to Nicoletto. "Let's start with you." He jotted down the man's full name, address, and other information. Yes, he was the former cop, now a writer and lecturer. "Your thoughts on this?"

The man, who'd said to call him Sully, grimly shook his head. "Based on what Rob told me, I'm guessing she opened her door for whoever it was. Meaning either she didn't feel threatened, or somehow knew the person. But I don't know anyone who'd want to do something like that to Laura. She's a good person, has a lot of friends in the community. Between all of us, we know a lot of people in this area in the lifestyle."

Everyone nodded in somber agreement as Sully continued. "We're a pretty tight-knit group. We look out for each other. I haven't heard any rumbles of anyone so much as speaking badly about her. I'm guessing you already went through her emails and FetLife account?"

"Done. Any theories?"

Sully met his gaze. "My gut tells me it's someone she came into contact with at her dive shop, or there in Englewood locally. While out shopping, eating, something. Maybe someone Rob knows who met her. She's a member of the Chamber of Commerce. She's spoken publicly at state and county meetings about fish and game laws."

His heart sank a little as he noted all of that. Yes, they'd had some pretty contentious hearings over the years about fishing regulations and restrictions, the latest one just a few weeks earlier. That was one thing Rob hadn't mentioned when they talked, although he didn't blame the man for forgetting it.

He'd have to talk to Rob again about his coworkers, if she'd had contact with any of them.

If any of them had started acting odd following the attack.

And they were already slowly working their way through interviewing customers and students at the shop, a very painstaking process considering just how many customers passed through her establishment on a daily basis.

Not to mention many of their customers were tourists, or part-time residents.

He went around the room, taking everyone's name and information and getting nearly the same answers from them with few new insights. Leah Erikkson mentioned that Laura had helped her, Tilly, and Loren with a Christmas charity drive in Sarasota. Loren offered up their regular "girls day" outings to get their nails done together and eat. Tilly's husband, Landry, mentioned that they all attended a Mote Marine charity event a month earlier, a dinner and special marine documentary film screening.

Shayla Daniels arrived straight from the hospital a little before ten, apologizing for being late and offering no new insights beyond what everyone else had already said. She did relate Laura had a few more recollections, but nothing relating to the attack.

Until he had the DNA results, any and every option still lay on the table, frustrating him. Once Laura Spaulding went home, very likely on Monday, she'd be vulnerable to further attack. He was already stretching his superiors' patience as it was by authorizing overtime for the deputies standing guard at her hospital room.

He closed his notepad and looked at everyone. "I appreciate you all coming here tonight to talk to me. Like I said, I'm not out to conduct a witch hunt. I just want to put this guy away for good before he hurts anyone else."

"You realize Rob loves her, right?" Shayla quietly asked. "And before this, she really loved him. She was looking forward to their wedding." Her husband draped his arm around her shoulders and she snuggled close to his side. "They were happy. I hope you've completely eliminated him as a suspect."

He shoved the wistful pang away. Daniels and his wife looked happy, in love. As did the other couples and triads. He nodded. "I do, and I have."

"He wouldn't be doing his job if he didn't ask us all this," Sully said, nodding his head toward Thomas. "He has to go through all leads."

"Thank you, Sully."

Sully was the first to stand, albeit slowly and with some obvious pain. He limped over to Thomas and extended his hand. "I wish I was still on the job so I could help out more."

Thomas shook with him. "So do I. I suspect we're going to need all the help, and luck, we can get catching this guy."

He said his good-byes and headed back to Charlotte County, calling dispatch to let them know he was off the clock and on his way home.

As he drove I-75 south, heading into the dark and desolate section south of the Clark Road exit, his thoughts returned to the night of the attack exactly a week earlier. The sight of fresh blood smeared on the wall, and all over the carpet and runner. The pictures knocked off the wall.

The shaken neighbor.

The door had been unlocked when the neighbor burst in after pounding on it. He tried the knob, found it open, and entered. He didn't pursue the attacker, who apparently knew about the back door and fled through it.

Now he understood the neighbor's stumbling over some of his answers when he'd interviewed him. It hadn't been simple shock, but an attempt to protect Rob and Laura's privacy.

I need to talk to him again. Tell him I know about the BDSM and see if he's got any other information that might be helpful.

But it would have to wait until tomorrow. For tonight he simply wanted to go home, get a hot shower, and attempt to fall asleep in his empty bed before his memories of Ella began to eat him alive once more.

* * * *

Despite his exhaustion, physically and mentally, Rob's spirits soared a little when Laura carefully made room for him in the bed and patted the mattress next to her.

"Are you sure?"

She smiled. "I'm sure. And you look exhausted. Rest for a few minutes."

He didn't argue, carefully squeezing himself against the edge of the bed, trying not to crowd her.

Before, it would have been irrelevant. The way they usually slept closely twined together, they could have been comfortable together in a twin bed.

Mindful of both her physical injuries and her lack of memories, he waited until she snuggled against him to fully relax.

"Don't let me fall asleep," he said.

"Why? I think you need to fall asleep for awhile."

"I have to be at work at six."

She pressed her face against his side before tentatively resting her hand on his chest. "Just a short nap. Please?"

He closed his eyes. Despite wanting to stay awake to talk to her, he couldn't help it. The afternoon had been one call after another, exhausting mentally and emotionally, including an accident victim who'd died en route to the hospital in Punta Gorda.

The suddenness of the dream might have shocked him awake had he not been so worn out. He relived the first night they'd spent in the house together, just a couple of months earlier.

He'd surprised her by borrowing one of Tony's smaller spanking benches and setting it up in the living room. She'd come home from teaching an evening class at the shop to find candles lit, music softly playing, and him sitting on the couch waiting for her.

He pointed at the floor in front of his feet.

With a sexy smile on her face, she left her purse by the door and stripped all the way across the living room, leaving a trail of discarded clothes behind her until she dropped to her knees in front of him, naked.

He stroked her hair. "Such a good girl," he whispered. He'd laid out her cuffs and play collar and quickly buckled them on her. "Ready to break in our new home, baby girl?"

In the dim, flickering light, her eyes appeared closer to sapphire blue, full of passion and longing as she stared up at him. "Yes, Sir."

Taking her by the hand, he helped her to her feet. "You're not going out on the boat tomorrow, are you?"

She grinned, knowing what that meant. "No, Sir." He didn't like to mark her up, regardless of her feelings on the matter, if she'd be taking a class out within a couple of days. A bathing suit didn't do much to conceal marks. And, unfortunately, he had to work the next day. They still had a lot of work to do in the house before they could live there full-time, but for tonight…

Tonight, they'd start making more memories and finally be able to enjoy letting loose in their own space.

He held her close, his hands stroking her back, down to her ass, where he grabbed her flesh and squeezed hard.

She draped her arms around his neck, nearly melting against him with a happy moan as his fingers dug in. He'd always had fantasies about tying up his partners and spanking them, but not until he'd met Laura had any of those fantasies—and more—come true.

Anything he'd wanted to do to her she'd met head-on and even improved upon. She'd talked him into trying knife play, wanting the sensation, not bloodletting, and even arranged for them to take a class on it at a club up in Tampa.

His trepidation had soon turned into sadistic glee as he watched her reaction to the feel of the blade smoothly sliding across her skin, the way lightly tracing patterns with the point of the knife raised gooseflesh on her.

Also not something they tended to do at the club or crowded parties, his professional safety concerns keeping it limited to at-home or small, private parties, where he didn't have to worry about someone bumping into him while he was doing it.

Limited to times like tonight, where, after he secured her to the bench with rope and then inserted a vibrating egg into her, he showed her the knife.

He didn't blindfold or gag her, wanting to look into her eyes and hear every sound she made.

When he held up the knife she let out a soft moan that had nothing to do with the vibrating egg inside her pussy.

He brought the blade close to her lips. "Kiss it, baby girl. Show it respect."

She did, licking her lips as she looked up at him.

Already his cock throbbed. Play sessions at home or a private party always ended in sex for them. They built up a head of passionate steam during a scene.

"Hold very, very still." He grinned and thumbed the remote control for the egg. It sped up, now slightly audible despite its location.

Moaning, Laura dropped her head back to the bench and squirmed a little despite herself. But when she felt the cool steel of the blade against her flesh, she fell completely still.

He knew she could be experiencing a wave of orgasms and still she'd force her body to remain completely motionless for knife play.

It also meant she'd practically tackle him in bed later if he didn't wear her out. Not that he minded in the least. It was one of the things he loved about her, that she didn't mind being aggressive with him when the mood struck her.

With his left hand he fisted her hair, ensuring she held absolutely still. With his right he slowly began tracing shapes across her back, down her spine, the tip of the blade not cutting but leaving faint red lines in its wake. He took his time, refusing to rush, stepping back when he finished to admire his work.

The words *PROPERTY OF ROB* could be clearly read in the temporary welts he'd left with the knife tip. Grinning, he snapped several pictures, walking around to show her.

Despite her glazed, subspacey expression, she finally managed to focus long enough to smile. "Yes, I am," she softly said.

He thumbed the egg's remote control again, bumping it higher. "You certainly are." While she rocked her hips against the bench, he picked up a cane. "Going straight to the hard stuff tonight," he warned. "Early morning tomorrow, and I want to fuck your brains out."

He started off with light strokes, to get her used to it before he increased the force. As pink welts began rising in the flesh of her ass and thighs, he felt his cock throb even more.

His. She belonged to him, and he'd be damned if he'd do anything to fuck it up. She was perfect for him, the love of his life.

Her fingers curled around the edges of the spanking bench. Tears trickled down her cheeks but she didn't safeword, didn't beg for mercy.

In fact, she arched her back to meet each stroke.

He couldn't stand it any longer. With marks crisscrossing her flesh, he put the cane down and untied her. Before she could reach for his zipper, he grabbed her by the hair and led her over to the couch. There, he put her on her hands and knees.

"Stay."

She froze.

He grinned, knowing she'd stay like that as long as he told her to. That didn't stop her from letting out a little noise when he fished the vibrating egg out of her pussy and shut it off.

"Don't worry. You won't be empty for long."

He quickly stripped and knelt between her legs. Lining up his cock with her cunt, he grabbed her hips. Then he sank his cock hard and deep inside her. "Come fast, baby. I won't last long."

Neither did she. Her fists clenched, her body meeting every hard and fast stroke when her first climax broke loose. He knew the feel of his thighs slapping against her stinging ass only served to make her orgasm that much harder.

She was happiest and came hardest when her orgasms were mixed with pain. He gave up counting at three and quit holding back. His release built, a tsunami of energy and need rapidly building inside him until the world shrank and focused on the feel of his cock fucking her cunt.

The explosion as his balls emptied his cum into her nearly took his breath away. He finished up by giving her several hard bare-handed slaps to her ass, across the cane marks. That pulled one last climax from her.

Winded, they collapsed onto the couch together.

His eyes snapped open at the sound of her voice. "Rob? It's almost midnight."

He looked around, disoriented, and realized where he was at. Not cuddled up with her on their couch.

In the hospital room.

She stared up at him. "I'm sorry," she softly said. "I shouldn't have let you sleep so long, but you looked so peaceful I didn't have the heart to wake you."

He sat up carefully, not wanting to hurt her. "It's okay, sweetie."

He also hoped she couldn't feel the erection pressing against the front of his pants. The dream had been a blissful diversion, a short trip into the past.

"You're not mad at me, are you?"

Shocked, he stared down at her. "No. Why would I be mad?"

"For letting you sleep."

He pulled her close, burying his face in her hair. "Sweetheart, I love you. I'll never get mad at you for having a chance to sleep next to you."

Chapter Ten

Saturday morning, Laura got the distinct impression that she must have been an early riser. This time she beat sunrise by about ten minutes.

As she started to get out of bed, a stray thought popped into her mind from out of nowhere.

That's why Sunday morning dives are always so freaking painful.

She froze, struggling to pull more from the recesses of her brain.

It was an absolutely true statement. The very depths of her soul told her it was.

Unfortunately, she had no idea what the hell it meant.

After a few minutes, when she realized no more was forthcoming, she let out a disappointed sigh before she continued her journey out of bed and to the bathroom.

Last night, watching Rob sleep, she felt relief that the pain she'd read on his face seemed to vanish. He almost looked happy, at peace.

She hadn't had the heart to wake him up, wanting to just lay there and stare at him. To have him to herself for a few minutes.

To see him free of the emotional pain this whole situation was obviously causing him.

After using the toilet and getting undressed so she could take a shower, she studied herself in the mirror. As it had so many times before, her hand went to her throat. It still felt like something important was missing, and not just a necklace, or a view of skin unblemished by bruises and stitches.

How could I be so attached to a necklace? But maybe she had been. Maybe it was very sentimental to her because Rob gave it to her.

Closing her eyes, she realized she had no trouble visualizing his face, hearing his voice in her mind. He had to work today but would stop by later that evening for an extended break, courtesy of his captain. Shayla was coming in that morning to stay with her, and Rob had arranged for Carol to stop by that evening until Rob arrived.

She felt a little nervous about Carol's visit. Despite knowing her relationship with Carol went back decades, she felt closer to Shayla, and not just because Shayla had spent more time with her at the hospital.

In her *heart*, she felt closer to Shayla. And she suspected this was something that pre-dated the attack.

She was now completely free of tubes and Hep-Locks, meaning she could stand in the shower and enjoy the feel of the warm water sluicing over her without any assistance needed.

Freedom.

A feeling of restlessness settled over her. She wanted to be out. To be free. Despite the risks presented by not having a deputy guarding her all the time, recovering a few memories yesterday had buoyed her spirits. The cards and flowers and even a few stuffed animals that now threatened to crowd her out of her hospital room were heartfelt and appreciated, but they did zilch to jostle any stubborn memories loose.

Maybe being home would trigger even more. Being able to lie in her own bed. Shower in her own bathroom. Cook her own food.

I'd kill for a grilled cheese.

Her eyes popped open again as she laughed. Another random thought she knew to be true.

It wasn't much, but she'd take the win.

* * * *

Laura was dressed and back in bed by the time Shayla arrived a little after seven thirty, once again fully loaded with food containers. The containers holding the cookies and other goodies from yesterday were still stacked on the bedside table next to the phone. Laura had been offering them around to the nurses and aides who came in, not wanting them to go to waste.

"Good morning, sunshine!" Shayla brightly greeted her.

Laura was about to answer her when the room phone rang. When she answered it, a hysterical man's voice yelled, making her pull the phone away from her ear.

"Laura? Laura, is that you? Are you okay? What happened?"

Fear hammered in her heart, freezing her. She was about to drop the phone when Shayla snagged it from her hand.

"Hello?" she demanded. "Who is this?"

Laura could hear the man's frantic tone but not make out his words. Shayla unloaded the food containers onto the bed tray table and walked around to the other side, the phone cord stretched to its limit at the end of the bed. "This is Laura's friend, Shayla Daniels."

As the man spoke some more, Shayla's expression relaxed. "Hold on." She pulled the phone from her ear. "It's your brother, Bill," she explained, before getting back on the phone to talk with him.

She spent a few minutes updating him about Laura's condition even as her own phone began ringing in her purse, Shayla ignoring it as she talked.

After a few minutes, she said, "Hold on." She turned to Laura. "He'd like to talk to you."

Her pulse had finally slowed to something resembling normal. "Did he calm down?"

She smiled. "Yes, he's calm." She held out the phone.

Laura tentatively reached for it. "Hello?"

The man breathed a sigh of relief. "Hi, Laura." He did sound calmer. "I'm sorry, sis. I didn't mean to scare you. I didn't get back until late last night and I finally played my messages. I tried calling Rob's cell, but it went to voice mail. He'd left the hospital information on one of his messages."

She tried to absorb all of that and couldn't. "Okay."

"Shayla told me you still don't have much of your memory."

"No." She tried to think back to the memories of the funeral and realized his voice did sound familiar. "Not much." Laura was aware of Shayla *tsking* at her cell, which she'd dug out of her purse. She stepped into the bathroom to make a call.

"Do..." His voice choked and broke. "Do you remember me?"

"A little. Not much. I'm sorry."

"No, don't apologize, hon. I'm going to make some phone calls as soon as it's a reasonable hour out here and shift some of my charters. Then I'll get a flight there as soon as I can."

She struggled to remember. "You're from Montana."

He sounded sad. "That's right. A little town at the northern entrance to Yellowstone called Gardiner."

She didn't know what else to say to him. "You might want to call Rob and tell him all the flight stuff. I'm…" She nearly choked up at the thought. "I'm sort of useless right now."

"I will. As soon as I have it." There was a moment of silence that felt so uncomfortable to her she knew it had to feel twice that for him.

She felt badly she couldn't console him, knowing it was her situation making him feel the way he did.

That she'd disrupted his life the way she'd disrupted the lives of everyone close to her.

Her fault or not, it didn't take the emotions away.

She thought about the psychiatrist's business card, which she'd tucked away in the drawer of the table next to her bed. "I'll tell Rob you called." That sounded lame to her ears, but she didn't know what else to say.

Shayla emerged from the bathroom, giving Laura the perfect excuse. "I need to go. I have someone here."

"Okay, sis. I love you."

She knew she had to say it back to him. The former version of her no doubt had loved him. "Love you, too."

She hung up and looked at Shayla, who wore a wry smile.

"Your other half was trying to call me to warn us your brother was going to call, and he might be upset when he did." She tucked her phone back into her purse.

Laura smiled. "A little late for that, huh?"

"Well, he was finishing up on a call. Eh, a run. They were working an accident and Bill apparently tried to get in touch with him just a few minutes before Rob got back into the ambulance. Rob tried to call here first but got a busy signal."

Laura's stomach rumbled. "So, breakfast?"

Shayla's smile widened. Laura could tell her friend took great pride and pleasure in bringing her the tasty food, so there was no way in hell she wouldn't eat it.

Besides, she was a great cook.

* * * *

Det. Thomas stopped by to talk with Laura after lunch. She didn't miss the glance Shayla gave him before excusing herself to go down to the coffee kiosk in the lobby.

Unlike the first time Laura talked with him, she felt no nervousness, no fear. Not about him, at least.

He offered up a warm, kindly smile. "I hear you've gotten a few memories back."

"Nothing helpful, unfortunately." She picked at the sheet on the bed. "I don't remember who did this to me." She finally raised her gaze to meet his. "Have you come up with anything?"

"Lab said DNA results may be ready as soon as Monday."

"That's good, right?"

"I don't know." He leaned forward, elbows on his knees, hands clasped together. "I need to prepare you. I suspect whoever attacked you might be involved in other crimes."

She froze as she stared at him, the chill settling deep in her core. "He's a serial rapist?" When he seemed to be searching for the answer, she added, "He's a serial killer."

She didn't need to phrase it as a question because she read the answer in his expression.

Eventually, he nodded. "I don't have confirmation yet. It's just a suspicion."

"But you wouldn't be mentioning it to me unless it was a pretty strong suspicion."

He nodded.

"How am I supposed to keep myself safe? Whoever did this to me might be someone I know."

He sat up. "I wanted to talk to you about getting a concealed carry permit."

"You want me to carry a gun?"

"And look into getting an alarm."

She let out a snort. "I don't even know if I like guns, much less if I've ever shot one before."

"Several shops in the area hold classes. And I can see if I can get a rush put on your concealed carry license paperwork."

"You think he'll try again."

He sounded like he was trying to pick his words carefully. "I'm saying that I think you should take every precaution you can. Including being proactive with your personal safety."

"Do you think he'll come after my friends? Or Rob?"

Thomas didn't answer at first. She was getting ready to ask the question again when he sat back in his chair. "I interviewed several of your friends last night. Ones that Rob said are the closest to you and him. I would suspect the men can handle themselves."

"That doesn't answer my question."

"I have no idea what might happen simply because we don't know who did this or what connection they have to you, or what knowledge they have about you or your friends. I strongly suggest taking whatever steps you can to protect your privacy, though."

"I didn't before this?"

"I didn't say that. Rob indicated you were pretty savvy in that regard and didn't share a lot of personal information online."

Shayla returned. Laura didn't miss how she glanced at the detective before looking away and taking another chair on the far side of the room.

Laura looked at her. "He says I should start carrying a gun."

She thought Shayla was going to choke on her coffee. "What?"

"Is that something I used to do?"

Shayla looked quickly back and forth between Laura and the detective. She had to ask it. "What are you not telling me, Shayla?"

Thomas spoke up. "Mrs. Daniels was there last night when I talked with everyone. I met with them at her house."

Shayla looked relieved not to have to be the one to admit it.

Laura sat up in bed. "Why didn't you tell me?"

"I didn't want to worry you."

Laura choked back her anger, not sure if it was even justified or not. "Well? What else should I know?"

"It's not a bad idea," Shayla quietly said. "I think Rob does have a gun. I don't remember you talking about shooting, but you aren't anti-gun as far as I know. And," she quickly added, "Clarisse said Sully taught her how to shoot. I'm sure he'd be willing to take you shooting and teach you. He's a retired cop."

A wave of exhaustion flowed through Laura. It felt like there were a million things she should know, beyond who attacked her, and the thought of relearning them overwhelmed her. She slumped back against her bed. "Whatever," she quietly said. "If Rob says it's okay, I'll do it."

Thomas stood and stepped closer, giving her hand a paternal squeeze. "I know this isn't easy—"

"*That* is the fucking understatement of the year."

He tried again. "Look, I know you don't know me. But the people I talked to last night, it's obvious how they feel about you. To a person they love you very much. Anyone would be lucky to have a fraction of that many people concerned about them. They're worried about you, and they want to do anything they can to help. They're just waiting for Rob to tell them it's okay to step forward."

She looked up at him. "So give me your professional opinion as a cop." She glanced at Shayla before focusing on him again. "What'd they think about Rob?"

He offered her a kindly smile. "They all agreed he'd die for you. And I suspect they'd all step forward to alibi him if your attacker turns up murdered."

Shayla let out a snort. "Screw that," she muttered. "We'd help him bury the fucker's body."

Laura started out laughing, but it immediately turned into more tears. She hated that, hated not being in control of her emotions on top of everything else.

Thomas chose that moment to take his leave as Shayla stepped forward to put her arms around Laura and console her.

"I hate this," she tearfully sobbed against her friend's shoulder. "I hate all of this. I want my life back."

"It'll happen," she said. "We'll get you there. He's right, there are two things you don't need to question. Rob loves you, and we all love you."

"I keep hoping someone's going to just pinch me and wake me up from this nightmare."

Shayla kissed her forehead. "Believe me, if we could fix this for you, we would. In a heartbeat."

* * * *

After leaving the hospital, Thomas headed back to Englewood to talk to the neighbor, Tom Edwards. Fortunately the man was home, even though his wife was out.

"I'd like to run through your statement with you again."

He didn't miss the caution in the man's face. "All right."

"Why didn't you head next door immediately when you heard the first noises?"

"Because…" His shoulders slumped a little. "I didn't think much of it."

He needed to play his hand. "Mr. Edwards, I'm aware of extenuating circumstances regarding Laura Spaulding and Rob Carlton's relationship. That is not a factor in my investigation. Would you like to restate, unofficially and off the record, what happened?"

Relief filled the man's face. "Let me tell you something, before I say anything else. We've had them over for dinner, and been to their place for dinner, several times. They're a sweet couple. I know Rob would not hurt her if his life depended on it."

"We have completely eliminated him as a suspect, Mr. Edwards."

The man nodded. "I heard the door slam, but it was the screaming that got my attention. She never screams. They don't raise their voices, either one of them. Ever. And it sounded like they were pounding on the walls."

"But you've heard other things?"

"Rob would never hurt—"

"I don't care if you've heard Rob spank her, all right?"

The man drew back a little, but nodded again. "Okay. Just so we're clear."

"We're clear. I've already discussed that with Rob. I need to know exactly what you heard and saw."

"Like I told you that night, his hair was lighter than Rob's, and I think he was a few inches shorter than Rob. He wasn't built like him, either. Thinner."

"Did you hear anything he said to her before the screaming and other noises started?"

"Not clearly. It was the yelling that caught my attention first. Like I told you, they never raise their voices. Well, laughter. I've heard that. Playful squeals from her. Never screaming. Never crying like that."

He shook his head. "I'm not saying they don't ever disagree with each other. They love to debate things. I've seen them go head-to-head at dinner sometimes. But even then, when Rob looks at her, you can see the love in his eyes. Pride. Like he thinks he's the luckiest son of a bitch in the world to have her."

Thomas tried to ignore that and the pain of loss it dredged up in his own soul. "And you've never seen anyone hanging around who didn't belong here?"

"No. They have friends over, but I've seen them all plenty of times. They're very friendly." He rubbed at his chin again. "I'm just glad we got home when we did. We'd been out of town for two weeks and got back home that morning. If we hadn't been here…" He shook his head. "Our cars were here while we were gone. A friend took us up, and we took an airport limo home."

Even though he'd left his card before, Thomas handed the man another one. "Thank you for your time, Mr. Edwards."

"I hope you catch him."

He glanced over at Laura Spaulding's door. "So do I."

Chapter Eleven

It was a little after six when Carol arrived, and Shayla and Laura had already eaten dinner. Shayla had run out and picked up a pizza for them, which they shared with the deputy on duty. Laura watched as Shayla seemed to act wary, maybe even careful around the other woman.

It felt like there was a whole layer of context she was missing out on and didn't even know how to ask about it. Or if she should ask in front of Carol.

Shayla introduced herself. "Shayla Daniels. We've met at Laura's shop before."

Recognition crossed the older woman's face. "Ah, that's right. Rob said you and your husband actually introduced him to Laura." She gave Shayla a warm hug and Shayla appeared to marginally relax. "It's good to see you again."

Shayla walked over to Laura's bed and gave her a hug. "Omelet tomorrow morning?"

"Are you sure I'm not imposing?"

Shayla smiled. "It's not an imposition, believe me. Besides, I have to be at work Monday. So take advantage while you can."

The thought that she wouldn't have Shayla there with her on Monday saddened her. "Thank you. Then I will."

When Shayla left, Laura honestly didn't know what to do with Carol.

Apparently, Carol felt the same. She nervously straightened cards and flowers on the windowsill and squared up the stack of photo albums. "Did you want to go through the albums again?"

"I think I'd like to talk."

"Okay." She walked over and sat in the chair Shayla had occupied most of the day.

It hadn't felt like this with Shayla. Forced, in a way. "Tell me about my parents."

They talked for a couple of hours. Actually, Carol did most of the talking, with Laura asking her questions.

Unfortunately, it stirred few new revelations, only a couple of old childhood memories.

It was a decided relief when Rob arrived a few minutes after ten. Laura wasn't sure what things in common she had to talk about with Carol before, but the conversation didn't flow easily between them like it had with Shayla.

Carol hugged her good-bye. Laura felt more than a little guilty about the tears threatening in the older woman's eyes. Laura wished she could have been a better conversationalist and hoped that under normal circumstances Carol hadn't borne the bulk of the talking.

Once they were alone, Rob sat on the edge of the bed and gently tucked her hair behind her ears. She wanted to lean into him, to snuggle with him.

"Are you okay?" he asked.

She closed her eyes. "You're here. I am now."

When he didn't reply, she opened her eyes. He looked sad. "I'm sorry I've got to work."

She grabbed his hand and pressed it against her cheek. "Please don't apologize."

His torn look ripped her own soul apart. "I...I don't know what to do when you come home. How to keep you safe."

"Det. Thomas came to talk to me today. He said I should get a concealed carry permit."

He slowly nodded. "That's one idea."

"How do you feel about it?"

"I won't force you to carry a gun."

"Let me rephrase the question. How would I have felt about it before?"

Dammit, I hate that word.

"You're not against them, if that's the question. You spearfish."

Right. She'd forgotten about that. "Shayla said one of our friends is a retired cop?"

He nodded again, even more slowly. "Sully. Clarisse's husband."

"When do I get to meet him? Them. All of them."

A sad sigh escaped him. "If they don't release you soon, I'll call them. Otherwise, I was thinking let's get you home and settled first and see if that jostles anything loose."

"Okay." She wondered if she always let him make decisions like this for her. It felt right, she wouldn't deny it.

Did that make her weak?

She scooted over on the bed to make room and patted the mattress next to her.

When he climbed into the bed, she immediately snuggled against his side as carefully as she could without hurting her ribs. She closed her eyes.

And burst into tears. Being next to him like this felt so right, so good.

So perfect.

He didn't say anything, simply held her, his lips pressed against the top of her head, his arms wrapped around her, comforting.

Familiar.

She didn't know much, but she knew she wanted to stay like this as long as possible.

When she eventually stopped crying, he reached for the box of tissues on the bedside table and handed it to her. "When do you have to be back to work?" she asked.

"Six. The captain's working with me."

"Tomorrow night?"

"I wish. In the morning."

She looked up at him. "I'm sorry."

His confused frown looked adorable. "Why are you apologizing?"

"Because you should be home getting sleep and you're here."

She hoped he didn't start crying, because that would totally finish her off. He brushed the hair from her face again. "Sweetheart, I'd walk through hell for you. A little sleep deprivation is nothing."

Still, at eleven thirty she gently suggested he should go home and get some sleep. She could see the exhaustion in his face, deep worry lines in the outer creases of his eyes and dark circles under them she suspected he didn't have a little over a week earlier.

He gave her a hug and a kiss before heading out. As she settled in to sleep, she thought about the warmth of his body, how right it felt being snuggled next to him.

I want to go home. With *him.*

* * * *

Sunday morning, they came to take Laura for another MRI early in the morning, before six o'clock.

She was already awake.

This time she didn't mind being in the machine without a nurse in the room because she knew the deputy would stay in the control room.

Am I finally accepting this?

It seemed hard to believe. Every hour that passed without more memories returning seemed one step closer to acceptance of her fate.

She didn't *want* to accept it. She wanted to beat this, to regain everything. She refused to believe she'd never have those memories again.

Of the Christmases and other holidays as a kid with her brother and parents.

Of her first days with Rob.

Of all the milestones in her life. She couldn't even remember her high school or college graduations.

Of working with her father at the shop.

She closed her eyes and listened to the music. Today, they had the radio tuned to a station playing light jazz and other easy listening music.

It wasn't possible to drift to sleep with the sound of the machine hammering away, or with the way the head brace dug into the back of her neck. She opted for trying to process her dreams from the night before.

Instead of being on a boat, she'd been kneeling at Rob's feet, naked. A feeling of utter contentment had filled her.

But...that's not normal. What's wrong with me? Something deep inside her wanted it more than anything despite her rational mind telling her it had to be an analogy for something else.

I can't even tell Shayla this. What would her friend think of her if she admitted something like that? Would she think she was weird? Would she distance herself?

She'd have to deal with it in her own way. *Maybe I should call Dr. Simpson's office tomorrow and make that appointment.*

At least the psychiatrist got paid to hear weird shit.

* * * *

Shayla was waiting for her in the room with a freshly made omelet and even more goodies. She greeted Laura with a hug. "Ready for breakfast?"

"You're spoiling me. I hope they let me out tomorrow or I'm going to hate tomorrow's hospital breakfast with a passion."

"How did your visit with Carol go last night?"

Laura pondered that as she savored the first bite of the omelet. "Good. But I didn't get any new memories."

"Sorry."

"No, it's okay." She forked another bite into her mouth. "But it was odd. I feel like I'm closer to you than I am to her." She looked at Shayla. "Does that make sense? I mean, I feel like I can talk to you all day with no problem. Last night, I felt like I had no idea what to talk to her about except to ask questions."

Shayla cocked her head as she considered her answer. "Well, we were...*are* pretty close. Carol is kind of like a mom to you. I know there are a lot of things I don't talk to my mom about." She shrugged. "And you saw a lot of her at work. She helps out in the shop. So you sort of had a different relationship with her than me."

"How do you get to the weekly girls' days you told me about?"

Shayla frowned. "I don't understand the question, hon."

"Your boss lets you?"

Comprehension dawned. "Oh. Sorry. Yes, because I usually work late Wednesdays and Thursdays anyway because Tony's frequently working late on those days with meetings. So I make it up. And I work at home and on the weekends a lot. He's a good boss. He lets us have certain things and we're happier and more productive for it."

"Do you enjoy being a reporter?"

"I love it. I love working for a magazine instead of a newspaper." She smiled. "It was one of the things we had in common, the writing. That really drew us together, I think."

"Is that how we met?"

Laura sensed another one of those missed meanings, a hidden context that escaped her as Shayla smiled a little too widely. "Yeah. You read one of my articles and contacted me and a friendship was born."

"Which one?"

"Oh, I don't remember. I'm sorry. It's been, what, over three years."

"Oh. Sorry."

Shayla laughed, a bright sound. "You need to quit apologizing for everything."

"Can we maybe do the girls' thing this week? If I'm out of here?"

She nodded. "If you're feeling up to it. I'll call everyone and tell them to clear their schedule. I'm sure Clarisse will want to come down, too."

"Does she bring her kids?"

"No." She grinned. "She says it's her mental health time with us."

"Do any of our other friends have kids? In this group, I mean."

Her smile faltered just a little. "No. Just Clarisse."

She wasn't sure she wanted to ask this question. "Did I want to have kids?" she softly asked. "Did Rob want them?"

"Oh, sweetie." She stood and leaned over, hugging Laura carefully so as not to make her spill her omelet. "You said you do, one day. So does Rob. You wanted to wait until after the wedding. You weren't in a hurry to start a family. You always said you wanted to enjoy being with Rob for a while first."

She stared at her food. "I'm just not sure if it's a good idea."

"Why?"

She shrugged, unable to meet her friend's gaze now. "I can't even remember most of my own childhood. Have I ever babysat? Changed a diaper? Did I have a good childhood?"

"You'll be a great mom if you decide you want kids."

"Do you want kids?"

Shayla pulled her chair closer and sat, but kept a hand resting on Laura's thigh. "No, Tony and I aren't having kids. We have cats."

"You didn't want them?"

She shrugged. "I really hadn't made up my mind. I wasn't even sure I was going to find a guy to spend my life with. He'd had a vasectomy before I ever met him, and he didn't want kids."

Shayla looked thoughtful for a moment. "I'm happy, and even more important, I'm content. I don't feel any sense of loss by not having kids. I know some people have an overwhelming desire to be a parent, and some have an overwhelming desire never to be a parent. I was in the middle. It didn't really matter much to me one way or another." She let out a little laugh. "I damn sure wasn't giving Tony up over it."

Laura pondered that for a moment as she took another couple of bites. She still wanted to talk about the dreams she'd had the night before, but couldn't bring herself to do it. She didn't want to say anything that might make the one person she really felt connected to as a friend think less of her.

"As long as you're happy," she eventually settled on saying.

Shayla's broad grin said it all. "I am," she assured her. "Happiest I've ever been in my life."

"I hope I get to that point."

The smile slowly slid from Shayla's face. "You are. Well, you were. I'm sure you will be again."

Laura took another bite but didn't respond. She wished she felt as sure as Shayla.

* * * *

The neurologist came in a couple of hours later, just before lunch. Laura asked Shayla to stay.

"Well," he said, "I'm thinking we'll discharge you sometime tomorrow. I'll have my PA check in with you, but unless anything else crops up, your MRI looks good. The mild swelling you had at first has completely subsided, compared to the MRI we took when you were admitted. You're a very lucky woman."

Laura let out a snort. "I don't feel very damn lucky."

His expression softened. "I'm sorry, Laura. I know it's frustrating—"

"You have no fucking *idea* what I'm feeling!" she shouted, startling both Shayla and the doctor and making the deputy stick his head inside to check on her. "You have no *fucking* clue what it's like to not know who I am or the people around me! So don't fucking tell me 'you know' what I'm feeling, because you don't."

The doctor slowly nodded. "I'm sorry. You're right. I don't know what it's like for you."

She collapsed back onto her pillows, her ribs aching in protest at the sudden movement. "Sorry," she mumbled. "I shouldn't have lost my temper like that."

"I saw in your chart that Dr. Simpson consulted with you."

"Yeah."

He glanced at Shayla, then back to Laura. "She's good at what she does. If anyone can help you, she can."

"Thanks." She couldn't roll to her side with her ribs, so she turned her face away from him.

She waited until she heard the room door open and close again to turn back to Shayla. "Did I used to blow my top like that?"

She slowly shook her head. "Not really, but I don't blame you. I'd probably be a basket case by now. I don't know how you're handling it so well."

"Well?" She wiped at her eyes, determined not to burst into tears for once. "Doesn't feel like I'm handling it very well from this end."

* * * *

Rob stopped by after lunch to see her for a few minutes. They'd brought a patient into the hospital and his partners on the ambulance crew shooed him upstairs while they prepped for their return to the station. When Shayla tried to step out to give them privacy, Laura and Rob both asked her to stay.

"Can you tell him what the doctor said?" Laura mumbled. "Please?" She was too comfortably snuggled against Rob's side to talk.

Shayla related the information but left out the outburst.

"That's great!" Rob said. "I'll tell the captain I need tomorrow off for sure."

"Tell him the rest," Laura said.

"What?" he asked.

She heard Shayla sigh before telling Rob about her outburst.

He gently palmed Laura's cheek. "Honey, look at me."

She forced her eyes open and wanted to sink into his sweet brown gaze.

"No one blames you for being emotional," he gently said. "No one. Especially not us, the ones who love you. God knows Tony and Seth had to deal with their fair share of listening to me rant and rave in the parking lot downstairs while you were unconscious."

She couldn't imagine Rob getting angry or losing his temper.

"So please go easy on yourself," he said. "If you need to scream, or rant and rave, or cry yourself out, whatever. Don't hold back. That's what we're here for, to help you through this. You never have to put on an act for us."

* * * *

It took every ounce of Rob's will to keep himself from crying. Yes, her bruises were fading, but she talked differently, acted differently, and her palpable emotional pain was something he couldn't fix.

He hated that. Hated not being able to do something to make this all better for her. To take her pain and tears away.

"I'll be here first thing in the morning and then I can take you home when they discharge you. Okay?"

She nodded, looking lost. Looking helpless. Forlorn.

If they weren't short-handed at the station, he would gladly take all of his banked vacation time and use it up over the next few weeks. But he suspected he'd need it spread out over the next weeks and months to go to doctor appointments with her.

"Bill is flying in late tomorrow night. Steve volunteered to drive to Tampa to get him. He's going to be here for two weeks. He'll stay with you while I'm at work."

"I don't need a babysitter," she mumbled half-heartedly.

"You do need someone who can handle a gun," he firmly said in a tone he hoped resonated with her. His "Dom tone" as she used to call it. "I want someone with you who can protect you until we get you trained and get you a gun."

He'd already called Sully and had that talk with him. Sully had volunteered not only to train her, but to have her stay with them, if necessary, to keep her safe.

It wasn't the best option, especially considering Rob didn't know how to break the news to Laura about their friends' poly triad. But if they still hadn't caught the fucker who attacked her by then, he would definitely give it serious thought.

Hell, Leah and Seth, as well as Ross and Loren, and Tilly and her guys, had all volunteered to keep her with them. Ross worked, but said Loren and Laura could come to the office during the day. Tony had volunteered to take weekend watches as necessary, or even evenings. Unfortunately with his job he couldn't watch her during the day or even bring her to work with him.

He didn't want to tell Laura all of that yet either. Yes, it was arranging a series of babysitters for her. Better that, and risk pissing her off, than taking the chance of the asshole getting another crack at her.

She finally nodded before resting her head against his chest again.

The deputy knocked before opening the door. "Rob, you have company."

He looked up as Craig and Sean stuck their heads in. "Hey, man," Sean said. "Sorry, but we need to roll. Punta Gorda got a call and we need to get back to the station to cover."

"Okay. I'm coming."

Laura sat up and wiped at her eyes. "Do I know them?"

Rob waved them in. "You've met them a couple of times before. This is Craig Jackson and Sean Bellows."

They stepped over and gently shook hands with her. "Hey, Laura," Craig said. "How you feeling?"

She shrugged. "Apparently I've had better days," she said.

Sean smiled. "Your sense of humor's still there."

Rob carefully untangled himself from her before getting out of bed, mindful of her ribs. He leaned in and kissed her. "I'll check in with you later, sweetheart."

"Okay."

He gave Shayla a hug before leaving and whispered in her ear, "Thank you."

She gave him a short nod before he headed out, Craig and Sean flanking him.

They stood waiting for the elevator. "I'm really sorry, dude," Craig said. He'd covered several shifts for Rob after the attack, and had been working with him that night when it happened.

"Yeah," Sean agreed. "Sorry."

Rob sucked in a deep breath. "Not a fraction as sorry as the fucker will be if I ever get my hands on him."

"Well, I don't think finding an alibi will be a problem if you do," Sean snarked. "Just make sure there aren't any video cameras around."

* * * *

Rob coordinated via phone with Tony, Seth, Leah, Tilly, Landry, Cris, Ross, and Loren. He'd given Seth a copy of the new keys for Laura's condo. They were converging on it that afternoon to clean it and remove all traces of the attack.

Shayla would stop by before they left to make sure everything was exactly as it had been, because she'd been there the evening before the attack watching a movie with Laura. Besides Rob, she was the only other person who would spot anything out of place. She'd also volunteered to go grocery shopping, knowing her friend's preferences as well as Rob did.

He took the jump seat in back while Craig drove them to the station. Giving up control of all of this had been almost as difficult as being unable to fix Laura's memory or battered body. It had taken Seth verbally shaking some sense into him over the phone the day before.

"Dude, let us help you. We *want* to help you. You can't do this alone, and you shouldn't have to. Believe me, if it wasn't for friends, Leah and I couldn't have handled what we went through. *Use* us. It's what we're *here* for."

Now he was on the phone with Seth again, mindful of his partners up in the cab.

"We've already got the carpet cleaner going," Seth reported. "I think we'll be able to get all of the stain out. And Leah, Tilly, and Loren are out in search of a new carpet runner and picture frames to match as much as they can."

"What about the walls?"

"Done. Cris and Landry tackled them first thing. You can't even tell there was any blood."

Rob closed his eyes as he pinched the bridge of his nose. He'd had a perpetual headache the past several days, between the stress, worry, lack of sleep, and poor diet. "You have no idea how much I appreciate this."

Seth's tone softened. "Like I told you yesterday, this is what we're here for. Use us. Hell, Leah and I would move you two in with us if I thought you'd say yes. At the very least until they catch the guy."

"Thanks. I appreciate it."

After getting off the phone with Seth, Rob sat back, eyes still closed. There was so much to think about. He knew Steve would also want to be involved with helping keep an eye on her.

While Steve and Carol had met quite a few of their closest kinky friends, for the most part he and Laura had kept their lives segmented. While their kinky friends were, admittedly, their closest friends, and the ones they spent the most time with, it was easier being able to be themselves around their kinky friends instead of subjugating all their kinky friends to having to watch every little thing they said and did in front of Steve and Carol and the others.

They'd even been planning on taking a page from Tony and Shayla's playbook and having their formal collaring and official wedding at the club, in front of all their kinky friends, and having the second, vanilla wedding later that evening with a mixed crowd of family, vanilla friends, and their closest kinky friends.

Fortunately for him, he didn't have to worry much about his own biological family. His parents had disowned him when he told them he wasn't following his father's footsteps and going into law like his two older brothers.

Well, his father had disowned him, and his mom and brothers didn't dare contradict him. Rob hadn't even bothered telling them he was engaged, much less about Laura's attack. The only contact he had with them was Christmas cards at the holidays.

Moving to Florida from Arizona to go to college had been a massive change of scenery. He couldn't have made it if not for the full academic scholarships.

And he didn't regret it in the least. He never would have met Laura, never would have met his friends, and never would have found the love of his life.

He'd also be miserably cooped up in a Phoenix high-rise office building every day. He'd take Florida's humidity and cool sea breezes over Arizona's blistering summer heat any day.

After they returned to the station, Rob stopped Craig and Sean when they got out of the ambulance. "Guys, I really appreciate you letting me do that and covering for me. I'm sorry if I haven't said that yet."

He hated the pity in their eyes, but appreciated it at the same time. "Dude," Craig said, "it's all right. I know you'd do the same for any of us."

Sean reached out and gripped Rob's shoulder. "Don't sweat it." He grinned. "Just be prepared to do more than your fair share of cooking for us when she's back to normal."

Rob managed a laugh. "You got it."

* * * *

Laura suspected whatever the nurses gave her to help with her pain was what made her sleepy, because her brain wouldn't shut off that night.

She lay there in bed, aware she was caught in a dream and unable to do anything about it.

In this dream she was seated at the desk in what she suspected was her own den, looking around at the bookshelves, the walls, finally at the desk itself.

Unremarkable, like any other mass-produced computer desk. The tower and monitor sat side by side on a low shelf while the keyboard slid underneath. Neat, tidy, nothing special.

In this dream she was relegated to mere spectator status with no control. Dream Laura reached out and turned the computer on. The screen came to life and she brought the email window up.

A message blinked at her and she clicked on it. Instead of text, a picture assembled like a jigsaw puzzle, forming a black skull inside a red circle with a slash through it. Once all the pieces were assembled, it blinked off and on, the skull's empty eyes menacing.

She jumped as she heard someone pounding on a door. In the dream she stood and walked down a hallway. Yes, she suspected this was her home. And as she stared at the door, it rattled in its frame, bowing in and out under the force of the blows as someone knocked, and knocked, and knocked again until it started to open—

Laura's eyes flew open and she let out a startled cry at the form bent over next to her bed.

The nurse put a hand on her shoulder. "It's all right. I'm sorry I scared you."

Her heart thundered in her chest, eventually slowing as she got her wits about her.

She was safe. In the hospital.

"What time is it?" Laura asked.

"A little after three in the morning."

She took a few more deep breaths and tried to go back to sleep, hoping there wouldn't be any more dreams like that.

Chapter Twelve

"This might sting a little," the PA warned as he carefully snipped at the stitches on her forehead Monday morning.

Laura winced, but kept her eyes closed, her hand clamped around Rob's. She was definitely going home today. Due to the size of the gash in her forehead and the urgency of her condition upon arrival, the doctors in the ER who treated her had used stitches that wouldn't dissolve.

The plastic surgeon's PA studied the result. "I think you'll have minimal scarring," he said. "But you need to follow the care instructions. You can call our office to schedule a follow-up appointment for us to evaluate it and go over your options."

She blinked her eyes to clear them after they'd watered in pain. "Thanks."

Rob took the sheet and glanced through it. "We'll follow it to the letter."

She squeezed his hand again. The comforting, protective way he'd said it only reinforced her trust in him.

He'd already packed everything, including the dozens of cards and the flower arrangements and stuffed animals, and loaded everything into his car. He'd also got the prescriptions for anti-anxiety meds and painkillers filled. All they were waiting for was the final paperwork releasing her. Even the deputy had been sent home.

"Det. Thomas will meet us at your condo," Rob told her once they were alone again. "He wants to be there when you get home in case any memories are triggered."

She nodded, nervous. As anxious as she felt to get home, she wasn't oblivious to the problems that presented. Her first firearm lesson was already scheduled for Wednesday. Sully would drive down and pick her up from the shop late that morning. Rob, unfortunately, had to work, but had assured her that Steve had met him before, and that Bill would go, too.

Left unspoken, she knew Rob meant Steve wouldn't let her go off with someone if he wasn't sure of their identity.

* * * *

Despite her nerves, and, admittedly, her fear, she couldn't help but be fascinated by the landscape as Rob drove her home to Englewood. Rob had taken charge of gathering all the release information for her. She was too overwhelmed and exhausted to process any of it.

It was a relief to have him there taking care of her, and she wasn't afraid to admit it.

Their little community was located on the Gulf of Mexico, straddling the thin strip of land between the northern end of Charlotte Harbor and the Sarasota County line.

"It's beautiful," she said as they crossed the bridge at El Jobean. When she looked past him, she could see south to the harbor.

"You love it here. You grew up here."

"Where did you grow up?" In retrospect she felt bad that they hadn't talked more about Rob's family and history.

She didn't miss his pained expression, but his voice hid it well. "Phoenix."

"Your family's there?"

"Yeah."

He didn't elaborate. "How long have you lived here?"

"I've been in Florida since I started college at eighteen. I went to USF up in Tampa. I moved here after graduation and getting a job with the county fire department. I've been here ever since. About eleven years."

"Have I met your family?"

His fingers tightened around the steering wheel. "No."

After a couple of minutes, she had to ask. "What happened with them?"

"My father is a big-shot attorney. My two older brothers didn't bother thinking for themselves and went to work for him. I didn't want to be a lawyer. They basically disowned me."

"That's horrible."

"Yeah." He took a deep breath and let it out before glancing over at her. "Your parents sort of adopted me when we started going out."

"Did we invite them to the wedding? Your family, I mean."

He let out an amused snort. "We were still debating it. You were of the opinion we should at least send an invitation. If nothing else, to let my brothers know about it in case they wanted to come. But neither of us held high hopes for my parents coming."

"And your opinion?"

"I could care less if they know or not. I think it burns my dad's bacon that I managed to put together a great life for myself without becoming a lawyer."

"Are you happy being a paramedic?"

They slowed to a stop for a red light. He looked at her and nodded. "Yeah. It's not the most pleasant job in the world at times, but I help people. I make a difference. Sometimes I save lives. The one life I save makes up for all the times I get puked or peed or shit on by a drunk." He smiled. "And if I hadn't stuck to my guns, I never would have met you. And I wouldn't give you up for anything."

* * * *

Det. Thomas was parked in front of her condo when they arrived. He stepped out of his car when Rob parked next to him.

Laura studied the complex from behind the safety of the windshield while Rob walked around and opened the door for her.

Nothing. It felt familiar, but beyond that, no memories.

Thomas walked over. "How are you feeling?"

She slowly nodded, her eyes on the building. "I'm okay."

The men stood there until she realized they were waiting on her to get out. She unfastened her seatbelt and slowly turned, both men reaching out to help her from the SUV.

Rob kept a steadying, comforting grip on her arm. "If it's too upsetting, you tell me immediately, okay?"

She nodded but didn't reply.

He led her toward the door, the unit in the middle of two others. After Rob handed the key to Thomas to unlock the door, she closed her eyes as the detective let the door swing open.

"Are you okay, honey?" Rob asked.

Laura nodded again before opening her eyes. In front of her lay the spot where she almost died.

Thomas walked in first and turned on the lights in the living room as well as opened the blinds. She hesitated at the door and steadied herself on the doorjamb. Then, after taking a deep breath, she carefully stepped through.

Bright sunlight filled the room while Laura stood in the front hall and looked around as if in a stranger's house.

Then again, I am a stranger.

But she recognized it. It was the living room she saw in her dream the night before.

Pictures lined the entry wall. Going from one to another, Laura touched each one in turn, whispering names to herself she'd learned while in the hospital. There was a picture of her and Bill standing in front of his airplane.

"That was taken when you flew out to visit him shortly after your parents' funeral," Rod softly explained.

It was obvious they were siblings, almost twins in appearance. He was two years older than her. According to Carol, they grew up with almost no sibling rivalry. She paused in front of it for a moment and caressed the outline of the plane.

Rob gently touched her arm. "Shayla went to the store for you and stocked your fridge. She got you everything we could think of that you like."

"Thanks." Laura focused on the rest of the living room. She let out a little laugh. "Laura. Loren. Leah." She turned to him. "How do you all keep us straight?"

He smiled. "We manage."

Her decorating taste ran to tropical pastels, corals and mints and light yellows. Her couch was upholstered in these colors, and the end and coffee tables were white with flecks of color.

"Everyone came over yesterday," Rob said. "They cleaned it up. They reframed a couple of the pictures that fell and broke. And..." She turned to him as his voice choked. "They got the blood cleaned up," he softly said.

She returned her focus to the pictures for a moment, trying to absorb everything. No hard and fast memories returned, but more static swirled around the abyss, as if pieces wanted to lock themselves into place and just couldn't quite fit.

After a few minutes she took a deep breath and turned to Thomas. "Please tell me what happened."

The men exchanged an uneasy glance before the detective spoke up. "We think you either knew, or recognized, or didn't feel threatened by the guy, at first. It looks like you opened your door for him.

"Your next-door neighbor said he heard yelling before he heard screaming. It looks like once the guy went after you, you fought back tooth and nail. We think maybe he hit you from behind and stunned you, but you had a lot of defensive injuries and fought back."

He pointed to her hands. "You peeled some of your nails down to the quick. That's why we think he ended up trying to strangle you first instead of raping you. You got in a few licks of you own. He probably wasn't expecting you to fight like that."

She looked at her hands, examining them while he continued talking. "We were able to get scrapings from under some of your nails for DNA evidence. Your neighbor heard the fight and came over, found the door unlocked, and rushed in. It surprised the attacker and he took off out the back door."

He pointed down the hallway. "We think since he knew you had a back door, he probably scoped out the place beforehand."

"Why would he attack me if I have neighbors?"

"He might have thought all your neighbors were either gone or wouldn't hear anything. The neighbor on the other side is a snowbird. They're not here. And Tom Edwards and his wife were gone for two weeks and returned that Friday morning."

She stared at her hands, the implication slamming into her. "I would have died," she whispered. "I would have died if they hadn't come home."

Rob protectively draped an arm around her shoulders. "Laura—"

"No, it's okay." She stared up at him. "I need to hear all of this. It happened. Not hearing it won't help me." She returned her focus to Thomas. "You think he came around before he attacked me. He thought I'd be alone."

Thomas nodded. "Likely. According to Rob, neither of you noticed any suspicious activity. If the guy knows where your shop is, he might have followed you home, watched for a day or two for patterns, and then struck when he thought you were alone."

"Wouldn't he see their car was back?" she asked.

"They said they took an airport limo home."

"Oh." She had a thought. "Is my car out there?"

"Yes, it's the Toyota," Rob said. "The truck. On the other side of where I parked."

She disengaged from his arm, went to the door, and opened it. There, next to Rob's Explorer, sat a silver Toyota Tundra with a double cab and a matching topper on back.

"That's mine?"

"Yeah."

She felt no recognition.

Disappointed, she closed the door and turned to them. "I don't remember anything."

* * * *

Rob struggled to keep his own emotions in check as he watched Laura walk over to her bookcase and study the contents. They were filled, floor to ceiling, with DVDs, CDs, and books. "You've got several boxes of books in storage that you didn't have room for."

When her parents had died in a car wreck a little over a year earlier, Rob had suggested she move in with him. She'd politely refused, not because she didn't want to, but because she said she was afraid of making the decision out of grief.

She was always strong and independent, two of the many things he loved about her. There was never any ego involved in their relationship. They were as comfortable together as they were secure apart.

She trailed her fingers over some of the spines. "I like a lot of different authors, huh?"

"That's an understatement." Her taste in books was as eclectic as her taste in music. She loved everything from Stephen King to Charles Dickens, and from Mozart to Meat Loaf. Her movies ranged from *Dirty Dancing* to *Butch Cassidy and the Sundance Kid* and *Alien*.

She was, before, unpredictable and indescribably unique. Willing to try almost anything once, both in their vanilla and kinky lives.

She stopped in front of a picture of the two of them with Doogie. "You said he's okay?"

"I decided to leave Doogie at my place. He's still a puppy, but he's a moose. I was afraid he might hurt you and didn't want to distract you right now."

"He's definitely a moose," Thomas said. "I've met him."

She stared at the picture. "In case it distracted me from maybe remembering something about the attack." She glanced at him.

He nodded.

Doogie was definitely a momma's boy and missed her terribly. Any time Rob mentioned her name, Doogie's ears perked up and he would run to the door, looking for his mom.

After a couple of minutes, Laura sat on the sofa and looked around. She sat like that for a while before speaking. "I can't remember any of it. Only what I already told you."

"That's okay," Thomas assured her. "If it comes back, it comes back."

"But you need me to testify."

"Believe me, we've got enough physical evidence, we can make a DNA conviction stick with no problem."

"If you find him."

"We will find him. There has to be someone out there who knows who he is. You put up a hard fight. He took a hurtin'."

"I didn't fight hard enough, apparently."

Rob walked over and knelt in front of her, taking her hands in his. "You are *not* to blame here. I want you to stop thinking like that."

"But I let the guy in, didn't I?"

"Laura," Thomas said, stepping closer, "we don't know who he is. He might have been someone you know. He might have worn a disguise, like a pizza man. It doesn't matter why you opened the door because he was here on a mission."

She took a deep, shuddering breath and let Rob help her to her feet. "Can you show me the rest of the place?" she asked.

It broke his heart how she sounded. Tentative, afraid. Weary.

Defeated.

"Yeah, sweetie."

It took her half an hour to make her way through the entire three-bedroom condo. One bedroom was her office.

He watched as she suppressed a shiver as she looked at the desk, and computer.

"Something?" he asked.

She shook her head. "I saw this in a dream."

There was a third room, a spare bedroom where her brother or other friends or relatives stayed when visiting. Her bedroom had a master bath, and she spent several minutes in there going over the items on the counter and in the medicine cabinet.

Before, she was a fairly plain dresser. Jeans, T-shirt or blouse, slacks, shorts. She wanted fast and functional, something she could wear around the shop. But she loved bright, wild nail polish.

Rob watched as she examined the various bottles with names like Smokestack, Passion Flame, and Indigo Dreaming.

"You said it was like having tattoos you could take off when you got bored with them," he offered when she didn't speak after several minutes.

She looked shocked. "I have tattoos?"

Rob laughed. "No, hon, you don't," he assured her.

The nurses had removed her nail polish while she was in the coma, after her nails had been scraped for DNA evidence. When Laura rubbed at her fingers, Rob noticed she had switched her engagement ring to her right hand.

Thomas caught his eye and slowly shook his head at Rob, his message clear. *Don't say anything.*

Rob took some comfort that Laura was still wearing it.

Thomas stepped out to give them a few moments alone. Laura looked at the other items—men's deodorant, shaving cream, an electric shaver, another toothbrush. Then she looked at Rob.

"I stay here a lot," he explained. "Depending on my shift. You've got a lot of stuff at the house, too. We go back and forth all the time."

Laura nodded. "That makes sense." He followed her back to the living room.

Det. Thomas looked at his watch. "I'm not trying to rush you, but maybe we should take her over to the shop."

When both men looked at her, she finally realized they were waiting for an answer. "What?"

Rob stroked her hand. "We're wondering if taking you to the shop will jog anything."

"Oh." She looked dazed, confused.

Overwhelmed.

Just when he thought his heart couldn't break any more, it did. He'd do anything, including taking her place, to fix this for her.

Unfortunately, he couldn't fix it. All he could do was swallow back his own emotions and provide the strongest support he could for her.

She nodded. "Okay. If you think that's best."

* * * *

Rob handed Thomas his car keys and asked him to take her out while he used the excuse of closing the blinds and turning off the lights. He also phoned Steve and told him they were coming, and asked him to warn everyone to not react to how she looked.

"I'll prepare the staff."

"Prepare yourself." He watched Thomas helped Laura into the Explorer.

"Yeah." He hesitated. "Carol said she looks pretty bad."

"Not as bad as she did." He yanked the blinds closed. "We'll see you in a few."

Laura's father had founded the dive shop over thirty years ago. Eight years prior, she bought him out and added bait and tackle. Its success grew, and she added on to the original building. She had four employees in the store, two boats, and a full-time captain who also ran fish and dive charters in addition to Steve Moss. Carol, who was a retired accountant, worked part-time and helped with bookkeeping duties.

Everyone stood waiting outside in the parking lot when Rob and Thomas pulled up. Before Rob could get out, Steve had already stepped forward and opened her door.

"How are you, Laura?" he practically screamed as he reached in to help her out.

"I got beat up, Steve. I didn't go deaf." Rob and Thomas both froze as they watched the interaction. Laura's eyes widened as stepped out and looked up at Steve. A smile lit both their faces. "I know you!" she squealed.

Rob felt a twinge of envy that her first spontaneous recognition of someone wasn't him, but Steve was over thirty years older than her and had been her father's best friend.

Laura began crying. "I know you." She wrapped her arms around Steve and sobbed. "I know you!"

Rob didn't intervene. If she had a memory, he didn't want to interrupt in case it stopped her from remembering more. Carol walked over to him and patted him on the back.

"He's like a dad to her," she whispered in his ear. "It's okay. Don't take it personally."

He nodded but didn't reply.

* * * *

Laura's spirits rose at the revelation, then quickly plummeted again when she realized she didn't recognize anyone else. When she walked into the store with Steve, closely shadowed by Rob and Det. Thomas, she remembered different items for sale and their functions.

Steve quizzed her about basic diving safety rules and she answered them all correctly. He moved into some more advanced areas and they discovered her knowledge remained intact.

"Well, it seems you're all right on your diving. At least you can teach," Steve laughed. He realized what he said and turned to Rob. "Sorry, son. It's just—"

"I know, Steve. It's a mixed bag. It's okay. I'm just glad she's alive."

Thomas patted Rob on the shoulder. "Call me if she remembers anything about the attack. You've got my cell. I don't care if it's in the middle of the night—call me."

"I will."

Rob ordered them all Chinese take-out for lunch. They ate it at a table on the dock behind the shop. When Carol and Steve finished they excused themselves and left Rob alone with Laura.

Laura's nervousness had abated somewhat in the quasi-familiar setting. At the condo, she felt like she'd walked uninvited into a stranger's home. Here, at least, she felt connected in some small way. She still knew her business, to a certain extent. And she knew Steve's name and a lot of things about him, even though some of her memories of him still seemed murky.

She'd caught herself looking at his hands for any signs of recent injury. Over the last few days in the hospital, any time a man came near her she looked at his hands, wondering who the attacker was. It could be anyone, including someone she knew well.

What scared her even more than the possibility of never getting her memory back was the thought that her attacker might be someone she dealt with on a daily basis. If so, as long as her memory was gone she could be exposing herself to danger.

Can I ever trust anyone again?

Chapter Thirteen

Laura felt more than useless as she watched Steve and Carol go through closing procedures at the store. When there was nothing left to do except lock up and set the alarm, she looked to Rob.

"What now?"

"I figured we'd go back to my place and pick up Doogie. I'm sure he'd love to see you. Then we'll go back to your place. Bill can drive you to work in the morning. He's flying in late tonight."

She nodded and remembered her thoughts. "I guess I'm a morning person, huh?"

Steve, Carol, and Rob all looked at each other before breaking into laughter.

"What?"

"You *hate* mornings," Rob said. "You're so used to getting up early that your body pretty much goes on auto-pilot, but you are definitely *not* a morning person."

"You don't get to the store until eleven on a lot of days," Steve said. "You usually close up. The only mornings you work are weekends when you have to go out on dives with us."

Rob helped her back into his Explorer and they headed over to his house. It felt familiar driving there, but didn't trigger any memories.

He helped her out of the SUV and to the front door. "Let me go in first," he said. "He's going to need a walk. Carol's husband came over and walked him, but he'll be excited to see you."

He slipped in through the front door, shutting it behind him. She heard a dog's happy barking and Rob's voice.

"Guess who's home? Mommy's home! That's right—whoa, hold on. Hold still. Doogie—*ow!*"

She'd started to reach for the door when he called out, "Okay, it's safe."

Cautiously, she eased the door open and peeked through. Rob had a large black Lab at the end of a leash, and seemed to have trouble holding him back.

"Are you sure they took stuff out when they neutered him?"

He laughed. "We've been wondering that ourselves."

"What happened?"

"He got me in the nuts."

"Ouch."

"Tell me about it."

The dog whined, his club-like tail frantically swishing back and forth at light speed as he tried to gain traction on the tile floor to reach her.

"Easy, Doog," he said as he took another wrap of the leash around his hand. "Let me get him outside real fast and then bring him in. Go ahead and sit on the couch. We won't be here long. I need to grab a couple of things." He headed toward the front door after she'd cleared the way. "Come on, puppy. Let's go."

She walked into the living room. It felt more familiar to her than her own condo.

Like she belonged here.

Rob said we spent a lot of time at each other's places.

Maybe that was the answer.

On the shelves flanking his flat-screen TV were an assortment of pictures. Quite a few were of the two of them, or of her, or her and Doogie, or her and other people. And a lot of the pictures were duplicates of ones she had in her condo.

She reached out and picked one up, the two of them walking along a beach near sunset. They'd been looking at each other.

If that wasn't love on both of their faces, she didn't know what was.

The front door opened. "Ready or not," Rob called out, "here we come."

She put the picture back and made her way over to the couch as Rob walked in with him, apparently throwing his weight back to hold onto the dog.

"Easy, Doog!" Rob let the dog approach.

She reached out for his head, and he quickly settled down and laid his head in her lap while she stroked his velvety ears. His large brown eyes flicked from Rob to Laura, happy to be back where he belonged.

"Labbybrat?" she asked.

Rob laughed. "Yes, that's what we call him. Sometimes he's the—"

Emotions and memories flowed through her, overwhelming. She felt the tears welling up in her eyes as the word came from somewhere. "Labbybratamooseasaurus."

* * * *

Rob couldn't help the bittersweet thought. *But she can't remember my pet name for her, or how I proposed to her.* He nodded. "Yes. The moose."

She buried her face in the dog's neck and breathed deeply. "He smells like oranges."

"The vet's groomer bathed him."

For his part, Doogie held perfectly still, just the very tip of his tail rapidly moving back and forth to indicate his pleasure.

"You gave him to me for Christmas."

She wasn't done, and Rob didn't interrupt her. How close was she? "No. Not Christmas," she corrected herself. "New Year's. You gave me a box with a rubber toy and dog cookies in it on Christmas day."

He knelt next to her and touched her shoulder. "Yes." He felt hope blossom inside him.

"And a piece of newspaper…"

She closed her eyes. It looked like it almost hurt her to think that hard, but maybe the memory was there, teasing her, resisting her efforts to pry it out of hiding.

"The classified section. With a breeder's ad circled in red ink." She paused. "He wasn't old enough to pick up on Christmas, and you wanted to make sure I wanted him. So on New Year's Day, the litter was eight weeks old and you took me there and I picked him out." She sat up in surprise. "He was the runt!"

He laughed. "You felt sorry for him getting stomped by his brothers and sisters."

Doogie scooted closer to Laura and pushed his nose against her hand, wanting more attention. "He got into the bathroom garbage that first night," Laura continued, "and I told him he was an oogie little doogie. And that's how we named him."

She cradled the Lab's head in her hands and looked into his eyes. "And you tried to hump the Edwards' poodle, you little gigolo! That's when I knew I needed to get you snipped!"

* * * *

With Doogie now settled, Rob let him off the leash and went to grab a uniform for the next day. While he was gone, Laura stroked the dog's head. He was content to sit there staring into her eyes.

"I wish you could fix all of my memory."

His tail continued swishing nonstop.

A few minutes later, Rob was ready to go. "I have your phone, if you want it." He handed it to her. "The cops went through it to see if there were any clues."

She stared at it. "Were there?"

He shook his head.

He helped her get back into his SUV, then loaded Doogie in the backseat before locking the house.

Back at her condo, she didn't miss how Rob quickly swept through the rooms and checked the back door before returning to the living room.

"Checking?"

He grimly nodded. "I'm not taking any chances." He grabbed his bag and started down the hall before he turned. "Are you okay with me sleeping in bed with you?"

His question filled her with a mix of emotions she couldn't sort through. Mentally, cognitively, emotionally, she knew this man was someone she had a strong, loving, intimate relationship with.

On the other hand, he was also still a stranger to her, except for all the good feelings when she thought about him.

But few memories.

He seemed to read her indecision. "If you say no, I'll sleep in the guest room. But I won't leave you alone in the apartment." He smiled. "Besides, Doogie missed his momma, and you aren't in any shape to walk him."

His playful, caring tone pulled at her. "You're good at pushing my buttons aren't you?"

His face transformed. For a moment, she thought he'd cry.

She hoped he didn't.

"That's what you always say."

Laura reached out and touched his hand. "I think we can try it. If I'm not comfortable, we won't do it again, for a little while at least. Okay?"

He nodded. "Deal." He hesitated, then leaned in and gently pressed a kiss to her forehead. She caught his spare hand and pulled him back in for another kiss, this one on the lips.

"Deal," she said, giving him a smile.

* * * *

Rob could tell Laura was tired and in pain, so he sent her and Doogie to go lie down on the couch while he fixed them dinner. He decided on macaroni and cheese with hot dogs. It was an easy and quick meal she usually preferred when she wasn't feeling well.

He watched over the pass-through as she turned on the TV and channel surfed. After five minutes she settled on cartoons. He smiled as he observed from his vantage point in the kitchen.

Some things hadn't changed. Laura was a kid at heart. Whenever she couldn't find anything else she wanted to watch, *Scooby-Doo* or *The Flintstones* or any of her other favorite cartoons were a preferred choice.

Rob put a pot of water on for the macaroni and leaned against the kitchen counter.

It'll just be a matter of time before she recalls other things.

Wouldn't it?

He held on to that thought like a magic charm. The possibility of her never remembering terrified him. The neurologist already warned him her memory could come back in strange ways, if at all. And anything she did remember should be considered a blessing and not an indication of its importance in her mind before the attack.

He'd seen proof of that today. But *Doogie?* Steve, he could understand. She loved him like a father.

But the *dog?*

The water boiled and Rob threw in the pasta. The hot dogs only took a minute to nuke. Laura looked at the plate before taking it from him. "I like this?"

"You used to."

Dubiously, she tried it, then smiled. "I still do."

He laughed. "Yanking my chain again."

"Gotta ring your bell—"

Rob froze, his fork halfway to his mouth, the hope nearly painful in his chest as his heart pounded. The look of concentration on her face bore silent testimony to the war going on inside her to retrieve the rest of the memory. He put his fork down and waited, hopeful.

Finally the frustration sent her into tears. "I'm sorry. There was something, but it's gone." She put her plate down and limped to her bedroom.

Doogie, torn between his upset mistress and a now-accessible plate of food, faced a moral battle known to dogs throughout history. He finally chose Laura and padded after her, casting one last longing look at the plate on the coffee table.

Rob's appetite disappeared. It was frustrating how she seemed to pull other thoughts from the past, but couldn't remember him or their relationship. Did it mean maybe she had second thoughts she never voiced before the attack? The neurologist's words gave him little comfort.

Despite Shayla's assurances that she'd been as crazy in love with him as he was with her, it still hurt.

He picked up the plates and carried them to the kitchen before going to her room.

The door was open, lights off. Laura had sprawled across the middle of her bed, Doogie lying next to her. She never used to let him get on the bed. Doogie didn't seem inclined to remind her.

The Lab looked up and gave him a "please don't tell her" look. Rob sat down and stroked the dog's fur.

"Want to talk?"

Laura shook her head.

"Want some company?"

She paused, then shook her head. "Not right now. I'm sorry. I'll be out in a little while."

He fought the urge to ask her to change her mind. Before, she would hunt him down to talk, curling up in his lap, ready and willing to share whatever was on her mind.

"Okay." He went back to the living room and channel surfed.

It was going to be a long night.

* * * *

She returned twenty minutes later, Doogie on her heels. He warmed up her dinner and sat with her while she ate. When she finished, he offered to take her plate for her, but she wanted to do it.

When she stood to walk to the kitchen, Doogie started to follow her but broke formation and trotted to the front door where he sat, looking from Laura to Rob.

"He needs to go out," Rob said. "I'll take him." He grabbed the leash and closed the door behind him.

Laura stood in the living room, realizing how empty the apartment felt without them. She noticed the blinds were still open and moved to close them. Looking out the dark window accentuated how vulnerable she felt. She jumped when the phone rang.

Following the sound, she located the base unit for the cordless phone on the kitchen counter. She picked up the handset and fumbled it. "Hello?"

There was silence on the other end, then a click and the dial tone. The phone felt icy in her hand and she dropped it without thinking. Racing for the front door, she nearly collided with Rob as he came in.

He calmed her down enough for her to tell the story. She didn't have a caller ID display on the older phone. Rob tried *69, but it came up an unavailable number.

He called Thomas to notify him of the hang-up call.

Thomas said it was probably nothing. Then again, with her attacker still on the loose they couldn't be sure. They had a standing order to trace all calls on her phone and would have to run it.

After the excitement died down, Laura wandered into her office and looked around before she sat at the desk. Rob followed her in.

"Want me to walk you through it?" he asked, and she nodded.

"Please."

He reached around her and turned on the monitor and tower. "I just left everything the way it was. I didn't delete your email or anything."

"That's okay. I've got to learn how to do this."

He showed her as he logged into her email. There were over a thousand new messages for her to wade through.

It wasn't until she had almost all the messages sorted that a new one arrived, with the subject line *Congratulations*.

She opened it.

You got lucky the last time. Don't worry, I'll be seeing you again. Soon.

Laura screamed.

Chapter Fourteen

Thomas personally responded to the call, dressed in shorts and a T-shirt with his badge hanging from a lanyard around his neck. Rob finally got Laura calmed down and asleep in bed with the aid of the anti-anxiety medication Dr. Simpson had prescribed for her, and a dose of the painkillers, with Doogie protectively curled next to her.

He stood in the living room and talked with Thomas in low tones so as not to disturb her. "So we're looking for someone who's not only psychotic and vicious, but also a computer expert?" Rob felt disgusted by the lack of answers and compounding questions.

He also fought his own rising panic that he might not be able to protect Laura from her attacker. He couldn't quit work to watch over her twenty-four-seven.

"Not necessarily," Thomas said. "There's readily available information out there about concealing your identity on the Internet. Whoever sent her that message knew how to mask his IP address, but it wasn't foolproof. It came up as a computer in a public library in Vancouver, Washington."

"You don't look convinced."

"I'm not. It's going to take some digging to determine if we can locate his true location."

"Aren't there people who can track freaks like this?"

"We've forwarded the information to the FDLE and they're working on it."

"That's not good enough. This guy's still out there getting his jollies tormenting her. Who knows if he's going to come back to finish the job?"

From the grim look on the detective's face, Rob knew he'd hit the nail on the head. "You're sure he'll come back, aren't you?"

"I've already spoken my piece that it might not be a bad idea to invest in an alarm system and get her a concealed carry permit as soon as possible."

"This is an active threat. Can't we get a deputy assigned to her again?"

"We don't have concrete proof it was from her attacker, for starters, even though it certainly looks like it. Our department is overworked and understaffed. There's no way they'll approve someone sitting on her now that she's home. Not unless you pay an off-duty officer. I had to pull strings as it was to keep an officer on her in the hospital."

Rob ran a hand through his hair. "We can't afford that."

Thomas looked at the wall of pictures in the entry way. He pointed to the one of Laura and her brother. "Didn't you say her brother lives out west? Send her out there for a while."

"She'll never go for it. And she just got out of the hospital. How am I supposed to help her get her memory back if she's out there?"

"I don't have any good answers for you. I'm sorry."

Rob managed to fight the urge to punch his fist through the wall in frustration. Finally, he turned to Thomas. "You find that fucker," he warned. "You find him before I do, because I'll kill him if he comes near her. There won't be a fucking trial, because I'll put a bullet in his goddamned brain."

The detective nodded. "I hear you. I also want to warn you that's not something you should be saying to me. Don't go off on a vigilante kick and hurt the wrong person."

"The only person I'll hurt is anyone who tries to hurt her."

After seeing Thomas out, he locked the door behind him and went to check on Laura again.

Despite his love for her, he also felt the most un-Domly of his life, considering his helplessness to protect her.

* * * *

Laura was still sound asleep when Bill called after midnight. He was in the car with Steve and heading back from the airport.

Rob closed the bedroom door so Laura couldn't hear. "I'll wait up for you." After hanging up, Rob settled on the couch to watch TV and await their arrival. He didn't dare leave the condo unlocked. That'd be stupid, considering what happened.

When Rob had finally talked to Bill, he'd broken down on the phone as he told Bill what happened. Both men agreed if they ever got their hands on the guy who did this to Laura, they'd take care of him themselves without help from law enforcement.

It was nearly one thirty in the morning when Rob heard a car pull up outside. He looked through the front window to see Steve parked there.

Stepping outside, Bill gave him a huge hug. "Sorry I wasn't here earlier," Bill said, his voice thick with emotion.

"It's okay. You're here now."

Steve and Rob helped him get his bags inside to the guest room before Steve took off for home.

"How's she doing?" Bill asked him.

Rob shook his head and filled him in on the evening's events. "Thank god the meds knocked her out."

"Jeez, they can't track the fucker?"

"It's complicated. And...don't get upset when you see her in the morning. She still looks pretty bad."

"How bad? Steve said he wanted me to talk to you about her condition."

"Bad. Just don't get all choked up or anything. I'm having a hard enough time keeping it together." They said good-night and Rob gently closed the bedroom door behind him.

Laura lay curled on her left side, on the left side of the bed. Normally he slept there and she slept on the right, but he wasn't about to disturb her.

Doogie, however, he had no qualms about evicting. He tapped the dog on the head and quietly snapped his fingers before pointing at the floor.

The Lab raised his head to look at him, thumped his tail, then plopped his head down again.

Suppressing the urge to make noise, Rob tapped him on the head again and pointed at the floor, more forcefully this time.

Doogie once again raised his head and must have realized Rob really meant it. With a disgusted sigh of his own, the dog slowly sat up and yawned before taking his sweet time jumping down onto the floor.

If it wasn't for the other circumstances, Rob would have laughed over it. But he carefully slid under the covers next to her. He'd opted to sleep in shorts, considering she'd gone to bed in an oversized T-shirt and underwear.

If it took time for her to get back to where they used to be, he'd wait. He'd do anything she needed.

Anything to prove to her how much he loved her.

He reached out and touched a strand of her hair. *I love you, baby girl. I love you so much it hurts. I just want you back, however I can get you.*

* * * *

The dream happened again, almost exactly as it'd started in the hospital. Sitting at the computer. The blinking skull.

The pounding on the door.

This time, she walked farther into the living room, knowing if she opened the door a large, black shadow would fill the doorway.

Fear filled her, along with anger. Whoever it was, they'd taken her life away from her. They hadn't killed her, but worse, they'd stolen the very core of her personality.

She started to reach for the door when she started awake, gasping as her heart thundered in her chest.

Next to her, Rob soundly slept.

Reassured by his warm presence, she reached behind her and put a hand on his hip before crashing back into sleep.

* * * *

When the alarm on his phone went off at five, Rob contemplated calling in for a moment. Laura slept through it, and he stared at her in the dim light cast by the nightlight in the master bathroom.

Doogie had crawled back up on the bed at some point and was curled at her feet.

The Lab looked at him but didn't move, apparently hoping he was invisible.

Rob got up and pulled on a T-shirt before moving to the door. With another quiet snap of his fingers, he motioned to the dog to come.

Reluctantly, after giving Laura and the now-empty real estate on her other side a longing glance, he jumped from the bed and padded after Rob.

Rob waited until he had the bedroom door closed to look down at the dog. "You're a mooch, you know that?"

Doogie wagged his tail.

He followed Rob into the kitchen and waited while he made the coffee before heading for the front door. Rob had just snapped the leash to the dog's collar when the door to the guest bedroom opened and Bill emerged.

"Please tell me that's coffee I smell," he mumbled.

"Yeah. I'll be right back."

Bill waved at him and headed toward the guest bathroom while Rob took the dog out. When he returned, Bill was standing in the kitchen with an empty mug in front of him on the counter and waiting for enough coffee to brew that he could pour a mug.

"You didn't have to get up this early," Rob said.

Bill nodded. "Yeah, I did. I think it'll be best if you wake her up before you leave."

"Why? I want her to sleep."

Bill sleepily arched an eyebrow at him. "I don't want to freak her out, her waking up to find you gone and someone she doesn't recognize here instead."

"Oh. Good point." He thought about it. "She recognized Steve. Maybe she'll remember you. And she's seen your picture."

"That's not the same." He grew tired of waiting and pulled the carafe out to pour himself half a cup. "You said she didn't recognize Carol and she's known her as long."

"True." Rob grabbed the mug he usually used and tried not to look at Laura's mug, which sat next to it. Oversized, it was bright lime green and bore the picture of Scooby-Doo. He'd given it to her two birthdays ago after finding out how much she loved the cartoon dog.

"She's tough," Bill insisted. "She'll get her memories back."

"I hope you're right."

* * * *

Rob grabbed his things and took a shower in the guest bathroom so he didn't wake Laura too soon. But as it drew close to time for him to leave, he knew he had to wake her.

He returned to the bedroom and sat on the edge of the bed after turning on one of the bedside lamps. "Laura, hon? I need to leave for work."

She mumbled something and tried to roll over, but then apparently the pain in her still-tender ribs jolted her from sleep.

Rob helped her sit up. "I'm sorry, sweetie. Bill's here. I wanted to make sure I…" He swallowed back the hitch in his throat and tried again. "He's awake. I wanted to make sure you were okay before I go."

"Bill?"

"Your brother."

"Oh." She slowly nodded, sleep still obviously in charge. "Okay."

She let him help her up and to the bathroom. He waited outside the door until she was done, then gave her his arm to hold onto as he walked her out to the living room, where he settled her on the couch. "I'll get you some coffee and your pain meds."

"Okay. Thanks."

Bill stepped into the living room. "Hi, sis."

Rob watched her brow furrow, her focus going from Bill to the picture of her with him on the wall and back again.

"Do you recognize me?" Bill asked.

She shook her head, staring at him. Eventually she spoke. "I've seen pictures of you. Rob and Carol and the others have told me about you."

Bill's eyes flicked toward Rob, then back to Laura. "It's been a while since we've seen each other." He walked over to sit next to her on the couch.

She studied his hands and he finally held them up for her. While tough and rugged, they were uninjured. "I've got an alibi." He smiled, and then when she looked away, he put them down. "Sorry, Laur. I guess that wasn't funny."

"It's okay." She finally looked at him again. "I don't have very many memories. I'm sorry."

Rob watched as Bill tried to smile, tried not to stare at her bruises. "I understand." Bill looked at him and met his gaze before returning his attention to her. "I'm sorry I wasn't here sooner, sis. I should have been here for you. I'm staying two weeks. A friend of mine is helping me out with my charters."

She nodded and looked away from him, as if afraid to meet his glance.

Laura normally would have been staring Bill right in the eyes and met him with a huge, friendly hug. She sat with her shoulders slumped, pulled in, trying to shrink away. Like a beat dog.

Then again, she looked like a beat dog.

Rob brought her a glass of water, a cup of coffee, and her meds. "It's getting late. I really need to go. Sweetheart, are you going to be okay?"

She glanced at Bill as she took the meds from Rob and swallowed them with a drink from the water. "I'm okay," she softly said.

Her weak tone of voice nearly broke his heart.

"I have to work a full twenty-four," Rob said. "But Bill's going to be with you. He'll take you to the shop later, if you want, and stay there with you. And the captain said as long as we're not on a call, I can take a long break and come home to have dinner with you."

"Okay." Doogie had rested his head on her lap and she reached out to stroke his head. "Can Doogie come to work with me?" she tentatively asked.

Rob had to swallow back another hitch in his throat. "He always goes to work with you, sweetheart."

"Okay. Thank you."

He took the water from her and leaned in to kiss her forehead. "And you can call me. If you get my voice mail, leave me a message and I'll call you back as soon as I can. Or you can text me."

"Okay."

He took the glass of water back to the kitchen and went to grab the bag he normally took with him to work, with spare clothes and shower stuff.

Bill followed him. "My god," he whispered. "She looks awful."

Rob nodded. "I know. I warned you."

"It's like I'm a stranger to her."

Rob nodded again. "I know."

"This is horrible—"

"You don't have to tell me that, Bill."

Bill stopped. "I'm sorry. I know you love her. I know this is rough on you."

"I almost lost her," he whispered, his voice hoarse. "She almost *died*. And now she doesn't even *know* me. That first day in the hospital when she woke up, she was afraid of me."

Bill reached out and touched Rob's shoulder. "She'll come back. She's tough. She'll get her memories back. I know it."

"I wish I was that sure. She can remember the dog, but she can't remember me." He glanced toward the living room. "I called her 'baby girl' in the hospital and it was like I'd insulted her. I can't even talk to her the same way. I don't know what to do for her, how to help her."

"Just love her, man. She'll come back."

Chapter Fifteen

Laura tried to relax around Bill. Intellectually, she knew if Rob trusted him, he was okay. She had few memories to rely on.

The fact that meeting him didn't trigger new memories depressed the hell out of her, although she wanted to hide that fact from the men.

"Well," Bill said once Rob had said his good-byes and left for work, "can I make you some breakfast?"

She nodded. "Thank you. That'd be nice." She followed him into the kitchen, Doogie on her heels.

"French toast?"

She thought about Shayla's omelets. "That's fine." She leaned against the counter to watch him as he searched for ingredients in the refrigerator and realized she'd be less than helpful.

She had no idea where anything was.

"Are you married?" she asked, unable to remember if she'd already asked that of anyone else.

He laughed from behind the fridge door. "No, happily divorced over six years now." He peeked at her from over the top of the door. "You despised her, so you weren't exactly heartbroken when it happened."

She felt her face heat. "Sorry."

"No, no need to be. She was a bitch. I just didn't see it at the time." He set eggs, milk, and a bottle of vanilla extract on the counter. "Mom and Dad didn't like her, either. Although I loved you all like hell for keeping your mouths shut about it at the time. I knew she didn't make a good impression, but you all still tried to welcome her to the family."

"Um, okay."

He found a loaf of bread in the pantry closet. "Don't worry. Mom and Dad loved Rob." He paused, a sad look on his face. "They adored him. They'd be happy to know you guys are getting married."

She stared at the engagement ring, that she'd put on her right hand. She didn't know why she'd moved it there.

He spotted it and met her gaze again. "Are you two still getting married?"

"I…" Her mouth snapped closed. Rob hadn't said anything else about it.

And she'd been too busy struggling to corral her free-ranging memories that she really hadn't thought much about it, either, other than her conversations with Shayla.

Bill didn't speak. She knew he was waiting for her answer.

She couldn't bear the weight of his gaze any longer and looked down to where Doogie was curled up in the corner of the kitchen, watching them. "I think so. Eventually." She shrugged and that hurt her aching ribs. "I guess so."

"Laur," he softly said, "if you have any doubts about Rob, don't."

"I don't. I guess. I just…" She closed her eyes and tried to condense her jungle of emotions into a coherent, short sentence. "I have doubts about me," she admitted.

"What?"

"I don't know who I am yet. What if he doesn't like the new me?"

When she finally looked at him again, the sadness in his expression nearly started her crying. "Rob will love you no matter what." He carefully engulfed her in a hug. After a few seconds, she relaxed into his embrace, familiar comfort, different than she felt with Rob.

"Let him be the one to decide whether he can love you or not," he told her. "Don't pull away from him because of all of this."

"He's so upset."

"Not at you. No one's upset at you."

"Because of me."

"No." He held her at arm's length. "Because of the fucker that did this. And that guy's a sick, sadistic bastard. Don't let him win like this by driving you away from Rob out of fear."

He pulled her close again. She closed her eyes and let her fractured mind drift. "Strawberries," she whispered, unsure what it meant.

"What?"

"Strawberries." This time she said it firmly as a mental picture tried to swim into focus.

"Yes?"

She held her breath as the puzzle piece went from fuzzy to solid and slid into place with a *click* only she could hear. "You love strawberries and try to get them every time you come home because they grow them up in Plant City."

She sucked in a breath, her words spinning out of her, faster and faster, Laura unwilling to reel them in until they twirled themselves out for fear of blocking the memory. "I make you strawberry shortcake from scratch whenever you come to visit."

Now her tears did flow. "I make it from Grandma's recipe, that Mom used to make."

He buried his face in her hair. "Yeah?"

"I made it for you when I came out and visited you after Mom and Dad died. We had to use frozen strawberries because we couldn't find them fresh out there." Her heart pounded, more memories sliding into place.

"When you came home after I called you about Mom and Dad, Rob drove me to the airport. When you made it into the terminal you hugged me and we both broke down crying right there."

"Yeah."

Pain echoed through her heart, feeling as fresh as it had that day. "You told me it was you and me and you'd always be there for me, no matter what," she sobbed. "No matter what."

He kissed the top of her head and she heard the tears in his voice. "Yeah, sis. No matter what."

Like a shattered mosaic pulling itself magically, seamlessly back together, a huge chunk of her childhood and teen years returned. She let out a gasp, her grip on him tightening. "I remember you." Her cries renewed. "I remember you, so why can't I remember Rob?"

* * * *

Bill wasn't sure he'd be able to get her calmed down at first. He helped her out to the couch where he sat, holding her while she cried herself out in his lap.

After getting her a handful of tissues, he said, "Why don't we just stay here today, huh?"

She sat up and shook her head, a familiar, determined look on her face. "No. I need to go to the shop. Maybe it'll trigger something. I'm tired of sitting around waiting for things to happen to me."

He brushed the hair out of her face. "I don't want you to stress yourself."

She took a deep breath. "Like you said, I can't let the fucker win."

He couldn't help but smile. "Well, at least your ability to argue to get your own way is still intact."

"Is that good?"

He hugged her again, unwilling to let her go after nearly losing her, his only living family other than some distant cousins. "Yes. Very good."

After he cooked her breakfast, she went to take a shower. When the condo phone rang, he picked it up. "Hello?"

A dial tone met him.

He stared at the phone for a minute, unsure what to do. Then he called Rob.

"Fuck, call Det. Thomas. Hold on." Bill got a piece of paper to write the info down while Rob dug the card out of his pocket. "Tell him about it. How is she?"

"In the shower. She doesn't know."

"I wouldn't tell her."

"I don't plan on it. In fact, I'm going to unplug the damn phone here, so call my cell." He hung up and relayed the information to the detective, who said he'd handle it. Then Bill reached behind the phone and unplugged the cord from the wall.

He went around and found two other bases and unplugged the phone cords from them, too. After trying her phone number from his cell and not hearing any ringing in the condo, he nodded to himself.

One problem solved. For now.

* * * *

Laura ended up giving Bill her cell phone and asked him to handle it for her. She kept getting texts from people who, while their names showed up in the contacts, didn't show up at all in her mind.

Except for Shayla and Rob, of course.

She paid close attention while Steve went through things with her, like showing her how to rebuild a regulator in the repair area in the back of the shop.

"I used to do this?"

Steve looked sad. "Since you were a kid."

"Oh." As she worked, more things came back to her until she was able to work on a regulator while Steve watched.

She showed him. "Like that?"

He hooked it to a tank they kept in back for that purpose and took a test breath from it. "Perfect." He offered her a smile. "Like you've never been gone."

Bill quietly sat on a stool at the other end of the repair counter and watched.

"I feel bad you're just sitting there," she said.

Bill shook his head. "Try making me leave, sis. You just keep doing what you need to do. I'm your shadow for the next couple of weeks."

She thought about Thursday. "I'm supposed to meet with Shayla and some others for a girls' morning on Thursday."

He smiled. "I know." He held up her phone. "She texted to confirm. Brunch and then nails."

Laura grinned. "Are you getting your nails done, too?"

He held his hand out in front of him, fingers spread, nails up. "I could do with a mani-pedi. They're in kind of rough shape."

Laura burst out laughing. This was the big brother she...

She took a hitching gulp of air before the tears hit again. Steve and Bill gathered close.

"What is it, sweetie?" Bill asked.

She let out a laugh that mixed with her tears. "Just more memories of you came through. Good tears, guys."

"You sure?" Steve asked. "I can't tell the difference."

She hugged them before wiping at her eyes with the back of her hand. "Yeah, good ones."

* * * *

Bill and Steve put their collective feet down around five o'clock that afternoon. Even though it wasn't closing time yet, they could tell Laura was exhausted. Steve helped herd her toward her truck, which Bill had driven them in that morning. Bill had Doogie by the leash and loaded him into the backseat while Steve helped her into the passenger seat.

"Am I being given my marching orders?" she quipped.

Bill nodded. "Absolutely, sis. I'm pulling big brother rank on you."

"And I'm pulling age rank on you, kiddo," Steve added. "Go home, get some sleep. Rob said you've got gun lessons tomorrow. Don't bother coming in. Go do that."

"I feel guilty not being here."

Bill slid behind the wheel and leaned forward. "You believe her?" he asked Steve. "The first vacation she's had in a while and she's fighting it." He smiled.

He took her home, keeping her distracted with the TV and by going through her photo albums again until he got dinner started in preparation for Rob's arrival.

When Rob returned, he gave her a kiss but sent Bill a look that told him Rob wanted to talk to him. Alone.

Bill followed him back to the master bedroom. "She okay?" Rob asked.

"Yeah. I unplugged the phones here, though."

"Good."

"She…" Bill felt horrible, but knew it was the situation. "She got some memories back about me."

He watched Rob's face as the man schooled it into professional neutrality. "Nothing about me?"

"It doesn't mean anything. Don't give it weight."

His shoulders slumped. "I know."

The three sat and talked after dinner. Laura yawned and looked at the time. "I'm sorry, but I need to go to bed. I'm really tired."

Bill and Rob both stood when she did. She hugged Rob. Bill watched as she reluctantly let him go. "When do you come back?"

He tucked her hair behind her ears. "Tomorrow morning. But then I need to go in at six tomorrow night to cover for one of the guys who covered for me."

"Okay." It looked like she was debating something, then she rose up on her toes and gave him a quick kiss, brushing her lips over his.

She hugged Bill. "Night, sis. See you in the morning."

When she closed the bedroom door behind her, both men heavily sat and stared at each other, the strain each felt mirrored on the other's face. Bill spoke first.

"She doesn't even sound the same," Bill said. "She talks differently. Did you notice that?"

Rob nodded. "Tell me about it. You want a beer?" Rob headed for the kitchen.

"Got anything stronger?"

"Jack Daniel's."

"Bring the bottle."

Rob reappeared with a glass of iced tea for him, and the bottle of liquor and a glass for Bill. "God, I wish I could have a drink," Rob said.

Bill held up the bottle. "Want some?"

Rob shook his head before he took a sip of tea. "Nothing stronger than this. I have to get back to work." He took a long swallow. "And I'm afraid if I start on that, I won't want to stop."

Bill started to pour his own drink and stopped at two fingers. "Good point." He capped the bottle and took a swallow, grimacing. "I don't know how you've managed to hold it together."

"I have to." Rob looked at his glass. "She's my life. If I lose her, everything else is pointless."

Bill studied him. "Don't give up on her, okay? I remember how she talked about you last summer. She's madly in love with you. As upset as she was, she told me the only thing that got her through losing Mom and Dad was you."

Rob looked away before he took another swallow. "I just wish I could believe that. You'd think she'd at least remember a few things about us if that was the case." He stared out into space. "She put her engagement ring on her right hand."

"Stop it."

Rob looked at him.

"Rob, she loves you. Trust me, she does. I talked to her, what, a week before the attack? She was raving about the fricking wedding invitations. At the time, I could have cared less. She was describing them to me, babbling on. She was so happy and I was just listening to her, letting her talk."

Bill stared at his drink, feeling guilty. "I wish I'd paid more attention now. I was just letting her go on and on. Man, you are her world. She has no doubts about you." He took another swig of whiskey and swirled the glass. "I know few things with certainty, but I have no doubt about her love for you."

* * * *

Bill was already up and watching TV when Laura awoke a little after five thirty the next morning. She felt comforted by the delicious aroma of coffee filling the condo.

Her night had been filled with nightmares about someone pounding on her door, waking up every time she reached for the knob.

Unfortunately, she hadn't had Rob's comforting presence next to her to soothe her.

After using the bathroom, she headed out to the living room. He sat on the couch, browsing on his laptop.

"Are you an early riser?" she asked.

He joined her in the kitchen. "Only because I set my alarm. Rob's supposed to be home soon. Wanted to make sure he got in okay. He also warned me you're suddenly an early riser." He smiled. "Despite a lifetime of hating mornings."

She stared at her coffee mug. Rob had fixed it for her the morning before, with milk and sugar. As she stared at the empty mug, it occurred to her that she didn't even remember how she used to take her coffee. Rob had brought her coffee. Shayla had brought her coffee.

They both knew more about her than she knew about herself.

She poured herself a mugful and picked it up, blowing a little across the top.

Bill frowned at her.

"What?" she asked. She took a sip, making a face at the bitter taste as Bill started laughing.

"That."

She put the mug down and added a generous amount of sugar. He reached into the fridge and handed her the carton of milk. She added enough to take it almost to the top of the mug and gave it a careful stir.

"You've taken sugar and milk or creamer in your coffee as long as you've been drinking it," he told her as he put the milk back.

"Apparently, I still do. It was an experiment." She carefully picked up the mug and took another sip.

Much better.

"Here's today's plan. Rob put me in touch with your friend, Sully. He texted me yesterday and said he'd be here by nine this morning."

Nerves took over, even though rationally she knew they shouldn't. "We're meeting him at the shop?"

"No, no need. He's coming here. We'll ride with him."

She tried to quell her rising panic. "But Rob said Steve's met him before. I don't want to have to wake Rob up."

He smiled and pulled out his phone, then showed her something. It was a picture of a man. "Rob sent me his pic."

She let out a relieved laugh as she looked at it. "He's thinking of everything."

He took the phone back. "Well, we're trying. It's a group effort. Apparently Sully suggested it."

She jumped when around six thirty she heard keys in the front door. Bill started toward it when Rob walked in.

Just the sight of him started her heart fluttering. She walked over with the intent of hugging him when she realized a strong, acrid aroma of smoke wafted off him.

He held out a hand to stay her. "Yeah, sorry. Wildfire. We had a couple of guys go down with heat exhaustion. Let me get a shower first, then I'll get my hug." He kissed her hand before heading toward the master bedroom.

"Coffee?" she asked after him.

"Yes, please." He disappeared, then stuck his head back out. "Milk and sugar, please." He disappeared again.

She nodded and headed toward the kitchen, trying to shrug off another round of tears that prickled her eyes.

She didn't even remember how Rob took his coffee, but she could remember Bill loved strawberries.

Bill followed her. "Stop thinking that."

"Thinking what?"

"That." He caught her hands and made her look at him. "Guilty. Stop it. You're trying too hard. I think more will come back if you stop trying to force it. Did you call and make an appointment with the psychiatrist yet?"

"No."

"Go take him his coffee. Then when you come back, I want that business card. I'll call her today and make the appointment for this week, if she can get you in."

"Okay."

Rob was already in the shower. She hesitated, but he'd left the door partially open.

"I have your coffee."

"Bring it in, sweetheart. It's okay."

She took a deep breath and walked in. His smoky clothes lay in a heap on the floor. The shower curtain, light fern green with leaves on it, hid his body from her. He pulled the shower curtain back and stuck his head out.

"Want to take a shower with me?"

She must have reacted badly, because his face fell. "Honey, it's okay. You don't have to."

Standing there, she finally put down the coffee on the counter, next to the sink. Stepping over his clothes she walked to the shower and leaned in.

"Maybe I want to," she softly said.

That earned her a smile, a smile that melted her soul. A smile she knew she'd do anything to see. A smile that seemed to instantly reverse the pain she'd read in his eyes over whatever expression she'd revealed after his comment.

She kissed him, slowly, sweetly, ignoring the spray from the shower lightly beading in her hair like condensation on a glass of iced tea in the summer heat.

His gaze traveled her face. "I don't want to push you," he said. "I know this is hard for you. The fact that you're willing is enough for now." He started to say something else, but a yawn took over. "And I hate to say it, but I'm exhausted. I only got about three hours of sleep yesterday total."

He kissed her again. "And you're meeting with Sully today."

"You mean I'm meeting Sully today."

He managed a tired smile. "I'd go with you, but exhaustion and firearms don't mix."

"Bill showed me his picture."

He kissed her once more. "I trust Sully with your life. He's a good man. Retired cop."

She cradled his cheek in her hand, felt the stubble there. When the mental spinning started again, she closed her eyes and waited to see if it would bring results or disappointment.

She stood with him, much like this morning, but in a different bathroom. "Does it have shells on the curtain?" She didn't want to open her eyes.

Hell, she didn't want to *breathe* for fear of losing it.

"Shells?"

"The shower curtain." Rob stood there in her mind just as plainly as he stood in front of her now. "And the carpet mat is beige." In here, there was only a white towel on the floor.

At the noise he made, she opened her eyes. She could tell from the way his eyes looked too bright that he was close to tears. "Yeah. The master bath in the bedroom at the house."

She threw her arms around him, not caring that she was getting wet. "It's not a lot," she finally managed, "but it's a start."

He buried his face in her hair. "Yeah, sweetheart. It's a start. And I'll take everything I can get."

* * * *

Laura hoped she didn't regret her decision to stick with non-prescription pain killers that morning. She couldn't imagine drugs and guns were a smart mix. And as long as she didn't make any fast, sudden movements, her ribs didn't bother her too much.

Sullivan Nicoletto wasn't quite as tall as Rob or Bill. Maybe in his late forties, his grey eyes seemed to take everything in. When he knocked, Bill had opened the door for him after looking through the peephole to verify his identity.

Bill shook hands with him and introduced himself after letting him in. Even Doogie seemed to recognize him, happily wagging his tail as Sully stooped to pet him.

Sully, as he'd asked her to call him, gave her a friendly smile she found reassuring. "How are you doing, Laur?"

She nodded. He felt familiar, but no concrete memories yet. "I'm okay."

"Nothing, huh?"

"Sorry."

"No, it's okay. I talked to Tony and Shay. They've been keeping us all posted so we weren't bugging poor Rob."

"He's asleep. He was on shift yesterday."

"That's okay. I don't want to wake him. Are you ready?"

"Am I dressed okay?" Bill had suggested she wear jeans. She'd also added a baseball cap and a pair of large, dark sunglasses to help conceal her bruises a little.

"You're fine," Sully assured her.

They headed east toward Pt. Charlotte, her in the backseat of his Jaguar while Bill rode up front. "I talked with Det. Thomas, who put me in touch with a gun range down here," Sully told them. "I've already talked with them. We're going to put you through a safety class this morning, as well as the concealed weapons class curriculum, then do range work. When we're done, we'll meet Thomas over at his office and get your fingerprints taken."

"Fingerprints?"

"For the license. Required. And we can stop anywhere to get your picture taken. He's going to personally handle your application to get your license rushed."

"Okay." She had a thought. "How much is all of this going to cost me?" She realized she had no idea how much money she had, much less how to access it. All of this might be beyond her budget.

If she even had a budget. Maybe the hospital bills had wiped her out.

Sully glanced at her in the mirror. "Nothing. I'm picking all of this up for you."

When she started to protest, he silenced her, catching and holding her gaze in the rearview mirror. "You let me do this for you, and for Rob. Consider it an early wedding present, okay? I'm sorry I couldn't be down here before this."

She realized he wasn't a man to be argued with. "Thank you," she said.

He smiled. "Besides, Clarisse would kill me if I let you pay."

The class work was easy enough, lasted about three hours, and before long they were in the gun range. Bill sat at a table just outside the range area, where he could watch through large windows.

Sully had brought three guns, two semi-automatics and a revolver, in a metal carry-case. From a duffel bag he produced two sets of shooting muffs and protective glasses.

With the instructor looking on, Sully showed her how all three guns worked and walked her through loading and unloading them. The weight of the guns in her hands wasn't familiar to her, but it wasn't altogether unpleasant, either.

Her aim wasn't the best, but it wasn't the worst. After shooting all three guns several times and growing more comfortable with them, Sully and the instructor both pronounced her capable enough to safely handle the guns.

Unfortunately, she also realized she should have taken a pain pill. She hoped the men couldn't see how much pain she was in.

"I'll make sure I get with you at least once a week to practice," Sully told her.

"I don't have a gun."

He smiled. "That's part two of my wedding present to you."

Sully helped her pick out a 9mm that felt comfortable to her. The instructor, who was also the gun shop's owner, let her shoot several magazines of rounds through it before Sully put down a credit card. She wouldn't be able to take it home for three days due to waiting period laws, but they got her fitted with two different holsters and a purse she could conceal it in. Sully also got her set up with a cleaning kit, showed her how to use it, and bought her a set of shooting muffs and glasses, as well as a range bag.

By the time they went for lunch, her application had been completed, her picture taken at a drugstore, and Thomas had personally supervised her fingerprints being taken.

And she wanted to break down and cry from the pain.

As they sat in the booth after the waitress took their order, Laura stared out the window.

"What's wrong, sweetie?" Bill asked.

She didn't look at them. "I'm okay," she softly said.

He reached into his pocket and pulled something out, setting it in front of her.

The bottle of her painkillers.

When she just stared at it, Sully reached across the table, glanced at the label, and then shook one into his palm.

"Hand."

Something about his tone of voice brooked no resistance. She held out her hand, palm up, in front of him. He dropped the tablet into her palm while Bill slid her glass of water over to her.

"She's stubborn," Bill said as they watched her take the pill.

Sully screwed the cap onto the bottle and returned it to Bill. "I know. She thinks she's a tough solder." He stared at her from across the table with a familiar intensity that didn't make her feel uncomfortable.

That bothered her in a way she couldn't understand. She looked down at her lap.

"I could tell how bad she was hurting," Sully said as he watched her. "But having dealt with my fair share of pain and that age-old question of do I or don't I take the meds now or later, I wasn't going to call her out on it at the range."

She looked up at him. "Why are you in pain?"

"Got shot in the line of duty. It's why I retired. Gut and leg. Most of the time, I'm all right. But if I overdo things and don't take my cane, I can end up needing some of those myself. I try to avoid getting to that point in the first place."

"I guess it makes it difficult with two babies, huh?"

He looked like he was about to speak, then changed his mind. It took him a moment to reply. "We get by. It takes teamwork."

It was definitely another of those missed context moments, like she'd sensed with Shayla in the hospital.

Lucky for him she was hurting too bad to pursue it. She just wanted the pain pill to kick in so she changed the subject rather than mulling it over.

"Is this what my life is going to be like now? Looking over my shoulder all the time?" She finally turned to them. "What kind of life is this?" she quietly asked. "Where I don't know who's who and might have to kill someone to protect myself?"

Sully reached across the table and laid his hands over hers. "If you need to, you're welcomed to come stay with us. I already told Rob that, but I'm telling you, too."

"But that's not *my* life." She looked out the window again. "I want *my* life back. At least the memories of it. If I had those, it wouldn't be so bad, I guess. Then maybe I'd know who did this to me. Or at least I'd have a good idea of who *didn't* do it to me so I wouldn't have to rely on everyone else to tell me who to trust."

"Do you trust me, Laura?" Sully quietly asked.

Something in her heart flipped over in a good way. Not romantically, but…familiar. The same way it'd felt when he'd ordered her to put her hand out.

She turned back to him and stared into his eyes. Grey, clear, understanding. He knew more about her than she did.

"Ask me again," she said.

His gaze never wavered from hers as he placed his other hand over hers on the table. "Do you trust me?" he softly asked, in a slightly different tone. Firmer, but…something specific she couldn't put her finger on.

She felt like she should know this.

She stared at him for a moment. Pulling air into her lungs suddenly became a difficult task, even more so with the pain. "Yes," she quietly said. "I trust you."

She wanted to add a "sir" to the end of that phrase but cut it off, all without understanding why.

He smiled and gently squeezed her hands before he released them and sat back. "Good. I'm glad you feel that way about me. Because yes, you're like family to us. I'll do whatever I can to help keep you safe."

Chapter Sixteen

Rob wasn't at the condo when they returned. After Sully dropped them off, Bill told her what he'd been up to. While they were shooting, Bill had called Dr. Simpson and set up an appointment. "Nine o'clock Saturday morning," he said. "She's coming in special to talk with you."

"I feel bad she's making an exception for me."

"Don't you try to wiggle out of this. I'm driving you there. Got it?"

She sensed the firm set of his jaw meant he wouldn't take no for an answer. "Thank you," she quietly said before retreating to her bedroom. She turned at the door. "I need to lie down for a little bit. Can we go to the shop after I wake up?"

"Of course, sweetie. Take as long as you need."

"Thanks."

* * * *

Bill watched as she closed the door behind her. He suspected once the pain pill fully kicked in that they wouldn't be leaving the apartment.

He was also telling Rob to put the kibosh on Laura going out with her friends in the morning. She was still in too much pain.

He slumped down on the sofa, idly stroking Doogie's head when the dog shoved it in his lap.

This wasn't their Laura. Nothing remotely like her. His sister would have taken to shooting that morning with a spirit of fun and adventure, pain or not.

Watching her with Sully had been painful. Like watching a dutiful child going through the motions, doing what they're told.

That wasn't his sister. Not his old sister. Not the Laura he grew up with.

His phone vibrated. He looked to see Rob calling.

"How'd she do?" he asked.

"Good, all things considered. Where are you?"

"The house. The alarm company is here now. I'll be back this afternoon."

"What about installing the alarm here?"

"Tomorrow morning. Don't worry, Steve said he'd come over while they do it."

"Won't be necessary." He told Rob about her pain. "I think we should either have them come here, or cancel it. She might get pissed off at me for that, but I don't care. She needs to rest."

Rob sounded exhausted. "I agree. I'll call Shayla. No new memories?"

He hated to be the bearer of bad news. "Sorry."

Bill checked on Laura several times. She never stirred when he opened her bedroom door.

It was after three o'clock when she finally made her way out to the living room, Doogie on her heels.

He looked up from the book he'd been reading as she carefully lowered herself next to him on the couch and put her head in his lap.

"Oh, little sis, you are sooo not going over to the shop today." He put the book aside and stroked her hair. "Sorry, but I'm pulling rank. You look like you feel horrible."

"I know," she softly said.

"How's the pain?"

"I don't want another pill. I hate taking them. My brain feels so fuzzy when I take them. I'm having a hard enough time without those on top of it."

"You need what you need to get through this." Although it didn't surprise him. Laura hated taking prescription pain meds even before all of this.

"I don't want one," she insisted.

He knew that stubborn tone. "I'll give you something nonprescription. Okay?"

"Okay." She laced her fingers through his. "Thank you for coming. For taking care of me."

"You don't have to thank me."

* * * *

Laura felt like she owed him more than just thanks. He was putting his life on hold to babysit her.

"I'm sorry."

He gently squeezed her hand. "No apologies. You're my little sister and I love you. You're family. The only family I've got."

She closed her eyes and thought about their parents' funeral. It wasn't the most pleasant memory to have back, but it least it involved Bill and Rob.

"Do you like Rob?"

"Of course I like him. Why?"

She opened her eyes and looked up at him. "Really? You *really* like him?"

He frowned. "Laur, listen to me. He's crazy about you. He loves you. We talked after you ordered your wedding invitations, because you were busting my balls about making sure…"

His voice faltered and he reached down to gently stroke her forehead. "You told me I'd damn sure better clear my calendar because I *would* be there to walk you down the aisle and give you away."

"Really?"

He nodded. "Really."

"Where is he?" She'd hoped Rob would be there when she woke up.

"He'll be back soon. The alarm company's at the house."

"Oh."

"And, news flash, Rob and I voted. You're not going tomorrow. Maybe next week. You need to heal up more."

She felt disappointed, but the amount of pain she was in then robbed her of the strength, or reason, to argue. "Okay."

They both looked up at the sound of keys in the door. Doogie lifted his head before running over to wait. Laura's heart sped up, fluttering in a pleasant way at the sight of Rob. Wearing a T-shirt that hugged his torso and showed off his physique, and a pair of cargo shorts, he carried a duffel bag.

He smiled when he saw her. "Hey, sweetie." He left the duffel by the door and walked over to the couch, where he knelt down next to her. "How are you feeling?"

She reached out for his hand and pulled it to her chest. "I'm okay."

Bill snorted. "She's lying. I told her she's not going to the shop today or to Sarasota tomorrow. And she won't take another pain pill."

Rob's gaze never left hers, even while Bill was talking. "Please take one. It'll make you feel better."

"It makes my head fuzzy."

He looked so sad. She tugged on his hand so he leaned in closer. She wished she could make the sadness in his eyes go away.

She brushed a kiss across his lips. It felt good, right.

He rewarded her with a smile. "I'm going to go put my stuff away. What do you want for dinner?"

She shrugged.

"Spaghetti and meatballs it is," he said.

She watched as he stood, retrieved his bag, and headed down the hall. Her libido wasn't exactly revving on all cylinders, but something tugged at her heart.

"Don't worry," Bill softly said. "You still look at him the way you used to."

She looked up into his smiling face. "I do?"

He nodded. "You do."

She rested her head in his lap again and closed her eyes. It would have to be enough.

For now.

* * * *

Laura brooked no resistance when Rob arched an eyebrow at her and held out the pill and a glass of water. Bill was in the kitchen helping with dinner, and she was watching the evening news on the couch with Doogie curled up on the floor next to her.

With a sigh she sat up, took the pill and water from him, and swallowed it down. "Happy?"

He pursed his lips. "I'm not happy this happened to you, no. But I'll do everything I can to take care of you, yes. I can't stand seeing you in pain."

"Unless you cause it?" Her jaw snapped shut and she frowned.

His face went blank as he took the glass from her.

"I…I'm sorry," she said, feeling mortified. "I don't know where that came from. It just popped out of my mouth."

"No, it's okay," he gently said.

She felt horrible. "Rob, I—"

"Laur, it's okay," he firmly said.

There was that tone again. The one Sully had used.

The one that told her Rob wasn't lying. He wasn't upset. If anything...

From the crinkles at the outer corner of his eyes, it almost looked like he was trying not to laugh.

But that couldn't be right.

Could it?

He didn't have to be at work until six in the morning. After dinner, she left the men to talk and went to curl up in bed. Rob joined her a short while later, leaving a pair of boxers on. She'd opted for a T-shirt and panties.

While rooting through the closet earlier, she'd found several corsets and slinky looking dresses, among other things, tucked in the far back corner.

"Can I ask you something?" she said, struggling to keep her head above consciousness over the effects of the pain pill.

He carefully rested a hand on her hip, trying to avoid her ribs. "Sure, sweetie. You can ask me anything."

"What are all those corsets and stuff for? In the closet?"

He didn't answer at first. "We...ah, we like to...play dress-up."

The little laugh didn't hurt her ribs. "You mean in bed?"

"Sure."

She tried to interpret that answer, but felt too tired to think about it. It made sense and felt right despite another of those missing-context moments, so she let it drop. "Okay." She'd almost fallen asleep when she had another thought. "You can scoot closer," she mumbled.

When she felt the comforting, firm warmth of his body molded against hers, she crashed into sleep.

* * * *

Rob lay there long after she fell asleep and listened to the sound of her breathing.

Next to hearing her in the throes of an orgasm, it was the best sound in the world when just a week ago they weren't even sure if she'd wake up.

Or what shape she'd be in if she did.

He hoped she didn't question him too much on his answer about the clothes, but he'd made a promise to himself not to lie to her in the process of trying to get her memory back. He couldn't tell her about the BDSM yet. Not when she was still trying to sort out her life.

He still wasn't sure how to broach the subject of Tilly's and Clarisse's poly triad relationships. Canceling tomorrow's get-together was a small blessing that bought him a little time to determine how to handle it.

I need to talk to Tony. Between work and getting Laura home and dealing with having alarm systems installed and everything else, he hadn't had a chance to sit down and call him.

Not exactly a call he wanted coworkers, Bill, Laura, or anyone at Laura's shop to overhear.

He also added another item to his mental checklist. *Get Laura to change her home phone number.* Thomas had asked him to wait a little while before doing that, to see if they could trap the caller.

I didn't check her email today. He'd forgotten to ask Bill to do it for her. Before, Laura would have practically had her iPhone attached to her wrist, responding to and deleting email throughout the day, texting with Shayla and others, and only using her laptop, iPad, or the home computer for writing or browsing.

Before.

He tried to erase those thoughts from his mind.

She will *get her memories back. I* know *it.*

He refused to believe anything else.

Hopefully, by the time Bill returned to Montana, Rob would have Laura talked into moving into the house. Just a couple of streets over from Carol, and less than a mile from Steve, they could help keep an eye on her for him.

Before, their routine on weeknights when he was home and not exhausted, they would play a little. Something to carry them both through until the next time. Sometimes a little over-the-knee spanking, sometimes more.

And then they'd fall asleep entwined in each other's arms, both of them naked except for Laura wearing her play collar, and her leather wrist and ankle cuffs.

He was afraid to move for fear of waking her or hurting her. He wanted to drape his arm around her waist and hold her close, wanted to bury his teeth in the curve of her neck where it met her shoulder. Something that usually had her begging for a good hard fucking.

He was afraid to even kiss her now. For fear of hurting her, or worse, scaring her.

In his mind he could feel the curve and weight of her breast in his hand as he dug his fingers in, making her gasp and squirm and beg for more.

He thought about the time in this very bed, just a couple of weeks before the attack, when he'd awoken in the middle of the night and rolled her onto her stomach. How he pinned her down by her neck, while he stroked her between her legs.

Even half asleep, she moaned and arched her back, spreading wide for him as he slowly finger-fucked her.

"Hands behind your back."

How she complied, without hesitation. He transferred his grip from her neck to her wrists and held on tightly, using her as leverage while he fucked her.

Reaching around her, he pinched her clit as he ordered her to come.

Her moans, muffled by her pillow as her body obeyed him, her pussy squeezed his cock even as she tried rocking her hips against him to intensify the feeling.

She made a soft sound in her sleep, bringing his thoughts back to the present.

Now...

He didn't know if he'd ever have his sweet baby girl back, or if he'd end up forging a new life with this new woman who, in so many ways, was nothing like the woman he fell in love with.

This new woman he still loved and would die to protect.

* * * *

After finally giving in to his exhaustion, Rob dreamed. Recalling one of their early nights together after they'd formalized their relationship, they were at his condo, before he'd sold it. He tied Laura facedown on his bed, arms spread, on her knees, ass exposed.

Still a little tentative, he'd spanked her bare-handed, enjoying the way she wiggled her ass for him, the way her pussy got wet, her clit swelling as her desire soared.

Then he donned a glove and picked up a bottle of lube. "Time for me to take possession of somewhere else."

Laura let out a little mewling sound of anticipation as he squirted lube down the seam of her ass and slowly began working it into her rim with one finger. He hadn't fucked her ass yet, but it was something they'd already talked about.

Something she'd asked him to do.

She softly moaned into the mattress as he gently breached her tight ring of muscle with one finger. Taking his time he carefully thrust, a little deeper each time, adding lube until after a few minutes he was able to easily slide one finger in and out of her.

Another moan escaped her.

"How's that, baby girl?"

"Yes, Sir!"

"That's not exactly the answer I was looking for."

"It's good, Sir."

"Want me to continue?"

"Please, Sir."

He grinned and leaned in to bite one ass cheek, then the other, hard enough to make her squeal and squirm and leave faint marks. "I'm going to completely own this sweet ass tonight." He'd ordered a harness and several butt plugs for her, but they hadn't arrived yet.

The thought of locking her in it for a weekend, with a vibrating egg in her pussy and a butt plug in her ass, made his cock throb.

As he made sure she was loose enough to continue, he noticed how she'd started rocking her hips in time with his movements, fucking herself back onto his hand. She'd done a little anal play on herself in the past, she'd admitted, but no one had ever fucked her back there.

Her virgin ass would be his.

After a few minutes he added more lube and a second finger. She whined a little bit as he slowly massaged and stretched her muscles with the tips of his fingers before repeating the process. Carefully, he worked the two fingers into her tight ass, scissoring them to help ready her for his cock.

It didn't take long for the discomfort to turn to pleasure. She soon started fucking herself back onto his hand again, her juices now dripping from her cunt. Her bare pussy lips were puffy.

He reached under her with his free hand and tweaked her clit, making her jump. "Just wait until I get you ready for my cock," he warned. "I'm going to park myself inside your ass and use the Hitachi on you. Make you come until I think you've had enough."

She whimpered, but her hips sped up.

That earned her a laugh. He withdrew his hand, mindful of her disappointed whines, and started over again with three fingers.

It took longer, but taking his time, he patiently worked on her until she was once again eagerly humping herself onto his hand.

"Such a good girl." After he thought he had her ready, he withdrew his hand again and stripped off the glove. He grabbed a condom and slicked his shaft with lube before drizzling more down the seam of her ass.

"Time for me to take full possession of this sweet ass." She fell still as he pressed the engorged head of his cock against her prepared rim. She froze, but soon started rocking her hips against him once more.

"Good girl." He let her set the pace, holding still as she began fucking herself little by little onto his cock, until his thighs were pressed against her ass and he was buried to the root inside her.

He grabbed the Hitachi. "Such a good girl. Good girls get rewards." He switched it on and reached around her to press it against her clit.

She exploded. The feel of her tight channel squeezing his cock nearly made him explode. He held back only through sheer force of will as orgasm after orgasm rolled through her.

Forced orgasm torture, he'd soon discovered, was a favorite of his. He loved nothing more than to watch her body writhe under his hands, under his control as he forced waves of pleasure through her.

He didn't know how long it was before he finally felt his own impending release subside enough he felt safe switching off the vibrator. Setting it aside, he grabbed her hips. "Mine," he whispered as he slowly withdrew before thrusting again. "All mine."

He slapped her ass. "Who does this belong to?"

"You, Sir!" He knew from the sound of her voice she was deep in subspace.

"Yes, it does. Such a good girl." He knew he wouldn't last long. Her ass was so tight, felt so good, that it wouldn't be long before he exploded. "Tell me what you want, baby girl."

"I want Sir to fuck and own my ass."

"Good girl." He sped up, harder, deeper, faster. Then it happened, an explosion rushing through his nervous system as his balls emptied into the condom, filling it with his cum. He braced himself, his arms on either side of her, and feathered kisses along her spine. "My good girl," he whispered. "I love you so much."

She turned her head enough she could force an eyelid open and look at him. She wore a sweet, sexy, sated smile. "I love you, too, Sir."

* * * *

Laura stirred when she heard the alarm go off Thursday morning, but then it silenced and she closed her eyes again. She hadn't slept well at all, even with Rob there, because of nightmares running on a repeating loop through her brain.

The only comfort she had was that she was now used to them.

When she next opened her eyes, Rob sat next to her on the edge of the bed.

Fully dressed in his uniform.

"Hey," he said. "Sorry. I didn't want to leave without saying good-bye."

"What time is it?"

"Twenty till six."

She started to sit up then winced as pain took over.

"Stay there." He left the bedroom, returning a few minutes later with a pain pill and water. "Take it."

That tone again. Even half asleep and hurting like hell it cut through her soul to some secret place that made her want to curl up in his lap and beg him to stay.

He helped her sit up enough she could swallow the pill and some water before easing her back down onto her pillow. "Why does it hurt more now than it did in the hospital?" she asked.

"You're not on IV meds anymore. And they were making you take meds on a regular basis in the hospital. Plus you were basically moving between bed and the bathroom and back again. You need to take it easy and not rush it."

He leaned in and pressed a sweet, lingering kiss to her forehead. He smelled good, his laundry detergent and soap and deodorant filling a gaping void inside her. She reached up and hooked her fingers into his shirt until he leaned close again.

Eyes still closed, she deeply inhaled several times. The laundry room came to mind again, the one she'd pictured before. "I want to go to your house again," she said.

"I had the locksmith change all the locks after…when he came to do your doors. I'll leave a key and a note for Bill. He needs to call me so I can walk him through the alarm."

She opened her eyes. In the dim light, his brown eyes looked dark, deep…

Sad.

"Thank you," she said.

His brow furrowed. "For what, sweetheart?"

"For not giving up on me."

He looked like he was on the verge of tears. He knelt next to the bed and gently cupped her hand in both of his and pressed his lips to it. "I love you. The only thing that can make me stop taking care of you is me dying, or you flat-out telling me you don't want me anymore."

With her free hand she caressed his cheek. Despite it hurting, she leaned in and kissed him on the lips, lingering, savoring it. "Thank you for being patient with me."

"Forever, sweetheart. I promise."

"I want you."

His jaw worked, as if he had to swallow. "I want you, too. More than anything."

"I don't know how long…until…I can…"

He kissed her hand again. "It doesn't matter. You're in no condition to even think about that, anyway. And if it takes weeks or months or even years for you to get to that point, then that's how long it takes."

"Did we…on our first date?"

He actually laughed. "No. For starters, I'm not like that, and neither are you. Secondly…" He let out another laugh and shook his head. "If I had time, I'd tell you the story. Let's say our first date was a true disaster. Fortunately, we kept trying until we got it right."

After one more kiss, he stood and carefully freed his hands from hers. "Do you need Bill to show you how to work your phone?"

She felt her face heat. "Yeah. I think so." She'd barely looked at it, overwhelmed. Frustrated that she knew she'd easily worked it before…

Before.

Everything before.

"I'll put that in the note, too. I walked Doogie already." The dog was curled up on the bed on her other side, in the space Rob had occupied. The Lab looked from him to her and back again.

"Love you," he told her.

She let out a deep breath she didn't realize she'd been holding. "I love you, too." That much she knew. She'd take it on faith despite whatever rumbles tried to traipse through her mind.

Deep in her heart, she knew she loved him.

She closed her eyes and let the pain pill kick in.

* * * *

Her stomach was growling when she pulled herself out of bed close to ten o'clock that morning. Bill was sitting in the living room and working on his laptop.

"There she is. How you feeling?"

She made her way over to the couch and eased herself down onto it before leaning over to rest her head against his shoulder.

"That bad, huh?" he asked.

"Yeah. Please don't ask me to take another pain pill. I want to go to the shop today."

"Your presence there is not requested. Steve and Carol said they'd both help load you back in the truck so I could haul you home."

She didn't want to cry. She'd done enough of that. She also didn't want to stay cooped up at the condo. Frustration set in.

"When do I get to decide what I do with my life? Or is this who I was before, just letting everyone tell me what to do?" Despite the pain it caused her, she stood and headed for the kitchen. "I'm sick and tired of everyone else telling me what to do. And worse, I've got a psycho who wanted me dead keeping me in fear for a life I can't even fucking remember!"

He followed her to the kitchen but she turned and pushed him out. "Go. Just...go sit down and leave me alone. I'll make my own breakfast. I'm not helpless."

She couldn't exactly storm, but she plodded over to the fridge and yanked it open, ignoring the pain in her side as she did.

Then she...stood there, staring at what was eye level.

Bill, who hadn't moved from the kitchen doorway, watched her without speaking.

She let the refrigerator door swing shut and rested her head against the cool surface as tears rolled down her cheeks. On the upper freezer door, there were several magnets. One from Yellowstone.

A magnet she'd bought on her trip out there after their parents died.

She remembered stopping in the visitor center by Old Faithful and buying it, one just like it for the fridge at the house, and several others for Shayla and...people she couldn't even remember. Maybe Sully and Clarisse had one on their fridge, too.

But she knew the one on Rob's fridge sat just a little lower than eye level, toward the right. The door handle, opposite of this one, was on the left, and it opened to the right. This one swung open to the left.

His fridge was stainless steel, and matched the stove and dishwasher. He'd taken her with him to pick them out when he bought them several months earlier.

"Laur?" Bill softly asked.

His voice shook her out of her thoughts and the remaining pieces swirled out of reach, once again, into the abyss.

"Take me to Rob's," she said.

"I can't. The alarm company will be here any minute. We have to wait until they leave."

She nodded as her eyes once again settled on the magnet. "I'm sorry."

He took a step into the kitchen. "It's okay," he said, his voice still low and gentle. "No one blames you for feeling out of whack. I'm surprised you're handling it as well as you are."

She reached up and touched the surface of the magnet, tracing its embossed image. "You took the time off then, too."

"Yeah." He edged closer, so he could drape his arm around her shoulders.

"Do you still have the horses?"

"You remember that?"

"I remember something about riding."

He smiled. "Yep. Those two big mooches are still hanging around."

She looked up into his eyes. "Will this get any easier?"

"I wish I could tell you that."

Chapter Seventeen

The alarm company was able to work fast and get everything installed in less than two hours. Her condo was much smaller and easier to equip than the house.

They went over everything with her, showed her how to program it, how to add additional users, and how to check trouble codes.

She stared at the keypad as she and Bill prepared to leave.

"What's wrong?" he asked. "Do you need help with it?"

She slowly shook her head. "I never needed one of these before, did I?"

"Well, you've had one at the shop for years."

"I mean here." Rob had arranged for the system and apparently paid for it out of his own pocket. He'd also instructed them to install a panic button in the master bedroom, and included not one, but two key fobs that also had panic button switches on them.

"No, you didn't. But this is different."

She picked up her purse, which she really hadn't looked through other than to study the contents of her wallet, and trailed a finger over the keypad. "I guess everything's different now."

* * * *

Bill went first out of caution, leaving Laura and Doogie in the truck while he got the front door unlocked and disarmed the alarm.

He had to help her out, the ibuprofen she'd taken not helping to kill the pain so much as strangle it a little.

Kind of like me.

She suppressed a snort.

"What's so funny?" he asked.

"Nothing." She looked around the yard. "Can we walk around?"

"Sure." He kept his arm out for her and she didn't argue with him. She held on for support, following him and Doogie as the dog sniffed every blade of grass and watered quite a few of them.

The back side of the property bordered a protected wetland area. With the exception of a two-foot swath outside the fence that Rob took care of with a weed trimmer, there was a ten-yard-wide section of overgrown grass and weeds leading to a thick area of pine trees mixed in with palms, palmettos, Brazilian peppers, melaleucas, and mangroves. The area was several hundred acres large. With the exception of the few homes on Rob's street there was no public access to the wildlife area except by boat from the water.

She stared out at the woodlands area and listened to the sounds of birds, insects, and the wind.

"I've spent a lot of time here, huh?"

"That's what Rob and you've both said."

"It's quiet here."

"Peaceful. That's one of the reasons you love it."

She closed her eyes and tried to remember something tickling at her thoughts. When she had it, she turned and looked at the back side of the house, where a screened-in lanai opened onto a wooden deck.

"He bought it from a bank. It was a foreclosure," she softly said. "I came to look at it with him. He built the lanai and deck."

Bill nodded, but didn't speak.

She stared, trying to pull images from the past, to merge and reconcile them with the present. "The yard was a mess. The kitchen had been gutted." She looked up at the new roof, variegated tan shingles. "The barrel tile roof was cracked and leaking."

Releasing Bill's arm, she walked over to the deck and stepped onto it. "We got a lot of stuff, including the kitchen cabinets, from IKEA."

She closed her eyes, teasing the last bit from her reluctant brain. "Seth was a contractor," she whispered, not understanding why Bill shouldn't hear that. "And Tony, Cris, Landry, Ross, Mac, they all came over and helped one weekend."

She opened her eyes again and, without waiting for Bill, headed around to the front of the house.

The laundry room. She had to see it.

With her heart pounding and Bill and Doogie on her heels, she pushed through the front door and trusted her feet. They unerringly carried her past the kitchen to a closed door.

Her fingers trembled as she reached out and twisted the knob, a sob falling from her as she recognized the laundry room. And on a low shelf over the washer sat a yellow jug of laundry detergent.

Ignoring the pain, she hurried over to it and yanked it from the shelf. Twisting the top off she held it up to her nose and took a deep breath.

Laughter flowed through her tears as she stood there, hugging the bottle to her chest and taking long, deep breaths.

Bill stood in the doorway, watching her. "You all right?"

"It's yellow," she said, eyes closed, the happiest she'd felt since the nightmare started. "I remembered. It's yellow. It's the detergent I use."

"Um, yeah. I think you have the same bottle at the condo."

She shook her head and kept her eyes closed in case more memories wanted to return. "No, you don't understand. I saw this laundry room. While I was still in the hospital. *This* room." Eventually, she opened her eyes and screwed the cap back on before returning the jug to its shelf.

"This room was in my thoughts. Meaning other stuff is still there. In my brain. It's just...locked up still."

"Sweetie, I thought we already established you remembered some stuff."

"I know. But *this* was one of the first things I remembered." She trailed a hand over the washing machine's lid. "If I can remember something as stupid and trivial as *this*, doesn't it mean I'll remember all the important stuff eventually?"

"I don't know. I'm not a doctor."

He stepped out of the way as she walked past him and to the kitchen.

A sense of peace settled over her. There on the fridge, exactly where she'd pictured it in her mind, was the other Yellowstone magnet.

* * * *

Friday morning, Bill drove Laura to the shop. Rob had come in a little after seven that morning, exhausted from working a serious early morning accident, and went to bed.

She'd spent the better part of a half hour before they left in the bathroom in front of the mirror, trying to mask the worst of the still-visible bruises with makeup. Fortunately, the swelling in her lip had completely gone down.

Another oddity. Bill told Laura she rarely wore makeup, due to the nature of her job. Unless she was going out somewhere with Rob.

She refused to take a pain pill that morning, the pain more tolerable and preferable to the fuzzy, groggy blanket that settled over her brain with the prescription drugs.

And work seemed to greatly help her state of mind. The more she dug into the paperwork and chores at the shop, with a little help from Steve and Carol, the more that came rushing back to her in terms of what to do.

Unfortunately, that didn't translate into a lot of personal memories. It also didn't help her with her writing. She'd forced herself to weed through her email again and found a note from an editor looking for a progress report on an article due to a magazine.

Feeling defeated, she asked Bill to call the editor at the number in the email while she retreated to the bathroom to have a cry in private.

Two steps forward, eight steps back.

* * * *

Bill sadly watched her exit the office before making the call and explaining the situation to the editor. The woman sounded sympathetic and told Bill she'd kill the article, but that if Laura regained her memory and wanted to submit it, she'd still take it.

Before, Laura was proud of her writing, of the freelance career she'd built up in addition to running the shop. She'd journaled every day as a teenager.

He wondered if that was a part of her life that would ever fully return, or if it was lost in the abyss forever.

In quiet tones throughout the morning, Bill, Steve, Carol, and the rest all talked out in the shop while they kept an eye on Laura. The Laura Bill grew up with was self-assured and confident. This Laura acted timid, reluctant to joke around. He wondered if that was due to the attack or loss of memory.

The Laura he knew smiled all the time, enjoyed life to the fullest.

This woman jumped at her own shadow.

Just after lunch, Sarah pulled Steve and Bill aside out on the dock, where Laura couldn't hear them talk. "It's not just her memories," Sarah said. "*She's* different."

Bill nodded. "I know."

"This has got to be killing Rob," Sarah said. "She's like a little mouse. I actually heard her apologize to a telemarketer before saying good-bye and hanging up."

"What?" Steve asked, incredulous.

Sarah nodded. "Exactly. And Cody was teasing her before lunch about putting a margarita machine on the big boat. She said she'd look into it."

Bill shook his head. Even he knew that was a long-running joke between Cody, their captain and die-hard Parrothead, and Laura. Old Laura would have tossed a funny comeback at him.

"How'd Cody take it?" Steve asked.

"I thought he was going to cry when he told me. First time I ever saw him that upset. He explained to her it was a joke, and she apologized for not remembering." She looked down at the dock. "He left a little bit after that. Said he had to get out of here before he lost it in front of her. He's really tore up about this. He's known her almost as long as Steve."

Steve glanced at his watch. "Take her home, Bill. She looks like she's in a lot of pain."

"I might need you all to help me. She's determined to figure things out."

Steve scrubbed his face with his hand. "She needs to go home. She needs to spend time with Rob. He'll probably be getting up soon if he's not up already. And honestly? I can understand why Cody left. I want to cry every time I look at her, too."

Sarah and Carol nodded their agreement, looking like they were pretty close to it themselves.

Bill took a deep breath. "Right. Someone wrangle Doogie for me. I'm going to need to move fast or she'll dig her heels in."

They trailed behind him as he headed for the office. Laura sat in front of the computer, staring at the screen.

"Well, I think it's time for you to call it a day."

She didn't turn from the screen. "Okay," she softly said.

He exchanged a worried look with Steve and walked over to her. Tears had left tracks on her cheeks, which she'd scrubbed free of the makeup after lunch, opting instead to stay hidden in the office, away from the prying view of customers.

"What's wrong?"

She pointed at the screen, which was opened to a sportsfishing magazine's website. The magazine whose editor he'd talked to earlier that morning.

One of Laura's articles, from three years ago, was up on the screen. It talked about grouper fishing and related a fishing trip she'd taken.

She shook her head. "I don't remember any of it," she said. "I read it several times, and I don't remember any of it. I don't remember doing the stuff in the article, and I don't remember writing it."

"Sweetie, you won't get everything back right away."

"Shouldn't I have gotten a hint?"

"Maybe not. Maybe it's like some of the other memories. Maybe you need to find something that triggers a chain reaction."

"Like what?"

He felt backed into a corner. "I don't know. Maybe your old journals."

She frowned. "What old journals?"

Bill looked for Steve and spotted him trying to step away from the office. "Steve. Do you know where Laura's old journals are?"

He shook his head. "Nope. I think her newer ones are on her laptop."

"What journals?" she asked again, frustration creeping into her voice.

"You used to keep a journal," Bill said. "Started when you were a kid."

"Call Rob," Carol suggested. Bill thought he heard her mutter, "Duh," under her breath.

Chapter Eighteen

Sarah helped Laura go through the shop computer, but there was nothing on it resembling a journal. Then Laura called Rob.

"Sweetheart, I don't know where your newer journals are. I went through your laptop looking for them after…" She heard him take a deep breath. "Even Det. Thomas had someone go through your laptop looking for clues. They're not there."

She rubbed at her forehead. "Steve and Bill said I had old handwritten journals."

"They might be in some of the boxes in the garage at the house. If they're not there, then they're probably at the storage unit."

"Storage unit?"

"Yeah, but that place is packed to the rafters. You can't go crawling around in there until your ribs are better." From his tone of voice she knew she couldn't argue with him.

Hell, she didn't *want* to argue with him.

Did I always let him dictate things to me?

How much of her life didn't she know about? At least she'd been able to sit down with Carol at the shop that morning. She'd gone through all the finances with Laura. She wasn't rich, but she had some savings and retirement accounts, and the shop paid her a salary every week. She also had a small joint account with Rob they'd recently opened, but it didn't have much money in it.

Her condo was paid off from her share of her parents' insurance settlement from the wreck and their life insurance. Bill told her they'd gone ahead and sold their parents' house because she hadn't wanted to live there alone, and didn't have time for the upkeep. Except for a couple of pieces of furniture, he'd given everything else to her to deal with, not wanting the hassle of shipping stuff to Montana.

So she'd gotten a storage unit and put it all there.

I didn't want to deal with it. That thought came to her with certainty. It'd been too painful, too draining. It had been easier to put it in storage and pay a fee every month, deducted from her credit card on file with them.

I didn't have to think about it.

"I'm going to cook us dinner tonight," Rob said. "Are you coming home soon? I don't want you wearing yourself out."

"Bill said we're coming home." She glanced over and spotted him nodding. "We'll see you soon."

Carol and Bill helped get Laura out to the truck while Steve brought Doogie on his leash. As they returned to her condo, she had a thought.

"Why do I have stuff stored in Rob's garage?"

He let out a little snort. "You planned on moving in together after the wedding," he added. "And it's not like you wanted to try to cram all that stuff into your condo. Which it wouldn't fit anyway. You told me you and Rob were going to deal with it all after the wedding and honeymoon."

Honeymoon. "Where were we going?" she asked.

He smiled. "Need you ask? You reserved a cabin at Old Faithful for a week."

She didn't blame Rob for not telling her all of that. He'd been busy working, and when they were together, and both awake, his focus had been on her, not slamming her head full of information.

"Besides, why wouldn't you put stuff at the house? It's your house, too."

"What?"

He glanced at her. "I thought you went over stuff with Carol."

"Bank accounts."

"You and Rob own the house together."

"What? Why?"

"Well, because you're marrying him, maybe?"

"But we're not married yet."

"You went in fifty-fifty on it. Hell, you're the one who found the house and told him you wanted it."

She closed her eyes, feeling overwhelmed again. "I did?"

"Yeah."

"Then why am I not living with him?"

"Well, because as of just three months or so ago, the house, as you told me, looked like a condemnable wasteland. You guys had friends come in and help you fix it up so you could even stay there. It's only been in the past two months the kitchen and bathrooms were done. I think Rob told me you guys just got the fourth bedroom painted three weeks ago. He was living with you off and on for a while as you guys did stuff to the house. He sold his condo over in Punta Gorda and used that for the down payment and renovations."

"Oh."

"Besides, you guys were back and forth all the time between the places. And if you had a dive trip or something and he was working, sometimes you weren't at the same house." He let out a laugh. "I used to joke with you that you needed a secretary to keep track of who was where."

"What was I going to do with my condo?"

"Rent it out, maybe. You weren't sure. You guys said you didn't want to get rid of it. But it was something you wanted to wait—"

"Until after the wedding," she finished for him.

"You remember?"

She sighed as she opened her eyes. "No. But it makes sense."

* * * *

Rob waited for Bill and Laura to return to the condo before he left to go to the house to look for the boxes for Laura.

What he left out was that wanted to stop by the shop before he went home so he could talk to Steve.

They stepped out onto the dock to sit and talk in private. "What's wrong, son? Other than the obvious, I mean."

"I don't know what to do. I'm afraid to say the wrong thing to her, but I'm going out of my gourd. I don't know how to help her. Apparently I'm not going to be able to protect her."

"She's made progress. It's just a matter of time."

"How much time? I'm afraid to leave her alone because that psycho might come back. Even if it wasn't for that, I'm afraid to leave her alone…" He sat back and didn't finish his thought.

"You're afraid she might not want you back."

He finally nodded.

"You have every right to be worried."

"Oh, yeah, thanks. That's a big help."

Steve leaned forward across the table and tapped the picnic table's weathered surface with his index finger. "Rob, listen to me. The doctors never guaranteed she'd get her memory back. It's a miracle she remembers as much as she does. Think of it this way. She picked you once, she'll pick you again."

"I'm afraid to come on too strong. Maybe she'll realize she wants someone different."

"Well hell, boy, sitting on your duff isn't going to solve that problem now, is it? How did you feel when you first met her?"

Rob thought back. For obvious reasons, Steve and Carol and the others had no idea how they'd met. All they knew was that Shayla and Tony had introduced them.

They always left out the part of it being at a BDSM club up in Sarasota.

"She was pretty. Smart. Funny, but not snotty or obnoxious. She was easy to talk to."

"Do you still love those things about her?"

"Of course."

"Then use your brain. Whatever you did before, if it worked the first time, it'll work again. Only this time you've got the special gift of hindsight not to repeat any mistakes you think you made you wish you could take back. You have the advantage of knowing what she did and didn't like about you. And, you have the advantage of knowing who she is and what she did and didn't like. That's a rare gift few ever get."

He thought about that for a moment. "Without her memory, she's not the same person anymore."

Steve nodded. "Neither are you."

* * * *

Rob returned to Laura's condo, empty-handed, over an hour later.

"I'm sorry, sweetheart. They're not there. I went through every box in the garage, and through the spare bedrooms. They aren't there."

Somehow, she managed not to cry. "Okay. Thanks for looking."

He gently pulled her to him and enveloped her in his arms. She felt a sense of peace settle over her in his embrace.

"I promise, once you're feeling better, we'll go over to the storage unit and look for them. All right?"

"Okay."

"Meanwhile, I know there's a lot of stuff on your computer. Older stuff you imported from your old systems, things like that. You didn't get your first laptop until about six years ago. After dinner, I'll help you look for the files. Okay?"

"You don't know where they are?"

"Sweetie, you are a private person when it comes to stuff like that. And I respect your privacy. The only time I've ever used your laptop was to check my email or look up stuff on the Internet, and even then only after I've asked you first."

"Can you check my email? You did it before."

"Well, yeah. I have your passwords. You have mine, too." She didn't miss how he caught himself. "Had," he softly said. "And can have again. We know each other's banking information, all of that. And anything you want of mine, anything you want to know, you tell me. But normally, no, I don't go into your email or other accounts unless you've asked me to for some reason."

She tucked her face against his chest again. "Okay."

"I have a little surprise. After dinner, Seth and Leah are coming over to visit."

"What about Shayla and Tony?" She desperately missed Shayla. She'd even texted with her a few times despite being nervous about using the phone and Bill helping her by removing a bunch of extra apps she didn't know how to use and didn't care about.

"Maybe tomorrow night. We're trying not to overwhelm you. All right?"

Part of her bridled against being handled like a child. Yet the majority of her loved him for his concern. And something about his tone of voice stirred something inside her in a good way. "Okay."

* * * *

Bill retired to the guest room to handle his email and watch TV after dinner, leaving them alone before their guests arrived.

Rob filled in a little bit of information about Leah and Seth. Shayla had told Laura about them, that Seth had been best friends with Leah's first husband, who'd died after a battle with pancreatic cancer.

Rob could tell Laura thought it was a little odd the two got together so soon after Leah was widowed, but he assured her Leah's husband had given them his blessings and even engineered their union.

"Really?" She studied Rob, her brow furrowed.

So much he couldn't tell her. So much he had to keep from her. He hated it. Hated not being able to tell her that Kaden had carefully trained Seth to take over as Leah's new Master following his death.

That Leah, for a brief, bittersweet time, had the triad she'd always longed for with the two men she loved, men who loved her.

A triad not unlike the ones Tilly and Clarisse both had, although in those cases the men had relationships with each other before meeting their women.

He'd called Tony for advice on broaching *that* subject. Other than agreeing that lying to Laura wasn't an option, Tony hadn't had any suggestions for breaking the information about their friends' triads to Laura other than just outright telling her about them.

When Seth and Leah arrived, he'd already briefed them over the phone about Laura's current condition. That they had to keep the conversation strictly vanilla.

Leah hugged him first before walking over to Laura. "Hi, sweetie."

Seth gave Rob a hug and whispered in his ear, "You okay?"

He gave a little shake of his head before plastering on a smile.

He wouldn't let Laura see him upset.

And he wouldn't let her see that the totally blank look she gave them as he introduced them to her threatened to rip his heart from his chest.

Yes, she'd been closer to Shayla, before. But Laura had been good friends with Leah, too. Next to Shayla, Rob would peg Leah as Laura's next best friend.

Leah sat on the couch next to her. Rob didn't miss how the smile on Leah's face probably matched the one he knew he wore in front of Laura.

The practiced face.

Hiding the pain inside.

Leah's green eyes looked a little too bright, like maybe she was on the verge of tears. "How are you feeling?" she asked Laura. "Rob said you're still having some pain."

"I'm okay." Rob watched as Laura stared at Leah's necklace, the silver chain with the heart locket that she wore as a day collar.

I need to get her another necklace. He hated the idea that the bastard who'd attacked Laura stole her day collar.

Rob and Seth mostly stayed silent, watching as Leah did her best to tease memories from Laura's mind.

When Rob stepped into the kitchen to get a drink of water, Seth followed.

He leaned in close. "It'll be okay."

Rob's shoulders tensed. He'd do anything for Laura to get her memory back and be safe, including giving up their Master-slave dynamic, if that's what it took.

"I'm not so sure," Rob whispered.

Seth squeezed his shoulder and returned to the living room. "Leah, it's late. We should probably let Laura get some rest."

Rob watched Laura nod.

The strong, feisty woman he'd fallen in love with was hidden somewhere inside the meek, mousey victim sitting on the sofa.

Damned if he knew the secret to finding her.

After hugs and good-nights, Rob walked them outside. Leah sniffled as she hugged him.

"Shayla warned me, but..." She sniffled again.

"Yeah."

Seth gave him another hug. "Seriously, if you need to bring her to our house, we've got the room. You can both stay with us as long as you need to. And Doogie."

Rob glanced around. There weren't any strange cars in sight, no one prowling the street. "Her brother leaves the Tuesday after next. If she hasn't got her memory back by then I might take you up on it. I'm scared to leave her alone."

When he returned to the condo, Laura wasn't on the sofa. He found her in her office, sitting in front of the computer.

"Sweetie, it's late. I think you should head for bed."

She stared at the screen for a moment. He'd thought maybe she hadn't heard him when she answered. "I keep having dreams."

He walked over to her and gently rested his hand on her shoulder. "What kind of dreams?"

"Bad ones. I start out sitting here and this image of a skull appears on the screen. Then someone's knocking on the door and I wake up before I answer it."

"You should talk to Dr. Simpson about it tomorrow when you see her."

She nodded. His heart jumped a little, in a good way, when she rested her hand on top of his and looked up at him. The blue flecks in her grey eyes looked darker, like sapphire chips. "What if she can't help me? What if I never get my memory back? Are you going to be able to love me like this?"

"What?"

"I saw the way you were watching me. And Leah. I could tell. I know I'm different now. I'm not the same."

He knelt next to her. "Laura, I love you. Nothing will change that. We'll get through this."

She looked down at the engagement ring on her right hand. "I wouldn't blame you if you wanted to call things off."

"*Stop.*" He used Dom tone on her. He immediately regretted it when her eyes widened a little in shock.

Or maybe it was fear.

He gentled his tone. "You are the love of my life. Whatever happens, we'll get through it together. I still want to marry you, if you still want me." That's when the horrible thought hit him. "Do you still want me?"

"I…" She looked down at the ring again. "This isn't fair to you."

Fear consumed him. "You let me worry about what's fair to me, okay?" He gently cupped her chin and tipped her face so she had to look him in the eye. "I will be right here by your side unless you tell me otherwise. Got it?"

Her eyes dropped closed. She nodded, then leaned against his chest as he engulfed her in his arms.

With his face buried in her hair, he said, "I swear, Laura, I will take care of you. I love you, and I will do everything I can to help you get through this. Just don't give up on me. Please."

"I won't," she whispered.

He breathed a sigh of relief. "Thank you."

Chapter Nineteen

Rob had to work a half-shift from six o'clock Saturday morning until six that night to fill in for a guy who'd covered for him while Laura was in the hospital. Bill drove Laura over to Pt. Charlotte to Dr. Simpson's office that morning.

Laura felt nervous, unsure, and even let Bill talk her into not just a pain pill, but one of the anti-anxiety pills as well.

She hated the fuzzy feeling in her brain with a passion, but she also knew she needed to be relaxed as much as possible when talking with the doctor.

Dr. Simpson's office was in a small medical complex near the hospital. She was part of a practice with three other psychiatrists and two psychologists. When they walked in, they found the receptionist's desk sat unmanned. The waiting room was a soothing blue and green combination, tastefully done, no doubt meant to put patients at ease while they waited.

Dr. Simpson heard them enter and stepped out of one of the offices. "Hi, Laura. Come on in."

Bill was going to sit in the waiting room, but Laura asked him to come in with her. Once Laura was settled on the couch, Dr. Simpson got them started.

"How have you been doing since I saw you? Have any new memories returned?"

"Some. Scattered."

"Nothing from the attack?"

Laura shook her head, and then detailed what she knew so far. Some of her childhood. Some of Bill, of Steve, and even little snatches of Rob, but the big things, the mile-marker events in her life, were still mostly missing.

"Are you having any more dreams?"

She took a deep breath and nodded. After explaining the dreams of the computer skull and the knocking on the door, she waited, hoping the woman would have some magical insight.

She didn't.

"What do you feel they mean?" the doctor asked.

Laura stared at her. "*Seriously?*"

"Yes."

She looked at Bill in case she was missing something, then back to Dr. Simpson. "I don't *know* what the hell they mean!"

"It's all right, Laura. Calm—"

"Oh, *soo* don't fucking tell me to calm down." She burst into tears. "This psycho is still out there, and you're telling me to calm down?"

Bill moved to sit next to her on the couch. "Laur, it's all right."

"No, it's *not* all right!" She stared from him to the doctor and back again in disbelief. "I think I've been pretty calm the past week all things considered, but I'm fucking sick and tired of trying to pretend I'm okay when I'm not!"

The outburst caught even her by surprise. Bill pulled her into his arms and Dr. Simpson handed her tissues as she cried herself out against him.

The doctor quietly spoke to Bill. "Has she been taking the anti-anxiety medication?"

"Not really. I made her take one this morning."

"I'm sitting *right* here," Laura snarked.

Bill patted her on the shoulder and continued. "She's really jumpy, the nightmares—she's not acting at all like herself."

"No shit, Sherlock."

"Laura," he said, big brother written all over his voice. "Please let me talk."

She shut up and blew her nose.

"I guess her friend Shayla was there when you talked to her the last time. She told Rob, who told me, about PTSD. I looked it up. She's showing a lot of the symptoms."

"I was strangled and beaten half to death," Laura said. "Wasn't exactly a walk in the park."

He continued as if she hadn't interrupted. "Rob's trying to find her old journals to see if they'll help with her memory, but so far we haven't located them."

Laura shut up. She hated feeling like they were treating her like a kid, but the fact that Rob was looking for the journals helped somewhat.

Dr. Simpson focused on her again. "We talked about this. That the trauma of the attack might trigger post-traumatic stress disorder. It certainly sounds like you're going through that."

"Look, can't you just give me that drug and see if it jogs my memory loose? Everything's obviously stuck in there somewhere. I remembered fucking laundry soap and a refrigerator magnet, for chrissake."

"I told you I'm hesitant to prescribe that. I'd rather you try other means first. I don't like using drugs for that purpose unless absolutely necessary."

"Getting my memory back *is* absolutely necessary."

"There is no guarantee it would work. It's not uncommon for there to be false memory retrieval. Dr. Collins is a psychologist, and a licensed hypnotherapist. Try working with her for a while, see if you make any progress. Give her a chance. I talked with her before you arrived today. She can fit you in at eight o'clock Monday morning."

Laura sighed. "Fine."

* * * *

Laura didn't speak on the ride home despite Bill trying to engage her. She wanted to go to the shop, but after Bill made her lunch she fell asleep on the sofa.

Unfortunately, she dreamed about the flashing skull and the pounding on the front door. Only this time she actually made it to the front door, where an ominous shadow raced toward her when she opened it.

When she awoke that afternoon, her pain had returned enough that she didn't want to go to the shop.

She damn sure didn't want another pain pill.

And the bad dreams had freaked her out and stolen her reserve.

What am I going to do when Bill leaves?

The thought terrified her, even as she chided herself. *I have to stand on my own two feet. I can't spend my life terrified.*

She was dozing again when the thought struck her between the eyes, so hard and sharp she woke up laughing.

"What's so funny?"

"Help me up."

He did, following her to the den where she powered up her desktop computer there and started going through it. Frustrated at first, eventually she found what she was looking for. Buried in a subdirectory in the Documents folder, she found a file called *journal.doc*.

The first entry was dated January first, six years earlier. Thinking she'd found the answer, she skimmed through to the end, when her hopes crashed again.

The final entry was dated December thirty-first, months before she'd met Rob.

She stared at the screen, another wave of depression setting in as she processed the defeat.

"What is it?"

She closed the file and started looking through the folders, hoping she'd missed something. "It's got to be here."

"What?"

"My journals. It doesn't make sense that I'd just stop."

"When you came out to visit me, you brought your laptop. You said you only kept the desktop as a backup. That you used the laptop for everything."

"Then where are my journals?"

"If I knew, believe me, I'd tell you."

He helped her copy the files. "You know, you should put this on your iPad. That way you don't have to juggle a computer while you read."

Confused, she stared at him. "What?"

"Your iPad. Email yourself the document file and read it on the iPad."

He made the same connection she did and beat her out to the living room, where the device sat on an end table, plugged into the charger. She watched as he went through it, looking at document files.

Nothing.

Defeated, she sat on the sofa. "It was worth a shot."

"You need to email yourself the file from the other computer."

"Can you please do it?" she quietly asked. "I left Gmail open."

He nodded and went to do it. A minute later, when she pulled up her email on the iPad, the file was waiting for her.

Bill returned to the living room and showed her how to download the file into her documents and open it.

She settled in to read from the beginning but feeling like she was stepping into the middle of a television series without any clue about the plot and cast.

Most of the entries were short and focused on mundane topics.

Others gave her brief insights about her parents.

We all got a good laugh today when Dad got a new cell phone…

She read until Bill's cell phone rang a little before six. He looked at it, frowning as he answered.

"Yeah. She's right here." He handed it over to her. "Rob."

"Hey."

"Hi, honey." He sounded exhausted. "Where's your cell phone?"

She winced. "Sorry. It's in my purse."

"Okay. Delete the five messages from me."

"Sorry." Apparently, before, she'd been pretty adept at dealing with technology. "Are you on your way home?"

"No, that's why I'm calling. We just finished working a wreck, but there's another one. We have to cover until the other crew comes back. I'm going to be late."

Laura fought back her disappointment. "Okay."

"Shayla and Tony are still coming tonight, though."

Part of her desperately wanted to see them.

Part of her wanted to hole up in bed and read and wait for Rob to get home.

"Okay."

"You don't sound thrilled."

"It's okay."

She thought he might have let out a sigh of frustration. "Are you in pain?"

"I'm fine." She glanced up at Bill, her gaze darting away from him.

"Let me talk to Bill."

She returned the phone to him.

Busted.

He stared at her while he talked to Rob. "She's in a lot more pain than she's letting on… Uh-huh… Yep. Exactly… All right. Here she is." He handed the phone back to her.

She fought the urge to stick her tongue out at him.

"Yeah?"

Rob did let out a sigh this time. "I'm going to call Shayla and Tony and ask them not to come tonight."

She wanted to argue but suspected from his tone of voice he wouldn't be swayed. "Okay."

"I'll be home in a couple of hours."

She returned the phone to Bill. "You ratted me out."

He snorted. "Duh. I'm your big brother."

* * * *

After the fact, she was glad Rob had canceled their plans. Bill cooked them dinner and she curled up on the couch to watch TV and tried not let Bill see how much pain she was in.

He wasn't buying it. "You need a pain pill. And you're going to take one." He held out one hand, the pill in his palm. In his other he held a glass of water.

"I don't want it."

"I don't care if you want it or not. I don't want to see you in that much pain. You're taking it."

She suspected he'd stand there all night until she did. Resigned, she carefully sat up, wincing as she did.

"See? You're in pain."

"Fine." She took it, washing it down with the water.

"Now go to bed and watch TV in there."

"Fine." She started to go when she turned and grabbed the stack of mail he'd brought in earlier and she hadn't gone through yet. "Can I take this and read it?"

"Yes, you damn smartass."

She curled up in bed. There were several bills, a couple of catalogs, and three get-well cards from people she apparently knew, but whose names she didn't recognize.

The last one she thought might be junk mail, because her name was computer-printed on the envelope, but there was no return address and the postmark was from New York City.

The outside of the card had nothing but a smiley face on it. Inside, in the same computer-printed font, was an inscription.

Welcome home, Laura. Sorry I wasn't there to greet you personally. Don't worry, it won't be long before I see you again.

The scream caught in her throat for a moment while she processed what it meant and let the card fall to the bed. When she finally let the scream rip, Bill burst through the bedroom door seconds later.

* * * *

Rob stood in the living room of Laura's condo with Det. Thomas and Bill. Once again, Laura was sleeping in the bedroom with the aid of an anti-anxiety pill.

The card and envelope now resided in a clear plastic evidence bag. "I'll be honest," Thomas said. "He printed it out, meaning it's pretty much untraceable. He mailed it from New York City. I'm willing to bet we don't find fingerprints on it, either."

Rob ran a hand through his hair. "What about DNA? From the flap, or the stamp?"

Det. Thomas shook his head. "Good luck with that. I'm still waiting on the rush job on the DNA from under her fingernails. I seriously doubt he was stupid enough to lick the flap. And the stamp looks like one of the self-adhesive kind."

"Can't we get a deputy assigned to watch the house?"

"I don't even have proof the same guy sent this."

Rob looked at him in disbelief. "Seriously?"

"Look, you and I can sit here and make wild guesses all night. I need proof to get those kinds of resources. Maybe it's time to think about moving her somewhere else."

Bill shook his head. "She won't go for that." He looked at the two men. "No, she's not the same person she was. But the stubborn streak is still there. She's going to want to stay here. In Englewood, at least. Rob might be able to talk her into going to friends' houses for a while, but she's going to dig her heels in eventually."

"She's got an appointment Monday with a hypnotherapist," Rob said. "Maybe she can help her get her memory back."

Thomas picked up the evidence bag. "Meanwhile, don't forget to stop by the gun shop. And make sure she carries it."

"She doesn't have her license yet," Bill reminded him.

The detective looked at him. "I don't know how you all do it out in Montana, but Florida is a castle doctrine state. She kills this guy in her home, I don't care if she has a carry permit or not."

"I thought law enforcement didn't espouse unqualified people carrying weapons?" Bill shot back.

The detective had reached the front door. He turned. "Then I strongly suggest Rob gets that friend of his back down here to make sure she's qualified. Either that, or she goes to live with them for a while."

Rob walked over and locked the door behind the detective. "I can take her back to Montana with me," Bill suggested.

"Like you said, she won't go for that."

"Do you have a better suggestion?"

Rob rubbed at his forehead, fighting the impending headache. "Not right at the moment, no."

* * * *

Rob found himself dreaming almost every night, about their life together, of times they'd spent together, sexy and otherwise.

The sexy times were the ones that usually stayed with him upon waking, bittersweet reminders of a life achingly just beyond his reach, one that Laura couldn't remember.

He crawled into bed with her, eventually falling asleep. Tonight his dreams focused on a night a few months earlier. He'd had a Saturday and

Sunday off, and Laura arranged to take the weekend off, too. They went to dinner at Sigalo's with everyone before heading to the club.

There, he and Tony had fun tying up Shayla and Laura with rope, an informal competition to see who could come up with the most inventive and decorative design. At the end of it, both women found themselves on the receiving end of forced orgasm sessions from their respective Dom.

Neither woman complained.

But the club rules prohibited sex. And despite taking Laura to the point where she finally safeworded because her clit got too sensitive, she still jumped him when they returned home to the condo.

After he returned from walking Doogie, she shoved him down onto the couch, where she straddled his lap and eagerly worked on his shirt buttons.

Laughing, he grabbed her wrists. "Did I give you permission to do that?"

"Please, Sir?" she whined. "I want to."

"You're not naked."

She leapt up from his lap, frantically yanking off her clothes before jumping on top of him again. "Please, Sir?"

He loved it when she got like this. "Oh, all right."

If he'd blinked, he would have missed how fast she rid him of his shirt. Then she started working on his belt.

"This would be easier if you'd let me do this myself."

Laura squirmed against him, rubbing herself against his thigh. "I like undressing you."

He fisted her hair and made her get up, keeping her bent over as he led her to the bedroom. "I know you do. But we're doing this my way."

After leaning her over the bed and delivering a stinging, bare-handed swat to her ass, he said, "Stay." She did, but he knew from the way she wiggled that she wanted to jump him again.

He kicked off his shoes and finished undressing. His erect cock led the way back to the bed, ready and willing for action. Stepping between her legs, he nudged her feet apart with his.

"Arms behind you."

She immediately complied. She still wore the leather wrist cuffs from the club. He leaned over and snagged a snap clip from the drawer of the bedside table and used it to fasten her wrists together.

"Good girl." He reached between her legs and found her, as expected, wet and ready for him.

Grabbing her wrists with one hand, he slowly fed his cock into her, both of them sighing with pleasure as he bottomed out inside her ready pussy.

"Who's my good girl?"

She tried to fuck herself back onto his cock but he leaned forward, pinning her against the bed.

"Me, Sir."

"I thought someone had more than enough orgasms earlier."

"I…did. But I'm horny again."

He tried to hold back his laughter. "Oh, are you? Should I get out the Hitachi?"

"No, Sir! Just your cock."

He playfully swatted her ass. "Good answer." Achingly slow, as slowly as he could stand, he fucked her, withdrawing until just the head of his cock remained inside her cunt before slamming forward again.

He knew if he did this long enough she would more than likely come at least one more time.

Whether he could hold out that long remained to be seen.

She felt so good, her pussy slick and grabbing at him, hot and ready. Perfection.

He fucked her for several minutes like this before pulling out and getting a disappointed moan from her.

He unclipped her wrists. "Don't worry, we're not done." He flipped her over and made her put her hands over her head, Then he reclipped her wrists and lifted her legs to his shoulders.

Now he fucked her this way, able to go even deeper.

It also allowed him to play with her nipples at the same time. She looked beautiful, eyes closed, skin flushed as she sought to get over one more time for him. He rolled her nipples between his thumb and forefinger, her little sounds of pleasure sending jolts straight through to his cock.

"Are you going to come for me like this?"

She nodded. "Yes, Sir. I think so."

He let go of her nipples and used his right thumb instead to lightly stroke her clit. He clamped his left around her calf and turned his head to nibble before he bit down.

That did it. She let out a cry as the walls of her cunt clamped down on his cock.

"Good girl," he grunted, fucking her hard and fast, catching up and coming with her. As he stood there staring down at her, she opened her eyes and smiled.

He turned his head again to kiss the marks left by his teeth. "Good?"

Her eyes drifted closed again, but the smile never left her face. "Very good, Sir."

Chapter Twenty

Laura jolted awake out of a nightmare early Sunday morning with Rob's body protectively draped around hers. As she lay there and waited for her pulse to slow to a subsonic rate, she tried to remember everything she could about the dream.

It started at the computer again. The pounding on the door. This time, she let the shadow figure in and fought with it, wrestling like it was a tornado of energy.

Next to her, Rob stirred and raised his head. "You okay?"

She let him fold her into his arms as she shook her head.

"Nightmares?"

"Yeah."

She closed her eyes and listened to the sound of his heart beating against her ear through his chest.

Another thing that felt oooh so right, even though she couldn't remember a damn thing.

He felt right.

If it wasn't for all the pain she was in, she would have given serious thought to kissing him and seeing where it went. She suspected they might have had a great sex life before.

There's that fucking word again.

She kept her forehead pressed against his chest. "What's on the agenda for today?"

He stroked her back. Through the T-shirt she wore, his fingers gently traced her spine as if he knew every ridge and curve.

Maybe he does.

"I don't have to go to work until tomorrow morning. I think for today we need to spend some time alone. Just the two of us. Talking."

She thought about the journals she'd found the night before, but compared to spending time alone with Rob, they took second place. "Okay."

Her voice sounded small and lost even to her own ears. What was it about him that did that to her? That his merely suggesting something sent her will spinning to do it without question?

He kissed the top of her head. "We need to talk about you taking a trip to Montana."

She stiffened. "No. I don't want to be away from you."

"I don't want to be away from you, either. But it's something we need to think about."

"Do I have to decide right now?"

"No." He kissed the top of her head again, then made her look up at him and pressed a kiss to her forehead. "But," he carefully said, "if I say you go, you go. Okay?"

There was that tone again. Part of her rebelled, wanting to scream no, it wasn't fucking okay, that she was an adult and she'd do what she damn well pleased.

The other part of her caved without hesitation, acquiescing. "Okay."

"Good g—" He cut himself off as if he was going to say more. "Good," he repeated, a single syllable.

She kissed him, her body coming alive when she felt his cock harden in his shorts, where her thigh pressed against him. He responded at first before pulling away.

"Sweetheart, we can't." His voice sounded hoarse, thick.

"Sure we can," she whispered, wanting more. The feel of her own body responding to him, something more than pain, she needed it.

Needed *him*.

He gently caught her wrists and pulled them to his chest. "Your ribs," he said. "We need to be careful."

"I don't care."

"You don't remember me much yet."

"I don't care. I want you."

His brown gaze bored into hers. "*I* care." He raised her hands to his lips and kissed them. "I love you, and yeah, I want you. But I think we need to do a lot of talking before we take that step."

"We used to sleep together."

"Yes, we did." He pressed her hands to his chest again. She felt his heart pounding against her palms. "And you don't know how much I want you. I don't want you to do this and regret it later."

"Why would I regret it? We were getting married."

He sadly smiled. "Exactly. Were."

Shock filled her. "Don't you still want to marry me?"

"Of course I do. But until I know you can speak of it in the future tense instead of the past tense, I think we need to take it slow."

A sadly resolute expression filled his face and she knew he wouldn't budge.

"What if I remember tomorrow? After the session with Dr. Collins. What…what if it's all better then?"

"Believe me, I hope that happens, sweetheart."

She wanted to reach up to her throat but she didn't want to pull her hands free from his gentle grip. She wished he'd never let her go.

She wished he'd roll her over onto her back, pin her to the bed, and fuck her brains out while holding her wrists trapped in his secure grasp.

She also knew he meant what he said.

"What did Det. Thomas say about the card?"

His expression darkened. "He doesn't hold out much hope for it giving him any leads."

"But he thinks the guy sent it, doesn't he?"

Rob nodded.

She buried her face against his chest. "I don't want to go to Montana," she softly said.

"I know, sweetheart." He released her wrists and put his arms around her again. "You don't have to go today. Today, I just want to spend the day relaxing with you.

* * * *

Bill made himself scarce. After fixing them breakfast, Rob drove Laura over to Englewood Beach on Manasota Key.

It was a sunny, warm Sunday, and the beach was filled with a mix of tourists and young families.

"We like going up to Middle Beach better," he told her as they walked along the water's edge.

"Middle Beach?"

"It's what everyone calls it. It's officially called Blind Pass Beach. It's quieter there."

"Why aren't we there?"

He didn't answer at first, but she figured it out. "You want to be where there's more people."

He gently squeezed her hand. "Yeah."

They settled in the shade of one of the picnic shelters and watched the water. She sat next to him, snuggled against his side with his arm draped around her shoulders. She'd let him talk her into a pain pill, but with the slow walk and the cool sea breeze blowing in off the Gulf, she didn't feel as groggy today.

Maybe it was his company that helped.

"I want to remember it all," she said. "I want to marry you."

He chuckled. "You don't know me very well yet."

"If I knew you well enough to want to marry you then, won't I want to marry you now?"

He smiled, but she couldn't get over how sad it looked. "I hope so, sweetheart. I really hope so."

* * * *

Rob had already left for work when Bill got Laura up and moving and in the truck early Monday morning for her appointment with Dr. Collins. When they arrived at the office, only a receptionist sat in the waiting area.

Bill walked ahead to check her in. "Laura Spaulding."

"I'll tell her she's here."

The receptionist had just hung up the phone when one of the office doors opened and a woman appeared. She wasn't as old as Dr. Simpson, but she wore a friendly smile behind her wire-rimmed glasses.

"Laura?"

She'd just sat down. She stood, trying not to wince. She'd adamantly refused any pain or anti-anxiety meds that morning. "Can my brother come in with me?"

"If that's what you want, absolutely."

They walked in and seated themselves in chairs near her desk. Dr.

Collins picked up a notepad and went through information she had from Dr. Simpson. "Is that all correct?"

Laura nodded.

Dr. Collins took her glasses off and put them on her desk. "You've been through a lot the past couple of weeks."

Laura nodded. "That's what they tell me."

"I'm not being facetious when I ask this, but what exactly do you want to get out of your sessions?"

"I'm hoping maybe I can get a few memories back. If nothing else, maybe I can get the dreams to stop. Deal with the stress. I'm not asking for miracles. I just want a little peace."

Dr. Collins nodded. "That's fair. Realistic. Tell me about the dreams."

Laura recounted every detail she could.

"I don't want to give you any false hopes. I think your dreams are memories trying to return. You probably already considered that."

"I didn't want to hope too much."

"From what you've told me you're already on the road to recovering your memories. I know your neurologist can't promise you anything and neither can I. But from what you've told me, I think you will at some point recover a bulk of your memories. Maybe not of the attack itself, and maybe not in the next few days, but hopefully soon and everything up until that point."

"What do I do now?"

"Are you open to trying hypnosis?"

"At this point, I'd dance naked in the middle of US 41 during morning rush hour if it'd bring my memory back."

Dr. Collins laughed. "I don't think that's necessary. Let's see how you respond to hypnosis." Laura consented to the doctor making an audio tape of the session.

Laura felt more relaxed reclining on the sofa. The doctor turned the lights down and sat in a chair next to the sofa. After twenty minutes, Laura was relaxed and responding to the doctor's questions.

The psychologist took Laura back to the dreams.

"Do you know the shadow?"

"I think I do."

"Is it someone you deal with every day?"

"No."

"Would you know the shadow if you saw it again?"

Laura frowned, concentrating. "Maybe. I don't know."

"Does the shadow ever say anything to you? Do you ever hear anything?"

She shook her head. "No."

"Okay. What did you say to the shadow?" Laura repeated her words from the dreams. "And what did you say to the shadow when he showed up at your door?"

"Hi." Laura's eyes snapped open. "I did know him!"

Bill tensed, resisting the urge to say anything.

Dr. Collins looked at Laura. "Do you see a face?"

She closed her eyes again. "Not yet."

"Does any name come to mind?"

She thought about it. "Dave maybe? I'm not sure."

"That's okay. Don't force it."

Laura lay there, then suddenly burst into tears. Dr. Collins got her a box of tissue and motioned to Bill to stay still.

"Laura, when I count to three, you're going to relax and be calm. You'll remember everything we talked about, but you'll be relaxed. Okay?"

Laura nodded.

"Okay. One, two, three."

Laura blew her nose.

"How do you feel?"

"I'm okay."

Dr. Collins patted her on the arm. "Good. Let's switch tracks for a while. I'd like to talk about what's been happening since the attack…"

At the end of the hour, Dr. Collins made Laura another appointment for two days later. "I have some ideas about how we might proceed from here. We'll talk more at your next appointment."

Bill escorted her out. Laura couldn't help but notice how he scanned the parking lot before leaving the building.

"Nervous?"

"About you? Absolutely. I can't afford to lose you, sis." He protectively put his arm around her and unlocked the car door.

She had a follow-up appointment with a doctor about her injuries. The only advice he had for her was to take it easy and keep seeing Dr. Simpson and Dr. Collins. There wasn't anything they could do for her injured ribs but prescribe rest.

Bill drove her back to Englewood. She only spent an hour at the shop before needing to go home and lie down. That also frustrated her. She knew she wasn't a person who normally sloughed off work.

Not that anyone apparently held it against her now, but she took it personally. The ribs didn't hurt as badly as they had before, even without the pain meds, but she knew she still had to take it easy or risk re-injuring them.

Fortunately, the only mail awaiting her was bills.

Her brother smiled as he tossed them onto the table.

"What?"

"Never thought I'd ever hear someone happy to say they received nothing but bills in their mail."

Rob had to work late, so they went to a restaurant in North Port for an early dinner. Despite the place being busy they were able to get a corner booth where they could talk privately.

"How you feel?" he asked her.

She shook her head as she looked over the menu. "Drained. Tired. I didn't like reliving some of that stuff."

He sipped his tea. "I'm sorry I wasn't here for you. If I'd known—"

She reached across the table and took his hand in hers. "Stop. Right now. You had no idea. I know you would have been here. It's not your fault this happened any more than it's Rob's."

Bill ordered them appetizers. Laura needed more time to decide on her dinner. Finally, she decided on a salad. She sat back in the booth. "I'm so tired."

"You've been through a lot, Laur. It's to be expected."

"I expect more from myself." He grinned. "What?" she asked.

"Nothing, but that's something you used to always say. Maybe more of you is coming back than you realize."

She played with her glass of iced tea. "I can only hope."

Chapter Twenty-One

Late Tuesday afternoon, after spending the day at the shop, Bill took Laura home. She fished her phone from her purse and realized she'd missed several texts from Shayla. Once she'd closed herself in her bedroom she opted to call her friend rather than text her.

"I'm sorry," Laura said. "I'm still getting used to technology."

"That's okay. So how are you feeling?"

"I'm...here."

"Rob told us you were wiped out Saturday. But can we come by tonight? We'll bring dinner."

She wanted to see her friend again. "Okay. Rob won't be here. My brother's here, though."

"Oh, good. We're looking forward to meeting him."

After a few more minutes, Laura felt exhaustion take over. She got off the phone and went back out to the living room to lie down on the sofa. "Shayla and Tony are coming over tonight."

Her eyes felt ready to cross from all the reading she'd done at the shop, and her shoulders hurt.

Maybe Rob can give me one of his neck rubs.

She froze. He'd never mentioned that to her. Was this a returning memory?

"Laur?" Bill asked. "You all right?"

Frozen, she concentrated, willing more to come. None did.

It was frustrating being teased and tortured by her own brain. Maybe she was a closet masochist and no one had ever caught on before.

She burst out laughing but wasn't sure why.

Bill stared at her with an odd look on his face. "You're starting to worry me."

"No, I'm okay."

"Then what's so funny?"

She rubbed the back of her neck. "I'm not sure."

* * * *

It felt good to sit down with Shayla and Tony in her own home. She knew, even though she couldn't remember, that they'd spent a lot of time together doing just this, talking, enjoying each other's company.

Only the other times it wasn't Tony and Shayla trying to help fill in the blanks of Laura's missing memories.

She watched the way Shayla looked at Tony, the love in her eyes as she glanced at him. The way she stood, without being asked, to refill his glass.

The way she obviously doted on him.

The way she leaned into him, his arm around her shoulders, as they sat and talked.

She wanted that with Rob. Maybe she'd already had it with him.

She wanted it back, if she had.

Bill stepped out of the room for a few minutes. Laura found herself saying, "You guys look like you've been in love forever."

Tony smiled down at Shayla. "I'm a lucky man."

"I'm a lucky p—girl." Shayla blushed and quickly smiled. "Girl. I'm a very lucky girl."

Laura wasn't sure, but it seemed like Shayla had started to say something else. Like she should know what it was Shayla had almost said.

Then Bill returned and Tony asked him about Montana and his job as a bush pilot, and Laura forgot what she was going to ask.

* * * *

Sully drove down Wednesday to take her to the gun range again. She'd passed the background check and was able to take possession of the 9mm.

He made her use it to practice. Practice included learning how to draw it, unloaded, from the holsters and the purse.

"I really recommend you carry in a holster, not in a purse. You want it on you at all times."

She nodded, not liking the idea but accepting it as a fact of life now.

After he was happy with her being able to draw it, he made her load and shoot it by herself.

Her aim was moderately better than it had been the last time. Sully's praise warmed her as he ran the target back to swap it out with a fresh one.

"Good job. Do it again." He smiled as he ran the target out.

"How do I know I can use this if I need to?"

He put his hands on her shoulders. "You know what he did to you the last time."

She nodded.

"Next time, he'll finish the job. You either shoot him, or he'll kill you. If you need to pull that gun, you don't hesitate, and you don't second-guess yourself. You pull it to shoot it. And you shoot it to save your life. And you figure that out by listening to your gut and staying vigilant."

"For how long?"

His hard expression softened. "Until either they catch the guy or he tries again. Think about it this way. If he does try again, if you don't kill him, he's liable to kill someone else later. So you shoot to kill. You don't shoot to wound, or shoot to warn. You shoot to *kill*. Understand me?"

"Yes, sir." She clamped her lips together as he smiled. "What?"

He shook his head, but he looked amused. "Nothing."

"I don't know why I said that."

His smile broadened. "It's okay, sweetie. Go ahead and shoot again."

* * * *

Thursday morning, Laura nervously fidgeted with her phone while Bill drove them to Sarasota to meet with her friends. Shayla had texted her a picture taken a few months earlier of all of them together during one of their girls' days.

It felt like a whole school of fish darting around in her stomach instead of butterflies.

This is going to be fine. At least, that's what Rob told her several times the night before when she worried.

She had Bill with her. She'd be seeing Shayla again.

It still didn't quell her nerves.

"It'll be okay, sis," he said.

"What if they don't like me?"

He let out a snort. "They're your friends. Of course they're going to love you. They *already* love you. Stop that."

"Sorry."

"Oh my god, Laur, stop *that*, too."

"Sor—" She clamped her lips shut on the word.

He glanced over at her and the wry look on his face made her smile.

"I'm that bad, huh?" she asked.

He reached across the seat and patted her leg. "You're just…different. You're coping the only way you can until you get your memories back."

"If."

"*When*," he firmly insisted.

Bill sat at an adjoining table during breakfast, close enough to keep an eye on them, but giving Laura privacy with her friends. They took up a large corner booth, and Shayla and Leah had sandwiched her between them.

Clarisse wasn't able to make it down that morning because the baby kept her awake half the night. But Tilly and Loren had joined them and were just as warm and welcoming as Leah and Shayla had been.

And yet…

There was still that underlying current running below everything, like she was missing some key thing that tied everything together. Something that might even give her an avalanche of answers if she could just figure it out.

She also knew on an instinctive level that it wasn't a bad thing. It just…

Was.

Like they constantly censored themselves around her.

When a stray thought crossed her brain, she spit it out, hoping it would trigger something. "Tilly, I know you're married to Landry, but who's Cris?"

She didn't imagine that all of the women paused, everyone looking to Shayla.

Shayla seemed to silently bounce the volley squarely back into Tilly's lap.

Laura had also noticed that while Leah, Shayla, and Loren all wore beautiful necklaces, Tilly wore a simple gold chain with a plain fluorite crystal pendant.

Tilly took a deep breath. "Rob didn't tell you about Cris?"

"I've heard his name mentioned before." She frowned. "I think. I'm not sure now. So much is muddied up, I don't know what is a memory or what I've heard."

"Well, it's complicated," Tilly said. "Landry, Cris, and I are poly."

As one, the other women's heads swiveled to watch Laura.

She would have found it amusing had Tilly's answer not confused her so much. "What? What does that mean?"

The other women looked to Tilly.

"Well, it means that I have a relationship with Landry and a relationship with Cris and they have a relationship with each other." She took a sip of her iced tea and watched Laura's reaction while the heads once again swiveled to focus on her.

I should know this. Something in her fractured memory pounded on a hidden door somewhere deep inside her brain and demanded release, but she couldn't locate it.

"And they're okay with it?" Laura asked.

Another swiveling of the heads back to Tilly.

Tilly kindly smiled. "Yeah. They were together before I met them. I got two for the price of one. And I wouldn't trade either of the big lugs for anything."

Laura sat back in her seat and considered things for a moment. The memories she thought she'd had when at the house with Bill returned to the forefront of her mind. "Landry and Cris came to help us work on the house, didn't they?"

"Yep."

She thought about it some more, then looked around. "So who's Mac?"

This time, everyone focused on Shayla. Shayla apparently realized no one was going to do the dirty work for her. She cleared her throat before smiling at Laura. "Mac is Clarisse and Sully's third. Sully and Mac were together before they met Clarisse."

Laura blinked. "Is this common?"

"Among our group it is," Tilly lightly snarked as she picked up her glass of water and took a sip.

Laura had a thought. "Am I and Rob…?" She couldn't finish it.

Shayla shook her head. "No. Rob doesn't share well with others. Neither do Tony or Ross."

Laura didn't miss what, or rather who, she'd left out. She looked at Leah.

Leah apparently knew it was her turn on the hot seat. "Kaden," she softly said, "my husband, was best friends with Seth. Since they were babies. When he found out about his cancer, he went to Seth and…" She shrugged. "I got to live my dream for a little while," she sadly said.

Suddenly, Laura didn't want to be talking about this anymore. Not if it made her friend look so sad. "I'm sorry." She took a deep breath and desperately wanted to change the subject. "So who wants to tell me what I'd planned for my wedding?"

After brunch the plan was to get their nails done, but Laura begged out. Her ribs were aching as she toughed out yet another day without the prescription pain pills, and her energy level had tanked.

She also wanted time alone to digest the poly relationship stuff. Was that the big secret Rob and everyone else had hidden from her so carefully? That they'd been worried she'd react badly?

After a round of hugs with all the women, Bill helped her into the truck.

"Are you all right, Laura?"

He hadn't been able to hear what they talked about from his table.

"Yeah. I'm just…thinking."

"Any new memories?"

"No. Just a couple of answers."

* * * *

Rob arrived home from work early Friday morning. Apparently he normally had more days off in a row, but he wanted to play catch-up covering for everyone who'd covered for him while Bill was still in town to help keep an eye on her.

She rolled over and draped her arm around him after he'd gotten a shower and climbed into bed with her.

"Can I ask you something?"

"Of course, sweetheart."

"Why didn't you tell me about Mac and Cris?"

She felt his body go rigid. "Who told you about Mac and Cris?"

"I had brunch with the girls yesterday morning. I had extra names running around in my head that I couldn't reconcile."

His body relaxed a little as he let out a breath he'd been holding. "They're our friends. We love them. We don't care what they do in their bedrooms."

She sat up and snapped on a bedside lamp. "Exactly. So why didn't you tell me about them?"

He looked exhausted. For a moment she felt guilty about slamming him with that right then, but she didn't want to let it wait and fester inside her.

"Sweetheart, I didn't know how to tell you. I didn't know how you'd react."

"Did I react badly when I knew them before?"

"No, of course not. You love them."

"Then why did you think I'd react badly now? Am I really that different?"

His hesitation in answering was all she needed. She threw the sheet aside and started to get up but he caught her hand. "Laur, please. I'm sorry. I just was so happy to have you awake, and then when you didn't have any memories, I was afraid to overwhelm you."

"Did you ever stop to think that maybe if you'd told me about them sooner, maybe it would have triggered more memories?"

From the look on his face, it was obvious he hadn't.

"When Bill took me by the house, I had some vague memories about people coming to help us. Maybe if I'd known who all those people were, maybe it might have triggered something."

She yanked her hand free and started for the bathroom.

He got up and rounded the bed faster than she could move and stopped her.

"Honey, I'm sorry."

"What else haven't you told me, huh?" She reached up to shove him out of her way but it was like trying to push granite. "What else are you hiding from me? How the hell am I supposed to trust you if I think you're hiding stuff?"

His eyes widened in shock. She suspected she couldn't have slapped him and elicited that kind of reaction.

He took a step back. "You don't trust me?"

Part of her screamed yes, that she trusted him with her life and her heart.

But she was mad. Mad and frustrated at life, and at her stubborn memory, and the guy who'd done this to her, and that Rob hadn't told her everything up front.

And he was, unfortunately, her target.

"How am I supposed to trust you when I have to find out something like that from people who are my friends? Something that the man I was supposed to marry should have told me!" She stepped around him and went into the bathroom, slamming the door behind her and locking it before she let the tears fall, hot and heavy.

He stood on the other side of the door, knocking. "Laur, please, sweetheart, you have to understand—"

"Go away, Rob. I'm too angry to talk to you right now." All she wanted to do was curl up in a ball and cry.

He tried a few more times to talk to her until she finally screamed at him to go away.

Silence.

She didn't know how long she stayed in there, but she went ahead and took her shower once she got the tears out of her system. When she finally unlocked the door and came out, Rob wasn't in the bedroom.

She walked out into the living room and found Bill sitting, bleary-eyed, at the table with a cup of coffee.

"Where's Rob?"

"I don't know, but I'm guessing since he asked me to make sure I didn't let you go anywhere by yourself, and that he had his bag with him, and that he looked like shit warmed over, *and* that you were screaming at him loud enough to wake me up that he probably went to the house."

She stared at him. "He...left?"

"Yeah. He left." He looked up at her. "Want to tell me what the *hell?*"

She slumped down into a chair across from him and told him.

He let out a sound that clued her in before he even spoke that he wasn't on her side on this one. "I can understand you being aggravated at him, but he didn't deserve for you to treat him the way you did."

"He lied to me!"

"No, he didn't. He just didn't tell you. Just like I didn't tell you about all the times you flew off the handle about stupid shit when you were a teenager and acted like an idiot." He arched an eyebrow at her.

Heat filled her face, but she didn't answer.

"He didn't tell you the same way I didn't tell you that you and Dad used to have lots and lots of conversations about your temper over the years when you were growing up, and even past college. He didn't tell you the same way I didn't tell you that, up until you met Rob, you were a pretty miserable person. Like you had a huge chip on your shoulder."

She slumped farther down in her chair. "I did?"

"Yeah. Like you were trying to prove yourself all the time."

She studied her hands. "If I was so bad," she muttered, "why do people even *want* to be friends with me?"

"Because people love you, Laura. As aggravating as you can be at times, you are ten times as generous and loving and fun to be around. You have your moments. We all do. In other words, you're as human as the rest of us."

She didn't have a reply.

He eventually spoke again. "The reason I love Rob is because I could see how good he is for you. How for the first time in your life you seemed to be relaxed and able to actually enjoy all of life and not drive-drive-drive yourself off a friggin' cliff. He's good for you. He gives you a sense of stability, a calm I've never seen you have in your life. Before…this, you looked like you'd finally found peace with him."

"I did?"

"Yeah. So I can forgive him for trying to not overwhelm you with stuff you might not be able to process. Especially a fact like that. I think you should, too."

"What if there's more he hasn't told me?"

"Guess what? There's probably a *lot* he hasn't told you. We can't regurgitate everything that's happened in your life or between us and you."

"I meant holding back deliberately."

"Like how you can be a pushy, judgmental bitch when your feelings get hurt?"

She glared at him.

He let out a snort. "Oh, don't give me *that* look, sis." He picked up his empty mug and headed back to the kitchen. "If looks could kill, believe me, you would have put me in my grave before you were ten."

Chapter Twenty-Two

Rob drove to the house, too tired to even think about the fight. He hated himself for not telling her sooner.

He also hated himself for not telling her about the BDSM.

Unfortunately, that was a very complex topic, and involved far more than simply explaining away friends' unusual relationship dynamics.

What he hated most of all was that he'd lost her trust, something he'd prided himself in keeping and cherishing and protecting beyond all else.

That hurt more than anything. She no longer trusted him.

And he knew he only had himself to blame.

He shut his phone off and climbed into bed. It felt weird to sleep here now. Especially alone. But from the way she'd gone off on him, he knew she needed to calm down, as did he, before they talked.

He was too exhausted to talk. Too exhausted to try to fix the situation.

Not to mention his heart hurt too much.

Maybe she needs time away from me. Time alone to rediscover who she is.

He'd always told himself, ever since he'd taken her on as not just his submissive, but as his fiancée, that if she ever wanted to leave he'd let her go. That he would never stand in her way. That he loved her enough he would never be one of those abusive fucks who held women hostage emotionally.

Now faced with the real possibility of her leaving, he wasn't sure he was strong enough to survive losing her.

* * * *

The crazy days working had taken a toll on Rob. When he finally awoke it was after three o'clock in the afternoon and he'd missed a call from Bill, who'd left a message telling Rob they were going grocery shopping and asking how he was.

Nothing from Laura. No texts, no calls.

He knew the shop would be busy but hoped he might be able to talk to Steve for a few minutes. Laura's truck wasn't parked out front when he drove up, so he stopped and went in.

Steve took one look at him and waved him outside onto the dock.

"What happened?"

They'd never gone into details about their friends' private lives with Steve, Carol, and other vanilla friends. They'd met some of their friends before, but that was it.

Keeping BDSM out of the equation, he told Steve what happened, and what he'd done.

Steve rubbed a hand over his face and stared out at the water for awhile. Both boats were out on dive or fishing charters, and the slips sat empty. A cool breeze off the Gulf blew through the mangroves on the other side of the channel from the docks.

Finally, he focused on Rob again.

"I can't say that I blame you for holding that back from her. In your shoes, I probably would have done the same thing."

"So how do I make it right?"

"Have you talked to her?"

"Not yet."

Steve looked out over the water again, slowly nodding. "She's got a temper on her."

"Yeah."

"You know, one thing I haven't seen much of since the two of you got together is that infamous temper of hers." He met Rob's gaze. "She's been the happiest I've ever seen in her life. Carol said the same thing the other day. You're good for her. Real good."

The older man leaned forward and tapped the picnic table again with his finger, as he had the other day when they talked. "I'm not about to get involved in your personal relationship with her. I don't know or care what the two of you do together. All I know is I really want to see her that happy again. So whatever it takes for you to make that happen, I'm all for it."

Steve sat back with a nod. "I was going to ask if you think a cookout would be a good idea. My house," he added. "Tomorrow. Invite all your friends, her friends. The closest ones."

"All of them?"

"*All* of them." He didn't flinch away from Rob's gaze. "Because maybe if we get them all in one spot together with her, it might help jiggle something loose."

"You don't mind?"

"Are they all consenting adults?"

"Yeah."

"Okay then. Not my cup of tea, but I'm not passing judgment on them. Especially since the past couple of years seem to have been the happiest of her life. They're part of that every bit as much as you are. If I recall, she met Shayla and Tony and all of them right before she met you."

"We...I met her through them."

He nodded again. "All right then. Tomorrow, five o'clock, my house." He stood and started to go inside.

"What do I tell everyone to bring?"

He turned. "Themselves and a side dish. I'll make burgers and brats." He snorted. "Maybe it'll help *your* brat." He headed inside.

It took every ounce of strength Rob had not to bust out laughing. Either Steve had just made one of the funniest unintentional jokes he'd ever heard...

Or maybe Steve knew more than he let on.

Just like he'd nearly busted a nut the other night over Laura's comment about him being the only one to hurt her.

It was a common private joke they shared, and had given him a little hope that she might be close to a breakthrough.

Either way, it didn't matter. He pulled out his phone and started making calls. Fortunately, he was off tomorrow night, because he had to work that night from six until six tomorrow morning.

* * * *

As the day wore on, Laura felt horrible about what she'd said to Rob. Bill was right, she didn't have a right to be mean to Rob, no matter how aggravated she'd felt. She also didn't feel up to going into the shop and facing Steve.

Somehow, she suspected he'd give her both barrels for yelling at Rob, too.

She also knew she deserved it.

Knowing Rob needed to sleep before another work shift that night, Laura wondered if he'd even come by the house before he left for work.

When she didn't call him, Bill did, leaving a message for Rob before they went grocery shopping.

Finally, a little after five, Rob stopped by, dressed for work.

She got up and went to him and put her arms around him, buried her face against his chest. "I'm sorry," she said. "I'm really, *really* sorry. I shouldn't have yelled at you."

Tension drained from him as he carefully hugged her. "It's okay, sweetie. I know this is stressful."

"Yeah, but you didn't deserve me going after you like that."

"We'll get through this." He made her look up at him. "But, seriously, can you trust me?"

She nodded. "Yeah. I do."

He kissed her. It made her want to cry again, the sweet tenderness of it.

"Tomorrow, at Steve's, we're having a cookout. All our friends."

"He knows about the fight?"

Rob smiled. "Yeah. I went over and talked to him to get some advice."

Now she really felt horrible. "Sorry," she softly said.

"It's okay. He offered to hold the cookout. I've already called everyone and they're coming down. Five o'clock."

"Everyone?"

He nodded. "Everyone that's a close friend. People from the shop, a few local friends. But yes, including Shayla and Tony and everyone."

A stray thought floated through. "What about Steve and Carol? Are they okay with…that?"

"It was Steve's idea." He stared into her eyes. "Okay?"

She nodded. "Okay. Thank you."

"You don't need to thank me."

"Thank you for forgiving me."

The way his expression shifted nearly broke her heart. The anguish lurking just below his surface made her feel even more horrible for the things she'd said and thought. "Laura, I'll do whatever it takes to make sure you're happy, and that you can trust me, and to help you get your memory back and keep you safe. If it means a few bumps in the road along the way, well, that's nothing. I'll go through that and more a thousand times over if it means I can take care of you and make you happy."

He leaned in and kissed her forehead. "I need to go to work. Love you."

She didn't want to let him go. "Love you, too."

"I'm going to the house in the morning after my shift. You and Bill meet me there and pick me up and we can ride to Steve's together. Okay?"

"Okay."

After he left, Bill returned from his room. She hadn't realized he'd left the living room.

"You all right, Laura?"

She shook her head and started crying. "What if I do something to screw this up with Rob?"

He hugged her. "If he could put up with what he's dealt with so far, sis, I think it's going to take a lot more than that to scare him off."

* * * *

After his shift ended Sunday morning, he returned to the house and collapsed into bed. Nearly every time he slept his dreams were filled with memories.

He didn't need to talk to a psychiatrist to know it came from his overwhelming desire to have their life back to the way it was before the attack.

This dream was an extremely fond memory. Early in their relationship, he'd had a Wednesday off, and a group of charter passengers cancelled a fishing trip due to a missed flight.

Not one to miss out on an opportunity, Laura had called him and asked if he wanted to go out on the boat with her.

That was a no-brainer.

Alone together, with snacks and cold soda on board, they took the smaller boat out into the Gulf on a beautiful day. By this time they'd done away with condoms, except for anal and on toys, and he'd wasted no time getting her naked and bent over a cooler once they'd reached their first fishing spot.

He'd enjoyed lathering her with sunscreen, taking time to tease her by playing with her nipples, ensuring he kept her horny and begging for release, to the point that he gave up trying to fish.

All he wanted was her.

Ditching his swim trunks, he sat on the cooler and crooked a finger at her. She dove for his cock, eagerly swallowing him to the root and nearly taking his breath away.

She was *damn* good.

He loved holding her hair, which she'd put into pigtails low on her head for him today. Two perfect handles with which to control and guide her.

"Spread your legs, baby. Wider." He watched as a thin string of juices dripped from her pussy onto the deck. "You're really horny, aren't you?"

She stared up into his eyes and mumbled what sounded like agreement around his cock.

The sound vibrated through him.

What she didn't know was he'd packed more than just fishing tackle.

"If you want to come, baby, you'd better make me come." She gave up all control, letting him take over with his hands in her hair while he fucked her mouth. Wrapping her hands around his thighs she held on, staying with him, eyes turned up to look at him.

He smiled down at her as he thrust, taking his time and enjoying the warm, wet heat of her mouth. "Such a good girl," he whispered.

She let out a little whimper of pleasure.

"When I come, don't swallow. Hold it."

Her mumbled, "Yes, Sir," is what triggered his climax. He fought the urge to drive deep into her mouth, not wanting to choke her. She sucked on him, pulling every last drop between her sweet lips.

When he could speak, he said, "Show me."

She opened.

"Good girl. Hold it until I say." He pulled her up off the deck and pushed her down over the cooler. After a quick glance around to ensure they were still alone, he began spanking her.

She whimpered, but didn't cry out, knowing if she disobeyed him, the "funishment" wouldn't be very fun.

Once her ass was pink enough for his liking, he grabbed the duffel bag he'd brought and dug through it. He quickly lubed up the butt plug, a small one she could easily take, and then lubed her rim before slowly sliding the plug inside her.

She moaned, this time with need, but didn't open her mouth.

Next he grabbed the vibrator. The rabbit-styled device was a little thicker than his cock, and longer. The added deviousness of the clit stimulator would only multiply the fun. He swung around, sitting on her and pinning her to the cooler, the final item in his hand.

A small wooden paddle.

"Okay, baby. You can come as much as you want, but don't you spill a drop, and don't you dare swallow. Understand?"

She barely got the mumbled, "Yes, Sir," all the way out before he turned the rabbit on, on its highest setting, and slid it home inside her cunt.

It was a good thing he sat on her. Before he'd thrust it three times into her, she'd had her first orgasm. And then he started smacking her with the paddle. Not as hard as he could, but hard enough he knew it stung and she had to struggle not to cry out.

Unfortunately for her, he'd put fresh batteries in the rabbit. He struggled to hold back his sadistic giggles as he fucked her with it, alternating between slow, deep strokes and hard, fast ones. Combined with the whacks from the paddle, she literally didn't know if she was coming or going.

And his cock quickly grew hard again.

He kept it up for nearly fifteen minutes, until her ass was a beautiful shade of red, tears streamed down her face, and he'd lost count of how many orgasms she'd had. Then he finally took mercy on her, removing the rabbit and shutting it off.

She went limp over the cooler.

"Oh, I'm not done with you yet, baby." He returned the paddle to the bag and turned, plunging his cock home. "It's time for round two for me."

Folding his body over hers, he fucked her, enjoying how she shivered and moaned as another series of orgasms washed through her. He played with the butt plug, too, tapping the base and gently thrusting it into her, adding to her torment.

But he couldn't hold back. He felt his own release build and gave in to it, grabbing her hips and fucking her hard until he'd finished, filling her full of cum on both ends.

He sat on the cooler and pulled her into his lap. "Show me."

Despite the glazed look on her face, she opened her mouth.

"Good girl. Swallow."

She did, curling up in his lap and resting her head against his chest. He enveloped her in his arms, loving the content sigh she breathed.

"Love you, baby girl." He kissed the top of her head.

She giggled. "Love you, too, Sir."

"Even if I'm a sadistic bastard sometimes?"

She trailed her fingers across his chest. "*Because* you're a sadistic bastard sometimes."

Rob startled awake and realized in his sleep he'd fisted his cock and now had a handful of his own cum. Dragging himself from bed to clean up and check the clock, he realized he'd only been asleep for less than an hour.

Maybe this time I can skip the dreams.

He was asleep seconds after returning to bed.

* * * *

Laura looked out the back window at the yard full of almost-strangers. In her mind, a swirling, ghostly cloud of isolated memories mirrored the mingling crowd in the backyard. So many vague, random things. Unfortunately, none fell into place and Laura nervously hid inside, watching through the window.

Steve's wife, Emily, walked into the kitchen. "What's wrong, honey?"

"There's so many."

Emily looked out the window. "People?"

Laura nodded. "He could be anyone."

Maybe this hadn't been such a good idea after all. Rob stood out at the grill with Steve, trying to not burn the burgers, while Sully, Tony, and Landry looked on.

"Laura, I've known some of these people for at least a couple of years. Rob and you have known the rest of them. I don't think it's possible any of them could have done this to you."

"You saw every one of them right after the attack?"

"No, but Steve said a bunch of people stopped by the shop after they heard what happened. Plus you're here with a large group of people. If anything, this is safe. You're surrounded by friends. No one is going to hurt you. Not here, not today."

There was a yell from outside. The women looked in time to see someone throw a glass of beer on a hamburger that had burst into flames on the grill.

Emily *tsked*. "Well, as long as you stay away from Tweedledee and Tweedledum and their fire pit of disaster, you'll be safe."

Emily finally coaxed Laura outside. Holding her hand, Carol took her around to all the guests she knew Laura couldn't remember and introduced them.

Earlier, Rob had taken her around and reintroduced her to the few of their friends she hadn't met yet. Like Tilly's guys, and Clarisse, Mac, and Ross.

Not many memories returned, but Laura remembered three people before Carol's introduction.

Rob watched from the grill, where Steve poked him, leaning in close. "Stop it, son."

"What?"

"You're frowning. No frowny time. Happy time. Happy, happy, happy."

He shook his head. "Easy for you to say."

"Come here." He grabbed Rob's shirt and dragged him through the kitchen door, closing it behind them. "Look, don't think this is harder on you than it is on any of us, all right? I know you love her, but we love her, too. I've known her a hell of a lot longer than you have. So has Carol. She's like a daughter to us, and you don't get to corner the market on being upset. Now get that friggin' head of yours on straight and go out there and look like you're enjoying yourself."

Rob leaned against the counter, arms crossed, staring at the floor. "She's like a whole new person. She talks differently. She walks differently." He finally looked up at Steve again. "What if she wasn't really in love with me?"

Steve stepped close. "Stop it. Quit feeling sorry for yourself. You know damn well that's not true. She is a different person because she doesn't have her memories. As her fiancé, you're the one who needs to take the lead and help her."

"I don't want to force her."

"Talk to her. Tell her how you feel."

Rob turned and watched Carol lead Laura around the backyard, from person to person. "What if she doesn't want to?"

"Well dammit, you won't know until you try, will you? You've got to start somewhere."

* * * *

Steve's house had a good view of the southern end of Lemon Bay. After dinner, Rob found Laura and got her alone for a few minutes. "Will you come watch the sunset with me?"

She nodded. He held out his hand and finally, timidly, she took it. He led her to the end of the dock, away from everyone else.

He sat down and patted the dock in front of him. She hesitantly sat, leaning against him and accepting his arms around her.

It felt right. She couldn't deny that.

As darkness fell, a snook hit the surface of the bay a few yards from them, rippling the water. She was afraid to break the spell, worried there might not be too many moments such as these again in her life.

"This isn't fair to you," she said.

"This isn't about me."

She turned to face him. "Half your life is gone. It's about you as much as it is me." From a few private conversations with Carol at the shop, and with Shayla while still in the hospital, she'd learned a lot about Rob, too embarrassed to ask him herself.

She learned they had been nearly inseparable, before. That she'd told Carol, Shayla, Steve, Bill, and others that he was the love of her life, but could she honestly say she loved him now when he was still a stranger in so many ways, regardless of how he made her feel?

Those thoughts led to more guilt.

Rob brushed a stray hair from her face. "Laura, I love you. I have loved you for years, and I will always love you. If that means I have to wait, I'll wait. You are my life. I will take whatever I can get. If that means sitting back and waiting, I can do that. I *will* do that."

Laura didn't know what to say. She leaned back against him and they watched the boats on the bay in the deepening dusk.

* * * *

Back at the house, Bill offered to go ahead and take Doogie home and left Laura with Rob to give them some alone time.

She hoped she hadn't screwed things up between them so badly that it couldn't be fixed. "Will you stay tonight?" she asked him. "At the condo? Please?"

"Is that what you want?"

She nodded.

He gathered her hands in his and kissed them. "Okay."

She relaxed a little, relieved. "Thank you for a nice evening. I appreciate all the trouble you and Steve and Carol went through to put that together at such short notice."

He nodded and looked at the floor. "You're welcome. I'm sorry you didn't get more memories back from it."

"It's okay."

"I need to go grab some stuff." When he returned he found her curled on the couch and listening to a CD. John McLean's *Better Angels* album.

"You like it?" he asked.

She nodded. "Did I always like it?"

He smiled. "It's one of your favorites. You ripped it to your iPod. You'd put it on and play it over and over while you were writing. You've got two kinds of music, writing and driving. This was one of your writing music selections."

"How can you put up with me when I don't know anything?"

He sat next to her on the couch and held her. "Because I love you."

Chapter Twenty-Three

Monday morning, Bill drove Laura to her next appointment with Dr. Collins. He sat in the room with her while Dr. Collins once again tried hypnosis. The nightmares about the door and the shadow hadn't stopped.

If anything, they'd grown more intense, the shadow gaining substance with every repetition.

Unfortunately, by the end of the session Laura hadn't recovered anything helpful about the dreams, or the rest of her life.

She made another appointment for the next Monday and slumped in her seat on the ride back to Englewood.

"Don't let it upset you," he gently chided.

"I need to figure this out."

"You won't do it driving yourself crazy. If it comes back, it comes back."

* * * *

She rode up to Tampa with Steve to take Bill to the airport Tuesday morning. After checking in, he stood with her in the main terminal near the shuttle that would take him airside.

She felt like she was losing one of her lifelines.

"I'm going to miss you."

"I'll miss you, too, sis." He hugged her close. "I'll come back in a few months." He laughed. "Sooner, if you decide to get married."

She laughed but pushed back the melancholy over that statement. It felt like she'd hit a stalemate in terms of new memories. But that evening, after Rob got off work, they were going to meet at a restaurant on Boca Grande that he told her used to be one of her favorites.

Maybe it would help trigger something.

Later that morning, while she was working at the shop, Det. Thomas called her to update her on the investigation.

"Well, do you want the good news, or the bad news?"

Laura closed her eyes. "Is the good news that you've got him?"

"No, but we know more about who he is."

She sighed. "What's the good news?"

"The DNA evidence we recovered from underneath your fingernails pinged several hits in the national database. We can link him to several crimes all over the country."

She swallowed hard. "What's the bad news?"

He paused. "The other victims were all raped and murdered."

Her heart pounded in her chest. "How many?"

"Do you really want to know?"

She forced the words out of her mouth. "Tell me."

"Fifteen. That we know of. Possibly ten others with the same MO, but either no DNA evidence or it was inconclusive. We don't have any reports of crimes with victims who survived."

No more untraceable calls had been received at her home line, and no fingerprints were found on the note she'd gotten in the mail. The possibility that the email and letter were just from cranks or a copycat was considered, but not ruled out.

The sheriff's office was also still running nighttime patrols along her street, usually once an hour if not more often.

"And I've got your concealed carry license here. Do you want me to bring it to you?"

She had difficulty processing that while still thinking about the fifteen dead women. "Can Rob get it?"

The detective must have realized how shaken she was. "Sure, just have him call me. Are you okay?"

"No." That number resonated in her brain. *Fifteen* dead women.

And she would have been sixteen.

Or twenty-six, if the others were related.

Her hands shook. "I have to go now. Thank you for calling." The receiver fell from her hand onto the phone. *Fifteen confirmed victims?* And she was the only one who survived?

Laura couldn't stand. Her legs shook too badly. Steve walked in and saw her. "What's wrong?"

She burst into tears as she related what Thomas said.

He hugged her. "Honey, you're lucky. You're a fighter. That will always keep you alive. You've been scrappy from when you were a kid. This guy isn't going to get another chance at you."

She couldn't stay in the shop and she didn't want to go home. She told Steve she was going out for a little while to get some lunch and drove into town. Despite his insistence on going with her, she refused.

She needed to be alone, and she'd be in public. What could happen?

Wandering through Merchant's Crossing shopping plaza, she passed a hair salon. Laura looked inside and saw they weren't busy, then studied her reflection in the window. The bruises had finally faded and she'd stopped wearing makeup.

Today, she had her nearly waist-length auburn hair up in a ponytail and braided. Before she could chicken out, she walked in and talked to a stylist. The woman made a few suggestions. Laura called Steve and told him she'd be shopping for a few more hours so he wouldn't worry, but didn't tell him what she was doing.

Three hours later, Laura returned to the shop.

When Steve saw her new hairstyle, his eyes popped.

"I thought you said you were getting lunch and shopping."

"Well, do you like it?"

"It's different." He stared. "Not bad different, it's just…I've never known you to do anything like this before. It'll take some getting used to."

The stylist had scissored Laura's hair to shoulder length. Still long enough to pull back into a ponytail when diving, but a drastic difference. After cutting it, the stylist colored it, lightening it a few shades and adding highlights, but not all the way to blonde.

Laura felt pleased with the results.

Sarah walked in and stopped short. "Uh. Wow. I mean…" She stared at Laura's new hairstyle. "Wow."

Steve still stared. "Rob's going to flip."

"Why?"

"He loved your hair long."

Laura considered that. "Is that why I kept it long? For him?" Mindful of Bill's comments about her temper, she reined in her irritation.

"No, hon. You kept it long because it looked pretty on you, and because it was easy for you to take care of. You only went to the salon maybe twice a year. You hated getting your hair cut because your mom made you keep it short and styled when you were little. When you were twelve she finally threw her hands up and let you do what you wanted with it, and you let it grow."

He let out a laugh. "You never do anything because someone else wanted you to, unless you wanted to first."

Sarah laughed with him. "That's the truth."

* * * *

Rob went to pick up Laura's concealed carry license from Det. Thomas. When he returned, his captain asked, "How's Laura doing? I haven't worked the same hours with you lately and have been meaning to ask."

"She's physically better. Her memory's still spotty. She can work and run the store. Steve hasn't got her back in the water yet to see if she can still dive or teach because of her ribs. She's got a lot of her childhood back, but very little recent memories."

"How are *you* handling it?"

He shrugged. "I'm just taking it one day at a time. I'm going to date her all over again. That's what I've got planned for tonight. She's meeting me over on Boca at a restaurant we went to all the time. I've already got it set up to have fresh flowers on the table and champagne chilling. Then I'm going to pop the question."

"You're going to propose again?"

"No. I'm going to ask her to go steady with me."

Once the captain quit laughing, he realized Rob was serious.

"She still doesn't know me. I'm not going to force her to put aside her reservations. I'm hoping she'll say yes."

"If she doesn't?"

He looked at the floor. Despite how they'd mended fences after her blowup, he didn't want to think about the very real possibility that things might not turn out the same between them once she learned about their BDSM dynamic. "I don't want to think about that."

* * * *

Despite a late accident call, Rob still managed to return to the station, shower, and make it to the restaurant with ten minutes to spare. He was sitting at the table waiting for Laura when a woman walked in who looked familiar. In the dim light, it wasn't until she was halfway to the table that he recognized her.

In his shock, he forgot to stand and pull her chair out like he'd planned.

"Hi, Rob." Her voice sounded timid, shy. Definitely not two words that would have described Laura before the attack.

"Um. Hi." He searched for words. That this truly wasn't his Laura anymore slammed home. She looked vaguely the same, but the drastic change in hairstyle emphasized the differences. She even walked differently, and not just because of her injuries. She didn't have the familiar confident, smooth glide.

Her face fell. "You don't like it, do you?"

He scrambled out of his chair and pulled hers out, helping her sit. "I'm sorry, honey. You look great. I just wasn't expecting it, that's all."

He stared at her for a moment and finally sat down. "What brought this on?"

She shrugged. "I just felt like doing it." She sniffed the flowers. "These are beautiful. Thank you." Looking at him she saw the shock still registering on his face and smiled. "Don't feel bad. Steve's and Sarah's jaws hit the floor, too."

He looked down at his menu. "I'm sorry. Was it that obvious?"

"It wasn't unexpected." She picked up her menu and studied it. The waitress took their drink order and appetizers. When they were alone, Laura put her menu down. She reached across the table and touched Rob's hand. "Why don't you order for me? Order me something I used to love."

"To be honest, I'm almost afraid to." He couldn't believe he said it, but now that he had, the emotions couldn't be rebottled.

She pulled back and frowned. "Why?"

"Because physically, you're the same woman I was supposed to marry in a few months. And that's about the extent of it. Even though I have a past with you, you're a stranger. You don't know me beyond what we've gone through the past few weeks, and I really don't know you anymore. Now I don't know what to say or do around you. I wanted tonight to be special. I was going to ask if you'd go steady with me. I know that's stupid, but I was hoping it would give you the time you need to make a decision about the future."

"Was?"

He didn't answer.

"Why won't you ask me? Just because I cut my hair?"

He tried to reply and couldn't. Finally, "I don't know. Would you say yes if I did?"

"You haven't given me the chance to answer. You're assuming I'll say no. Don't you have enough respect for me to give me the chance to make up my own mind? Is this the kind of relationship we used to have, where I just went along with you no matter what?"

That shocked him into silence. The waitress reappeared to take their dinner orders before he could answer. Laura handed her the menu. "I'll have the grouper Florentine with a baked potato, extra sour cream please, and asparagus."

She looked at Rob as his grin spread ear to ear. Somehow that seemed to annoy her. "What?" she snapped.

"That's what you always ordered."

* * * *

Laura reined in her temper, not wanting a repeat of their fight Saturday morning. She apologized, he leaned over and kissed her, and they moved past the incident to settle into a comfortable conversation. Rob pulled her concealed carry permit out of his pocket and handed it to her.

"And here's this." He smiled, but she noticed it held no humor. "You're now legal."

She studied it. Yes, she'd been carrying the gun, actually feeling vulnerable when she took it off for a shower, or to put it in the drawer of the nightstand to sleep. "Thanks." She slipped it into her wallet. "Not sure if I should hope I do or don't need to use it."

Once their food arrived he broached the subject again.

"Would you consider seeing a jerk like me exclusively?"

She laughed, nearly choking on a bite of grouper. "Is that how you asked me the first time?"

"No," he admitted. "But I feel pretty vulnerable right now, so I felt honesty was probably the best approach."

She tilted her head, considering. "I guess since you saw me looking like something out of a George Romero flick and still wanted me, I should give you a chance."

His jaw fell open.

"What?" she asked.

"That's something you used to say. You love his movies."

"Really?"

He nodded.

"See? There's hope then, isn't there?"

He smiled. "I hope so."

"Then yes. I think we should."

"Should what?"

"You aren't chickening out on me already are you?"

"Huh? Oh! Sorry." He laughed. "No, I'm not chickening out on you." He took her hands in his and gently squeezed them. "I would never do that."

* * * *

After dinner they walked along the beach, by the Boca Grand lighthouse. It was a beautiful, cloudless night. Under a quarter-full moon, and with only the inky Gulf out to the west, the stars shimmered overhead like a magical blanket. The warm evening was tempered by the cool breeze coming off the Gulf. There were a few boats out in the Pass getting in some night fishing, but other than that, they were alone.

Rob risked feeling for her hand and she let him take it. Almost like old times.

Almost.

Before, he would have taken her home and they would have made love before falling asleep entwined like an ancient puzzle.

Before, they would have deeply kissed before parting and said "I love you" to each other.

Before.

Rob wanted to kill the bastard who took not only Laura's memory, but his life. His future. The old Laura might never return, and neither might the happiness he used to know.

They stopped by the ruins of the old phosphate docks and she looked across the pass toward Don Pedro Island. "What's that?"

She hadn't been out in the boat yet, Steve refusing to take her out on the water until her ribs were completely healed. Rob explained it to her, pointing out landmarks. She never needed a chart close to shore before. She used to have every barrier island, every fishing cove, every sandbar committed to memory.

There was that word again. While her dive knowledge was intact, apparently her navigational expertise was still MIA.

The no-see-ums swarmed and she asked to go home. They returned in separate cars to her condo. Steve had brought Doogie home for her from the shop. When Rob reached for the leash to take him out, she stopped him.

"I'll take him."

"Are you sure? I don't mind."

"It's okay. I can handle it." She patted the small of her back. "I'm legally packing, now, remember?" She smiled, but it held no humor.

She clipped the lead to the Lab's collar and they went out. Rob kicked his shoes off by the door and waited nervously until they returned a few minutes later.

"See?" She smiled. "I'm getting better all the time."

They watched TV until the eleven o'clock news. Laura yawned and couldn't stop. "I have to go to sleep or I won't be able to wake up in the morning."

He nodded. "All right. I'll be right there. I want to check the locks and get the coffeepot set for in the morning."

She patted his leg and after hesitating for a moment, kissed him on the lips. "Good night, Rob."

"Night."

His eyes followed her down the hall. It was strange watching her walk away from him with not only a different gait, but now a different look, too. She wasn't his Laura.

Then a chilling thought struck him—could *he* get used to the new Laura?

Chapter Twenty-Four

When Rob awoke the next morning, Laura had already left for the shop. A note lay on the counter next to a fresh pot of coffee.

Maybe we could have dinner at your place tonight? Bring Doogie by the shop if you need to. - L.

His stomach knotted. It was *their* house. They owned it together. They'd thought of it as theirs, not his.

They had agreed she would rent out the condo after the wedding and move in with him.

Before.

He slammed his fist against the counter hard enough to rattle the glasses in the drainer. Doogie ran into the kitchen, worried.

"It's okay, boy." He spent a moment loving the dog before going to get a shower.

* * * *

"You're in awful early, kiddo," Steve observed.

Laura set her coffee cup on the desk. "I woke up early." The truth was, she wanted to be out of the house before Rob woke up. She didn't want to face him, afraid he'd sense the mood she was in.

Despite having his comforting presence next to her in bed, nightmares plagued her. Not just the one about the door and the shadow, which she'd sadly come to expect every night. But dreams about other men, sexy, strange, odd dreams involving bondage and spankings.

And orgasms.

And Rob hadn't been in them.

She didn't want to be faced with trying to explain all of that to him when she didn't even understand it.

Steve puttered around the shop for ten minutes before finally planting himself next to her desk.

"So?"

"So…what?"

"Laura, you never could play that game with me. How did Rob react to the new hairstyle?"

She shrugged. "I think he was a little freaked out."

Steve waited for her to continue but she didn't. "And then what happened?"

"Not much. We had dinner, took a walk, went home. That's about it."

He shook his head. "For a writer, you aren't a very good storyteller."

The fact was she hadn't done any writing since the attack. She spent several hours going through her past articles and the journals she'd found, but she worried perhaps that part of her was gone forever.

"I've just got a lot of stuff to do. That's all."

"You were never a good liar, either. Did you have a fight?"

"No, no fight. Really."

He finally left her alone. She didn't want to think about it. Yes she did want to "date" Rob. Going "steady." Sounded pretty sophomoric. Considering she was rebuilding her life from the ground up, maybe it wasn't a bad idea. She still hadn't found the missing journals. Rob said he never snooped and never had a need to know where she kept them or what she wrote in them.

So he said.

Not that she had a reason to not trust him, the truth was, she didn't know if she could or not no matter how much she wanted to. If she could find the journals, the path back to her memories might be shortened considerably. Over the past couple of days, she had noticed little odd snippets suddenly appearing in her memories after reading through the old journals. As if seeing it in black and white made a difference.

What concerned her was she had no idea what kind of person she was in her relationship with Rob other than what people told her. Was she really in love with Rob and had accepted his proposal because she wanted to spend her life with him, or did she accept to remove the loneliness from her life? Was she strong and self-directed, or was she a totally codependent wuss, afraid to stand on her own two feet?

A journal could open a lot of doors for her that secondhand retelling could never unlock.

Later that afternoon, a man walked in and browsed the dive gear.

"Can I help you?"

When he looked at her and smiled, she felt something tighten in her gut.

"Actually, yes," he said. "I need new gear plus a refresher class. My ex-wife got all my stuff, and it's been about five years since I last dove. I finally got moved into my new place and I'm ready to start diving again."

He was maybe in his late thirties. Tall, dark blond hair, almost brown. Looked like he worked in an office but he wasn't pale. Trim. Piercing green eyes.

Do I know him? "Sure. What's your price range?" With business to conduct she pushed all emotions out of the way and went to work. It wasn't until he was out the door with a complete new rig and signed up for a weekend refresher class she realized how odd she felt. A rush she couldn't explain. It wasn't that she was attracted to him, although he was a fairly decent-looking guy, but there was something else there she couldn't name.

Steve came in from the dock and looked over her shoulder at the charge copy of his receipt. "Wow. That guy must be made of money. Did you make sure the credit card wasn't hot?"

"Yeah. It's okay."

"What's wrong?"

She shook her head. "Nothing, I guess. Just a strange feeling."

Steve looked out the window but the customer had already driven away. "Why? Did you recognize him or something?"

"I don't know. He didn't act like he knew me. It was just strange."

"Don Kern. Don't know the name." He grabbed the phone book and thumbed through it. "No listing for him, either."

"He said he just moved into a new place. Besides, he'll be here on Saturday morning for his refresher class. You'll be teaching, so you don't have to worry about the big, bad wolf."

"You think I'm going parental on you? Well *excuse* me, but anyone who expresses an interest in you at this point to me is a prime suspect."

Carol and Sarah had told Laura that men used to hit on her all the time in the shop. It was an occupational hazard, and both Sarah and Carol said she'd been confidently adept at turning away unwanted advances without causing offense.

Before.

Laura noticed when that happened now she usually blushed and got flustered and tried to pretend it didn't happen, or she'd sputter that she was engaged.

She wished she had that same self-confidence back now.

The phone rang, giving her an excuse avoid the conversation. Steve stormed into the back room.

It was Rob. "I saw your note this morning."

"Yeah, um, I thought maybe we could eat at your place tonight. Is that okay?"

"Sure. What do you want?"

"I don't know. Whatever you think. Surprise me. I was just thinking I ought to spend more time over there, you know? Maybe it will help trigger something."

Rob paused. "Sure, honey. What time?"

"Are you all right?"

"I'm fine. Is seven okay?"

"That's fine." She paused. "Would you mind taking Doogie over there with you? Is it okay to have him there?"

* * * *

Rob gripped his phone tightly, trying to control his voice. "No, of course I don't mind. You always brought him with you."

When they hung up, Rob stared at the phone. In fact, he and Doogie were already over at the house. He had a ton of chores to catch up on and wanted the dog's company.

He went outside and used the weed trimmer for an hour to get rid of some of his pent-up emotions.

She felt she had to ask permission to bring Doogie with her?

She was timid. She was shy. She jumped at noises and wasn't much of a talker.

The polar opposite of who she was.

Before.

* * * *

Laura looked at the phone. She did want to spend time at Rob's. At the same time, essentially, she had never lived by herself, that she could remember.

Maybe I should.

She fingered the solitaire on her right hand. Rob had been very good about not saying anything, even though she noticed him looking at it. It had to be difficult for him.

The day crept by. When she finally called it quits at five she was more than ready to go home. Steve shooed her out the door, offering to lock up.

After two wrong turns she finally found Rob's driveway.

She didn't admit to him that she got lost.

The house was filled with a wonderful garlicky aroma and he presented her with fresh shrimp scampi on angel hair pasta, broccoli au gratin, and homemade garlic knots. Everything tasted delicious, and they sat on the couch after dinner to talk.

He played with the label on his bottle of beer. "I want to be honest with you. My life was all planned. Our lives were planned. We were getting married, I was happy, I thought you were happy. Then this all happened. I love you as much now, if not more, than I did before this happened. That hasn't changed, it won't change."

Doogie put his head in her lap and she petted him while carefully choosing her words. "I don't even know who I am, who I was, what I wanted to be. I have no history other than what people tell me or I see in pictures or what little I read. I have no true idea of the future I'd pictured for myself or us. I don't know how much I lost or how much I had to gain when I lost it."

She took a deep breath and forced the words out. "I think maybe I need to live by myself for a little while. Try to figure things out."

His face shifted into an unreadable mask. "You don't want to see me anymore?"

"I *do* want to see you. And that's *not* what I meant." She struggled to force the words out. "I need time to figure out what my next step is."

"Can't you trust me when I tell you what we were to each other?"

"That's not fair." She stood and walked over to the windows to stare out at the wetlands silhouetted against the setting sun. "I'm not saying I doubt you. It's just I don't know to what extent I used to let you influence my decisions. I still have to figure out who I am. Can't you understand that?"

He pointed to his head. "Up here, yes." He pointed to his chest. "In here, it feels like someone's ripped out my guts and stomped them. Every day I see you, I'm afraid to touch you, I'm afraid to say things to you that weeks ago I took for granted. I can still picture the last time we made love like it was yesterday, can still feel your fingers on my back, can still hear the sound of your voice, remember the way your hair smelled. That's not going away anytime soon. You have a lifetime to remember. If I lose you, I have a lifetime to forget."

Laura wanted to cry. She was torn between what she wanted to do to make him feel better and what she had to do to continue her life. "I'd better go. I'll talk to you tomorrow." She whistled for Doogie and was out the door before Rob could say anything.

* * * *

He spent the next couple of hours pacing the house, walking back and forth between standing at the wall with their picture on it and working on an email message to her that he'd never send.

Was this truly the end? Should he just try to get on with his life and hope that she caught up with him, or should he keep trying to make something out of nothing and end up hurt anyway a few months or years down the road?

Could he spend the rest of his life in a vanilla relationship?

Then his words to her in the restaurant came back to him. He caressed her image in a photo.

He'd made a promise to her, as her Master, to always protect her, to take care of her.

If this was how she needed him to care for her, he'd do it. He wouldn't back out on a promise just because she couldn't remember it.

"No, Laura. I won't chicken out on you. No matter how long it takes for you to make up your mind, I won't give up."

Chapter Twenty-Five

Thursday morning dawned grey and cloudy, perfectly matching Laura's mood. She didn't bother making coffee, instead getting one at a gas station on the way to the shop.

She was alone, so why make a full pot?

It was a bittersweet thought.

She missed having Rob at the condo. It felt wrong without him there.

Maybe I made the wrong decision.

She brought Doogie to work with her and took some comfort in his quiet presence.

Steve arrived at the dive shop at seven, marveling in her early arrival. "Two days in a row. Are we working on a record?"

"What?"

"You are not a morning person."

"I'm not the girl I used to be."

Steve grimaced. "I didn't mean it like that."

"I know, but I'm getting tired of people telling me how I was and wasn't, how I should and shouldn't, and you know what? I'm beginning to wonder if this wasn't such a bad thing that happened to me after all."

"You don't mean that."

"Maybe I do." She defiantly glared at him until he shook his head.

"Oh, yeah, that's real smart, Laur. You used to be pretty bright, but now you're saying getting beaten to a bloody pulp and left for dead on your living room floor was manna from heaven? Screw your head on straight. And in case you haven't figured it out yet, I've known you long enough that I have the right to tell you when you've got your head stuck so far and firmly up your ass that you need a pry bar to remove it."

He stormed out the back door, slamming it so hard the glass rattled. She reddened, feeling stupid and chastised. Ten minutes later she gathered enough guts to follow him.

"I'm sorry."

He didn't look up from the bait tank where he was fishing dead shrimp out with a net and tossing them to waiting pelicans in the water.

"Yeah, well I'm sorry this happened to you, but we're all doing the best we can. We didn't take the physical beating you did, but it hurt us like hell seeing you like that and then having to get used to this new you."

He returned the net to its hook. "I'm not trying to say we're suffering more than you. That's *not* what I mean. You have got to be the bravest person I know, and I respect you for it. You just can't take your fear out on us because you've changed and we haven't. I know you don't know what we used to be like. We only want what's best for you, and we wouldn't lie to you."

She broke down as he held her, letting her cry on his shoulder as if she was ten years old again. After a few minutes she stepped away and wiped her face with her hands. "I'm sorry, Steve. It's just that I'm so scared."

"We all are, honey. It's not just your life that's lost. We're all kind of adrift here, too. You are a big part of all of our lives, and it hurts us to see you like this." He kissed her on the forehead and walked inside to ring up a customer.

She stood on the dock for a few more minutes, watching boats in the Intracoastal heading toward the Boca causeway bridge. This was one of the few things that felt familiar. She must have spent hours in this very place doing the same thing. The phone rang and after a moment, Steve opened the door and called her in.

"Who is it?"

He shrugged and she picked the receiver up. "Hello?"

"Hi, is this Laura?" The man's voice sounded vaguely familiar.

"Yes? Who's speaking please?"

"Oh, I'm sorry. This is Don Kern. I was in yesterday."

She thought back and it clicked. Those green eyes. "Oh, yes. Hi."

He cleared his throat. "Listen, I feel kind of stupid asking this, and you're probably going to say no, but before I totally lose my nerve would you mind having lunch with me today?"

It caught her totally unprepared.

So did her answer. "Sure."

They agreed on a restaurant in town and she said she'd meet him there at one. She hung up the phone before Steve returned, and when he asked who it was she said it was just a question about Saturday's class. He returned to the workroom and didn't notice how preoccupied she was.

She didn't know why she lied. And while it probably wasn't the wisest thing to do, having lunch with a stranger, it was in a public place.

There was something about Don Kern. Like her mind was working on a puzzle and didn't want to let go. She hadn't felt this way about anyone since the attack, and instinctively she felt she had to meet him, talk with him.

If it wasn't for customers she wouldn't have got any work done. The mysterious Don Kern clouded her mind. She didn't know if the troubling aspect was because she knew him or because she didn't.

He hadn't acted like he knew her, but she couldn't be sure. Her story was well-known around town. People came up to her in public and introduced themselves. Some of them people she'd known for years or went to school with, or who were friends of her parents, or customers. From their reaction, she guessed her shop was a fixture in the area.

At twelve thirty she hollered she was going out and left before Steve could question her. She made it to the restaurant with a few minutes to spare and grabbed a table. Don Kern showed up on time. He spotted her and smiled, and she watched him as he walked over.

She didn't feel the same emotions she had when she first met Rob in the hospital. And now she regretted this meeting.

Just...something she couldn't put her finger on.

"Hi." He sat at the table. "I can't believe you said yes."

His green eyes transfixed her. They were a supernatural intensity. She wondered if the color was natural or contacts. Regardless, there was something there, some feeling.

She couldn't say it was bad, but the longer she sat in his presence, she definitely wouldn't label it good.

"Well, I figured no harm, no foul," Laura lied. The waitress came and took their order and brought them water. "Dutch okay?"

"I asked you," he said, "so it's my treat."

"No offense, but I feel better paying my share."

He didn't argue the point and they spent the next few minutes chatting.

"Listen, I have to tell you something," Laura said. "I get the feeling that

I know you, but to be quite honest, you're not going to believe this."

"What's that?"

She related an abbreviated version of the story, and he looked shocked in the appropriate places. So far, so good. His hands didn't appear to be scarred, but this many weeks after the attack, that was a useless barometer.

"That's horrible. God, you're lucky to be alive."

"Sometimes I wonder."

He looked sheepish. "Okay, I have to admit, I do know you."

She tensed, feeling the comforting weight of the gun pressing into the small of her back against the chair. "Aha."

"We took a class together in college. USF, in Tampa."

She relaxed a little. "Go on."

"You sat in front of me in the lecture hall, three rows down, and I spent the entire semester looking at the back of your neck and too scared to ask you for your phone number."

Her tension levels dropped a little. "Why's that?"

"You were dating my Psych professor. I was afraid I'd get flunked if I hit on you. When I walked into the shop yesterday, I wasn't sure it was you. Then I realized it was, and it's been eating at me ever since. I figured I wasn't in college anymore and it was time to grow a set, you know?"

Whew. That explained a lot and made sense. She remembered reading something in the journals, reminiscing about dating a guy in college. "So tell me about yourself."

He expounded on the divorce story. He was a pharmaceutical company rep, based in Pt. Charlotte. Travelled on the road a lot, but the pay was good. He came home early one day and caught his ex in bed with someone else. When he asked for a divorce, she took all of his stuff and sold it or gave it away while he was out of town on business.

"So now I'm starting out all over again." He looked at her. "Well, okay, not in the same way you are. I guess I shouldn't feel sorry for myself, should I?"

"Actually, I don't feel too sorry for myself. I'm alive. I have people in my life who love me very much. I have a good job and financial security. I just have to create a new identity for myself if my old one doesn't return."

"What did the doctors say about that anyway?" He seemed hesitant to ask, but then again, so did most people who asked her that. "Will you get your memory back?"

"They say that the longer it takes the less likely it is it will."

"That sucks."

They finished about an hour later. When he asked her if he could take her out to dinner the next night, she fibbed and told him she already had plans, but they could talk after Saturday's class. He wrote his private cell number on his business card and handed it to her.

"Needless to say, you'd probably never catch me at home. You can always call me on my cell."

They settled the bill and he walked her to her car. "So, I guess I'll see you at class?"

She nodded. "Yep."

He extended his hand and she took it, briefly. His grip felt delicate, dry and soft, like shaking hands with a mannequin with balsa wood fingers. "Thanks for a wonderful lunch, Laura."

He closed her door for her. She drove back to the shop feeling strange, like a play had occurred in front of her and she had a central role in it but didn't know a single one of her lines.

And no one had cared.

She felt out of control. Nothing was going the way she thought it should, and why in heck was she even *having* lunch with this guy when she already told Rob she'd date him exclusively? Not to mention Kern was a total stranger to her.

It wasn't a date though. Just lunch.

Yes, just lunch. So why had she hid it from Steve? Did she used to cheat on Rob?

That scared her. She pulled over before getting to the shop and sat tightly gripping the steering wheel. Maybe there was a good reason why her memory wouldn't come back. Maybe there were parts of her life she didn't *want* to recall. Stuff she never even told Shayla.

Maybe there were parts of her personality best left undisturbed in the dark abyss of her missing mind.

Something like that, she couldn't imagine she'd even confide in Shayla about it had it happened.

What if her mind refused to release her past because it wasn't a very good past? What if she'd led some sort of dark double life?

Do I even deserve *Rob's love?*

If only she could find those journals.

Then again, maybe she was better off if she didn't.

Laura continued on to the shop and managed to make it through the rest of the day despite her knotted stomach. Then she had a thought.

She'd forgotten about going to the warehouse. Forgot since Rob told her about it, that was.

She went to Steve. "Do you have a key or whatever to get into the warehouse?"

"No, but you have it on your key ring." She brought it to him and he showed her which ones. "You feeling up to doing it?"

"Yeah. My ribs are fine. I need to find those journals."

"You want me to take you over there?"

"Please."

They left Sarah to close up the shop. Laura followed Steve in her truck. The warehouse complex was buried on a side street near Rotonda, a huge wagon wheel-shaped subdivision that looked deceptively easy to maneuver through on a map until you were actually inside it. He drove to the last building where the largest storage units were and took her key ring from her.

"Rob's got a set, too, and there's a spare set somewhere at your place. I don't know where you keep them, though."

He tried several padlock keys until he found the right ones. There were three units altogether, right next to each other, and she matched up her keys to the ones on his ring.

He opened all three doors for her. The units were jammed full with hundreds of boxes wedged in with walls of furniture. No wonder Rob hadn't wanted her coming here before.

Laura's breath left her. "Oh. My. Fucking. God. How am I supposed to sort through all of this?"

"Don't worry, sweetheart, you knew all this stuff when you put it in here. You numbered all the boxes and made a list with the contents so you could find stuff. If you'll look, you'll see they're stacked in numerical order."

They were. "I did?"

"Yep."

She breathed a sigh of relief. "Oh, good. Where's the list?"

"I don't know. Probably in your office at home."

She felt her spirits sink again. There would be no quick search with a successful outcome. She wondered if she was impatient in her former life.

"No idea for sure, huh?"

"You were pretty methodical with things like this. You have a file somewhere with all your stuff in it like your will, business and insurance paperwork, things like that."

As Laura thought about it, a light switched on in her brain. "You're right, I do. I remember seeing it. It's a red folder, the only red one. I didn't go through it because it was in the front of the 'morgue' drawer. I guess I considered all my clippings important, too."

"Every hurricane threat, that's one of the first things you packed. It makes sense you'd put that folder in with them. To you, those clippings were important."

Were. It almost sounded like she was dead and had just forgot to stop breathing. She'd even noticed more people taking about her in the past tense from before.

She mentally shook that thought off. "Okay, I'll have to find it and come back and look later."

"No problem." He locked the doors and she followed him out to Placida Road before going their separate ways. Doogie had been very patient while they were at the warehouse, sitting quietly in the passenger seat.

She looked over at him. "Feel like coming back here tonight and helping me search?"

Just the tip of his tail wagged. Anything his mistress wanted, he wanted. Labs were willing to follow.

She dug her phone out, which was still on silent from lunch. She'd missed several calls from Rob throughout the day and he'd left her two voice mails.

In one way it comforted her. On the other hand it annoyed her for some reason. She wasn't sure why.

Then she felt guilty. And that *definitely* annoyed her.

Was Rob controlling? Did he used to keep tabs on her every move?

Then again, he had good reason to be worried about her without Bill to keep an eye on her. Except she had the comforting weight of the 9mm in the holster against her back.

She couldn't spend her life waiting for people to babysit her.

And if that's what she needed to use to rebuild her life from the ground up, carrying a concealed weapon so she didn't spend every spare moment focused on what might happen, she'd do it.

But first, she wanted to find that list before she did anything else. Back at the condo, she found it in the red folder in her desk. Also her will, business papers, insurance policies, and other important documents. She changed into jeans and an old T-shirt and called Rob.

"Hi. I was afraid you'd forgot me."

She felt another twinge of guilt over lunch with Don Kern, and then anger and resentment for feeling guilty, and right on top of that guilt for feeling angry and resentful.

She suppressed a nervous laugh. "No, just had a busy day, that's all."

He sounded hesitant. "Did you want to have dinner or something tonight? Maybe go see a movie?"

"I'm sorry, but not tonight. I've got some boxes of stuff I want to sort through from the warehouse. I want to find the old journals."

"Do you want any help?"

She gripped the phone tightly. He sounded hopeful, but she wanted to be alone. She didn't know what she'd find in the journals, and if it wasn't something good, she didn't want Rob around.

"I'm not trying to blow you off, but I really want to do it by myself. I *need* to do it by myself."

"Are you sure it's okay to go over there alone?"

"I'm taking Doogie. And the gun. Steve already ran me over there earlier. It's fine."

He was quiet for a moment. "I understand." He sounded like he didn't understand, but was doing his best to give her the space she asked for.

She didn't want to leave him sounding hurt. "Listen, tomorrow night, here, I cook dinner for you. It's time to see if I can make something edible. Okay?"

His voice lightened. "That sounds good. What time?"

They agreed on a time and she hung up. Locating a flashlight, she leashed Doogie and grabbed her list.

The storage yard was open twenty-four hours and the manager lived in an apartment on the second floor of the office. Laura used another key to open the lock on the gate, and she locked it behind her, feeling a little more secure knowing a random stranger couldn't get in.

Her ribs didn't protest too much when she opened the door to the third storage unit, where her list indicated the boxes were located. She found a light switch and two sets of fluorescent four-bangers flickered to life. It wasn't as bright as she would've liked, but it was light enough to see. The list indicated boxes seventy-six through seventy-eight were her journals.

She searched through the stacks and realized the boxes she needed were buried in a back corner. It took her nearly an hour to unbury them, and she ripped them open.

Even the journals were numbered. Starting in her junior high years and going all the way until the computer journals started. From the number and the short date range each one contained, she wondered where the newer ones were. Based on everything she'd seen, she journaled nearly every day, even if it was only a couple of sentences about the weather or what she ate. It had been an ingrained habit for years.

It didn't make sense she would stop.

But where did I put the damn things? She didn't have time to think about it. It was almost dark and she wanted to get home. The three large boxes fit in the backseat of the truck. She locked the unit and loaded Doogie. A quick shower to rinse off the sweat and grime, then she spread out on the living room floor in an oversized T-shirt with a cup of hot tea and Doogie by her side.

Surreal did not begin to describe it. Laura decided the best way was to start at the beginning since she was missing the last few years anyway. The early journals were filled with handwriting that looked vaguely familiar, a narrow script that eventually morphed into the penmanship she now used.

Well, used *before*. Even her handwriting was different now when compared to notes and signatures on paperwork at the shop from the days before the attack.

She had normal teenage experiences, hated math, loved English. A crush on a boy a year older than herself. Then a month later, he was the anti-Christ. Two months after that, she accepted his invitation to a fall dance.

I don't understand why boys are soooo childish. They just drive me absolutely nuts. They are immature and absolutely not worth wasting time on. Why are they so cute?

Laura couldn't help but smile at the words. They brought back ghostly images—memories or fantasies, she wasn't sure. There was an easy feel, a flow to the rhythm of the narrative that entranced her and gripped her. Steve was right—she was a good writer. Even in junior high.

There was no school today, teacher work day (hurray!). I took the flats boat out by myself. I didn't go far, just out to Bull Bay. Didn't even take a fishing pole with me. I had my notebook and a pen. I wanted to write, work on my poetry and get a few ideas for my stories. I was the only one there, no one looking for snook, no one trolling for tarpon.

The air was heavy, sweet with the fecund smell of the mangrove roots and mud and salt. I watched a school of baitfish come in, followed soon after by a school of snook. Wished for a pole then! I watched them dancing on the surface, turning and spinning and ripping across the water. The only sounds the lapping of the water on the fiberglass hull, the fish splashing, the cry of a gull hitting the leftovers on the surface. Far away, the drone of an outboard had no more effect than a mosquito near my ear.

Wait, that was a mosquito near my ear. Remember the deet next time…

Laura made it all the way to her freshman year at Lemon Bay High when she yawned and looked at the clock. It was nearly two in the morning, and she realized she was about to fall asleep where she sat. It didn't make any sense to force herself through them all in one night.

She went to bed with Doogie on her heels.

Chapter Twenty-Six

There wasn't a girls' day that week because Leah, Tilly, and Loren had a meeting for a charity project they were involved with. When Laura awoke shortly before dawn, she returned to the journals.

At seven she called Steve and told him she wouldn't make it in and why. By eight o'clock, she'd worked her way to her junior year of college and had progressed from simple daily events to interspersing poetry and snippets of fiction. The writing improved as well.

Sunlight on the water,
gulls over the beach,
magical, a moment forever suspended in time
by the sheer power of its renewal
We should be so lucky
that nature could bring us back
to such beauty on a daily basis...

It was different from the magazine articles she'd already read. This was real and held a raw, magic quality that couldn't have been evident to her as a teenager, or even as an adult fresh into college. Maybe not ever. Why else would these have been sitting buried in the warehouse?

Perhaps before she didn't realize how good her writing was.
She?

Laura wondered if this was how people with multiple personalities felt. Even with most of her childhood intact, as well as other memory fragments returning, she still saw herself before as a different person whose mind she couldn't decipher other than what she read on the paper in front of her.

She also read, yes, about the guy she'd dated back then. A professor older than her by fifteen years. So at least that part of Don Kern's story matched up.

When Laura took a break at ten to stretch her back, she realized while she was trying to get her memories back by going through her old writings, she'd yet to look up any of Shayla's.

After a quick search on her laptop, she found the website for the magazine Shayla worked for. She started with the most recent entries. One was about a marine research facility in Sarasota, Mote Marine.

A few memories trickled back as she read, something about a charity dinner.

She closed her eyes. Rob was there, dressed in a nice suit, as were their friends. Tony and Shayla, Seth and Leah, and the others.

But nothing more than a few stray memories from that night.

Still, she'd take the win.

She kept reading the articles, regardless of the subject matter, hopefully desperate for another recent memory including Rob to slide home and lock into place.

It felt like all she did lately was search for elusive clues to who she used to be. Like trying to find a missing person standing right in front of her.

Maybe that's another reason Shayla and I are such good friends, because we're both writers.

That made sense. Even better, it felt right.

She spent two hours working through the magazine's online archives, sometimes getting sidetracked from Shayla's articles by another article that caught her eye.

Unfortunately, nothing she read was enough to trigger a lot of memories, but stray fragments gathered like dust to static electricity. That gave her hope.

Then she accidentally closed the search result page and had to run a new one on the site. She typed in Shayla's first name and hit enter before thinking about it.

Several new articles appeared, with a different last name of Pierce, but showing earlier dates than the first batch of articles.

Oh, stupid. That's her maiden name.

She immediately giggled as she realized what she'd thought, adding one more hash mark in the win column for the tiny victory.

I remembered her maiden name!

Pleased with herself, she continued reading, latest articles first and working backward through time.

When she reached the last several articles, apparently some of the first ones Shayla wrote for the publication, Laura realized they were part of a series.

She froze as she jumped back farther in time to open the first in the series.

Part of her wanted to close the browser window, forget she ever saw it.

And yet, something kept her reading. Refused to let her stop.

As her heart pounded, thudding hard and heavy in her chest like a gorilla trying to break free, she took a deep breath and started over from the beginning.

Last weekend, a group of friends gathered around a table at a local restaurant and discussed their week, their jobs, their lives, graciously inviting this writer into their inner circle. Nothing distinguished them from anyone else in the restaurant.

Except that an hour later, after dinner ended, they all met up at a local private BDSM dungeon club to continue their evening...

She wasn't an idiot. As she read, despite the way Shayla had disguised the identities of the people she met and talked with along the way, she easily recognized them.

Mental pictures flashed through her mind, of her friends, dressed in a wide variety of sexy clothes.

Or maybe I'm remembering?

Now she wasn't sure if that was a good or bad thing.

Her mind pulled her back to finding the corsets in her closet.

A numbing chill settled over her.

And the description of the man Shayla had paired up with—mentor and teacher at first, progressing into Dominant—left no doubt in Laura's mind it was Tony.

Several times during reading, she caught herself feeling at her throat for the necklace no longer there.

A necklace much like Shayla's, which Laura now suspected was a day collar.

Information and memories and emotions flooded into her brain, small chunks interconnected by their topic.

Confusion set in, overwhelming. As she finished reading the series she didn't realize she'd stood. It felt like she'd climbed almost to the top of an incredibly high stone wall hiding the answer to her prayers on its other side, and all she needed to do was get a little nudge to make it over and finally see what lay hidden.

She had difficulty trying to pull all her thoughts together. But she knew she couldn't talk to Rob about this. He'd never mentioned *any* of this. And Shayla had obviously been in on keeping this information from her.

As had their other "friends."

Of all of them, she suspected there was only one who would give her an unvarnished, completely truthful telling, answering any and all of her questions with blatant, perhaps even painful, honesty.

She grabbed her phone, which she put on silent mode and shoved into her purse, and her keys, and headed out the door after walking Doogie and setting the alarm.

* * * *

She had to stop and buy a street map, the tiny map app on her phone confusing her even more. After looking up the address, she headed north to Bradenton until she turned in at the driveway and pulled up to the guard shack marking the main entrance of the sprawling campus housing the national headquarters for Asher Insurance.

The guard held an electronic tablet. "Name and photo identification, please."

She swallowed hard, fighting back the panic struggling to take hold in her brain as she handed over her driver's license. "Laura Spaulding."

"Reason for your visit?"

"I…I'm not expected. I'm here to see Tony Daniels." It struck her that maybe she should have called first. What if he wasn't there? Or in a meeting.

She didn't care. She needed her questions answered by someone other than Rob.

By someone who, at an instinctive level, she trusted would not lie to her.

By someone she trusted, *period*.

She didn't know where that trust in Tony stemmed from, but it felt right. For now, she'd go with that.

The guard tapped her information into the tablet, walked to the back of her truck, presumably to note the tag number, and then snapped a picture of her driver's license with the tablet's built-in camera. "Just a moment, please."

He disappeared into the guard shack and returned less than minute later with a plastic ID badge. He handed it and her license to her, along with a paper parking pass. "Put the pass on your dash. He's in building C, which is that one there." He pointed it out, along with where to park. "Make sure to wear the badge while you're on campus. When you leave, we take them both back from you here."

"Thank you." He opened the gate for her and she found a parking spot not too far from the building.

Why am I here?

Now she wasn't sure if this was the greatest idea. So many things floated through her head, confusing, emotions and memories and overwhelming loss and need.

It threatened to swamp her.

She suspected of the people she'd met so far, it would be Tony who could help her make sense of it all.

Honestly.

The unvarnished truth.

Before she confronted Rob about any of it.

She left her phone and purse locked in the truck and made herself walk to the building. The front door was locked, but a man working at a reception desk raised his head and hit a buzzer when she rang the doorbell.

The lock clicked and she had to force herself to tug on the handle to open it. Somehow, despite no longer being able to feel her feet, she managed to walk across the lobby to the desk.

The man immediately frowned. "Are you all right, ma'am?"

No, I'm less all right than I can ever remember being in my life.

She choked back a snort of laughter at that, considering she could only clearly remember the last couple of weeks since waking up, with everything else disjointed and shattered across the realms of her mind.

Tears threatened. It was all she could do to force the words out. "I need to speak with Tony Daniels, please. It's...important."

He kept a wary eye on her while he grabbed a phone and spoke into it. "He'll be out in a minute," he said. "You can sit over there, if you'd like." He pointed to three chairs lined up on the other wall, but she shook her head.

"I'm okay. I'd rather stand."

Laura hated that she involuntarily flinched when she heard the inner door latch click loudly before it swung open and Tony walked out. When he spotted her, he immediately crossed the room to her side.

"Laura? What's wrong? Are you okay?"

Tears were imminent. She shook her head, not trusting her voice.

He grabbed her by the elbow and led her to another door. "No interruptions," he barked over his shoulder as he opened the door to what was a small conference room. He flipped on the light and closed the door behind them before guiding her to the nearest chair.

He pulled another chair around so he could sit in front of her. "Laura, what is it?" he asked, grabbing her hands. "What happened?"

Ragged sobs broke through. "I...read. I read Shayla's articles..." That was all she could choke out before she lost it, her fear and anger and loss pouring out of her like the rushing tide through the Boca Grande pass.

He let out a deep sigh but said nothing. Instead, he gently put his arms around her and let her cry on his shoulder. She didn't know how many minutes passed while she cried the worst of it out, until she finally sniffled back snot and tears and slowly sat up.

She let out a sharp laugh when he glanced down at the wet spot on his shirt before smirking at her.

"Does Rob know you're here?"

She shook her head while wiping at her cheeks with her hands.

"Stay here. I'll be right back."

He left the room. Alone with her thoughts, she realized this was probably not the greatest idea.

Ironically, it didn't escape her that she had no clue whether or not it was her *worst* idea ever.

He returned a few minutes later with a laptop case slung over his shoulder and a handful of tissues, the latter of which he passed to her. Then he held out a hand. "Give me your keys," he softly said.

She passed them over without comment.

"Where are we going?" she asked.

"To talk. I told them I had a family emergency." He shoved the keys in his pocket and held out his hand to her again. "Come on, sweetie. Let's go."

She felt a deeply embedded trust in him. She took his hand and let him lead her out of the building.

"Where are you parked?"

She pointed and he changed direction to lead her there. "What about your car?" she asked.

"Shayla can bring me back later to get it. Or she can bring me to work in the morning. You aren't an employee or a vendor. If we leave your truck here tonight, they'll tow it."

He walked her over to the passenger side and unlocked the door for her, waiting until she was in to close it. Then he walked around to the driver's door, put his laptop in the backseat, and climbed behind the wheel.

After turning in her parking pass and visitor's badge, he drove. She didn't speak, unsure what to even say.

Somehow she felt it was better to wait until he could give her his undivided attention.

He stopped at a convenience store, where he bought them a couple of cold bottles of water, as well as a small box of tissues. After another twenty minutes of driving, turning off a main road and into a residential area, they pulled into a park. It felt familiar, but the sign at the entrance identifying it as the De Soto National Memorial rang absolutely no bells in her memory.

There weren't many cars there, so he had no trouble finding a shady spot to park a ways from everyone else. Still feeling no need to fill the silence, she grabbed a wad of the tissues and followed him as he carried the bottles of water and led her toward a shaded bench near the water overlooking a bay.

Once they were settled on the bench, he cracked the top open on one of the bottles and passed it to her. "I texted Rob," he said. "I told him simply that you were with me and safe and that I'd call him as soon as I found out what was going on." He took a swallow from his own bottle. "And that he needed to not panic." A wry smile curved his face.

Laura had no trouble recognizing what Shayla saw in Tony. He exuded a presence that calmed her simply by being near him. Steady as a rock, ready to deal head-on with whatever he had to face.

Much like she felt about Rob.

Volume deserted her voice. She pushed the words out. "I need to know."

"We need to back up. You read the articles Shayla wrote about…?"

He didn't finish. She made herself look up at him. "BDSM."

He slowly nodded. "And?"

There wasn't any reason to try to hide her tears. "I need to know."

"About?"

"Can't you make this easy for me?"

"No," he gently said. "I won't lie to you, but I won't spoon-feed you your past, either. If you want me to tell you about my relationship with Shayla, I will. If you want me to tell you what I know of you and Rob, I will. If you want me to detail what happened between you and Rob, I can't, simply because most of your relationship happened beyond my view."

Carefully drawing in a shuddering breath, she asked, "How did I really meet you and Shayla?"

"Now *that*," he said in the same gentle tone, "is something I can tell you." He recounted, from his point of view, how Laura had emailed Shayla only a few months after they'd married. She'd read Shayla's articles and, like many others, finally grew the nerve to reach out for more information.

"We invited you to join us and Ross and Loren at dinner one evening. You looked like you were frightened out of your wits." He smiled. "Shay draped an arm around your shoulders and it was like the two of you had been sisters all your lives.

"We sat there talking for several hours, until nearly midnight and the restaurant was trying to close. You and Shay and Loren exchanged phone numbers and email addresses, and you were texting and calling each other until that weekend, when you came to Maria's Submission 101 class at the Venture.

"That's the name of the club," he clarified. "Shay and Loren met you there, and you went to dinner with all of us after class."

He took another swallow of his water. She didn't interrupt him while he gathered his thoughts. "You really wanted to throw yourself head-first into BDSM. Fortunately, the girls helped you temper that. Shay asked me if it'd be okay to offer for us to step forward as your protectors."

She had to ask. "What's that?"

"In terms of protocol for some, it means people had to go through me or Shay before they could play with you. That we were the ones who vetted your play partners. It didn't stop asshats on Fet from trying to contact you, but you had no problem dealing with and blocking those creeps on your own."

"Fet?"

"FetLife." He frowned. "You don't know any of this?"

She shook her head.

He slowly nodded before continuing. "Shay and I, jointly, gave you a collar of protection." He shrugged. "Again, just a formality. You didn't answer to me like a submissive, but it was an easy out for you to blow off people who gave you the creeps in real life. And it gave you a sense of safety."

Her hand once again went to her throat. He noticed.

He pulled out his phone, tapped and swiped through it, then held it up so she could see it.

It was a picture of her, Shayla, Loren, Leah, Tilly, and Clarisse. All of them wore bright, happy smiles, and they were dressed in corsets.

And they all wore collars.

Her hand went to her throat again as he took the phone back.

"I played with you a little. Nonsexual play," he quickly added. "No orgasm play. Landry did a little of that with you, but that was only at our private parties, not at the club. Panties on," he amended. "Fairly tame stuff. I did shibari on you, because you really enjoyed rope. Landry, Tilly, and Ross played with you some, impact play. You asked Seth and Leah to use a singletail on you."

Her hand stayed at her throat, her fingers wrapping around and resting there, a poor imitation for the ghostly feel of the collar she knew with certainty had been burned into her soul.

"After about six months, Rob started coming to the club with a friend of a friend. The two of you met. Even though all of us were cautious at first, we knew you'd met someone special. Rob was new to the scene but eager to learn. Responsibly. He took every class he could fit into his schedule. If work interfered with him going to a class, Ross, Seth, Landry, and I included him in some private parties at my house where we could work with him, and you, together."

"And?"

He smiled. "Shay said it best. Said she got the good kind of chills watching the two of you figure this out together. And even better, he didn't resent you deferring to me and wearing my collar of protection. He didn't ask me to hand you over, he didn't pressure you to say something to me. He just…"

He rubbed his goatee and moustache with his hand, apparently pondering his next words. "You two did start dating. I waited a couple of weeks after that to have Shay invite the two of you over to our house for dinner. Just the four of us. While you and Shay were in the kitchen, I took Rob out to the playroom on the pretense of wanting to show him some techniques. And he and I had a talk."

He took another swallow of water. The day was warm despite their shaded spot and the cool breeze. She watched as a small bead of sweat trickled down his temple.

"I cut right to the chase and asked him what he wanted to do with you. His answer was that he was willing to wait as long as it took for me to decide he was worthy of you. That he wasn't going to ask me, or you, to uncollar you. That he wanted to know you wanted him, and that I felt sure he was safe enough of a player to not to harm you."

A soft laugh escaped him. "In other words, he wanted you badly and was afraid of screwing it up. So I called you and Shay into the playroom and had you kneel in front of me and I point-blank asked you what you thought about Rob."

Another laugh, this one a little louder. He met her gaze. "Your face turned the deepest shade of red I've ever seen. Your voice got really soft and you said you were attracted to him. When I asked you why you hadn't told me before, you said—"

"I didn't want to make a mistake," she whispered. The words had magically appeared in her brain, even though she wasn't sure yet if she was truly remembering the night or just reliving it through Tony.

He cocked his head at her. "Yes. Go on."

She didn't think about it. She opened her mouth and let the words surprise her. "I wanted to wait until you said something to me about him because I was so attracted to him that it scared me."

He nodded but didn't interrupt.

The words continued. She didn't want to stop them in case the memories ceased. "I feel safe with you, and Landry, and Ross, and Seth. But I can't be with any of you and I know that. There's something in me that doesn't want to leave Rob's side after we play."

She closed her eyes, reliving it, looking up even as she'd looked up at Tony that night. "I was scared to ask you because of how right it always feels being with him. I was afraid he didn't feel like that about me. Or that I was mistaking sub frenzy for real feelings."

"Tell me what he said to you."

Tears squeezed out from under her closed lids and rolled down her cheeks. "It was a question. 'Do you think you can trust a noob who still isn't sure he knows what he's doing?'"

"And your response?"

"I trust Tony."

His voice sounded like it came from down a long tunnel. "Then what?"

She was no longer sitting on the bench. She was kneeling on the floor of a room she'd never seen, yet knew was Tony and Shayla's private playroom. "You reached down and uncollared me and said you felt perfectly safe entrusting me to his protection, if that was what I wanted. But that if I ever didn't feel safe, I was to come back to you, or Seth or Ross or Landry or Cris or Sully or Mac, any of you. I was to come to whoever I could get to first and tell one of you. That if you found out I wasn't safe and didn't say anything or come to one of you, that you would personally ensure that I would definitely regret it."

"Then what happened?"

"You turned to Rob and told him he had your full blessings and permissions." She laughed, finally opening her eyes. "You also told him they'd never find his body if he harmed me." She looked at him as she wiped at her eyes.

He wore a gentle smile. "And then?"

She started crying again. "He held out his hand to me and asked if I'd please consider being his submissive. And I said yes."

The large, gaping void of her memory was still there. Now, however, it felt like a safe, sturdy outcropping had suddenly appeared, holding the treasured memories safely in place, no longer swirling and lost in the abyss with so much else.

He opened his arms to her and she collapsed against him, sobbing again. "I said yes," she whispered. "I said yes and he pulled the necklace from his pocket and put it on me right then. He'd bought it a few days earlier to have it in case he ever got the chance to be with me."

Tony gently stroked her back. "Go on," he urged.

"We..." She stumbled, the memory a little blurry for a moment until locking firmly in place. "You and Shay stepped out for a few minutes," she said. "He promised to own up to mistakes, that he'd never violate a safeword, and he'd never lie to me. Then he admitted he thought he was falling in love with me."

She closed her eyes. "We hadn't had sex yet. And he promised to wait as long as it took, that he wouldn't pressure me to do anything I didn't want to do, and that he wouldn't control who I could or couldn't see or talk to, as long as I never lied to him."

Her eyes flew open. "Oh, *shit!*"

He laughed. "Yeees?"

She sat up, feeling heat fill her cheeks. Her hand flew to her mouth as she stared at Tony. His green eyes twinkled with devilish amusement.

"You came in to tell us dinner was ready and caught me giving him a blow job. I'd pushed him onto one of the spanking benches and yanked his zipper down."

He nodded, roaring with laughter. "Yes, you definitely weren't in a mood to wait. Lucky for you, he's perfectly happy with having a sexually aggressive submissive."

Her hand didn't move from her mouth. "Holy crap."

He reached out and tucked a strand of hair behind her ear. "Sweetie, in the past couple of years, believe me, that's one of the *tamest* things I've seen the two of you do at our private parties."

She finally dropped her hand. "That's what Shay meant." She realized she was calling her Shay now.

"Meant by what?"

"In the hospital, after the chaplain had left, I asked her if I was religious. She made a comment about..." She laughed. "Now I understand."

Tony smirked. "I've heard a lot of, 'Oh, gods!' come from you group of ladies. And some of the men."

She nodded, still laughing. "Yeah. I get it now. And now I get why she looked freaked out. Like she'd spilled the beans."

"Please don't be angry at Rob. Or Shay. Just like with the poly stuff, he didn't want to overwhelm you. I told her to handle this however Rob thought was best. That's what we all did."

Laura felt tears close again. It still surprised her that her moods could swing so wildly. "I'm not upset. I get it."

He glanced at his phone. "Speaking of, wait here." He got up and walked a few yards away before answering his phone and talking. After a few minutes, he ended the call and returned. He held out a hand to her. "Come on."

She let him help her up. "Where to?"

"Home. My home. Rob gets off at six and he's going to come straight to my house for dinner after he walks Doogie."

Chapter Twenty-Seven

A few more memories piggybacked on top of what she'd just rediscovered. As she looked out the passenger window while Tony drove, she considered all of it.

It all felt *right*.

It didn't tell her who attacked her, and it didn't give her back the bulk of her relationship with Rob, but it did make a few things flip into a different perspective that felt right. That had felt desperately missing in a way she hadn't been able to put her finger on before that moment.

To her, that was every bit as important as regaining all of her memories.

It also left her with a sense of peace she'd known had been missing in her life, but that she had attributed to her fear over the attacker still wandering around out there somewhere.

The overwhelming feeling that something besides her memories was missing.

She'd been missing her Master.

She no longer felt alone.

Closing her eyes, she took a deep breath.

Yes, the fear still hung there, dark and foreboding without memories to light the mass from below.

Now, however, instead of feeling like she walked along the edge of a crumbling cliff, risking a deathly plunge into the abyss, she felt securely tethered to a rock that wouldn't move.

Tethered heart and soul to Rob.

And to her adopted kinky kin.

Another deep breath filled her lungs with hope every bit as much as it did with air. No, she wasn't alone now. Her parents were dead, and she had Steve, Carol, and Bill, among others.

But her *family*, the ones she knew would drop everything to rush to her side, the ones she would do the same for, they were back in her heart, if not completely in her memories yet.

She had enough. She had enough to remember them, the love she had for all of them and the love she knew they had for her, and for Rob.

The trust they had for Rob to take care of her. To love her. To treat her well.

And she knew if they all had that kind of faith in him, so would she.

Shayla wasn't home yet and wouldn't be for at least an hour. He walked down to their bedroom and closed himself in to call her, leaving Laura alone in the living room.

She sat on the floor while Bagel and Cream, Tony and Shayla's cats, crawled all over her, head-butting her chin and rubbing their heads against her hands in their search for attention.

"Doogie's going to be all over you when you get home." She'd been sitting with her back to the hallway and Tony's voice startled her a little.

She looked over her shoulder at him and caught the smile on his face. He'd changed out of his jeans and work shirt into shorts and a T-shirt.

"He'll get over it. He's smelled them before…"

There was that head cock again as Tony watched her. Finally, when she didn't speak, he asked, "Another memory?"

"Sort of." She gave the cats one last scratch each before gently moving them from her lap so she could stand. "Some things aren't really memories, but when I say them it just feels right. Does that make sense?"

"I'm not a psychiatrist."

She thought about the appointment she'd been putting off making with Dr. Simpson. "I need to make another appointment with my shrink."

He nodded. "That would be the prudent thing to do."

She blurted it out. "What if I don't like who I was…before?"

He cocked his head the other direction. "I doubt that's going to be a problem. We all love you. Think of it this way. If you do find out stuff about yourself that you're not happy with, this is the perfect opportunity to make changes that will make you happy."

"Will Rob love the new me?"

He'd started walking toward the kitchen but stopped in his tracks and turned to face her. "Sweetie," he gently said, "Rob already loves you. I don't think there's much you could do to make him stop loving you."

* * * *

Laura felt more familiarity coming back as she helped Tony get dinner ready. To the point she was about to playfully run him out of the kitchen to get him out of her way when he recognized what was going on.

"You think you've got this under control?" he teased.

"Yeah, I think I can make baked ziti without help."

He grinned and took his glass of iced tea to one of the barstools pushed under the counter, where he took a seat to watch her. "Then go for it, missy."

She giggled, another memory falling into place. It had been his nickname for her once she wore his collar of protection. And still was. "Yes, *Sir*," she teased right back.

That got a full-throated laugh out of him. He held his glass up in a mock toast. "Now *that* was a great thing to hear come out of your mouth. I was wondering if we ever would."

They talked while she cooked. The few times she fumbled and paused, unable to remember where something was, he waited until she asked for prompting instead of jumping in to save her.

It didn't escape her notice that she was more familiar with their kitchen than she'd been with the one at her condo, at first.

"I spend a lot of time here with Shay, didn't I?"

"You do. It's been weird not having everybody together like we're used to."

She stopped, hands braced on the counter. "I'm sorry," she quietly said before another storm of tears surprised her.

He rounded the counter to hug her. "I didn't mean it like that. We just—"

"Didn't want to overwhelm me."

"Yeah." He made her look up at him. "Rob asked us to keep the BDSM stuff from you. And of course we did it. Because we were all willing to do whatever it took to help him and you."

"I hope this gets easier."

"I wish I had an answer for you there."

"Can we go to the club this weekend?"

He pursed his lips. She realized she recognized the expression but wasn't sure what it meant. Finally, he said, "That's up to Rob. I'm thinking no. It's too soon."

"But what if it helps me get my memory back?"

"But what if it doesn't, and overwhelms you?" He rested his hands on her shoulders. "Look, I'll talk to everyone. Maybe we can have a private party here Saturday night. I'm sure Shayla will be up for it. That way, it's a small, controlled environment, and you and Rob can have privacy as you need it."

She nodded.

Shayla rushed in from work and practically knocked Laura over as she threw her arms around her. "Are you okay?"

"I'm okay. Sorry I borrowed Tony."

"Hey, it's all right." Shayla frowned. "Did anything else come back?"

"I think enough did. For now." She took a deep breath. "For starters. It has to be enough."

Shayla went to put her things away and change clothes. As her friend reappeared in a tank top and shorts, with a leather collar locked around her neck, Laura once again reached up to her own throat.

She felt naked despite her clothes.

The irony did not escape her.

Tony watched her. "You all right?"

She slowly shook her head. "No." She felt tears welling up in her eyes again and silently cursed her inability not to cry. "He took my day collar. That fucker stole it." She walked over to where they kept a roll of paper towels hanging under the upper cabinets and ripped off a couple of sheets. Angrily, she blew her nose.

Tony rounded the counter, but didn't touch her. "Do you remember him?"

She froze as she realized why he'd asked it, but another wave of frustration washed through her. "No." She blew her nose again. "I can't remember a face. Just that it was a guy." She thought about it some more. "Shorter than Rob but taller than me."

They watched her, not interrupting.

She closed her eyes and the memory of opening her front door and having it shoved open, surprising her, came to mind. But the person in the doorway still remained a large, human-shaped shadow.

"That's all," she finally said. "I did open the door for him. He caught me by surprise when I did, but I don't remember him."

* * * *

Rob forced himself not to speed. Once Tony had convinced him Laura was safe and with them, and that they wouldn't let her out of their sight until he got there, he calmed down.

Tony's latest text indicated she'd remembered a few more things but didn't elaborate.

Recriminations swam through his mind. *I should have told her. I should have been up front with her.*

Would she now hate him for holding so much back, regardless of his reasoning?

He felt the bulk of her play collar in his pocket, rubbing against his leg. Had he totally botched their future together? Should he have severed ties with all their kinky friends until she'd decided if she even wanted him?

He would have hated doing that, but he'd do anything for her.

It was nearly seven when he pulled into their driveway behind Laura's truck and parked. He didn't bother knocking when he got there, going straight inside.

The three of them were standing in the kitchen talking. As soon as Laura saw him, he started to say something but she flew into his arms, crying, clinging to him.

Tony walked over and grabbed his upper arm. "Come on."

He was shocked when Tony led them through the laundry room into the playroom that sat just off the garage.

Shayla trailed behind, not saying anything, but carrying a box of tissues in her hand.

"Rob, I want you to stand right about…here," Tony said, positioning him.

Tony took Shayla's hand and made her release Rob. "You, kneel here."

Rob's heart pounded in his chest as he watched.

Laura knelt in front of Tony.

"Laura, look at me."

She looked up at Tony.

"Tell him what you remembered."

Shayla ducked in to hand her a tissue before darting back to Tony's side.

Laura wiped at her cheeks as she looked up at Rob. "I remember that night."

"The attack?"

She shook her head. "No."

Suddenly, he couldn't suck in a breath. He didn't dare risk interrupting. His gut tightened and his knees felt like they'd let go any second.

"*Tell* him, Laura," Tony said.

Rob realized he was using his "Dom voice." The tone he used in a scene.

Tony hadn't used that tone with Laura since…

He swallowed hard.

Tears rolled down her cheeks. "The bastard stole my day collar. The one you gave me that night. When you asked me to be your submissive."

He started to reach for her but Tony held out a restraining arm. "Wait," he softly said. "Let her say it. It might help."

"Tony took his play collar off me that night and you gave me my day collar." She wiped at her eyes again. "Ever since I first saw Shay in the hospital, it felt like something was missing. You said it was a necklace, but it felt like more. Now I know why."

Rob nodded but didn't speak. He felt the collar through his pants and slid his hand into his pocket to wrap his fingers around it.

"I trust you," she said to Rob. "I trust you, and I want it back. I want your collar. I *need* it. I want at least that feeling of safety back because I don't want that bastard to steal that from me, too. I want to be your submissive."

Her expression froze for a second, her body rigid. "I…" Her eyes closed.

Every muscle in his body tensed.

"I was going to ask you…" She faltered over the words as she struggled with the memory. "I wanted you to make me your slave," she finally whispered before looking up at him again.

He nodded.

"Is that what you want, Laura?" Tony asked. "You need to tell him."

* * * *

Laura stared up at Rob. "I've never wanted anything more in my life," she said.

Tony dropped his arm. "Rob?"

Rob pulled something out of his pocket and held it up for her to see.

A blinding flash of memories swept through her, of all the times he'd buckled that same play collar around her neck, at home or before going to the club, or at a private party here or at Seth's or at Tilly's or anywhere with their friends.

Their family.

Rob's voice sounded choked. "Will you please do me the honor of being my slave?"

She nodded. "Yes, Sir."

He knelt in front of her, his eyes never leaving hers as he buckled the collar around her neck. Then the corner of his mouth quirked in a smile. "I should beat your ass for getting your hair cut."

She laughed and fell into his arms, crying happy tears this time. "I'm sorry, Sir. I plead amnesia."

It felt so good, his arms around her, holding her, his hands stroking her back.

Her Master.

"It's all right, sweetheart," he said. "I forgive you. I'll always forgive you."

She wasn't sure exactly when Tony and Shay stepped out to give them privacy, but Shay had left the box of tissues on one of the spanking benches. Rob stood and helped her to her feet. "You're still my beautiful baby girl. If you want it short, you can have it short. It's your hair."

She rested her head against his chest. "No, Sir. I don't want it short." She'd forgotten how good it felt when he grabbed a handful of hair in his fist and led her around by it. "Why haven't you called me that before?"

"Called you what?"

"Baby girl."

"I did, in the hospital, when you first woke up. When you sort of reacted badly, I thought I shouldn't."

Thinking back, she remembered she had. "I'm sorry."

He kissed her forehead. "Stop apologizing."

Now there was something she wanted to do to round off the recovered memories. No, not everything was there with her relationship with him, but one thing was.

She looked up at him before pushing him back against one of the spanking benches. She grinned as she sank to her knees again and worked on his belt.

He grinned, too, and didn't bother stopping her. His cock instantly grew hard, making it difficult to work the zipper down, but she finally had him freed from his briefs.

Slowly, she wrapped her fingers around his shaft. Their gazes locked as she flicked her tongue out and licked at the head. The past and present merged as she remembered what she'd said to him that night.

"I've been dying to do this to you, Sir." She slowly engulfed his cock in her mouth, licking, teasing, tasting, her gaze not leaving his.

He reached down and stroked her cheek. "Such a good girl," he cooed.

It only served to fire her need. She sucked him deep into her mouth, her other hand cupping his sac and gently rolling it against her palm as she worked his cock. She wanted to make him come, wanted to drain his balls.

Wanted to taste him.

It didn't take long before his shaft tightened and his entire body tensed. "Get ready," he warned just before she felt his balls draw up tight and fill her mouth with his cum.

She closed her eyes, moaning as she swallowed, enjoying this, savoring it, wishing the moment would never end.

Then he laughed.

"What?" She looked up at him.

"At least Tony didn't interrupt us this time."

* * * *

Rob wasn't done, however. He wasn't about to waste a moment's time. He ordered her to strip and bent her over the same spanking bench, where he placed his left hand on the back of her neck to pin her down before spanking her with his bare hand.

When he began lightly slapping her pussy, she closed her eyes and moaned, arching her back to get more contact.

"Such a good girl," he said. "Don't move." He left her side. She heard him rummaging around for a moment before he returned. Then the sound of plastic rustling.

She glanced back and saw he was hard again and had rolled a condom onto his cock.

She looked up at him. "Sir, we don't use condoms."

"Are you on the pill again?"

She started to answer, then her mouth snapped shut. No, she'd seen the packages in her medicine cabinet, but hadn't thought about them. "Sorry, Sir."

He laughed and slapped her ass, a little bit of sting but making her pussy clench again with need. "No apologies tonight."

He stood behind her and she held still, moaning as he slid his cock deep inside her.

This was something they hadn't done that first night, but it was something they'd done plenty of other times, right here on this bench.

And *damn*, did it feel *good*.

He filled her, big enough to make her pleasantly ache in the good way as his cock stretched her cunt.

Once he was buried deep inside her, he fell still and she felt him reach for something.

She barely had time to process the sound of the *click* before a low hum filled the room and he pressed the vibrator against her clit.

The moan that rolled out of her as her orgasm exploded came from a totally primitive place inside her. Her fingers locked around the bench's uprights as she fucked herself back onto his cock. He refused to let up, making her take it, forcing several orgasms out of her.

"You can do it, baby girl," he urged, amusement tingeing his voice. "You've taken this and more. You're just a little out of practice is all."

He was right about that. It wasn't uncommon for him to tie her up and force her to come for a solid hour or more before finally giving in to her begging and fucking her.

He took a couple of hard strokes inside her, triggering another round of orgasms that threatened to take her breath away.

"That's it. Such a good girl. Fuck my cock, baby."

She did, knowing she had no choice but to obey him and let him do what he wanted to her body.

She wouldn't have it any other way.

She didn't know how long he kept her there, forcing her to come with his cock buried inside her, but she collapsed onto the bench when he turned the vibrator off, set it aside, and grabbed her by the hips.

"I'll take it easy on you tonight." He fucked her, hard and fast, and again she had to hold on to the bench, this time to keep from falling off as the sound of his thighs slapping against her ass filled the room.

One more sweet shudder rolled through her as her pussy clamped down on him again.

"Oh, *good* girl," he managed, breathless. Then he plunged hard and deep one final time, a groan escaping him as he fell still inside her. He braced himself against the bench, the front of his shirt rubbing along her naked back as he nibbled the nape of her neck.

The feeling of his breath against her flesh felt so good, so right, she wanted to cry.

This is what she'd been missing above all.

Him.

After he caught his breath he got up and stepped into the powder room to clean up before returning to her and gathering her into his arms. "I could not have made it through dinner if I didn't do that to you first," he said with a playful smile.

She rested her forehead against him. "Yes, Sir. Me, either."

* * * *

Tony looked amused when they emerged from the playroom a few minutes later. Rob had helped Laura clean up and get dressed, but he made her wear her play collar.

Shay rushed into the kitchen. "Well?"

"*Pet*," Tony called in a warning tone from the living room, where he sat on the couch watching TV.

Laura threw her arms around her friend. "It's all good," she assured her.

After dinner, Rob followed her back to the condo. While she waited at a stop light, she looked down at her hands.

The solitaire glittered in the dim light. She held out her hands, palms down, and stared at them. The pale circle of flesh she'd had when first waking up in the hospital had blended into the rest of her finger on her left hand. She thought about it for several minutes and switched the ring from her right to her left.

That felt better.

Much better.

Chapter Twenty-Eight

They'd collapsed into bed when they got home, both of them exhausted. Friday morning, she was awake a little after five in the morning and watched Rob while he slept.

Her Sir. Her Master.

Unfortunately, he had to go to work that morning to work two back-to-back shifts, and he wouldn't be home until Sunday morning.

In everything that happened the night before, she hadn't told him about her lunch with Don Kern and knew she had to do it as soon as possible. The more she thought about it, the worse she felt even though she hadn't done anything improper.

She climbed out of bed, naked except for her collar, and went to start the coffee.

When Rob made it out to the kitchen a short while later, he gave her a kiss and then stared at her for a moment. "What's wrong?"

"Is it that obvious?"

He nodded.

She told him the story, starting when Don Kern walked into the dive shop. Rob looked troubled and stared at the floor for a moment before speaking.

"Is he someone you want to go out with? Because if you do—"

"No, Sir!" She grabbed his hand and squeezed. "Just the opposite. The good thing about all this is that it made me realize something."

"What's that?"

She held her left hand up. "I needed to put this back where it belonged."

Tears flooded his eyes as he folded her into his arms and held her. She stood with him like that until Doogie decided that his people needed cheering up and stuck his cold wet nose against Rob's bare ass.

"Hey, personal space, doggie." He ran his hand up her back, to the base of her neck where he grabbed her hair. His tone changed, dropping. "Who do you belong to, baby girl?"

Need and desire swept through her. "You, Sir," she said in a tiny voice.

Now she recognized it. The beginning of subspace. Rob had always been able to get her there just with his tone of voice.

He nuzzled the base of her neck. "Who owns you?"

A soft, mewling sound escaped her. "You, Sir."

He feathered his lips along the base of her throat, up to the side of her neck, where it met her shoulder. He gently nipped. "Who do you want to own you?"

"You, Sir. Only You."

His breath felt hot against her flesh. When he bit down, hard, she let out a little cry and had to hold on to him because her knees wanted to give out. She felt her juices coating the insides of her thighs, her need thick and heavy for him even as the sweet pain swept through her. He bit and sucked and she knew by the time he finished she'd be sporting one hell of a hickey there that would last for several days, at least.

It wouldn't be the first time, although usually he did it where her clothes would cover the mark.

When he finally released her with his teeth, he examined his handiwork with a pleased smile on his face.

"Today and tomorrow, if you go into the shop, you wear a shirt that will show off that mark nicely."

She clung to him, wishing she could keep him there with her all day. "Yes, Sir."

"Sunday, I want you to arrange to stay home."

"Yes, Sir."

He kissed her, hard and deep and full of the passion she hadn't felt until yesterday. "Sunday, we're going over to the house after I wake up. All our toys are over there. And I'm going to give my girl one hell of a spanking. You're going to feel it for several days every time you sit down."

She wanted to feel it right then! "Yes, Sir!"

He hooked a finger through the D-ring on her collar and tugged on it, leading her over to the kitchen sink, where he pushed her forward over the counter.

"Legs spread."

She did, her breath coming in hitching gasps. She heard him open a drawer and rummage around before closing it again. Then the feel of his hand on the back of her neck, fingers around her collar, holding her down.

"This is just a reminder." She knew immediately he'd grabbed a wooden spoon, and he smacked her several times with it on the ass, stingy, but not nearly hard enough to leave marks.

Then she heard him lay it on the counter. His free hand appeared between her legs, gently probing.

"Oh, you're a very wet girl." He sounded amused.

"Yes, Sir," she admitted.

He plunged two fingers inside her cunt, still holding her in place with her collar, and finger-fucked her hard and fast.

"Don't you dare come, baby girl," he warned. "If you do, you're going to get some not-fun strokes from my belt."

She tried to hold on to the sink, her knees weak from his words and tone and even the threat. He also knew exactly where to thrust, what sweet spots inside her would take her over the edge, and his other fingers hit her swollen and throbbing clit with every stroke.

Just when she wasn't sure she was going to be able to obey him and hang on, he stopped, making her gasp and whine when he pulled his hand from her cunt.

He yanked her up from the sink. "Knees."

She dropped like a sinking stone in front of him, looking up.

His cock jutted out, rock hard, a drop of pre-cum pearling at the slit at the end.

She wanted to lick it off and knew if she didn't wait for permission that could mean more punishment.

She didn't care. She wanted it all.

"Open."

She did, and he stuck his fingers in her mouth. She knew what he wanted and didn't lose eye contact with him as she licked her juices off his fingers.

His cock twitched in time with her mouth, making him smile. He cradled her chin with his other hand. "Such a good girl," he cooed, sending another flood of juices to her pussy.

When he pulled his hand out of her mouth he replaced it with his cock.

This time, he gathered her hair in his hands and took full control, fucking her mouth the way he liked while she wrapped her hands around his thighs and held on.

"Get ready," he grunted just before his cock hardened and exploded, rewarding her with a mouthful of his cum as his balls emptied.

She felt him shudder. He grabbed one of the chairs and pulled it over, not removing his cock from her mouth, cradling her head in his lap. He stroked her hair. "Good girl," he whispered. "Such a good girl."

Her eyes dropped closed. She could do this for the rest of her life, sitting collared at his feet, doing this.

Doing anything he asked of her.

This was the peace that had been missing in her life, beyond the memories. *This* was the missed context, the ability to discuss all things vanilla and kinky with her friends and knowing they understood exactly where her mind was at.

It was *this*.

It was *Him*.

She let out a content sigh.

After a couple of minutes, he tapped her on the head and made her sit up and look at him.

He leaned forward in the chair and caught the ring on her collar with his finger. "Such a good girl."

"Thank You, Sir."

He grinned. "Oh, you thank me *now*." He reached between her legs with his free hand to play with her clit. "You don't get to come until Sunday."

Her breath caught. "What?"

"Is that a problem?"

Her clit throbbed, especially since he was now rolling it between his thumb and forefinger. "But…"

"Do you accept this punishment, baby girl?"

She didn't have a choice. She wouldn't disappoint him. "Yes, Sir," she whispered.

He released her clit, but then started tormenting her nipples, going back and forth between them until they were both taut, aching peaks.

"No playing with yourself unless I tell you to. And no orgasms. If you come without permission, it's twenty-five hard ones with the big paddle.

Got it?"

At that point she was so horny she thought it might be worth it. "Yes, Sir."

He kissed her. "Good girl."

* * * *

Rob sent Laura frequent text messages all throughout the day, making sure to keep her horny and on edge. As instructed, she wore a shirt that would expose the hickey, but she left her hair down and other than Sarah giving her a friendly ribbing about it, no one else commented.

Friday night, without Rob's comforting, solid presence in bed next to her, dreams plagued her unlike any other.

These weren't mere dreams, though. She suspected they were true memories of past events. When she awoke Saturday morning, she was reluctant to leave the bed for fear of not recovering any more information. Most of what she picked up was older stuff, college years, but included some very fond memories of her parents and Bill.

And Rob.

She brewed a pot of coffee, then it hit her.

Don Kern.

This was the morning of his class.

The thought filled her with trepidation. She didn't know what she felt about the man with the green eyes, but now that she was rebuilding her relationship with Rob she didn't feel right about seeing Don Kern, even platonically.

She didn't want anyone but her Master.

At class she would simply tell him she wouldn't feel comfortable making plans with him. He would either understand or not.

Besides, Steve was teaching the class. She could easily make herself unavailable.

A hope filled her that she had begun to think wasn't possible. The light at the end of the tunnel was no longer an oncoming train.

It was conceivable she'd make it through this okay.

She took her time getting ready. By the time she reached the shop, Steve and the class were already on the boat and gone.

Sarah laughed. "Boy, there was one guy who seemed disappointed you weren't teaching the class."

Laura froze. "What do you mean?"

"What's his name, Don? He asked for you specifically. I guess he thought you were teaching."

A chill settled over her, wiping out the morning's progress with her mood. "If he doesn't like it, that's tough. I never told him I was going to be the instructor."

"Hey, don't get upset. He just seems to have a thing for you is all. He's not the first and won't be the last, you know that. Sometimes we get people like that. They get their card, they go out a couple of times on the boat, and once they realize diving's not *Sea Hunt* and that you don't have the slightest bit of interest in them other than making sure they don't die on their check-out dive, they quit being creepy."

"Yeah, you're right." One of the things she remembered was Sarah was someone she could always talk to and confide in without worrying about it getting around. "Listen, I've got to talk to someone."

"STS?"

"Huh?"

Sarah laughed. "Sworn to secrecy stuff?"

"Yeah, something like that." She recounted Don Kern's initial visit to the store, the call, and her lunch with him. She also mentioned recovering a lot of her memories about Rob, while leaving out the BDSM aspect.

When she finished telling it, Sarah let out a breath.

"Well, that makes it a little different." She looked at Laura. "Why the hell did you go to lunch with him and not tell anyone?"

Laura shook her head. "I don't know. I wish I hadn't now. I just had this…feeling."

"Were you attracted to him?"

"Not like that."

Sarah chewed on her lip. "He might really be bent out of shape then."

"I laid it all out for him at lunch. And I never promised him dinner. I said we'd talk after class, that's all."

"Yeah, but the difference in what you said and what he heard could be the equivalent between English and Swahili for all you know." She thought about it for a moment. "Do you want to blow and let me handle him for you?"

"Is that something I would have done?"

Before?

The word was implied but ever-present.

"No, you would have told him to go take a flying jump off a really short pier." She smiled. "Or you would have introduced him to Rob, who would have assisted him off the pier himself. You also probably wouldn't have gone out to lunch alone with the guy, either."

"Is Rob jealous?"

"Oh no, that's not what I meant at all. Rob's always very secure with you. You're joined at the heart, not the hip. He's just...you own his heart. If you asked him to bring you the moon on a string he would hijack the space shuttle without a second thought."

That made her feel worse, not better. *Guilty guilty guilty.* "Why don't you just tell Mr. Kern that my fiancé came and picked me up?" Laura grabbed her purse and some paperwork and headed for the door. "And don't give him my home or cell number."

"Duh and a half. Besides, you're unlisted."

It surprised her that Sarah knew. "What?"

"Well, yeah. Everyone here knows that. It's SOP. No one gives out your home number or your private cell. Something about a creep a few years ago wouldn't quit calling you."

Frozen in her tracks, she forced herself to turn completely to face Sarah. "What?"

Sarah saw the look on her face. "What's wrong?"

"Why did you say I got an unlisted number?"

Sarah realized Laura didn't know this. "Years ago, before you met Rob and when you were still living with your parents. You dated some guy in college, but then later, you dated him again for a little while. When you broke up with him the second time, he didn't want to take no for an answer at first. Your dad got the house number changed and had it unlisted. When you moved to your condo you kept your number unlisted. Rob and everyone who works here know that."

She hadn't read anything about the second relationship with the guy in the journals. Then again, there was still a lot she hadn't read through yet, in both the older handwritten journals and the newer computerized ones. "Are you sure they knew? I mean about why it was unlisted?"

She thought back. "I'm pretty sure."

"Do you remember the guy's name?"

She shook her head. "No, not offhand. Steve might. He threw the guy out of the shop one day when your dad wasn't here and the guy wouldn't leave. That was before I worked here." She frowned. "You're not thinking Don Kern is that guy, are you?"

Laura considered it. "No, I guess not. If Steve threw the guy out, I'm sure he'd remember him."

On the way home she checked her mirror every few seconds. Any car that pulled out behind her she watched like a hawk, and almost rear-ended someone when she took her eyes off the road for too long. When she walked in the door she called Det. Thomas and left a message asking him to call her. She double-checked her locks, set the alarm, and called Rob. When she got his voice mail, she left him a message to call her.

Who made the hang-up call after she got home from the hospital? They assumed it was the attacker. Was it? If the number had been changed, that meant it would rule out the old boyfriend, right? Or was her attacker someone close to her who she gave her phone number to? Or was it just a coincidence?

Her cell phone rang ten minutes later when Thomas returned her call.

"Listen, this might not be anything. I just found this out today and thought I should tell you." She related the conversation with Sarah and her thoughts on the situation.

"You're talking about"—she heard papers rustling—"Kevin Baldwin. Psych professor at USF in Tampa. Steve and Carol already told me about him and we checked him out. He was in front of a class of fifty people that ended at eight o'clock that night, and went with a group of other professors and students to a local bar after. His wife swears he was home by twelve, the friends say he didn't leave until after eleven, and his credit card receipt for the bar tab was date stamped 11:20 p.m. There's no way he could be your attacker. Tampa's a good two-hour one-way trip. Plus he was uninjured. I saw this guy myself. Unless he killed you first, there's no way he could have hurt you the way the attacker did. This guy's maybe one-fifty soaking wet, about five ten. He's a beanpole. If he turned sideways, he'd disappear."

"Okay, I get the message." She sighed. "I'm sorry I bothered you."

"No, listen, anything you think of, and I mean anything, call me. It might not be important, but then again it could turn out to be the one thing we need to break the case."

"No new leads yet?"

"I'm afraid not."

"Okay then. Thanks for your time." She ended the call feeling disappointed and somewhat relieved.

A smile crept across her face as she stared at her engagement ring, finally back where it belonged on her left hand.

If nothing else, at least she had her priorities straight and had Rob back where he belonged in her life.

Chapter Twenty-Nine

Rob called her an hour later, out of breath and sounding hoarse. "Hey, what's wrong?"

"Nothing's wrong, Sir. I just wanted to call. Are you okay?"

"Yeah, got a lungful of smoke at a brush fire over in Gulf Cove. I'm okay. Good news is Cap's sending me home early. How about you call us in a pizza and we watch zombie movies on the couch?"

She'd meant to tell him about playing hooky from the shop to avoid Don Kern, but the news that they would get to be together sooner than she thought shoved it out of her brain. "Don't tell me." She thought about it. "Sausage and mushrooms?"

"That's my girl." She couldn't tell if he sounded hoarse from the smoke or just choked up. "I'll be there at five. Love you, baby girl."

She squeezed the receiver tightly. "Love you, too, Sir." She no sooner ended the call when her cell rang again from the dive shop's number.

Sarah sounded the all clear. "I think Steve was wondering what was going on but the guy seemed to take it okay."

"What did you say?"

"He asked me if you were around and I told him that you had been here, but your fiancé picked you up earlier."

"That's it? Wow, that was easy."

"He did ask to have you call him. Left me a card with his cell number."

"Ugh. Not so easy."

"This guy doesn't strike me as easy to blow off." Sarah paused. "Tell you the truth, there's something not nice about him."

"Why's that?"

"I don't know. It's just a creepy feeling I get. Like the smile on his lips doesn't go any further than his teeth, you know what I mean? It's a mask."

"I won't be in tomorrow. Rob's got the day off and I really need to spend the time with him. Can you guys handle the shop without me?" Laura had learned it wasn't uncommon for her to work weekends and take days off during the week, especially if Rob was on duty. She'd always tailored her schedule around his as much as she could. Weekends were their busiest time, but there were plenty of others to fill in for her absence.

"Sure, no sweat. Take it easy, lay low. I'll handle Mr. Green Eyes if he comes back."

* * * *

She met Rob at the door wearing one of his T-shirts, her collar, and nothing else, which made him smile in a way that thrilled her.

He hooked his finger through the D-ring in the front of the collar and pulled her in for a kiss. "That's a beautiful sight."

"Thank you, Sir."

"The only thing better would be naked."

"The pizza hasn't arrived yet."

He grinned and delivered a playful swat to her bare ass, which the T-shirt just barely covered. "Then you'd better lose that shirt as soon as it does."

It felt like she was once again complete, even without the missing memories. "Yes, Sir."

Rob grabbed a quick shower. Once the pizza was delivered, she ditched the shirt as ordered. They sat at the coffee table and she asked him about his day while they ate. He told her about the fire, and a wreck earlier that morning that sent a teenager to the hospital with non-life-threatening injuries.

He studied her. "Okay, tell me what's going on. There's something on your mind."

She filled him in on what Sarah said about Don Kern.

He frowned. "Do you want me to call this guy for you?"

"No, Sir. I think it'll be okay. I just wanted you to know."

"Good girl." He paused. "Where's your gun?"

"In the drawer next to the bed."

He nodded. "New order. No matter what, until this is settled, if you're not home you better be wearing that gun. Unless, you know, you're at the courthouse or airport or something. But other than that, I catch you without it, you're getting fifty with a cane. And I don't mean funishment. Got it?"

She quickly nodded. "Yes, Sir." She hated punishment with the cane. And she knew from the serious look on his face that he meant it.

He smiled. "Wait for me on the bed. Hands and knees."

She jumped to do it, her clit throbbing as she heard him putting the pizza away in the kitchen. Her juices were already flowing, her libido in a constant simmer since the blow job the morning before.

A few minutes later, he walked down the hall and stood in the doorway.

"Now there's the most beautiful sight in the world."

She heard the sound of him dropping his clothes to the floor. He walked behind her and reached out and stroked her ass. "Light play tonight. It seems Tom and his wife next door can hear more of our play than we thought."

Her face heated, but not from anticipation. "Yikes."

"Yeah." He lightly slapped her ass once, then stroked her again. "And I'm pretty tired. Tomorrow, at the house, we'll make up for lost time."

He stepped away and returned a moment later. He rolled a condom on and knelt behind her on the bed. "You can come as much as you want, baby girl."

She let out a gasp as he drove his cock home, hard and deep inside her.

That made him chuckle. "Surprise you?"

"Uh-huh!" She thrust back against him, trying to get him to start moving again, but he wasn't ready to. He reached around and found her clit with his fingers.

"That's what I wanted," he said. He started pinching it, rolling it between his fingers and quickly making her explode around his cock.

She buried her face in the pillow to muffle her screams. Damn it felt good to come! It felt even better to come impaled on his cock, her cunt walls squeezing it against her G-spot while he forced another orgasm out of her.

Pleasure and pain. She loved just a pinch of sadism with her sex, enough to push her over the edge again and again as he forced her to take what he wanted her to take, trusting him to know her body better than she did.

Usually he did it with a vibrator, but tonight she was so horny and desperate he'd had no trouble using his talented fingers on her.

After she'd lost count, he slapped her ass and started fucking her, hard and fast. As she had on the bench, that made her come one more time.

"Good girl," he said, grunting the words as he thrust until he came and filled the condom.

They flopped over onto their sides, his cock still inside her. He wrapped his arms around her and held her. "It's good to have you back, baby girl."

"I'm not back all the way, Sir."

"You're back enough. That's all I care about. I have *you* back."

After a few minutes he got out of bed and cleaned up. She ducked into the bathroom, too, then climbed back into bed next to him. They fit together perfectly, like a couple of spoons.

His left arm was under her pillow, his right around her waist and gently holding her hand. He kissed her on the back of the neck. "Sweet dreams, baby girl."

"Dream a little dream of me." It was something they'd used to say to each other.

She heard his sharp intake of breath. "You are remembering more."

Soon his breathing evened out, and she felt all of him relax.

We had plenty of fun nights that started like this. Bits and pieces of memories floated in, and before she knew it, daylight streamed through the window and Doogie had his chin resting on the bed about four inches from her face.

"Are you trying to tell me something, goofball?"

"Who are you calling goofball?" Rob hadn't moved during the night, his body still draped around hers. She also realized more memories had returned.

She rolled over to face him. "I can't promise you riches," she recited from memory. "I can't promise you a fancy house or new cars every year. I can't even promise you I'll be home every night because of my job. But I can promise you a true heart that would die for you if you asked."

He stared at her for a moment before he finished the rest. "This ring isn't just a piece of stone in a metal band. It's my love for you that will never die."

"You said you practiced weeks so you could say it without choking up."

He brushed a strand of hair out of her eyes. "I still did."

"It was the most romantic thing I ever heard in my life."

He buried his head against her shoulder. "Are you coming back to me?"

"In bits and pieces." She tilted his head up. "Slowly but surely."

"Maybe I should thank that guy Kern," he said.

"Why?"

He smiled. "Apparently it's triggered something."

She brushed her lips lightly across his. The feeling electrified every nerve ending in her body. She felt his cock stiffen, but he made no move toward her, letting her take control.

She wrapped one leg around his and kissed the tracks of his tears, then his cheeks, his forehead, tracing a tender line down to his ear.

"I want you, Sir," she whispered. "Please?"

"You don't know how badly," his voice broke.

She pulled away and sat up to change position, but he stopped her.

"What's wrong?"

"We've got a problem."

"What?"

He motioned to Doogie, who still hadn't moved. "Him for one. He's probably about to pop. Two, I'm out of condoms."

She let out a frustrated groan.

"I only grabbed one extra from Tony's because they're joined in pairs. I stuck the extra in my pocket. We never needed condoms except for toys. I moved all of that over to the house…right after. Didn't want anyone poking around in it. Unless you want to get pregnant, which I don't think is a good idea at this exact time, we need to get more condoms."

"Hell."

He laughed, pulling her on top of him and kissing her. "Hey, I had a case of blue balls for the past few weeks. I think you can survive a couple of hours."

They grabbed a shower—together, and she shaved her pussy for good measure—and headed out to brunch. Then they returned to the condo to grab their stuff and Doogie and went to the house.

Rob smiled as soon as they were inside with the door securely locked behind them. "Do I need to remind you?"

She grinned and stripped, a little giggle escaping her as he buckled her play collar around her neck. Then he hooked a finger through the D-ring and led her into the bedroom.

With a smile he shoved her back onto the bed, where she landed with a bounce.

"Stay," he ordered before kneeling down. He pulled stuff out from under the bed and she realized it was their storage tubs full of toys and other gear.

He triumphantly held up a condom. "Aha!"

"Yay!"

He also tossed her leather wrist and ankle cuffs onto the bed.

Then he stood, the Hitachi vibrator in his hand. "I think you know what I want to do with this, don't you?"

She nodded, swallowing hard. "Yes, Sir."

"Good girl." He put it on the bed and rummaged around a little more to find what he wanted. He produced one of the less stingy paddles, a small riding crop, and several clips. "On your back."

He used the clips to fasten her wrists and ankles together, then made her lift her legs and used a short piece of rope with clips at both ends to clip her wrists to her ankles.

She was essentially hog-tied, her pussy exposed.

He stripped and knelt in front of her, his eyes gleaming with mischief. It was such a relief to see that expression on his face instead of the sadness, or anger on her behalf, that he'd worn for the past few weeks.

He bent his head to her pussy and swiped his tongue along her shaven flesh. "By the way, don't forget to keep yourself shaved from now on."

She tried to focus, but she already felt herself slipping into subspace. "Yes, Sir."

"Good girl." He licked her again, swiping his tongue along her clit and making her moan. She felt him pick up the paddle and knew what would come next. "You may come."

He continued licking her, even as he lightly slapped at her thighs with the paddle, not painful, just a little stingy, enough bite in each impact to send her over the cliff again and again as he sucked and licked her clit.

Then he sat up and gave her several hard whacks along her ass cheeks, in the crease where they met her upper thighs, making her howl.

"Aw, my poor girl." Before the sting had even faded he bent his head and began licking her again, turning her howls into plaintive whimpers as he drove her toward pleasure.

He repeated this several times, until he was ready for something different. He put down the paddle, picked up the Hitachi and the riding crop, and changed position so he was sitting next to her, his back to her, and the arm holding the Hitachi rested against her restrained legs.

"Again, come as much as you want." He flicked the Hitachi on and pressed it against her clit.

She didn't bother trying to stifle her moans as a larger orgasm washed over her. He started slapping at her ass with the riding crop even as he forced orgasm after orgasm out of her until she sobbed and screamed and moaned and couldn't tell pleasure from pain anymore.

He finally switched off the Hitachi and turned, a gorgeous smile on his face. "Any more complaints about being horny?"

She rapidly shook her head. "No, Sir."

"Good girl." He knelt in front of her, rolled the condom on, and got into position.

Slowly, savoring it, he slid his cock inside her.

He smiled down at her. "Such a good girl you are. *My* good girl."

He took his time, building up and slowing down until she realized he was waiting for her to come again before he let his own release happen.

He cocked his head at her. "Do you need a little assistance?"

She finally nodded.

He grinned and stopped moving. She was about to change her mind and tell him no, she thought she could go over, when he grabbed the Hitachi and switched it on, pressing it against her clit.

He leaned forward, driving his cock deep inside her as she came. She closed her eyes and rode it, arching her back, helpless to do anything but lie there and take what he gave her.

She didn't bother counting how many. It wasn't until he laughed and switched it off again and started moving that she opened her eyes. He grinned as he fucked her, hard and fast, until his eyes fell closed and he came with a final thrust before falling still.

Winded, she lay there, eyes closed, happy.

He finally withdrew. She heard him in the bathroom before he returned and unclipped her.

Crawling into bed, she curled up in his arms, never wanting the moment to end.

"I love you, Sir."

He kissed the top of her head. "I love you, too, baby girl. I love you so much, you have no idea."

* * * *

Monday morning, they slept in a little and Rob was glad he didn't have to go to work. He made the coffee while Laura let Doogie out the back door into the fenced yard. She walked around with him, watching him sniff until he decided on the exact spot. When he took an interest in one corner of the back fence, she followed him over.

"What is it?"

He let out a little growl, his attention focused on the wetlands beyond the fence.

Coming out of the mangroves, through the Spanish needles and tall grass, easily visible in the dew-laden morning, was a freshly beaten-down path. It stopped near the corner of the fence and looked like someone or something had stood there for quite a while from the size of the area and the way the grass and weeds were pressed down more than the actual path.

Laura turned and looked at the house. The living room and master bedroom windows faced this corner.

And they hadn't closed the blinds the night before.

Terror erased all thoughts of romance. She grabbed Doogie's collar and raced for the house with him in tow. She shut the door and locked it behind her, closing all the blinds in the living room. Rob walked in and looked at her.

"What's wrong?"

She pointed out the path, visible from the living room window. He disappeared into the bedroom and came back with her gun.

He slipped into a pair of sneakers and went out the door. "Lock it behind me." She did, watching from the window while he jumped the back fence and followed the path out of sight.

Fifteen minutes later she was about to call 911 when Rob emerged from the underbrush, apparently unharmed. She unlocked the door for him. He walked in, locking it behind him.

From the grim look on his face she knew he'd found something. "What is it?"

"The trail leads to a small sandspit in the mangroves. Looks like someone dragged a small boat up out of the water. The tide hasn't come in yet, meaning it's recent."

He put his hands on her shoulders. "Laura, I don't want to scare you, but nobody ever comes into these mangroves. It's too shallow for any decent fishing, and there's too many mosquitoes."

Her throat felt dry. "You're saying someone watched us last night, Sir?"

The grim set of his mouth was all she needed to confirm her suspicions.

"We need to call Det. Thomas," he said. "Let me get some stuff together and we'll go back to the condo and decide what to do. Steve's got that seasonal rental house over on Manasota Key. I'm sure if it's vacant he'll let us use it."

While Rob packed, she called Thomas and left a message asking him to call her on the cell. Rob made a point of making sure all the doors and windows were locked and all the blinds closed before they left for her condo. Her cell phone rang as they walked through the door and she handed the phone to Rob, still too stressed to talk.

Thomas was there in twenty minutes, along with a deputy in a marked cruiser. It looked like they'd gotten Thomas up early because he was dressed in jeans and a T-shirt, his badge clipped to his belt and his pistol tucked into a holster in his back waistband.

Leaving a deputy to watch Laura, Thomas had Rob take him to the house and show him the area. They returned an hour later, Thomas looking grim. He waited while Rob got in touch with Steve and got the okay to use the rental house. Steve called Carol and she brought the keys to them. Laura packed a weekend bag, her laptop, the journals, and got Doogie's food and toys ready to go.

"Give me your keys and the alarm code," Thomas said. "I'll spend the next couple of nights there at the house. I want you to leave Laura's truck there, too. Maybe we can bait this guy."

"So you think it was him watching us last night?" she asked.

He nodded. "It's a reasonable suspicion. This guy didn't just fade into the woodwork. He didn't get to finish what he started. I think he'll try again, sooner or later. You're a threat to him if you get your memory back."

Carol spoke up. "How about Rob's Explorer? Won't the guy know it, too? They can take my car if someone can take me home. I can use my husband's truck."

"That's a good idea," Thomas said. "We'll leave Rob's truck here." They made the arrangements and a deputy in an unmarked cruiser followed them to the key.

Chapter Thirty

Manasota Key had a split personality. For years, Charlotte County commissioners let developers run rampant on the southern end, while on the north end Sarasota County stymied them. Therefore, when you reached the green and white sign reading *Now Entering Sarasota County*, the demarcation line was obvious by the sudden lack of condos, beach houses, and trailer parks, replaced by greenbelts of mangrove and oak trees native to the island. There were still houses built there that had no business being on a barrier island, but at least it was more pleasant to the eye and you could kid yourself that the developers weren't running the show.

Steve's rental house sat nestled in a thick tangle of mangroves, oaks, and palm trees on the Intracoastal side of the key, with a Gulf beach right-of-way access across the road. A two-story stilt house, with a screen porch circling it, it sat almost completely hidden from the road by trees.

It was completely furnished but empty of food. A deputy stayed behind with Laura while Rob went out for provisions.

Doogie wasted no time exploring the new territory. He proudly brought Laura a desiccated lizard he'd found that had gotten trapped inside. He presented her with the mummified reptile, his otter tail wagging so hard his whole body wiggled with glee.

"Out. Give it." He spit it into her hand and she praised him, wasting no time throwing it away and washing her hands.

Rob finally returned and the deputies left, promising to return after dark.

"What'd you get, Sir?" Laura tried to peek inside the bags but he gently slapped her hand away.

"Don't worry about it. You'll find out later." He wouldn't let her help him put up the groceries, so she sulked into the den and set up her laptop to catch up with her email. Rob made frequent checks of the property with Doogie, and at one point he returned and found her curled up on the couch with one of her old journals.

"How are you doing?"

"I'm up to my senior year of college."

He tried to read over her shoulder but the handwriting made him dizzy. "You're going to go blind reading that."

She looked up at him. "I'm used to it, remember?"

"Good point." He left her alone.

I can't believe it's almost over. I made it through. One of the girls in my BizAd class laughed when I said I was going to take over Dad's shop. I'm sure she thinks it's funny, never lead anywhere. She's the kind of person who has visions of a corner office and corporate Jag. She wasn't laughing so hard when I casually mentioned the two freelance writing contracts I'd already snagged will probably pay me more in the next six months than she'll make in the next year—if she manages to get a job that entails more than asking if you'd like fries with that. Graduates are a dime a dozen. Good solid careers are rarer than perfect emeralds. She'll learn that soon enough.

I have to admit that I felt a little smug. Most of what my classmates learned, I was raised on. Balance sheets, employee management—been there, done that. I did learn stuff, but some of it was applicable to larger businesses. Still nice to know.

I'm glad Dad insisted I stay with it. I know I can make money with my writing, and that's a dream I'm dearly grateful for. The shop is security. I don't resent taking it over like some might. Why should I open my own business when I'm doing what I'm happy doing? Some people would say I'm not living up to my fullest potential. Screw that. I'm happy, I pay my bills, and I enjoy going to work every day. How many people are that lucky? Not very damn many.

Even back then she had determination and spirit, direction, foresight, self-confidence. That was the person she wanted to know—to be—again. She didn't feel anything like her now.

Rob finished cooking and brought out delicious pork chops and risotto.

"Are you some sort of gourmet chef or something, Sir?"

He laughed. "No, but sometimes we've got a lot of time on our hands at the station. Firemen are notoriously good cooks."

"The guys must love you."

"Yeah, John Baker's been standing in for me, and everyone said they need stock in Mylanta."

A knock on the door startled Laura. Doogie barked, sounding the alarm.

"Too late, dingbat," Rob chastised the dog. "The Visigoths have already arrived." He peeked through the side window and opened the door. It was a deputy. "Want some chow?"

"No, thanks. Just wanted to let you know we're down there."

They spent the evening in companionable silence, watching TV. For once, Laura didn't want to talk. She just wanted to absorb all she'd read and focus on the newly-recovered memories. She started yawning around eleven.

"Time to turn in." She looked at Rob, wanting him to suggest something, anything.

He brushed the hair away from her forehead and stroked her cheek. She started to speak and he gently touched his finger to her lips, silencing her. He took the remote control and turned the TV off, changing the stereo to a soft rock station.

He stood and made a "wait" motion to her and disappeared into the bedroom. A moment later he returned and stood in front of her, holding her play collar. He buckled it around her neck before offering his hand.

She let him take her into his arms. They swayed in time with the music and he made no move to kiss her, content to stare into her eyes.

Dropping her head to his chest she closed her eyes, feeling safe and warm and cherished. It finally hit her she didn't have to have all of her memories back to enjoy life with him.

He kissed the top of her head, burying his face in her hair as they danced. The song changed and he stepped back, taking her hand and leading her down the hall. In the bedroom, several candles bathed the room with their dancing glow. She smiled and folded back into his arms as they danced at the foot of the bed for several tantalizingly long minutes.

The passion rose in her and she kissed him harder, running her hands down his back until she could pull his shirt free and trail her fingers along his smooth skin. She pulled him against her and could feel from his stiff cock how ready he was, but when she tried to unfasten his shorts he wouldn't be rushed and stepped away.

He had her lie on the bed and gave her a back rub, fully clothed. After working up to her shoulders he slowly teased her shirt up, kissing her bared skin as he exposed it.

Laura shivered, wondering if it had always been this good, or just especially so this time. There was no fear or trepidation in her now as a warm flood of familiar sensations washed over her. This was different than their sadistic playtime. This was vanilla lovin', and it was every bit as good as the kinky stuff.

She rolled over, pulling her shirt the rest of the way off. He sat up and removed his and lay down next to her, his skin hot to the touch. She traced gentle circles on his chest and then reached up and grabbed him by the neck, pulling him down on top of her. His cock was pressed hard against her and his breath quickened. She wrapped her legs around him, wanting him inside her.

Rob eased her shorts off and kissed her just below the navel. She trembled with anticipation and softly begged him not to stop as he slowly worked his way south, until he was licking and sucking on her clit. He pushed her legs apart and settled in, slowly thrusting into her pussy with two fingers as he worked her swollen nub with his tongue. It didn't take him long to get her over the edge and make her cry out with pleasure as her orgasm vibrated through her.

He sat up and peeled his shorts off. She reached for him and he paused, getting a condom from the nightstand.

She helped him roll it onto his stiff cock. Then he slowly entered her, enjoying every second. They moved together in a slow, passionate rhythm, until she was soon crying out again from yet another orgasm.

This felt like sweet perfection. He quickened his pace while she matched him thrust for thrust, until she felt his cock harden inside her, swelling, throbbing as he filled the condom. Only then did they collapse together, spent, happy, exhausted.

He went to clean up. When he returned to bed he took her into his arms. "Do you have any idea how much I love you, baby girl?"

She yelped and jumped closer to him. Doogie, his tail wagging with happy doggy joy, had goosed her with his wet nose.

He also had something in his mouth.

"Damn," Rob yelled. "Leave it! Drop it!" Rob jumped over her and chased the Lab out of the bedroom. She was about to follow when she heard Rob catch him.

"Give it. Give *it*!" He must have, and a moment later she heard the guest toilet flush, Rob washing his hands before returning to the bedroom.

"Let's try this again." He slipped under the covers with her.

Her curiosity would not be denied. "What did he have, Sir?"

Even in the dimming candlelight she saw his face redden.

"Come on, Sir. Tell me."

He finally told her and she roared with laughter while Doogie crept back into the bedroom.

"He fished it out of the damn garbage. I told you we never used those things, except for anal and on toys," he muttered.

She snuggled into his arms, still chortling every few minutes, quietly talking and asking him questions about things she was starting to remember. Pretty soon her breathing slowed and deepened, and when he looked she was asleep, wearing a contented smile.

He carefully extricated himself and put out the candles. Before extinguishing the last one he glared at Doogie. "You're just mad because I'm the one who suggested it was time you got snipped, aren't you?"

Doogie's tail thumped once.

* * * *

Tuesday morning, Rob awoke before Laura. She didn't stir from her peaceful sleep when he got out of bed. Kissing her on the forehead, he grabbed a pair of shorts and leashed Doogie for his morning walk. He didn't have to work this morning, but would go in that night.

At least there'd be deputies at the house to keep an eye on Laura for him.

He met one of the deputies on his way down the stairs. "Hi, Rob, I was just coming up to tell you we were leaving. We'll be back around dark."

"Any problems last night?"

"No. I haven't heard back yet if they got anyone at your house or the condo, though."

"Okay, thanks."

He let Doogie explore the yard for a few minutes. It was around seven-thirty he thought, but he hadn't checked the clock. Boats cruised past in the ICW, and he smelled the tangy Gulf air. It wasn't just muggy. You could wring the mist out with your bare hands. Once the sea breezes picked up later in the day and the sun rose, the key would dry out.

Doogie reluctantly followed Rob up the stairs. Laura still slept. He made coffee and turned on the TV, sitting on the couch to watch. She stumbled out of the bedroom a few minutes later wearing his T-shirt, her collar, and nothing else. With the deputies standing guard, he'd relaxed the naked rule a little.

"Do you want coffee?" he asked.

She shook her head and crawled into his lap, her head on his shoulder. "I just want to go back to sleep, Sir. I had the most wonderful dreams."

He smiled and kissed the top of her head. "I think my dream's finally coming true."

"There are still big holes in my memory. I think a lot of it is starting to come back, though. I can remember a lot from when I was a kid, Mom and Dad and Bill, stuff like that. I remember things from a few years ago. Like our first date."

Rob groaned. "You would have to remember *that* fiasco, wouldn't you?"

What started out a journey to a formal Chamber of Commerce dinner banquet ended with Rob in the back of an ambulance, performing CPR on an accident victim—who later died. Two cars collided head-on in front of them on their way to the banquet, and Rob immediately jumped out to help. Laura followed the ambulance to the hospital, driving Rob's Explorer. By the time Rob finished filling out paperwork and they gave their statements to the trooper, it was too late to make the banquet. They drove through Checkers and parked at the fishing pier by the Tom Adams bridge.

"Despite everything that happened that night," she said, "if nothing else, it showed me what a dedicated, compassionate person you are. You didn't have to do what you did. You could have stood back as soon as the crew arrived on scene and we wouldn't have missed the dinner. But you cared, and you stayed, and you tried your best to save that man." She kissed him. "I think I fell in love with you that night, Sir."

He hugged her. "You amaze me."

"Why?"

"Most people find it hard to live with people who work the kind of hours and shifts I do."

"Yeah, but I love all the time you're home." She rolled over and unfastened his shorts. His cock hardened at the attention.

"We'd better go into the bedroom." He made her stand and led her down the hall.

With everything going on, all he wanted was to make love to her, to show her with his body everything in his heart beyond the kink, beyond their dynamic.

Just the pure love.

He rolled her on top of him and buried his face in the juncture of her thighs, enjoying the sweet taste of her juices. He flicked at her clit with his tongue, happy to know the old techniques still had the same effect on her even without all her memories. When she found his cock and took it into her mouth, he moaned loudly against her flesh, enjoying her echoing moan around his cock.

He reached up and wrapped his hands around her ass, holding tight and digging his fingers in when she tried to wiggle away until she gave in. Alternating fucking her with his tongue and licking and sucking on her clit, he kept her coming, every gasping moan filling his heart until he was satisfied he'd pleasured her enough.

He rolled her off him and pulled her up the bed. "Don't you ever try to make me stop making you come," he teased. "I'll stop when I'm damn good and ready."

She laughed. "Yes, Sir."

He grabbed a condom, rolled it onto his cock, and knelt between her legs. Then he lifted her ankles, resting them on his shoulders and leaning forward, pinning her. Sliding his cock inside her, he paused and reached up to grab her wrists and hold them over her head.

Okay, so maybe a little kink.

He smiled down at her. "Look at me, baby girl." The blue flecks in her eyes looked dark as she focused on him.

"Who do you belong to?"

Her voice sounded tiny, subspacey. "You, Sir."

He slowly thrust, knowing today he wouldn't be able to hold out very long after the way she'd been sucking on his cock. "Yes, you do. Whose good girl are you?"

She writhed beneath him, happy. "Yours, Sir."

"Such a very good girl." He started thrusting, his release catching him by surprise with only a few thrusts. His cock pulsed, throbbing, exploding as his balls emptied into the condom. After a few moments he rolled to his side, enjoying the feel of her stretching out next to him.

"Let's take a nap, sweetheart."

She draped her body over his. "Yes, Sir."

* * * *

A few hours later they showered and leashed Doogie for a long walk down to a convenience store.

Laura's stomach growled. "What do you want to eat? I don't know about you, but I'm getting pretty hungry."

"I'm going to make you one of my world-famous omelets."

"World-famous?"

"Okay, well, maybe not world-famous, and not as good as Shay's, but the guys at the station like them." They picked up a newspaper and returned to the house. Laura wasn't worried about the shop. Tuesday mornings were always pretty slow.

Rob fired up the stove while Laura checked her email. She scrolled through her messages when she spotted one with the subject *Getting Closer*.

"Rob!"

He ran in and looked over her shoulder. Reaching around her, he clicked to open the message.

You are running out of time, Laura.

It was sent late the night before.

Laura made a strange sound and Rob turned to her. Pale and trembling, she bolted for the bathroom. He followed her, holding her shoulders and pulling her hair away from her face while she was sick, then helping her clean up. Her tears flowed and he held her there, sitting on the bathroom floor, while she sobbed.

"Why can't he leave me alone? Why does he want to ruin my life? Who the hell is he?"

"I don't know, honey, but he's going to be one sorry bastard if I get my hands on him."

Det. Thomas probably broke several speed laws to make it there as fast as he did. This time he came armed with FDLE agent Bruce Hutchins, also working on the case. At his advice they left the computer alone after opening the message. Hutchins sat down at the computer and got to work. They left him to his business and went to the kitchen. Laura's appetite had deserted her, but Rob coaxed her into eating a few bites anyway.

Thomas sounded as frustrated as they were. "Laura, have you remembered anything about the attack?"

She shook her head. "I don't remember anything from a couple of months up until the attack. That's still mostly a complete blank. There's little stuff coming back from before that, and some big chunks from several years ago, but nothing that would be any help."

"This guy has to be someone who knows you or had some sort of contact with you. He's got your email address for crying out loud."

"That doesn't mean anything," Rob interrupted. "Her email address is usually listed in the tag at the end of her articles, and it's listed on the shop's web site. It wouldn't be hard for someone with even a little computer knowledge to find that out."

"I've got it," Hutchins called.

They returned to the living room and looked over his shoulder. He had set up his own laptop and was running a program on it. "I fingered the IP of the email message. Originated from a server in New Mexico."

Laura blinked. "New Mexico?"

He nodded. "That doesn't mean anything. He could have logged into it from somewhere else. What I have to do now is contact the server and have them run traces on their end."

Det. Thomas turned to Laura. "Do you know anyone who has this kind of computer experience? Anyone at all you can think of?"

She sat down and concentrated, finally shaking her head. "No one I know of." She snorted. "Not that *that* means anything."

The agent finished his work and packed up his computer. "Whoever he is, he's using the same code name."

Upon getting the emailed threats, Laura had been too distraught to think, much less analyze them. "What's he calling himself?"

"MedicineMan."

"Did anything happen last night at either place?" Rob asked.

Thomas shook his head. "Nothing. All quiet."

"That's a pretty strange coincidence, don't you think?" Rob noted. "We disappear, and all of a sudden she gets another message."

Thomas didn't say anything at first. It was obvious to Laura the detective was reluctant to say anything in front of her.

Laura stared at them. "Are you two saying that this guy's been watching me all this time?"

"We think that's a possibility, yes. It's one we've strongly considered for a while now."

"And you think this confirms it?"

Thomas nodded.

She stood and went to the window. "This is bullshit. First this freak tries to kill me, and now he's stalking me. I can't live my life like this. I don't want to be in fear for the rest of my life, and I refuse to run."

Anger rapidly displaced her fear. "Who the *fuck* does this asshole think he is?"

Chapter Thirty-One

After Thomas and Hutchins left, Rob drove Laura to the dive shop, taking a long, winding route north off the key, then down 776 to the eastern end of Placida Road, and around the south end of the peninsula before heading north again to the shop.

Laura went straight to her office and worked on some accounting, Rob refusing to leave until he absolutely had to for work. Now the question of the missing current journals seemed more important than ever. She leafed through the last few books. There were almost daily entries, many quite detailed. It would stand to reason she wouldn't change her habits.

An answer to this entire nightmare might be there if she could find them.

Sarah went out to pick up some office supplies and lunch for everyone when Steve put down his foot and refused to let Laura leave. When she returned an hour later, she raced into the shop. Steve was out back working on one of the boat engines. "Watch out, Laura, Mr. Green Eyes alert. He pulled in right behind me."

"Damn."

"What?" Rob looked like they were speaking a foreign language.

Laura whispered low enough Sarah couldn't hear him. "*Sir*, that guy."

His jaw tightened before he grinned from ear to ear. "Don't worry. I'll handle this. You both stay in here." He stepped out into the shop, leaving the door cracked open enough the women could hear.

They heard the bell jingle on the front door as it opened, followed by Rob's voice. "Hello! Can I help you with anything?"

Sarah and Laura looked at each other and tried not to laugh. The tone of Rob's voice sounded so fakely cheerful it was almost comical.

Laura heard Don Kern's voice. "Is Laura here?"

"Sure. Can I tell her who's here?"

"Don Kern."

"Hold on, I'll get her."

They expected Rob to open the office door, since it was located behind the counter. Instead, Rob bellowed as if she was outside on the dock. "Honey! There's a Mr. Kern here to see you!"

The women almost lost it. Laura waited a moment before leaving the office, as if she had been outside. Sarah followed close behind, not wanting to miss the fun.

"Did you call me, sweetie?" She stretched up and kissed Rob, letting out a squeal when he reached around and goosed her ass.

"Yes. This gentleman here asked to see you."

For a second, Don Kern wore a surprised expression. Then a mask slipped over his face and he was the model of professionalism. He asked about booking a dive trip. Laura gave him all the details before Sarah took over and finished the transaction. Rob followed Laura back to the office, goosing her again before she could get through the door.

With the door closed behind them Laura laughed. "You're just plain mean, Sir!" she whispered.

He took her into his arms and kissed her before reaching up and getting a handful of her hair, pulling her head back and melting her. "No," he said as he nibbled the base of her throat. "I'm protecting what's rightfully *mine*."

She wanted to lock the door and beg him to fuck her on her desk. "Are you jealous, Sir?"

"Oh, please. Of that guy? Not a chance. I just don't trust anyone with an interest in you." He sat down in her chair and pulled her into his lap. "Let me tell you something. I'm sure everyone we know will back me up on this. I've never been jealous. I trusted and I still trust you. I know it's an occupational hazard that men are going to stare at you. I say let them eat their hearts out. But this guy just doesn't seem to take a hint very well. Most men would have dropped it after the other day."

"And how do you know he wasn't just coming in here to book a dive trip and that's all?"

"Because I saw the look on his face when I yelled for you. It was a look that said, 'Crap! This is the boyfriend.'"

"And they say men aren't psychic."

Sarah opened the office door. "All clear."

Rob's curiosity got the best of him. "How did he act?"

"He didn't say anything, if that's what you mean. Seemed to have forgotten the entire thing."

"That's good." He looked at Laura. "Are you ready to go? I want to take you home before I go to work. Thomas said a deputy will meet us there."

Laura grabbed Doogie and her stuff and quickly loaded up into Carol's car. She noticed Rob turned the wrong way when they left the shop's driveway.

"Where are we going?"

He headed south around the point and back up the other side of the Cape Haze peninsula. "I'm taking the long way again. With a twist."

Casting a glance behind them Laura realized what he was worried about. "Do you think we're being followed?"

"Don't know. Makes sense to not take chances though, doesn't it?"

They rode in silence. When he hit the east side of Rotonda, he turned in and wove through side streets inside the circle.

"I guess that's one good thing. You know your way around here."

"Hey, any fireman or deputy who has to work this area knows these streets by heart."

They emerged from the maze on the north side of Rotonda and took 776 all the way up to the north entrance to Manasota Key. Laura couldn't help but notice Rob constantly checking traffic behind them.

"Did we give them the slip?"

"Not funny. I don't see anyone, so I guess we did."

The deputy arrived minutes after they did. Rob checked all the doors and windows to be on the safe side. Everything was still locked up tight.

After seeing Laura safely inside, he kissed her good-bye. "You get the deputy's attention when you walk Doogie. Understand?"

She nodded. "Yes, Sir."

"I only have to work a half shift tonight. I'll be back early in the morning. You keep that gun on you, or in the drawer by the bed. Understand?"

"Yes, Sir."

He kissed her one more time before walking out. He waited until she locked the door behind him before heading downstairs. She watched through the window as he talked to the deputy for a minute before getting in Carol's car and heading north.

She went to the couch and sat, depressed. She'd been run not only out of her life, but now out of the condo, and the house—*their* house—by this psycho.

Part of her did hope he showed up at the front door.

Just so I can blow the fucker's head off and end this for good.

* * * *

Laura startled awake before dawn. Doogie stood on his hind legs at the bedroom window, his front paws on the sill, looking out.

She glanced at her cell phone. It was only a little after five. She walked over and stood next to Doogie and looked out.

Nothing seemed out of place but she studied the dog. Doogie remained alert and frozen, his eyes fixed on a point out beyond the porch.

"What is it?" she whispered. The dog softly chuffed, as if in reply, and continued his vigil.

The hair on the back of her neck stood up. Something wasn't right. Doogie was young, but he rarely alerted like this, and never at night.

It reminded her a lot of his reaction to finding the trail in the backyard at the house.

She slipped into shorts, grabbed the gun, and told Doogie to stay. Totally unnecessary, as it turned out. Whatever he was focused on, he wasn't leaving that window. Without turning on any lights she moved into the living room. She couldn't hear anything except the hum of the A/C air handler coming to life.

The front door was still locked. Outside, the screen door was still locked and intact. The light switch next to the front door turned on porch, stair, and walkway lights. She flipped it on and cautiously unlocked the door.

The deputy met her halfway up the stairs, his expression serious, his hand resting on the butt of his holstered gun.

"Go back inside, Laura."

"What's going on?"

The deputy's radio came to life and he spoke into his shoulder mic.

Then to her. "Go inside, lock the door, keep the lights on. We'll be up in a little while."

She looked around, felt her hackles rise again, and hurried back up the stairs. She locked the screen and front doors behind her. Doogie met her at the front door, then raced back to the bedroom. When she followed him, she found Doogie alerting at the same window.

This time the black Lab let out a low growl totally out of character for the gentle dog.

She screamed at the sound of someone pounding on the front door. "Laura! It's me."

She raced back to the living room to let Rob in, breathing a sigh of relief to have him in her arms. He kicked the door shut behind him and locked it. "What's going on? The deputy sent me up here and there's three more parked downstairs."

"I don't know. Doogie woke me up. When I went outside, he told me to get back in the house, lock the door, and leave the lights on. He said he'll be up in a little while."

She got dressed and made them a pot of coffee. They heard yet another car drive up and a dog barking. Laura hushed Doogie when he replied with barks of his own.

Rob looked out the front window. "It's a K-9 unit."

They watched the officer unload a large German shepherd and head around the back of the house. He circled around, came up the stairs, went back down again, and then into the woods behind the house.

Thomas arrived a moment later. The deputy in charge talked with him, pointed behind the house, and then they hurried off.

Twenty minutes after that, Thomas finally came upstairs and explained.

"The deputy heard a boat idling along the shore, then it stopped and there was a splash like someone got out in the water. He walked down there and found a little skiff. When he identified himself and told whoever it was to show themselves and come out, he heard someone take off running through the brush. That's when you came out. He was calling for backup."

"But he didn't see anyone?"

"No."

There was more. Rob was determined to hear it. "What did you find in the boat?"

Thomas looked at Laura, hesitant.

Laura spoke up. "Tell us. I want to know. This lunatic's after me. I want to know what's going on."

"We found a bag, one of those cheap nylon backpacks, like a gym bag. Inside it was duct tape, a roll of rope, and a knife."

Chapter Thirty-Two

Rob watched as Laura blanched. "This house isn't safe either, is it?" she asked.

"We need to get you out of here," Thomas said. "Right now, while he can't track you."

"What if that's what he wants?" Rob asked. "What if this was a deliberate attempt to get us to move Laura again?" Rob couldn't believe he even said the words. The paranoia grew like a tumor in his gut.

"Whoever this guy is, now he's on the run. He's not going to be tailing you in the next little bit. We're going to get you out of here, get you safe. That's my priority."

"I don't think there's anywhere's safe enough," Laura said.

Rob had a flash. "Maybe there is."

It was 3:00 a.m. in Montana when Rob called Bill. After the problems last time, Bill had given them several alternate numbers, including his girlfriend's house and cell phone, the airport he worked out of, neighbors, even the local sheriff's office. Fortunately, Bill was home. He quickly awoke when Rob explained the problem to him.

"Let me make some calls. I'll get her a ticket to Denver, meet her there, and fly back with her."

"Okay, call me right back."

Laura balked. "Oh, no. You are *not* shipping me up to Montana. I won't go without you."

"Laura, you have to. I'll take some vacation time in a week or so. I'll drive and bring Doogie with me. I can't just leave right now."

"Neither can I."

Thomas stepped in. "Laura, you don't have a choice in the matter. If I have to send you to the airport handcuffed to an armed deputy, I will."

She looked at him. "You don't have the authority to do that."

The detective stared her down. "You want to try me?"

She managed not to burst into tears.

Barely. "I can't believe this is happening."

She was in the shower when Bill called back with the flight arrangements. "I'll meet her in Denver for her connection to Bozeman."

Rob wrote the flight information down and read it back to Bill for confirmation. "Okay. I'll get her on that flight."

Bill had arranged a non-stop from Tampa to Denver. It left TIA at ten, which didn't give Rob much time.

He helped Laura pack and the deputies escorted them back to her condo so she could get the clothes she'd need for the northern climate. It was fairly warm there this time of year, but still chilly by Florida standards.

Rob loaded her suitcases into Thomas' unmarked patrol car. She'd changed into jeans and had a lightweight jacket to carry on. She carried her laptop and iPad and had the rest of the journals she hadn't read yet in her checked bags.

Rob hated the look on her face when he had to remind her to leave the gun behind. Leaning close, he whispered in her ear, "It's all right, baby girl. I'm giving you permission not to carry it. You'll be safe out there."

She broke down. "I don't want to go."

He forced himself to stay strong for her. "I know. I'm sorry, but I'm ordering you to go. And you *will* stay out there until I say so." He took her play collar from his pocket put it in her hands. "Take it with you. Keep it in your pocket. Even when you can't wear it, remember you have it and remember who owns you."

She tearfully nodded. "Yes, Sir."

Laura knelt and hugged Doogie. The Lab licked her face but acted listless, apparently knowing his mom was leaving. One of the deputies volunteered to take him to Steve at the shop for her, and she fought back tears as they drove off, Doogie racing back and forth in the back seat while looking out the rear window.

Rob sat with her in the back seat of Thomas's car. She remained silent most of the way, and when asked a question she answered mostly in one-word sentences. Upon their arrival at the airport, Thomas pulled up to the departures curb and requested an airport police officer be summoned. He identified himself, and three more airport officers arrived to escort them.

They were rushed through the ticket desk. TSA agents gave Rob and Thomas special clearance to go to the airside terminal with her and the airport police.

With a few minutes remaining before her flight boarded, Rob said his good-byes there and kissed her one last time.

"You'll be fine, baby girl. I'll be there before you know it. You'll be safe."

"What good is it if I'm forced into exile from my own life?"

He caressed her cheek. "I love you."

"I love you, too, Sir," she whispered.

One of the officers escorted her down the gangway and they lost sight of her around a turn. When the officer reappeared, they started boarding the other passengers.

The airport police and TSA agents stood there with them while Thomas and Rob watched until the plane left.

Rob was assured that an airport police and TSA escort would be awaiting her at the gate when the plane arrived in Denver, and would stay with her until she and Bill caught their flight out.

That left Rob feeling a little better.

Neither man said much on the ride back south.

"You know this is for the best," Thomas said after they'd crossed the Skyway. "You know this is the only way to keep her safe for now."

"I know."

"We'll figure this out and find him."

He nodded.

Thomas tried again a few minutes later. "He's going to screw up. He took a big risk trying to get to her. He's desperate. That means we'll catch him."

Rob looked at him. "I'm warning you, if he shows up I'm shooting him before I call for help. If I have my way, he won't go to trial."

Thomas nodded. "Can't say I blame you there."

* * * *

A deputy returned to the Manasota house with Rob and waited while he finished collecting their things, then drove him to the house where he picked up Laura's truck. It was better if he went home for now. The general consensus felt Laura was the primary target.

Steve was understandably upset when Rob arrived to pick up Doogie. "How long is she going to stay out there?"

Rob shrugged. "Don't know. I don't want her out there, but I don't want her dead, either. If they can find this whacko, she can come home. If not, she won't be safe here." He stroked Doogie's head. "And you can't tell anyone where she is. No one. Not even Carol or Sarah. Don't even say she's out of town. Just say she's not here and you don't know when she'll be in. If someone accidentally lets it slip where she is—"

"Don't worry. We won't."

Rob took Doogie and went back to the condo. He felt as empty as the rooms there without Laura waiting for him. He had to call Shayla and tell her the news and not to spread it around. The only thing she could tell everyone was that Laura wouldn't be around for a while. That Shayla didn't know where she'd gone, or when she'd return.

Which was the truth, because he didn't tell her where he'd sent Laura even though he suspected she'd easily guess Montana.

* * * *

Bill didn't skimp on his little sister. He'd arranged first class for her, and since the airline had been notified of the special circumstances, Laura had the row to herself. She curled up by the window and watched the ground sweep past as they took off. The plane veered northwest, over the Gulf.

In an hour, they were flying over oil rigs and the Mississippi Delta outside of New Orleans. The landscape changed from green to brown as they approached the Midwest. She watched mountains, fields, and strange cities and towns slowly pass beneath her. At one point she dozed for a little while, then a flight attendant asked her to come to the front of the plane.

She kept her play collar in her hands the whole time, rubbing her fingers over the soft leather.

It was the only thing keeping her from crying.

The head steward approached her. "Ms. Spaulding?"

Her heart froze, sure that he was going to tell her Rob was dead. That something horrible had happened and MedicineMan had struck.

"Yes?"

"TSA told us you're to deplane first. Your brother is already at the airport. The airport police will make sure your baggage is transferred to your connecting flight, and officers will stay with you until you make the plane change."

"Okay. Thank you."

Laura felt eyes on her as she made her way back to her seat. No doubt there were curious passengers who heard some of her exchange with the crew. She hated the attention and wanted to know when she would wake up from the nightmare.

The flight attendants were very kind, and one even sat next to her for the landing. Officers were waiting when the door opened and the gangway was attached, Bill standing close behind them.

He didn't recognize her at first and she had her first genuine laugh of the day as he did a double-take over her new hairdo. He held out his arms and she fell into them, enjoying the hug.

"Don't say it."

He smiled. "You went and done it." He took her knapsack and laptop case from her. The officers escorted them to the next gate and helped them board. Once the plane was in the air, she relaxed for the first time that day.

Denver fell away behind them, the landscape giving way to the Rocky Mountains. When she felt the plane descend toward Bozeman, Bill took her hand and squeezed it. "You okay?"

She closed her eyes and shook her head, tears rolling down her face. She'd just started recalling memories about her and Rob, and now she didn't have him, either. Her life had been put on hold, and she felt terrified.

The breakdown loomed despite doing her best to stave it off. Bill helped collect her luggage and then they traveled across to the private aviation section of the airport, where he loaded her and her luggage into his plane.

That's where she finally let loose, sobbing in his arms, crying, screaming in the small cockpit while she vented the terror and anger from her system.

The flight to Gardiner from Bozeman didn't take long. From there they drove to his house, a few minutes north of town.

Gardiner sat just outside the north entrance to Yellowstone. Bill's house was located on fifty rolling acres in a valley surrounded by hills and pine trees, a large but cozy log cabin with all the amenities. His three dogs, all mutts, came running from the porch to greet them when they pulled in. She sat down among them and let them sniff her, enjoying their furry presence.

It was the first comforting event that had blessed her all day.

She called Rob and reached his voice mail. She also left a message for Thomas that she was safe. The dogs gathered around her once more, so she spent time playing with them and wishing Rob would call.

Bill discussed making dinner and Laura looked at the sky. "Is it that late already?" She glanced at her watch.

He laughed. "Jet lag and an unfamiliarity with Montana summers. It's after seven."

"You're kidding." She looked at his watch and reset hers with a twinge of regret. It was one less connection to home. It felt like a week had passed instead of hours. It was still only Tuesday afternoon.

Nothing exciting had happened to him since his return from Florida. He flew tourists, hunters, supplies, mail, and medical patients between the Livingston and Bozeman areas to and from more isolated locales.

His career started after he graduated from the Air Force academy. While training to be a pilot, he was injured in a football game after hours, nearly breaking his neck. The injury was life-threatening and enough to keep him out of a fighter cockpit.

He had a medical discharge, flight training, but not enough to get him a job with a large airline. He opted for private enterprise and a friend of his hooked him up with a charter company in the northwest. Within a year he opened his own company with two other pilots working for him. He lived well and didn't miss the hot Florida summers.

"The bugs are nasty though. You wouldn't believe."

"Nastier than Florida?"

He laughed. "Laur, we've got mosquitoes the size of pelicans."

* * * *

The evening grew chilly. After dinner, Bill lit a fire and they sat with the dogs and talked. Mostly Bill did the talking. Laura asked him questions, recalled fragments of memory, and had him clarify things. He talked about their parents. He told her about her fifth birthday, when she tried to play

Rocket J. Squirrel to his Bullwinkle and nearly impaled herself on a fence when she jumped off a tree stump. He told her about grandparents, an aunt and uncle, a couple of cousins.

When the phone rang Bill answered it, passing it to Laura.

"Hi, honey. How you doin'?"

Rob's voice was a welcomed sound. Bill discreetly left the room while they talked. Doogie missed her terribly, Steve and Carol said hi, and the police didn't have any new developments.

"Have you checked your email lately?"

Her heart skipped. "Why? Do the police think he's sent one?"

"No, silly. *I* sent you an email."

She laughed. "Oh. Sorry. I guess I'm just super-suspicious."

"With good reason." They chatted for a few more minutes before he said good-bye. "I love you, baby girl. I'll be out there soon, okay?"

"Okay, Sir. I love you, too."

Bill returned a few minutes later. "I've got tomorrow off so it doesn't matter if I pull a late one, but it's got to be way past your bedtime."

Laura looked at her watch and did a fast calculation, suddenly yawning. "I guess I am tired."

He hugged her and they said good night. The double bed in his guest room, without someone next to her, felt huge.

She tried to put it into perspective. *At least I'm alive to complain about it.*

Before crawling into bed, she retrieved her iPad and punched in the password to hook it up to Bill's wireless modem. She checked her email.

Sure enough, there was Rob's message.

My sweet baby girl,

I promise I'll do everything I can to get out there as soon as possible. I love you, and I miss you, but I also promised when you agreed to be Mine that I would protect you.

And I meant it.

Here are My orders: I want you to carry your collar with you everywhere. If you can wear it at night, do so. If not, that's okay, but keep it with you in bed. Always carry it in your pocket or your purse, where you can touch it when you feel sad. And when you touch it, you think of Me. You think about how much I love you, and how once we're through this, I'm going to stand up in front of all our friends and collar you as My slave before I marry you.

Email Me every morning when you wake up, and every evening before you go to bed. I know cell reception isn't great out there, but if you can text Me, too, do that as well.

your loving Master.

The screen went blurry as she cried, tears rolling down her cheeks as she silently sobbed over the message. The collar lay on the bed next to her. She picked it up and pressed it to her lips, inhaling and smelling the comforting, familiar scent of leather.

The scent of *Him*. Of the leather cuffs he buckled around her wrists and ankles before they played, of the leather floggers he used on her, of the black boots he sometimes wore to the club and she'd kneel with her forehead pressed against them.

It was his leather boots she dreamed about as she cried herself to sleep, alone.

Chapter Thirty-Three

Wednesday morning, she awoke to a message from her stalker in her email. She sat, numb, while Bill called Det. Thomas and reported it.

Sorry I didn't get to play with you before I was interrupted. We could have had a lot of fun together.
Don't worry, we still will. I'm very, very patient.

She buried herself in the old journals she had with her, going through everything in an attempt to escape the hell her life had become.

Thursday, Bill had to get back to his schedule. Laura flew with him a few times over the next several days on shorter delivery runs when he had passenger space. She wasn't keen on flying, but she took her camera and snapped some breathtaking aerial shots.

Bill even coaxed her into taking the controls for short periods of time in calm conditions. While she enjoyed the feel of flying, she thought it wasn't something she would do on her own.

Montana was different. Rugged landscapes, towering mountains, a literal polar opposite from everything she knew in Florida. It would have been a good kind of different under better circumstances.

A week later, she was pining for home and Rob. Unfortunately he couldn't leave yet. The wife of one of the guys at the station had a baby and needed to take a couple of weeks off. He'd filled in for Rob while Laura was in the hospital, so Rob felt obliged to do the same.

Heartbroken, Laura agreed. They talked, at least briefly, every evening his time. Between those all too short conversations they e-mailed and texted.

There were no more emails from MedicineMan.

Bill owned two gentle horses he rarely had time to ride. Laura made a point of going out with them for a couple of hours each day. Determined to renew her journaling habit, she decided to go old-school and purchased a new notebook and package of pens during a shopping trip into town.

She rode out to a beautiful overlook every day and wrote whatever came to mind. Much of her childhood and adolescence was again intact. There were still gaping holes in the past several years—including some of her time with Rob the past several months.

Perhaps it was fear of losing what she'd regained, perhaps it was several months of writing skills lying dormant, she didn't know. Within a week she had filled the first journal and started a second. Soon she wrote not just during her rides, but anytime she thought of something.

Obsessing over the missing journals wasn't healthy for her, and she wasn't too oblivious to realize it. She decided to go back to some of her old journals and take notes from story ideas she jotted down in the past. As a result she came up with a story idea she wanted to expand upon.

Over the next several days she generated close to twenty thousand words and felt there might even be a good novel in it. If nothing else, it kept her mind off her loneliness.

One evening Bill noticed her going through an old journal and then writing something in a new one.

"Putting the puzzle back together?"

She nodded. "Something like that."

"You always have been big on that, almost religious. Every day. Never stopped. Did you find the missing ones yet?"

"No."

"You looked all over your office?"

She nodded. "Through my computers, everywhere."

"You'll find them. Or you'll get enough memories back that you'll remember where you put them."

She wasn't so sure. "I hope so."

Rob called her later that evening.

"I miss you, Sir."

"I know. I miss you, too, baby girl."

"I want to come home."

His voice changed to Dom tone. "We've had this conversation. It's not safe."

"How do we know he's not just laying low until I return? What if you leave and he follows you out here? I'm tired of putting my life on hold like this."

"Let's give it two more weeks. If nothing else happens, I'll come out and get you and we'll drive home together. All right?"

"*Two* more weeks? No, Sir, I don't want to—"

"*Laura.*" The firm sadness in his voice silenced her as much as his Dom tone. "I don't like this any more than you do. He almost took you from me once. I'm *not* letting him have a second chance."

She couldn't respond.

"Are you there?" he asked.

"Yes, Sir," she whispered.

"This is for your own good."

"Yes, Sir." They said their good-byes and she returned to the living room, dejected.

"What's wrong?" Bill asked.

She couldn't look at him. "He said at least two more weeks."

"Hey, sis, if it's what needs to happen, then that's it. No argument."

She picked up her latest journal and pen and started writing to escape her misery at missing Rob and everyone else. Rob had ordered her not to tell Shayla or the others where she was, or to email them for fear of that somehow giving away her location. She was allowed to text message with them only, but the cell reception was spotty, meaning most of the time she couldn't even do that.

When she went to send Rob her evening email, she found he'd surprised her with pictures of Doogie and him on the shop dock. She smiled, missing them all the more, wanting her life back.

This isn't how my life should go, away from home and hiding from some faceless psycho.

She cried herself to sleep.

* * * *

The next morning, Laura forced herself to go riding. The horses loved her for it, but her mind didn't make the journey with her. She was once again too focused obsessing over the missing journals.

Despite Bill and Rob both telling her to try to relax about it, it was all she could think about.

Nightmares once again plagued her dream, the shadow bursting through the front door. She couldn't help but think it had to be key to solving the mystery.

On Sunday, Bill announced he had a surprise for her.

They drove out to the airfield where a friend of Bill's gave aerial tours of Yellowstone. It was breathtaking and took her mind off her problems. Later, they went on a drive and he showed her a lake not far from the house where bald eagles nested. She watched them hunt, swooping down and plucking fish out of the water with surgical precision. By the end of the day she felt tired but happy.

Rob got the short version on the phone. Later, she curled up with her laptop and sent him an email detailing her day's adventures. She hit send and shut the computer down, ready for bed. Rob would answer by morning. Sleep eluded her, and a half hour later she decided to go back and read over some of her old articles again in hopes that maybe it would trigger something.

Anything.

Two hours later, it hadn't. Dejected, she set the computer on the nightstand and tried to sleep.

Nothing looked clearer the next morning, either. Bill noticed her foul mood at breakfast.

"What's up?"

She told him.

"You'll figure it out eventually, sis. They have to be somewhere. You didn't just stop or lose them."

"Well, where the hell are they?"

"You'll find them," he insisted.

* * * *

There was only one week left in her agreed Montana tenure when the note arrived in her email one morning. After opening Gmail she scanned the inbox and felt her stomach tighten.

MedicineMan.

Det. Thomas was at his desk and put her on hold while he got in touch with Hutchins. The tech logged in and accessed the newest threat.

Thomas returned to the phone. "What does it say?"

"I don't know. I haven't read it yet. I'm almost afraid to."

"Go ahead. I've got Hutchins working on it on his end."

Hesitating, she finally forced herself to click on the message.

Her voice trembled as she read it to Thomas.

"Where have you been? I'm really missing you. Can't wait for you to come home. I have big plans."

"This guy is obviously stalking everywhere he knows you usually are."

"Have you been keeping an eye on Rob?"

"This guy's after you, not him."

"He would probably go through Rob to get to me."

"I won't lie and tell you no. He's proven how vicious he is."

"Did you ever find anything out about the boat?"

"The skiff was stolen from a snowbird couple's house on the other end of the key. The guy must have used gloves, because there were no fingerprints that didn't belong there."

"When can I come home?"

"I can't legally keep you from returning. Unfortunately, I don't have the manpower to guard you indefinitely."

"I realize that. I'm not asking for an armed guard. I need to live my life, what I can of it. I can't spend the rest of my life hiding in Montana. I have a business, a home, and family. I want my life back." Her hand reached up to her throat. In her pocket, as Rob had ordered, she kept her leather play collar.

"I want my friends back. They're my adopted family. This guy took my past. I'm not letting him take my future, too."

* * * *

Rob called an hour later. Thomas had updated him and Rob was adamant. "Honey, you can't come home."

"Either you come out here and get me next week, or I'll fly home and rent a car in Tampa. I'm *not* staying here."

"*Stop.*" Dom tone.

She would have nothing to do with it. She walked into the bedroom and closed the door behind her and dropped her voice. "Sir, I don't care if you give me two hundred with a goddamned cane. I'm sick of hiding and not being able to live my life!"

"It's not safe."

"What happens when he finally figures out where I am and he comes looking for me here? The police are a good fifteen minutes away at the very least. If the weather's good and they're not off on another call. At least at home I can bet on someone responding in a few minutes. And I can carry a gun there."

"And you could be dead by then, so what difference would it make?"

"At least I would be home. Goddammit, you're not hiding me up here forever." She did something she didn't think she'd ever done since accepting his collar. "Sir, I'm sorry, but if you're not up here in seven days, I'm flying out of Bozeman and coming home. Do you understand me?"

She hoped she hadn't pushed too far. He was quiet for a moment. "I'll talk to the captain about getting off. I'll come get you. You're *not* coming home alone, understand? I waited for you. The least you can do is wait for me. All right?"

She breathed a sigh of relief. "Yes, Sir. Just hurry, please?"

* * * *

Rob called her the next day. "I'll leave on Thursday. I figure if I drive straight through, it'll probably take me four days."

Thursday was only four days away, meaning he should be there by the following Monday. Hopefully.

"Yes."

Cabin fever of a sort had set in. She missed her life, her business, her home, her dog, and her fiancé. She wanted it back, what she had of it. A risk she was willing to take.

While she was gone, Rob had installed motion-detection floodlights outside the house and rented a Bush Hog to clear out the tall grass and underbrush just beyond the fence to increase visibility. And in a move Laura called overkill, he had an electric fence installed.

"I considered burying a few land mines, but I thought Det. Thomas might not like that idea."

She laughed, missing his sense of humor more than ever.

* * * *

Laura spent the next day riding and journaling. She would miss Bill and the serenity she found in Montana but she was ready to go home and face whatever happened. In her forced exile, her fear had turned into anger.

There was no way MedicineMan would ruin her life. She wouldn't let it happen.

Rob left on time, calling her every day with his progress. On Monday, right on schedule, he pulled into Bill's driveway and Laura nearly tackled him before he climbed out of the Explorer.

She wrapped her arms around him and kissed him, crying with relief and joy. "I'm so glad to see you, Sir!"

He picked her up and held her, Laura breathing in his scent and absorbing every single moment.

When Doogie nosed the back of Rob's neck, he turned. "Someone else missed you, too."

Doogie's entire body wagged with joy as she hugged him. He'd grown in her absence, at least ten pounds heavier than when she last saw him.

When Bill's dogs realized the visitor had brought a new playmate, they came over and said hi. She let the Lab jump out and go play.

"Will they be okay?" Rob asked.

"Oh, yeah. All I'll have to do is ring the dinner bell and he'll come running with them."

She led him inside and showed him around. Doogie forgot his new friends in his eagerness to follow his mom. She helped Rob unload his bags and Doogie's gear and when Bill returned they went out to eat in Gardiner. Despite Laura's desire to start for home immediately, she agreed to Rob's request let him rest for a couple of days.

"You know, it's not easy putting up with seventy-five pounds of wiggly Lab for several thousand miles."

She laughed and hugged him. "I guess I can wait that long. With you here, I'm sure I can think of something to fill the time."

They went to bed early, except they remembered to lock Doogie out of the bedroom.

Rob wasted no time. He began yanking his clothes off before the bedroom door even swung shut behind him.

"Naked," he ordered in full Dom tone. "Now."

She took mere seconds to strip.

He extended his hand and snapped his fingers. "Collar."

She grabbed it and fought the urge to sob with relief when he pointed at the floor by his feet. She held her hair out of the way while he buckled the collar around her neck.

Hooking a finger through the D-ring on the front, he tugged, urging her to her feet. After backing her to the edge of the bed, he put a hand in the middle of her chest and gently pushed.

She fell to the bed with a bounce, giggling.

He smiled. "You laugh now. You just wait." He rolled a condom onto his cock and straddled her on the bed, grabbing her wrists and pinning them over her head with one hand while he lined up his cock at the entrance of her pussy with the other.

"Hard and fast, baby," he hoarsely said. "Because I can't fucking stand not to be inside you."

He wasn't kidding. She let out a soft cry as he thrust hard and deep, her swollen clit rubbing against his body with each stroke.

Burying his face in the crook of her neck, he said, "Come for me, baby. Come now."

Then he bit down on her shoulder. Hard.

She cried out, her orgasm popping like an overloaded circuit. She thought he made a little growling sound, but then another orgasm washed through her as he kept biting her, the pain serving to amp up her release.

"One more," he gasped, slamming his hips into her.

Laura wasn't sure she could handle another one. Maybe it was the forced separation, but it felt like every nerve ending in her body sizzled. With his cock driving hard and deep inside her with each thrust, her body responded. As her cunt clamped down on his cock he let out a grunt of his own she knew meant he was coming, too.

He fell still, his lips now kissing at the spot on her shoulder she suspected would be nice and purple the next morning.

If she was lucky.

"Love you, baby girl." He released her wrists and she wrapped her arms around him.

"Love you, too, Sir. I missed you."

It sounded like he sighed. "I missed you, too, baby. You have no idea how much I missed you."

Rob dragged himself out of bed to clean up and returned a minute later. Exhausted, he fell asleep curled around her. She lay awake for a while, listening to him breathe, remembering what she could of life before the attack.

He woke her early the next morning by burying his face between her legs and quickly erasing all vestiges of sleep from her system. After making her come, he pinned her wrists over her head and fucked her, hard and fast and with a smile on his face that she would have gladly killed anyone for interrupting.

Later, after Rob drifted back to sleep, Laura pulled on some clothes and went outside to feed the horses.

She would miss them. They were a comfort and a path to healing through the quiet rides. After filling their feed buckets she sat and softly talked to them. Maurie, the piebald gelding, nickered to her and nuzzled her foot with his nose. She stroked his fur, laying her face against his neck and smelling his sweet scent.

When a noise startled her she whirled around. Rob stood in the barn doorway, silhouetted by the morning sun.

"Sorry. I didn't mean to scare you."

"That's okay."

He knelt next to her and reached out. The gelding cautiously sniffed his hand, blowing a few times before nuzzling him and then reburying his head in the bucket.

"He's a big Lab, that's all," Rob laughed.

"Horses are the ultimate Labs. They'll eat themselves sick."

"We could always buy the lot next door, fence it in, and build a pole barn. Our area's zoned for horses."

She scratched Peter, a buckskin gelding, behind the ears. "I'll think about it." Then she had another thought. "After we get this other stuff behind us." The horrifying thought of going out one morning and finding a dead, mutilated horse nauseated her.

And with MedicineMan still on the loose, that was a possibility she didn't doubt. There's no way she'd ever let Doogie out of her sight outside at the house, much less leave him outside in the yard alone.

They walked back inside, hand and hand. They talked about showering but drifted into bed first. After an hour they rose once more and finally made it into the bath. Rob finished first and made a fresh pot of coffee for Laura. When she emerged, wrapped in Rob's robe, he pulled her into his arms and kissed her.

"I had an idea," he said.

"Let's hear it."

"I know you said you still wanted to follow our original wedding plans, but how about we fudge a little and go ahead and get married here, before we leave?" He pulled a box out of his pocket and opened it for her.

It was their wedding bands.

She looked at him. "In Montana?"

"Well, unless we're in outer Mongolia, yeah, Montana." His face turned somber. "Look, I almost lost you once. And who knows what's going to happen when we get home. I know I said I wanted to collar you and marry you in front of our friends. But I love you, and I'm bound and determined I'm going to marry you no matter what. I can't think of a more beautiful place to honeymoon than here. Hell, we were going to honeymoon here anyway."

He dropped to one knee and held her hand. "Please marry me. I can't beg or grovel any more than that." He smiled. "Besides, I put up with Doogie all the way up here. You damn well owe me, baby girl."

She playfully shoved him. "When?"

"When do you want to do it? How long will it take us to get a license?"

"I don't know." She managed to get in touch with Bill at the airfield before he left for a trip and he told her who to contact. By the time he returned home that evening, they had a marriage license.

A friend of his was a notary public. Bill called a couple of his friends, people Laura had come to know during her stay. The next day they drove into Yellowstone. Three hours later, on the boardwalk overlooking the terraces at Mammoth Hot Springs, Laura officially became Laura Carlton.

One of Bill's friends videotaped the ceremony for them while a second photographed it. They all went out to dinner after, and they returned to Bill's tired and happy. Bill went home with his girlfriend, leaving Rob and Laura alone.

"Go bring me your collar, baby girl," he quietly ordered.

She nearly tripped over her feet in her run for the bedroom, earning her a gentle laugh as he watched her. She brought it to him, presenting it.

He took it and pointed at the floor.

This felt beyond right, beyond perfect. Kneeling at her Master's feet, the world at large nowhere in sight. Just *Him*.

He buckled it around her throat before gathering her hair in his right hand and tipping her head back so he could look into her eyes.

"Who do you belong to?"

"You, Sir."

He smiled, breaking her heart with its perfection. She knew she could never deny him anything he asked, ever, if it meant earning that smile from him.

Not a hint of the sadness, the pain, that he'd worn so heavily in the early weeks after the attack.

"That's right. You do. My sweet, beautiful baby girl. All mine."

Without releasing his hold on her hair, he urged her to her feet. He gripped the back of her neck firmly with his other hand and lowered his lips just above hers.

"You belong to me. I'll die before I let anyone hurt you. You know that, right?"

She nodded, transfixed by his sweet gaze. "Yes, Sir."

He teased her, making as if to kiss her but not letting her close the gap, earning her another of those smiles. "Tell me what you want."

This was something else that felt right. She wasn't sure what to say, but the words magically appeared in her brain. "I want you to own me completely, Sir. I want to be your slave. I want you to own my heart and my body."

He never looked away, his gaze holding hers. "For the rest of our lives."

"Yes, Sir."

"That means taking punishment if you disobey me."

Her breath came faster. "Yes, Sir."

He completed the kiss, setting off explosions inside her. He kissed her hard, crushing, fucking her mouth with his tongue as she did her best not to let her knees turn to jelly. She had to wrap her arms around him for support.

He took and tasted, giving her no choice, holding her there and stealing her breath with the ferocity.

Just as suddenly, he used his grip on her to pull her away from him with a playful smile. She gasped, reeling, and he used her discombobulation to spin her around and deliver a bare-handed swat that stung even through the seat of her jeans.

"Go start a fire, baby girl. I have plans for you tonight."

She raced to do it.

Laura kindled a fire while Rob opened a chilled bottle of champagne he'd bought the day before. They curled up in front of the fireplace and linked arms.

He gazed into her eyes as she felt the first true, deep peace she had since the nightmare began. "I love you, Laur," he said. "You are my life."

She leaned over to kiss him, nearly spilling her glass. This set them both giggling and they barely managed to take a sip before having to untangle themselves and put the glasses down.

"Tell me the truth, Sir. Was I always this klutzy?"

He smiled. "Yes, but it was one of the things I loved about you." He brushed a strand of hair away from her eyes. She hadn't had the color touched up. It had grown out a little and she was back to wearing it like she used to. "Someone so beautiful and talented and yet as human as the rest of us." He stroked her cheek. "You used to always joke you wear your food well."

"There's still a lot I don't remember, you know."

He nodded. "I know."

"Are you okay with that?"

"I wouldn't be here if I wasn't." He hooked a finger through the ring in the front of her collar and pulled her close. "Tonight you don't think about that. Tonight, you completely belong to me, and I'm going to make up for lost time." He kissed her before pulling her into his arms.

She settled against him and watched the flames dance in the hearth. "I want it all back, Sir," she whispered. "I want all my memories back. I want to know everything." She paused. "I want those *goddamn* journals!"

"*Stop*. That's an order. Do not think about it. Not tonight. Regardless of whether or not your old memories come back, we're going to make new ones, right?"

She nodded.

"Okay, then. Let's make some right now." He kissed her, slowly, refusing to be rushed. She folded against him, opening herself to him completely, her body pressed against his. She'd missed this, being with him, contact with him. Especially when they'd just begun rekindling this part of their relationship.

When she pulled him down on top of her, he stopped her.

"What?"

"Hold on a minute." He got up and disappeared into the bedroom, reappearing with blankets and pillows, as well as a duffel bag.

"What's that?" she asked.

He grinned. "You'll find out, baby girl."

A thrill ran through her. He obviously had something up his sleeve. She had a strong suspicion what that something was.

Once they spread the blankets and pillows out on the floor, he held his arms out to her and drew her close. "That's better."

He took his time. It was sweet, slow torture as he traced her neckline with tiny kisses and carefully unbuttoned her shirt. As he kissed her bared skin she pushed away all thoughts that these last few days could be the beginning of the end if the stalker had his way.

She moaned softly while he slowly, carefully, explored every inch of her flesh. When she tried to work on his waistband he gently pushed her hands away. With a sigh she lay back and closed her eyes, enjoying the feel of his body against hers.

He made her feel beautiful, in a way she'd thought she might never feel after seeing her reflection in the mirror at the hospital. She'd come away, physically, with just a tiny scar on her forehead.

Emotional and mental scars, however, weren't something she wanted to ponder. Not tonight.

Feather-soft, his fingers traced patterns on her skin, making her shiver with anticipation. He nibbled on the top of her shoulder, at the junction with her neck, nipping her just enough to make her squeal with pleasure and pain.

"Such a sweet sound," he whispered against her flesh before he did it again. And again.

Her clit pulsed, throbbing. He knew her body better than she did, it sometimes felt like.

Then he reached for the bag, hooking the strap with his finger and dragging it close. He unzipped it and held up her leather wrist and ankle cuffs. Slowly, after grazing his teeth across her flesh at every point, he buckled each cuff around her.

"Now that's the way I wish I could keep you dressed all the time," he said. He grabbed her wrists and pulled them up and over her head, pinning her down. His stiff cock pressed through his jeans, hitting her perfectly against her clit. "Wearing nothing but my cuffs, my collar, and my wedding ring."

She nodded, barely able to breathe with the anticipation coursing through her body.

He reached into the bag again. He withdrew a coil of royal blue rope and held it up. "Tonight, we do things my way."

Laura caught her lower lip under her teeth. She felt close to coming just from the raging passion in his face. She nodded.

"Good girl." Using her wrists, he pulled her up into a sitting position. "Arms up."

She immediately complied as he set to work, weaving a chest harness around her torso. He took his time, the rope sliding over her flesh as he trapped her breasts, making them stand out.

Pausing, he leaned in and sucked her left nipple between his lips.

She let out a moan and started to put her arms down to hold him but he let go. "I said arms up."

Dom tone. Her arms shot skyward again.

"Good girl." He sucked her right nipple into his mouth. An accompanying bolt of liquid need coursed straight to her aching clit.

He continued fashioning the chest harness, then added her arms to it, binding them snugly to her sides and leaving her unable to move them.

Rob stood and admired his handiwork. "Good." He pushed her down onto her back. Leaning over, he pulled something else from the bag. She recognized it as an adjustable spreader bar. He clipped it to her ankle cuffs and then pushed her legs up and back, using the rope to secure it to the chest harness and leaving her open and vulnerable.

"Someone got mouthy with me on the phone, didn't they?"

Unable to trust her voice, she nodded.

He *tsked* at her and reached over to pull something else from the bag.

A short rattan cane.

He held it up for her inspection before reaching down, tormenting her nipples with the tip. "What do bad girls get when they disobey or get mouthy?"

"The cane, Sir." The whispered response had appeared from the depths of her brain without conscious thought on her part.

He touched her clit with the tip. "Yes, they do." He reached up and held it close to her mouth. "Kiss it. Show it love. It's for your own good."

Eagerly, as if his cock, she wrapped her lips around the thin rod, flicking her tongue over it, sucking on it.

He smiled. "Such a good girl. Now ask me for it."

"I need punishment, Sir. I disobeyed you."

"Tell me details. What did you do?"

She felt the prickle of tears in her eyes. "I talked back to you on the phone, Sir."

He knelt next to her and grabbed her chin, forcing her to look at him. This wasn't Rob the playful paramedic that most everyone else saw.

This was her Master, and this man was all business.

A ferocity had taken over his expression. "Do you understand why you are being punished?"

She nodded. "Yes, Sir."

"Tell me."

"I…because I talked back."

He shook his head. "No."

Confusion filled her. She struggled for the words even as his grip tightened on her chin, almost painfully, and he leaned in closer.

"You were going to disobey me," he quietly said. "When I'd given you a direct order that related to keeping you safe. What is the first and most important rule I have for you?"

This, too, came unbidden to her lips. "That I obey you, Sir," she whispered.

He slowly nodded. "What is the first rule I told you applies to me?"

Now she felt the tears rolling out the corners of her eyes, her vision blurring. "That you will always take care of me and put me first, Sir."

He nodded, his expression softening. "Very good, baby girl," he whispered, leaning in to kiss her. "You remembered."

She did, but that small achievement paled in comparison to her personal shame.

She'd disobeyed him.

She knew viscerally that never in their relationship since she'd become his submissive had she ever so blatantly challenged and disobeyed him.

As if reading her mind, he asked, "What is our rule regarding talking?"

Another answer from the abyss. "If I don't agree with you, I calmly ask to take a time-out to talk, and we will."

"Did you?"

She almost couldn't bear to say it. "No, Sir."

He nodded. "That was very disappointing to me, that you did that. Do you feel you've earned punishment?"

"Yes, Sir."

"Say it."

Her breath hitched, now from crying instead of passion. "I disobeyed you by talking back to you, and by not asking to talk about it."

"Do you understand why I have to punish you for that?"

It didn't help her feel any better about it. "I was going to disobey you and put myself at risk."

His grip on her chin eased. He leaned in and kissed her. "Yes. Exactly. How many do you think you've earned?"

They never had a set number before. She rarely earned anything more than a hard, bare-handed swat across her ass, or, a couple of times, five with his belt.

He rarely punished her with a cane, although the threat of it as punishment went a long way toward keeping her focused. She hated the cane, which was why he liked to include it in their play sometimes. She'd take it for him in play, because he wanted her to.

But punishment was different.

She'd disappointed him.

That was something she couldn't bear.

"Fifty, Sir."

He arched an eyebrow at her. "Fifty?"

She nodded, unable to speak it.

He leaned in and pressed a long, lingering kiss to her forehead. "Ten," he said. "Ten hard ones. These are going to hurt, and they're going to leave marks."

"Yes, Sir."

"I'll give you time between each stroke to process it, but you will take all ten without a safeword. This is punishment. Do you agree?"

She nodded.

"Say it."

"No safeword, Sir. I'll take them." She knew damn well if she sat up and said stop, game over, he would. And he wouldn't hold it against her.

She also knew she'd never be able to live with herself if she did that. She *wanted* this, wanted to be his.

That meant she took her earned lumps.

And she knew she'd earned them. That he was going to go easier on her than she would have gone on herself made her feel worse, not better.

He reached into the bag and pulled out a rubber ball gag. "Do you want this?"

"Yes, Sir." It would be easier to take the strokes, having something to bite down on.

He put down the cane. "Before we do, I want you to say it all, exactly why I'm doing this, and ask me for it."

She'd rather take extra cane strokes, but she spoke, her voice trembling. "I earned punishment for talking back to you on the phone. I was going to disobey you and put myself in danger, meaning I would have made you violate your rule to keep me safe. I need to be punished to remind me who is in charge…"

She froze as a flood of memories about another night when they'd had a similar conversation flowed back into her brain. They felt foreign, but right, as they slipped into place.

He frowned. "Laur?" Their most basic safeword was to use each others' first names when deep in a scene.

She shook her head to quiet him. "I…" She swallowed hard, not wanting to stop to process it and interrupt things. "I get mouthy. I get pushy. I lose my temper and Sir has to remind me when I get like that, because…"

Another sob as her talks with Bill and Steve and others about her infamous temper came to mind.

And about how much happier they all noted she seemed to be once Rob came into her life. "Because I *need* Sir's strength to keep me taken in hand and keep me grounded. I'm happiest when Sir's in charge. And I don't want Sir to let me slide and let me get out of punishment."

He put down the gag and reached over as if to untie the spreader bar, but she shifted, moving her bent legs away from him and putting the knot out of reach. "I *need* punishment," she rapidly said, "because I *want* you to be in charge of me. I *need* someone stronger than me. *Please*, Sir. *Please* give me my punishment."

He froze. "Laura, do we need to stop and talk about this?"

She shook her head. "No, not now. Please, not now, Sir."

He hesitated, considering.

She knew if he decided to stop, that was it, they'd stop.

She didn't *want* him to stop. "*Please*, Sir," she begged. "Please."

He sat up again, considering. "Legs back," he ordered.

She shifted toward him again.

Like a flash, his hand shot out and snagged the ring on her collar. He pulled her head up, leaning in eye-to-eye. "Don't you *ever* pull away from me like that again. Do you understand me?"

She wanted to laugh with relief. "Yes, Sir. I'm sorry, Sir."

He nodded. "Good girl." He leaned in and kissed her forehead before releasing her collar. "That's an extra stroke for that."

She eagerly nodded. "Yes, Sir." Relief flooded her. He wouldn't stop. It also explained why he hadn't shed his clothes yet. Unless it was something that happened when he'd already got naked, he never undressed before he got her punishment out of the way.

"Sir?" she whispered before he fitted the ball gag into her mouth.

"Yes?"

"I miss my maintenance spankings." Every morning they spent together, before, even if he was running late, she got at least a quick, bare-handed spanking over his lap, usually once he was already dressed.

Somehow, that made it even hotter for her, to be naked across his thighs, feeling the fabric of his cargo pants rubbing against her flesh while he firmly pinned her down by the neck with his left hand and smacked her ass with his right.

Even if it meant waking her up and rolling her over to deliver several stinging swats to her ass, she got them.

She'd needed them.

She'd *wanted* them.

If they had the day to spend together, or he wasn't running late, he took his time and sometimes even used a paddle or other implement to make it sting even more. On his days off, he'd give her spankings so good she was still feeling them that evening, and usually spent her day wet because she'd wiggle in her office chair just to feel the burn in her ass.

His stern expression dissolved as he burst into laughter. "Is that what you just remembered, sweetheart? Maintenance spankings?"

She nodded.

He leaned in and kissed her forehead. "Then starting tomorrow morning, you'll get your maintenance spankings again. It'll be my pleasure."

He fit the ball gag into her mouth and waited until she had it positioned where she wanted it to buckle it behind her head.

Then he shifted positions, sitting next to her, his back to her and his left arm pressed into the backs of her knees. He picked up the cane with his right and looked at her. "Ready?"

She nodded.

She felt him slowly rub the cane up and down the backsides of her thighs, the crease where they joined her ass cheeks, and down her ass. Up and down, building the tension.

Then he paused it in that damn crease and she took a deep breath.

Zwwip. The snap as it struck her there, all the way across, tore a scream from her as she bit down on the gag with her jaw tightly clenched.

He looked back at her, once again calm and stern, all playfulness gone. "One," he said.

She nodded, tears of pain coursing down her cheeks.

He hadn't been kidding when he'd said they would hurt.

She couldn't have loved him any more or harder in that moment if she'd tried. He wouldn't let her get away with disobeying him. He was in charge.

He *owned* her.

He waited until she settled down for a moment, once again stroking the cane up and down her flesh. Where he'd stop and take the second stroke, only he knew.

Zwwip. Right across the center of her ass cheeks, every bit as hard as the first. As she struggled to process it through her scream of pain, she delighted in the fact the welts from that stroke would still hurt in a couple of days.

If she was lucky.

"That's two." He drew it out, all eleven strokes hard and biting and leaving her a screaming, sobbing mess by the time he finished and put down the cane.

"There's my good girl," he cooed, his fingers softly stroking and soothing her flesh.

Then they came to a stop over her clit. In a flash, her sobs turned to moans as he slipped two fingers inside her pussy as deeply as he could.

"You are a very, very wet girl," he said. "You have really missed your spankings, haven't you?"

She forced her eyes open and nodded.

The grin on his face only made her clit throb harder. "Such a good girl."

He reached into the bag and pulled something else out. She couldn't see exactly what, but then she heard a soft *click* and a hum.

Rob left her no time to process that. He filled her pussy again with his fingers and pressed the vibrator against her clit with his other hand.

The scream around the ball gag this time was far louder, and not from pain.

Her back arched even as her body betrayed her, humping against his hand and the vibrator as much as she could immobilized.

"Such a good girl," he cooed again. "You took your punishment so well, you earned a reward."

She threw her head back and moaned, the orgasm expanding, overwhelming. Yes, punishment was always followed by a reward, even when the maintenance spankings weren't on a daily basis if he didn't have time.

Her Master wasn't an idiot. He'd learned well from Seth and Tony and the others, meting overwhelming pleasure with overwhelming pain and rewiring her body to crave every bit of it.

She had no idea how long he kept her coming. All she knew was she gave thanks it was a battery operated vibrator and not the more intense—and electrically powered—Hitachi.

Eventually, he let out a chuckle and switched the vibrator off. Panting, she tried to catch her breath, eyes closed.

Even through the last echoes of pleasure she felt the stinging, burning stripes of the cane marks across her flesh.

And, despite the gaping holes in her memory, she finally felt complete.

* * * *

Rob had to force himself to give her all eleven strokes. Seeing her obvious distress before he started was the only thing that made him hold on to his reserve and follow through.

His memories of their hours of conversation, hundreds of hours, maybe, with her curled in his lap and talking. About her asking him, before, to never let her talk her way out of punishment, especially if he thought she'd earned it.

Her begging him to never let her get away with anything or push him around.

The memory of Steve confiding in him just a month after Rob collared her that he didn't know what Rob had done to Laura, but to never stop doing it. That she seemed relaxed and peaceful for the first time in her life.

How his initial reluctance to take the firm control she told him she craved had eventually morphed into *his* need to keep her in hand, as much for his own sake as for hers.

In a career where he controlled very little, where he witnessed so many bad things on a daily basis, where chaos and even violence caused others pain and suffering that he frequently felt helpless to stop, *this* was the blissful center of his universe. Keeping her happy and loved. Controlling what happened and ensuring that peace and calm ruled their household.

She strictly ruled the rest of her world, her business. Lives literally depended on that exacting level of control she had, inspiring and training students who could die if they didn't do what she told them, how she told them, and when she told them.

She needed the release from the stress. She needed him to be someone she could always count on to retain that control, even if she pushed the boundaries and tried to test him.

They really were two halves of a kinky little whole.

After removing the ball gag, he held the vibrator up to her lips. Without coaxing she opened, licking and sucking it clean and earning herself another laugh.

"That's my good girl."

He released her legs from the spreader bar and untied the rope harness, freeing her. Then he finally shed his own clothes and lay down next to her, kissing her neck, nibbling on her ear.

"I want you, Sir," she gasped. "Please." She sat up and swung a leg over him but he stopped her.

"Wait." He reached behind him, trying to get to his pants.

She pulled his hand back. "No."

Their eyes locked. "Laur, we need—"

She silenced him with a finger on his lips and shook her head. Her eyes smoldered in the firelight. "*Please*, Sir. No."

There was a determined set to her jaw he knew all too well. He let her pull his hand back and place it on her hip. His other followed suit and she leaned forward and kissed him long and tenderly. Sitting up, she smiled and teased him with her hips, gliding the length of his engorged cock back and forth through her wet folds.

She still remembered how to do that.

"Are you sure this is what you want?" he asked.

"Don't you?"

He smiled. "Mrs. Carlton, you know what you're doing to me, don't you?"

She nodded, closing her eyes and enjoying it. "Having fun, aren't you?" she asked.

He laughed. "Oh yes."

"Okay then."

He tried one more time just to make sure. "I know we discussed this…before. Are you sure this is what you want?"

She nodded.

He grabbed her hips and lifted her, then settled her down onto the full length of his cock. He had to hold her still for a moment, not wanting to explode just yet. Her slick cunt tightly gripped his cock, a perfect fit.

Everything about them seemed to fit perfectly together.

Once he knew he had himself under control, he let her take the lead. In a few minutes, when he knew he couldn't take it anymore, he began thrusting up into her, rocking together, easily finding a rhythm.

She still knew how make him moan. He gently stroked her clit with his thumb, bringing her almost to the edge. When he knew she was ready he thrust up hard, met her strokes, their eyes locked.

He waited until her eyes dropped closed, letting out a soft cry at the same time her pussy clenched around his cock. That's when he finally let go and moaned, exploding inside her and filling her with his cum. When it was over she collapsed on top of him and he wrapped his arms around her, drawing a blanket up over them.

The fire crackled beside them, defining their entire world. No fear, no worries, no hurts, only them entwined and the comforting house and the fire to warm them. Just when he thought she was asleep she kissed the side of his neck.

"I love you, Sir."

He hugged her. "I love you, too, baby girl."

She paused. "You did want kids, right?"

He laughed. "Now's a pretty bad time to ask, doncha think?"

He rolled them over and stared down at her, loving her, wishing he could freeze the night and capture the moment forever. "You do remember you said I could name a boy Iggy, right?"

She laughed, reaching up to tickle him. He pinned her arms as he kissed her, feeling himself stiffen inside her once again.

She glanced down. "Looks like you've got something that needs taken care of, Sir."

"Then why don't we?"

* * * *

It was nearly midnight when they drifted to sleep in front of the dying fire.

Laura woke in the middle of the night. The fire was almost out and the house had chilled. She wiggled free of Rob's arms and turned the thermostat up. The dogs were all asleep in the kitchen and nothing seemed amiss.

Then why am I so jumpy?

She retrieved Rob's robe from the bedroom and made the rounds of the house, making sure all the doors and windows were locked. At the front door she flipped on the outside flood lights, carefully looking around before turning them off again.

Something had woken her.

She went around to the back door and turned on the light. A shadowy shape huddled on the ground out at the farthest reaches of the light. She couldn't tell what it was. Looking around, she unlatched the door and stepped out onto the porch, taking a few steps out.

It was Peter. The buckskin was lying down. That didn't make sense, because she'd latched the stall doors before they went out to dinner.

She called to the horse, not getting a response. Her breath frosted in front of her and that's when she realized the gelding wasn't breathing.

Forgetting caution, she rushed forward, her bare feet hitting something damp. When she looked down she saw the ground was covered in blood. Fighting her nausea she approached the horse and saw his head lay at a grotesque, unnatural angle to his neck.

Because its throat was cut, the head nearly completely severed from its neck.

She opened her mouth to scream and felt hands grab her shoulders, shaking her.

That's when she sat up and realized she was still on the floor in front of the fire and Rob was trying to break the nightmare's spell. Outside glowed the soft twilight of a Montana summer dawn.

Relief washed over her and she collapsed, sobbing in his arms. He finally got her to tell him about the dream and he made a point of checking on the horses. They were fine, the dogs were fine, everything was fine.

They moved into the bedroom and she tried to go back to sleep. Just when she didn't think sleep would be possible she woke up to Rob kissing the back of her neck and whispering breakfast was ready. The nightmare faded into memory and she made the decision to forget it and enjoy the day.

But before she could eat breakfast, he rolled her onto her stomach and examined her ass, stroking her with one hand while pinning her down at the neck with the other.

She instantly felt wet.

He laughed. "Okay, baby girl. You wanted maintenance spankings to resume, didn't you?"

"Yes, Sir," she mumbled into the mattress.

He gave her five fast, only slightly stingy swats, across her ass. "You've got some nice welts, baby girl. I'm going to take it easy on you until those heal up. But I promised you maintenance spankings."

"Thank you, Sir."

He rolled her over and kissed her. "Breakfast." He grinned and left the room before she could protest that now she wanted a hard fucking instead of eggs and bacon.

After a quick stop by the bathroom, and running her hand over her flesh in the mirror and smiling over the now-purple welts marking her flesh, she headed to the kitchen to join him.

Rob wanted to go riding after breakfast. So after he kept her horny while making her give him a blow job in the shower, they set out over the hills on the horses, taking a lunch with them.

Riding proved an added sweet torture, her ass reminding her with every step of the cane strokes.

But happiness and peace filled her. She was his. Utterly, completely.

And he'd more than proved it the night before.

Rob caught her up on events at the shop in person better than he could through email or over the phone. They talked about their past, she asked him about things she remembered. Several times she looked over and stared at the gold band on his left ring finger, and the wedding band now surrounding her engagement ring and felt a warm thrill run through her.

He wasn't only her Master. Finally, he was her husband.

They had to file the marriage certificate Monday morning, but except for that they were legal. Instead of a ceremony like they originally planned at home, they would show the video and throw a reception party. She played with the rings on her hand, getting used to the pleasantly different feel.

One of the many memories still missing was the day they'd picked them out.

They lunched at her overlook and even watched a bald eagle swoop down and pluck a salmon out of the stream below.

"Wow, that's awesome." Rob said.

Laura nodded. "I love this place. I think this is the only thing that's helped me keep my sanity this entire time."

He put his arm around her and kissed the top of her head. "I'm sorry about sending you off, baby girl. It was for your own good."

She nodded. "I know, Sir. I don't like it, but I understand. I just can't wait to get home."

"I think I can." He leaned over and nuzzled her neck, sending shivers through her.

They would have gone further except Maurie walked over and stuck his nose in their faces, sniffing them.

"Thanks, Maurie," Laura laughed, gently pushing the gelding away.

Rob groaned, falling back on the ground. "First Doogie, now him. What is it with animals insisting on interrupting my love life?"

Chapter Thirty-Four

Monday morning, after Rob gave her a quick maintenance spanking, Rob, Laura, and Bill went out to eat breakfast before they filed the marriage certificate.

"So when do you want me back in Florida?" Bill asked with a smile. "I don't want to miss the reception."

"Anytime you want, for as long as you want," Rob said. "I can't tell you how much I appreciate all you've done for us."

"Hey, family's family. I tell you what, when they catch that psycho, you and me are going to save the State of Florida the cost of a trial."

Rob stuck out his hand. "Agreed, brother."

Laura looked at her "boys." "Well ain't the testosterone thick this morning?" It was gratifying they cared that much about her, even though she knew most of it was bravado.

She hoped. She didn't want either of them in jail.

And truth be told, *she* wanted the first shot at MedicineMan.

After breakfast, Laura and Rob filed their certificate and spent the morning touring the town. Laura enjoyed playing guide and they finally made their way back to the house for lunch in the afternoon. Rob fixed them some sandwiches while Laura checked her email.

She spotted it sitting in her inbox and called out to Rob. He reached out and clicked on it to read it.

Apparently your boyfriend's disappeared, too. Come out, come out, wherever you are. Let's play hide and seek. I'm It.

You can't hide forever.

I'll still be waiting.

* * * *

Rob handled the call to Thomas. Thomas put Rob on hold while he contacted Hutchinson.

When Thomas returned to the line, Rob asked, "Where the hell are these emails coming from?"

"We haven't been able to track this guy. He's masking his MAC address in addition to his IP."

"I don't understand what that means. What about the email account he's using? You can't track it?"

"He's using a free server but gave totally false information when he opened it. The server offered to block the account, but he'll just open another one under another name. This way at least it's easier to track him down. He has to know we're trying to track him and thinks we can't."

"Easier? You don't even know who he is yet."

"It's easier to keep track of one persona versus four or five."

Laura felt her confidence slip as she listened in on the speaker call. Maybe Montana wasn't such a bad place after all. Talking tough was one thing. The constant worry was almost too much for her to take. The hypervigilance she would need upon returning to Florida intimidated her, to say the least. All it would take was one wrong move, one minute of inattention, and she could die.

Maybe her decision the night before hadn't been the right one. She didn't think it was the right time of the month for her to get pregnant, but anything was possible. Perhaps it would be best to take precautions.

Then again, it was her life. If she could figure out what she did with the other journals, maybe something in them would solve this whole problem.

If they even existed. Unfortunately, she was beginning to doubt they did.

Laura found it hard to believe some random psycho managed to target her in Englewood. It was a sleepy retirement town filled mostly with snowbirds and fishermen. While it was true the population was growing quickly and new people were moving into the area, it still wasn't the kind of place that spawned stalkers.

She hoped.

While on the phone with Rob, Thomas told him they had an FBI profiler working on the case since he was linked to the other killings. Hopefully that would give them a lead to work with, or at least a way to eliminate people from the suspect list.

Not that they had any suspects to begin with.

Once Rob was off the phone, she spoke up. "I want to leave tomorrow, Sir," Laura said. "I can't live like this anymore. I want it over with, one way or another. Either this son of a bitch is going to come after me or he's full of hot air and gets off by sending me messages. I don't care anymore. I want it settled. Please, Sir?"

"We could be talking your life here." He looked at her belly and laid his hand on it. "Or more."

"Sir, I promise, I'll carry that gun twenty-four-seven. If he's stupid enough to try something, I won't hesitate to blow his friggin' head off. You know I can do it, too." While in Montana, she'd started practicing with Bill's guns.

She'd gotten good. *Damn* good.

They spent the afternoon packing. Laura took one last short ride on the horses while Rob changed the oil in the Explorer.

She hoped she'd be around to visit next summer. It was very chilly now, totally unlike what she was used to in Florida. At home she would still be in shorts and tank tops and sweating to death in the humidity. The AC would be running full blast, with no relief in sight for at least a month.

But she loved it. And she would remember how much she loved it while Bill regaled her of stories over the winter of Montana's frigid temperatures.

* * * *

Tuesday morning, Bill had breakfast ready for them by the time they'd finished their shower. After eating, they loaded up the last of their belongings and Doogie.

Laura hated saying good-bye and watched Bill disappear in the distance through the rear window.

Rob reached over and patted her on the thigh. "It's okay. He'll be back down in a few weeks."

"I know." She watched the landscape pass outside the window. "I want to go home. I just wish they'd catch him."

No need to clarify.

They took their time. Rob had vacation time to spare and felt no rush to return to Florida. Neither did Laura. With maintenance spankings every morning, they took a leisurely route and made a point of stopping at places of interest along the way.

Two days later, Laura's period started, effectively deciding that concern. Rob hugged her. "You know, when it happens, it happens."

The trip wasn't difficult physically. Mentally was a different matter. The closer they got to Florida the larger the knot in her stomach grew. Traveling made her feel vulnerable even though she knew there was no way MedicineMan could possibly know where they were.

This ought to be the easy part. Still, she found it difficult to relax.

She did, however, enjoy their hours together. They talked and she even read to him from the journals while he drove. More memories returned, mostly from several years prior. Every day drew her closer to Rob, and despite her missing memories she knew deep inside her decision to marry him was the right one.

The decision to give herself to him as his slave even more so.

They stopped one last time, their ninth day, in the Florida Panhandle, near Apalachicola. Laura had amassed a bag full of postcards and refrigerator magnets from stops along the way. Even Doogie sensed how close they were to home. It could have been the smell of the Gulf or just a feel in the air, but the Lab acted tense and on alert most of the evening.

Steve called them later the next day when they were just north of Tampa. "You planning on coming home any time soon?"

"We should be home in a few hours." The sun sank low in the west. She wasn't sure what time it really was because she hadn't reset her watch. Her body tried to stay on Montana time, but her brain was wide awake.

"We'll have the troops waiting."

Laura wondered if he was kidding.

There were two unfamiliar trucks parked in Rob's driveway when they arrived. Laura tensed until Steve emerged from behind the house, waving. She laughed and jumped out, running into his arms and letting him swing her around like she was ten again.

"You look good, girl." He shook Rob's hand. "Congratulations, son. Welcome to the family."

Rob looked at the house and the other two men turning the corner. "Any problems?"

Steve shook his head. "Nope. Just wanted to make sure there wouldn't be." He introduced the men, Bob and Pat, and something clicked in Laura's brain.

"They're your brothers."

Steve smiled. "Yep. Just wanted to check the place out for you."

That's when Laura spotted the bulge of the revolver in a holster under Steve's shirt. "You came prepared."

"You'd better believe it. You're not the only one with a concealed carry permit now."

The men helped them unpack before leaving them alone. Laura went to the fridge. When she opened the door she startled. "Sir!"

He came running, scared by her tone of voice.

Someone had stuffed the fridge full of food.

"Did Steve tell you he was going to do this?"

He shook his head. "No. Surprise to me."

"Remind me to make him a red velvet cake, okay?"

Rob nodded before they realized what she'd said and hugged each other. One more memory recovered. Another small victory.

* * * *

Rob knew that next to the memory loss, the hardest thing for Laura was the actual piecemeal recovery of information. Like a jigsaw puzzle that was impossible to assemble because she didn't have a picture to guide her. There were interconnected memories with no clues between them to attach them, which gave them no more significance than space junk orbiting the earth. Unless something spectacularly large happened to survive the descent through the atmosphere, it was barely a blip on the radar screen of recognition.

Later that evening before they went to bed, Rob wanted to talk.

"I think we need to have a discussion."

She didn't like his tone. "What, Sir?"

He took her hand. "No, not like that. Equals."

She sat up. "Okay."

"Don't you think we ought to wait to have a baby until we get this settled?"

Laura pushed down her rage. One more aspect of her life on hold because of the madman. "Is that what you want?"

Rob knew from her clipped tones she was close to breaking. "Honey, it's not what I want. I want us to have a family and be happy. It's hard enough for me to risk your life. It wouldn't be fair to risk a child. And if you get pregnant now, that's going to make you that much more vulnerable."

Finally, she said, "All right, Sir. Whatever."

"No, not 'whatever.' I told you, this is Laura and Rob, not Sir and slave. Laura, look at me." She finally did. "Honey, what happens if you get pregnant and then this guy sees you pregnant? It could set him off. The next time he tries he could kill you. And that would be more than I could handle, knowing that not only did I lose you and a baby, but that it was my fault."

"What happens if they don't catch this guy for months, years? What then? Do we never have children and live in fear hoping this guy will get caught? We put our lives on total hold and never break free? I live the rest of my life with a gun strapped to my hip and watching families take dive classes and wishing we could have kids? Or we go back to Montana and start over there, giving up everything we have just because this maniac's still on the loose? Dammit, that's not fair."

Rob wrapped his arms around her. "It won't take years. I know it won't. I have a feeling you're going to find the missing journals and the answer's going to be there. If not that, then he'll slip up and the cops will find him. Either way, they will get him."

They curled up together. Exhausted, Rob soon fell asleep.

Laura lay awake and an hour later turned on the TV. Her body was worn out but her mind raced. Not for the first time, she wondered if there wasn't some key clue she had overlooked because she didn't recognize its importance.

And where were the journals?

For once, she wished Rob had been nosy and knew where and how she wrote her journals.

The enormity of the situation hit her and she broke down and cried, first upset but then angry and finally enraged.

Who the fuck *is this guy to think he has a right to interrupt my life? Why does he think he has the right to torment me like this? And why the* fuck *is he picking on* me*?*

There was no doubt of the crossroads before her. Either she hid until MedicineMan got bored and left her alone, or killed her, or she needed to fight back.

Rage stewed and boiled and finally bubbled over. Storming out into the living room, she opened her laptop and turned it on. Her fingers flew across the keyboard and she quickly re-read her message before punching the send button. Going to bed didn't feel like a good idea, and there was nothing good on TV. After a few minutes she checked her email.

Nothing.

Of course he probably wouldn't reply tonight, if at all. It was late and whoever—wherever—he was, it wasn't likely he'd seen the email yet.

I hope I didn't just screw up.

Whatever happened, she would go down fighting. It felt clichéd, it scared her to death, but to fully reclaim her life meant facing this madman down and she was tired of running.

When the yawning started she finally felt satisfied enough to try sleep again.

* * * *

The dream centered on the condo once again, different than the ones she'd had before. It felt more like watching a TV show than living through a memory or a creation of her own subconscious. There was no way to tell if this was recall or simply terror spilling over into her imagination, but unlike the Montana dream, she recognized it as such and let it play out even though she knew it would scare her.

She watched from above and to the rear, like a camera on a boom, as her dream self toured the condo. Dark stains streaked the walls, pictures were knocked askew or broken on the floor, the back door stood open. A coil of rope lay tangled on the floor near the sofa.

Her dream self turned, looking around. The condo lay empty except for her and the mess. A dark shadow crossed the threshold in the back hall and stopped short in the doorway. Facing it, dream Laura shouted, "I'm not afraid of you!"

The shadow settled there, motionless, silent, more like a dark fog than an absence of light. A vague outline of a person coagulated somewhat, nothing recognizable.

The coil of rope slithered toward her and she kicked it, sending it skittering across the carpet back toward the shape.

"You already attacked me. What do you want?"

The shadow made no noise as it faded out of sight. Then the rear door slammed shut.

* * * *

She woke with a start, breathing heavily. Next to her, Rob still slept and Doogie lay undisturbed on the floor. Nothing. Outside the sky lightened slowly with dawn approaching, and there were only fifteen minutes left before the alarm was set to go off.

No more sleep for her. Coffee sounded good and she walked out into the kitchen. Then she remembered the email message and did an about-face for the living room. The laptop was still set up on the coffee table and she checked her email.

Nothing.

The wait was worse than anything. What if he didn't reply at all? There was a gap of several weeks before. He might be tired of the game. Or with her replying he might get scared off and decide not to play the game anymore.

Or she might have enraged him and he was plotting his attack at that moment.

Coffee. She finally got the pot going and a few minutes later Rob stumbled into the kitchen.

"Good morning, sweetheart," he greeted her. She kissed him and he hugged her. "How'd you sleep?"

She shrugged. "Dreams. Nothing I can do about them."

"Not good ones?"

"No, Sir. Not this time."

"Memories?"

She shook her head. "Not really. But I've decided I'm not going to let this guy ruin my life." She told him about the email message she sent MedicineMan and Rob winced.

"Don't you think you should have cleared that with Thomas first?"

"Why? I'm sick of this game. If this guy wants me, he's going to have to come get me."

He let out a sigh she recognized as him trying to be patient. "Let me see it." Dom tone.

She opened up the email program and brought the message up.

Hey asshole, let me tell you something. I'm beginning to think you're all talk and no balls. You aren't going to get a second chance, but I sure hope you try, because I've got something special waiting for you. Tag, motherfucker.

He looked at her. "Tag?"

"Remember he said he was it in one of the messages?"

"Oh, yeah." He looked back to the screen. "I still say you should have cleared this first."

"Easier to get forgiveness than permission."

"Yeah, but the stakes usually aren't this high." He turned and put his hands on her shoulders. "Promise me you'll call Thomas first thing this morning and tell him what you did."

She started to protest then snapped her mouth shut on that. "Yes, Sir," she finally said.

He smiled. "Well, that wasn't meant as an order from Sir, but good girl."

He gave her a morning spanking that helped calm her while they were waiting for the coffee to finish brewing. Once the coffee was ready, they both took a mug and headed to the bathroom for a shower. They ended up in bed before getting there and enjoyed the moment before finally making it into the shower. Rob had to work and Laura wanted to go to the shop. Rob walked Doogie. Nothing seemed amiss outside and he watched Laura get in her car and drive off before resetting the alarm and leaving.

Steve was already at the shop waiting for her. She made her phone call to Det. Thomas to report the e-mail she'd sent.

"I wish you'd have run that past me first."

"I'm sorry. It's just that I'm sick of this."

"I understand, but you can't cut us out of the loop and hope he comes through your front door so you can blow his nuts off."

"Why not? Sounds like a plan to me."

"Please work with me. Let me know if he replies and then we'll decide how to go from there."

She reluctantly agreed. Sarah arrived as Laura hung up. She wanted to see pictures and hear updates.

"Oh, Mr. Green Eyes came in a couple of times while you were gone."

"He did?"

She nodded. "He's hitting on me now."

Laura laughed. "Not interested in me anymore, huh?"

"Doesn't seem to be. He hasn't even asked about you. Sorry."

"Ah, you can have him, Sar."

"Don't worry. I don't *want* him. He's not my type."

Laura caught her up on paperwork and class schedules and they did some other work until lunchtime. Steve brought lunch in and they sat out on the dock. Laura had her laptop set up in the office and had been checking her email every few minutes.

Still no reply from MedicineMan. On the one hand, she was relieved. On the other, it was like waiting for a decision on a Florida election outcome—no apparent end in sight.

Det. Thomas arrived later and looked over her shoulder while she checked her mail again. Still no reply.

"Well, that doesn't necessarily mean anything," he said. "He could be out of town or working or just not answering."

"I know. It's the waiting that's hardest."

"Think of it this way—every moment you're waiting is a moment you're still alive."

She turned to stare up at him. "But what kind of life *is* it?"

Chapter Thirty-Five

The days, and then weeks, crawled by. Laura sent two more taunting messages with no replies. Thomas instructed her not to send any more until something else happened. Laura still carried her gun with her, although her sense of urgency dissipated. Bob still checked in on her when she had to be alone at the house, and deputies still patrolled their quiet street at night.

Business picked up and a heavy class and dive trip schedule monopolized her time. To take her mind off the missing journals, she worked on the novel she'd started in Montana. The manuscript was up to nearly fifty-thousand words and still going strong.

Her memory recovery hit a brick wall. She continued to dream, though not about the attack and not about anything that triggered significant gains for her. During a routine follow-up with her neurologist, she asked him for a prognosis.

"I think you already know the answer."

"Give me a guess."

He sat down. "It's been several months now. Unless you have some sort of massive trigger event, I doubt you'll recover many more memories."

"That's not written in stone."

"No it's not. It's not even written in pencil. It's possible you could wake up tomorrow with everything intact. It's also possible I'll hit the lotto Saturday night."

"Not very probable though."

"I'm afraid not."

* * * *

The next afternoon, Sarah brought the shop mail in and laid it on Laura's desk. Around closing time Laura finally got a chance to go through it. Sifting through the envelopes one in particular caught her attention.

The unstamped, uncancelled manila envelope bore the shop's address but no return label. The font looked computer-generated and it was addressed to "Laura Spaulding."

A cold chill crept through her as she grabbed a letter opener. After poking at it and determining it didn't appear to contain anything but paper, she carefully slit the end open. She carefully held the opposite end with just the tips of her fingers and shook the paper out onto her desk where it landed print side up.

It was set in large-scale print in landscape mode.

TAG! I'M CLOSER THAN YOU THINK! ;)

She screamed for Steve.

* * * *

Thomas donned a latex glove to pick up the envelope and paper and put them in an evidence bag. Rob was comforting Laura in the other corner of the office.

"He had to put it right in the mailbox. That means he was outside. He could have been one of our customers today!"

"I know, honey. I know." Rob was out of words and wishing he'd never took their peace for granted. The idea of the attacker being that close to Laura both scared and infuriated him.

"Laura, have you checked your email lately?" Thomas asked.

She shook her head.

"Could you, please?"

She nodded and sat down in front of the laptop. Sure enough.

So how'd you like it?

Thomas ordered another trace of the message and told her to send a reply.

Laura thought about it. "What do I say? That he'd succeeded in freaking me out? That I'm scared again?"

"Say whatever you want, Laura," Thomas urged. "I'll tell you if it needs to be changed."

"Maybe his game isn't to finish me off, but to keep me in terror for years unless I regained my memory."

Rob watched her set her chin and start typing. He read over her shoulder while she composed and Thomas approved it before she hit send.

Hey, chickenshit. Why didn't you just come in and say hi? I've been looking forward to having a talk with you.

If she'd written any more her rage would have spilled out into the message and the stalker would have the satisfaction of seeing how disturbed she really was. As she'd left it, she came off only sounding really pissed.

"It's bad enough I feel like a prisoner."

"Then you give any ground and reveal how you truly feel," Thomas said.

They provided Thomas with a list of all the day's customers before Rob followed Laura home and waited for her to lock the door and arm the alarm. He had to return to work for a couple of hours, although he was beginning to wonder if he shouldn't look into paramedic jobs in Montana.

* * * *

Laura tried watching TV before she finally gave up and went to bed. Exhaustion took over and she dropped off in a few minutes.

The condo dream returned. This time the shadowy form solidified a little more.

Not enough for her to recognize.

Over the next couple of nights, the dream reoccurred until, finally, she couldn't take it anymore.

Laura wanted the condo emptied, and whatever wouldn't fit in the house they packed and moved to the warehouse. Before closing the door one last time she completely searched every cabinet and closet just to make sure the journals weren't there. Lately, she spent every spare moment she could looking for the journals.

A week later, and still no reply from the stalker.

"I don't know how much more of this I can take, Sir."

Rob wrapped his arms around her, trying to comfort her. "I wish I had answers for you. Hang in there, baby girl. They'll catch him."

"I wish I believed that."

There'd been several false alarms. Once, Thomas told her, they had a lead in Michigan, just to discover the computer they tracked the email to was owned by a single, elderly, retired woman who used to teach biology in a middle school. Not only did she not know Laura, she'd never been to Florida, and she was the only one who ever used or had access to her computer.

When Rob suggested delaying their wedding party plans, Laura nearly took his head off.

"I'm *not* living my life around what could happen!"

"Laur, all I'm suggesting is we take some time—"

"Look, we changed our life because of this madman. We live in a friggin' fortress, I can't even walk my dog without having a loaded gun in my hand. I am *not* giving up our wedding party!"

She stormed down the hall, slamming the bedroom door behind her hard enough to rattle the windows.

Rob went after her and found her lying facedown on the bed, sobbing.

He lay down next to her and rubbed her back. "That's three with a cane. In the morning."

She nodded. "Yes, Sir," she whispered before she rolled over and curled up next to him, eventually falling asleep in his arms.

* * * *

The dream came again. This time she didn't wait for the shadow to appear. Storming down the hallway, she stood in the spot where the shadow always appeared.

"Well, come on! What's wrong? Are you afraid of me?"

The shadow began to coalesce and she reached out, grabbing for it. When her arm passed through thin air she screamed, "Come on, you bastard! What are you waiting for?"

The shadow drifted back out the door, wafting away into sunlight.

Rob startled when she sat up, now wide awake.

"Honey, are you okay?"

She nodded, slightly disoriented. "I'm okay."

He watched her. "You don't look okay."

"I'm fine." She wasn't. Stress ate away at her and she knew she wouldn't rest in peace until she had some sort of resolution.

Or maybe *she* would be resting in peace if she didn't find some sort of resolution.

* * * *

Outside of spending time alone with Rob and work, her writing was Laura's only true relief. With other people around her all day and customers to take care of, she could shuffle her problems and stress to the side.

She was teaching a Saturday afternoon class when Don Kern walked in. The students were watching a video about underwater navigation in the darkened classroom. Laura scooched her chair back a little so she could observe him through the darkened classroom window without being seen.

She watched as Sarah talked with him. He appeared to ask her a question and she answered, pointing to the regulators. He smiled and walked over to the display and browsed.

Laura knew there were only a few minutes left on the video.

Wait a minute. This is my shop. Why should I be nervous?

When the video ended, she covered the rest of the material. Then she followed the students out into the showroom after class and headed for the counter.

"Laura."

She fought the urge to stiffen and turned to face him. "Yes?"

The green eyes still struck her as odd, indefinable. "How are you?"

"I'm fine, thanks. What can I do for you, Mr. Kern?"

"I wanted to get some class information for a friend of mine."

"Oh, that's good. Did Sarah get you set up?"

"Yes, she gave me the information." He glanced at his watch. "Listen, how are you doing?"

Haven't we covered that question? "I'm just fine. Got married a few weeks ago."

"Oh? Congratulations."

"Thanks."

He acted like he wanted to say something else. Then, "How are you doing with that other—"

"I'm sorry, was there anything else you needed, Mr. Kern? I have a lot to get done today."

His brow furrowed, but he shook his head. "No, just wanted to say hi."

"Thanks."

He left and Sarah walked over to her. "Well?"

Laura shrugged. "I chopped him off at the knees. I didn't give him a chance to say much."

"Didn't hit on you or anything?"

"Nope. Said he just needed some information."

"Yeah, I gave him a class schedule." She looked out the window. "Hey, he drives a Beemer."

Laura dismissed the incident and went back to work. She still had several details to finalize for the wedding party. Rob met her at the shop and they went out to dinner. She filled him in on the day's events, culminating with her visit from Don Kern.

Rob got "that look" on his face, the one Laura knew meant he was going to delve into super-protective Sir mode. "I really don't like the idea of that guy in the shop."

"He's a customer." She regretted saying anything to Rob about the visit.

"I don't like him."

"Getting jealous are we?" She knew what buttons to push.

"No. You know me better than that."

Yes, she did.

She smiled. "Don't worry, Sir. I'm staying safe."

He smiled. "Good girl."

* * * *

She spent the rest of the day working on finishing paperwork for the shop. Bill was due to arrive in three days. Laura wanted to spend her time with him, not worrying about work.

She also knew Rob was counting down the days until Bill's arrival, glad to have one more set of eyes watching over her. They had no way of knowing if MedicineMan would really attack again or not, but he wasn't willing to take chances with her safety.

It also meant they hadn't gone up to the club or over to their friend's houses since their return from Montana. They were afraid if MedicineMan was paying close attention to Laura that he might start stalking them, too, as a way to get to her.

Or as a way to gain information to blackmail Rob and cost him his job.

Laura settled for lots of phone conversations with Shayla and the others.

The day before Bill's scheduled arrival, Laura set out to clean the house. With a young Labbybrat around, it didn't take long for fur balls to breed under the sofa. The kitchen first, and she worked her way through the living and dining rooms, their bedroom, the spare bedroom, and finally to the office where the greatest clutter accumulated.

She'd tried to put the missing journals out of her mind, but they were always there, close to the surface.

What the hell did I do with them?

For the first time, another answer occurred. What if somehow her attacker had them? But that didn't make sense. How would he have gotten them?

Unless he knew what he was looking for.

Once again that brought her around to the possibility the attacker was someone close to her. And that just didn't seem possible.

* * * *

Rob drove Laura to Tampa to meet Bill's plane. She took a notepad along to work but got carsick and had to put it aside. By the time they arrived in Tampa she felt better, and when Bill arrived she was overjoyed to see him. They ate dinner with Steve and Carol. The next day, Rob was relieved to leave for work and not have Laura alone.

Laura decided to take time off from the shop. Probably a good thing, because with the stress she thought she was coming down with something. After dinner that night, she hugged her brother and Rob good night and headed for bed.

The condo dream returned. This time she started out with the condo clean and tidy, carpet runner in place on the floor. There was a knock on the door and she went to answer it. A voice she couldn't understand said something, and when she opened the door a black shadow raced in.

She screamed, waking both Rob and herself. Bill knocked on their bedroom door a moment later.

Rob went to the door. "She's okay. Just a dream."

Rob blocked her view, but Laura knew from Bill's stance he held a handgun.

"Sure?"

Rob nodded. "She's okay."

Rob closed the door and sat next to her. "Don't you think it's time you went back to Dr. Collins or Dr. Simpson?"

"I don't have time."

"Laura, you're under a lot of stress. Tomorrow morning, call and make an appointment."

Her anger subsided. He was right. Maybe it would help. It wouldn't hurt. "All right. Fine."

* * * *

The next morning, Rob enjoyed the feel of Laura's hands on him. In an instant he was awake, kissing her. Apparently Bill was up, too, because he smelled coffee brewing in the kitchen. Suddenly, Laura bolted out of bed and raced for the bathroom. He followed her, worried. She leaned over the toilet, looking green, not actually getting sick.

"You okay?"

She nodded. "I just had a rough moment there."

"You sure? You don't look good."

"I think I'm coming down with something. I haven't felt good the past couple of days. Or it could have been what I ate last night."

At her insistence, he went back to bed. He heard the water running and a moment later she was in bed with him. This time, she didn't leave.

He stopped her. "No spanking this morning."

When she started to argue, he silenced her. "Sick is different. I'm not flipping you over on your stomach and spanking you." He kissed her. "Don't worry, we'll make it up tomorrow."

She teased him and taunted him until he couldn't hold back any longer.

He retrieved a condom from the side table drawer and enjoyed making love to her. Later they got up and showered, taking their time. Rob didn't have to be at work until later that afternoon.

Bill sat at the kitchen table with the paper, Doogie at his feet. "Well good morning, folks."

"Shouldn't you have jet lag?" Laura poured Rob and her cups of coffee.

"I'm fine. Doogie decided he wanted to sleep with me. He woke me up this morning to go out. You guys decided to sleep late."

Rob grinned. "Who said we were sleeping?" Laura playfully swatted Rob's shoulder and he ducked her.

Then he ratted her out. "I told her last night she needs to make an appointment with Dr. Collins or Dr. Stephens. Can you—"

Bill gave him a thumbs-up. "I'll make sure she does it."

"Thanks."

He nodded. "You better believe it."

She'd started a dream journal, writing down anything she thought of or any dreams she had. There wasn't much she remembered from the night before. She found an empty note pad and jotted down some thoughts anyway.

After breakfast she left Rob and Bill at the table while she went to get her morning dose of dread, as she thought of it, while her mail downloaded.

Nothing. After making an appointment with Dr. Collins, who had an opening for the next day, she returned to the living room and sat and talked with Bill, going through albums again, until she started yawning.

"You okay, Laur?" Rob went to her.

"Just tired. I'm going to lie down."

They watched her go to the bedroom.

"How is she really?" Bill asked.

Rob shook his head. "I'm surprised she's held up as well as she has. Everything's catching up with her now that she's slowing down and being forced to deal with it."

Rob followed her to the bedroom. She lay on the bed, Doogie beside her. He shooed the Lab off the bed and curled up next to her. "You okay?"

She nodded without opening her eyes. "I'm okay. Just tired. I've been so busy."

"Listen. Why don't you just hire an extra person part-time at the shop and stay home? Write, relax, give yourself some time. You really haven't had much in the way of downtime since…you know."

"No, just the better part of a month in Montana."

"Laura, that's not fair. Not to mention it wasn't what you could call a vacation. You were under almost as much stress there as you would have been here."

Laura kissed his hand, held it to her chest. "I know. I've been thinking about taking some time off anyway. The novel is coming along pretty well."

"We can afford it. Don't worry." He curled up with her on the bed and she dropped off to sleep.

He watched, gently brushing a strand of hair from her face. There was still a scar on her forehead, not noticeable unless you were looking for it. It enraged him, always reminding him of the brutal attack, how he should have been with her, would have been with her if it hadn't been for the accident he had to work.

Bill looked up from the TV when Rob returned. "She okay?"

"Yes. She's just totally exhausted." He looked at his watch. "Damn. I need to get to work. Call me if…" He didn't want to finish.

"She'll be okay, Rob. She's tough."

"Sometimes she thinks she's tougher than she really is."

* * * *

Laura slept. Bill checked on her periodically. She seemed restless, disturbed. One time he heard her moan in her sleep and he considered waking her. He let Doogie into the room with her and the Lab carefully climbed up on the bed and protectively curled up next to his mistress. That seemed to comfort her and Bill left her bedroom door open so he could hear.

Laura felt sucked down into the depths of her dream. She knew she was dreaming, and that was the extent of the control she had. It was the apartment again, before the attack. This time was different. The rooms were dark and possessed an unearthly quality that never came through before.

The knock on the door. Thunderous, wall-shaking. The fear hit her and she realized that no matter what she did she would open that door. Despite turning to run her feet betrayed her and she slowly moved toward the front door.

Suddenly, Doogie appeared at her side, calming her. He growled at the door, bearing his teeth, something the gentle dog never did before. Taking comfort in his presence she willed herself to reach out and grab the doorknob. The door swung open.

Nothing.

Doogie pushed himself in front of her, between her and the open doorway, still growling.

Laura stepped back and closed the door. Doogie pushed into her arms and licked her face.

The scene changed. Still the apartment. The otherworldly aspect was gone and it was back to before the attack. Once again there was a knock on the door. Doogie looked up and gently took her hand in his mouth, leading her away from the door.

The rear door swung open, the shadow filling the doorway. Doogie bristled, advanced. Laura tried to hold him back without success. The dog stalked the shadow, and when he reached the back door he leapt, attacking. The shadow blew apart and the door slammed shut. Doogie walked back to her wagging his tail and letting her stroke his ears.

That's when she woke. Doogie looked over at her. She smiled, petting his head. "Good boy."

His tail thumped once on the bed.

* * * *

Laura retrieved her dream notebook and wrote furiously. The dream was so different from what she'd had before. Maybe Doogie's presence had something to do with it.

She wouldn't take any chances.

Bill cooked her dinner and they watched TV. Laura sat in listless silence.

"You want to talk?" He knew she'd had rough dreams that afternoon.

"No. It's just the same old stuff."

"You're so stubborn, sis."

"Doesn't it run in the family?"

He laughed. "Yes, it does. And you got a heaping share."

Chapter Thirty-Six

Laura woke before dawn. She walked to the living room and peeked through the blinds. She found out she used to jog. Not religiously but usually once or twice a week, preferring early morning when the sun wasn't hot.

Before.

She used to go to work and take out classes, dive by herself on pleasure trips, enjoyed her lifestyle.

Before.

She used to take long walks with Doogie, enjoyed taking him to the dog park, loved riding around.

Now, she felt like a hostage, always looking over her shoulder, feeling guilty and resentful at the same time because everyone she loved felt responsible for her safety.

Doogie woke up and walked to her side. He nuzzled her hand.

"Gotta go out?"

He wagged his otter tail.

Her robe hung over the back of the bathroom door. She slipped into it and put the gun in the pocket, knotting the belt around her waist to keep the gun's weight from pulling it down.

She slipped the leash on Doogie and turned off the alarm before they went out the back door. It was nearly dawn and she cautiously looked around the yard while Doogie sniffed the ground. Every sound, every movement set her on edge. She smelled the methane from the rotten vegetation in the mangrove swampland on the other side of the trees, heard a raccoon rummaging in the brush, a mockingbird sounding off in a nearby tree.

"C'mon, Doog. Get it done."

"Laur?"

She jumped at the sound of Bill's voice. "Yeah?"

"You okay?" He was barely awake, and had Rob's gun in his hand, held along his thigh.

"I'm fine. Just walking the brat."

"Want me to finish up with him?"

At that moment Doogie decided he was done and led Laura back toward the house. "I guess not."

He locked the door behind her and reached down to pet the dog. "Rob wouldn't like you going out there by yourself." He reset the alarm.

"I'm going stir crazy."

Her appointment with Dr. Collins didn't trigger any new memories, unfortunately.

But with the way she was feeling, she finally let Bill talk her into seeing her general practitioner about her other symptoms. Her regular doctor was out of town, so she had to see one of his partners, whom she'd never seen before. The doctor examined her, including taking blood work and a urine sample. After he was finished, Bill returned to the exam room to wait with her.

The doctor walked in with her chart and smiled. "Congratulations, you two."

Bill and Laura looked at each other in confusion. Bill spoke first. "Sorry?"

The doctor smiled at him. "You're going to be a father."

Laura's jaw hit the floor but Bill recovered first. "Uh, this is my sister, not my wife."

The doctor blushed. "Oh, I'm sorry, I thought—"

Laura shook her head. "I can't be pregnant. I had my period a few weeks ago."

The doctor was still trying to recover from his error. "I thought the nurse said you were married, Laura."

"I *am* married. My husband's at work. My brother is visiting us for a few weeks. Are you sure? I mean, I had my period."

The doctor nodded. "Yes, we're sure. It's not uncommon for a woman to have one or more episodes that look like periods in their early pregnancy."

Laura did the math and closed her eyes. "Crap." She'd be about five weeks along, or less.

Bill reached over and took her hand. "I thought you guys wanted—"

"We do. We did. Then we decided to wait for a while, see if they can catch the psycho first."

"Oh."

She looked at the doctor. "Oh, god, I've had wine—"

The doctor smiled. "As long as you're not doing any drugs or smoking or anything like that, chances are, the baby's fine. Since you're here, let's do an ultrasound and some more blood work, okay?"

She nodded, numb. The doctor left to order the tests and she looked at Bill, her eyes wet. "What am I going to do?"

"I'd say the first thing is to tell Rob."

She closed her eyes. "He's working until tomorrow. Double shift."

They quietly waited until the doctor and nurse returned. An hour later they were finished, but the doctor recommended she not do any diving considering the fairly recent trauma she'd been through.

"Better to err on the side of caution," he said.

* * * *

Bill waited for Laura while she checked out and made a follow-up appointment for a few weeks later. He browsed a fishing magazine in the waiting area when he heard a man's voice speak Laura's name.

Bill looked up and saw a man in a suit emerge from the back. Laura visibly bristled.

"Oh, hello," she said.

Bill stood, waiting for a cue she needed him to intercede. The guy looked like a salesman, probably a pharmacy rep. Two others had come and gone earlier while they awaited Laura's turn.

The nurse behind the counter handed Laura an appointment card and some paperwork. "Mrs. Carlton, do you want any brochures, or need a referral to a Lamaze class?"

"No, that's okay. I'll get that from you next time."

The nurse turned to the man. "Hi, Don. Didn't see you come in. I thought you weren't due until next week. Did you need anything else?"

He smiled, but Bill didn't like the look of him. "No, I'm okay, Della, thanks. I was in the area, thought I'd pop in. Tell the doc I'll stop by next week to see if he needs anything." He turned to Laura. "How are you?"

Laura forced a smile. "I'm fine, thank you." Then she turned back to the nurse. "Am I all set?"

Della nodded. "Yes, we'll see you back in three weeks."

"Thank you." Laura turned to walk away. "Nice seeing you, Mr. Kern."

Bill fell into step beside her and sensed her agitation. In the car he quickly locked the doors once they were inside. "Okay, sis. What's that about? Who was he?"

She filled him in. "Customer from the shop. It unnerved me seeing him there until I remembered he's a pharmaceutical sales rep. And Englewood is a very small town."

"So he's just creepy?"

"Yeah, but apparently he's got a girlfriend now. Sara said he brought a woman in with him for a dive last week." Laura groaned and smacked her leg. "I can't dive!"

"What?"

"I'm supposed to run the check-out dives this weekend. I can't do water classes. Crap!"

"Why?"

She looked at Bill. "Duh. What'd the doc just say?"

He winced. "Sorry, sis. I'm not used to the fact that I'm going to be an uncle yet." He drove. "Where to?"

She closed her eyes and leaned back in her seat. "What time is it?"

"Noon."

"Let's go to Rob's station."

"I need directions."

* * * *

They found Rob at the station. He was happy to see them until he got a good look at Laura's expression. "What's wrong?"

"We need to talk," she said quietly.

Rob looked at Bill. Bill shook his head. No help there.

Rob took her hand. "Come on."

Bill followed them inside and sat in the lounge to watch TV. The captain let them use his office, where Rob sat her down.

"Okay, tell me what's wrong, baby girl. What did the doctor say?"

Her tears finally broke through the shock and she sobbed, unable to speak.

He put his arms around her, trying to soothe her. "Honey, please, what's wrong? You're scaring me." His imagination pictured the worse. Was it cancer? Was she dying?

It took her several minutes to calm down enough to sniffle her answer against his shoulder, and he couldn't understand what she said.

"Sweetheart," he whispered, "*please*. Whatever it is, we'll get through it together. I love you. Tell me."

She sat up and wiped her eyes with the back of her hand. "Sir, I'm pregnant."

He stared at her, sure he misheard her. "You're not sick?"

She looked at him. "What?"

"What did you say?" He must have misheard her, as upset as she was.

"I'm pregnant, Sir," she whispered. "About six weeks."

The words finally made it through to his brain and he felt his dread lift. He grabbed her hands. "We're going to have a baby?"

She nodded, and he grinned. "That's fantastic!" He hugged her, "Jeez, I thought you were going to tell me you were dying! You scared the crap out of me! I should beat you on general principle just for that."

She finally laughed and managed to pull free. "No, Sir. Not dying."

"That's great! A baby—" He processed the look on her face. "What's wrong? Is there something wrong with it?"

She shook her head. "No, Sir. Not that I know of."

Rob studied her and finally understood how upset she was. He lowered his voice and dropped into full-on Dom tone. "Baby girl, why do you look like you've received bad news?"

She looked down at her lap. "Because we decided to wait, Sir."

"It's okay." He pulled her to him again. "It'll be okay sweetheart. Don't you still want to have a baby?"

"Yes."

"Then tell me what's wrong."

She shrugged. "I'm just… It was a shock, Sir. It hasn't sunk in yet."

He kissed her. "Have you told anyone else yet?"

"Bill was there when the doctor told me." She barked out a laugh. "He mistook Bill for you and we had to explain he was my brother."

He caressed her cheek. "I love you so much. You have no idea."

She rested her head against him. "I don't want to tell anyone else yet, Sir."

"Why not?"

She shrugged. "I don't mean not tell Shayla and our close friends, or Steve and Carol and Sarah. I just don't want it to be public knowledge."

He studied her face. "Okay," he agreed.

* * * *

Bill stood when they finally emerged from the office a few minutes later. "Are you okay?"

She nodded. Rob held her hand and walked them out to the car. He hugged her before opening the door for her. "Sweetheart, this is okay. This is *good* news."

She wished she felt the same. "I know." She forced herself not to call him "Sir" in front of Bill.

Rob held the door for her while she got in, and he leaned in and kissed her one last time. "Take it easy, all right? Don't wear yourself out." He closed the door and watched them pull out of the parking lot.

"Where to, sis?"

She sighed. "Let's pull through somewhere, get something to eat, and take it to the shop."

There were no customers when they arrived at the shop. Steve put down the regulator he was working on when she walked in. "What's wrong?"

Bill laughed. "Who says anything's wrong?"

He frowned and pointed to Laura. "I've known this girl since she was a kid. What's going on?"

Laura shook her head. "Where's Carol and Sarah?"

"They're out back. Why?"

"I want to say this once and get it over with." They took the food outside and found Carol and Sarah at the table.

"Honey," Carol said, "what's wrong?"

Bill shook his head. "Does everyone have this weird psychic stuff?"

"About her, yes," Sarah said. "What's wrong?"

Laura sat and started to unwrap her burger. "I've got something I need to tell you all. And you can't tell *anyone*. It needs to be between just the three of you. Bill knows, obviously. And Rob."

"What is it?" Steve asked.

She looked at him. "I'm pregnant."

Sarah grinned. "That's great!" She studied Laura, her smile fading. "That's not great? Why do you look upset?"

Laura glared at her. "Psycho guy after me. Sort of preempts the baby buzz."

"Oh. Yeah." She looked at the table. "You're right."

Carol patted her arm. "This will be fine, honey. I'm sure. But why don't you want anyone to know?"

"What if it sets this psycho off?"

"Oh."

They all fell silent. Steve finally spoke. "Well, you're dry-docked for the duration. We'll need to come up with a story for a while. But it'll be awfully hard to hide a baby bump once you start to show."

"I already thought about it. We can tell people I've got a perforated eardrum. That'll explain me being sick to my stomach, blame it on vertigo. That'll get me through a few months. Hopefully this creep will be in custody by then."

"What about Cody? You don't want to tell him or the others?" The boat captain was a friend, but she didn't trust him or the others to keep her secret. They might likely reveal it accidentally, not intentionally.

She shook her head. "Not yet. Not right now. The fewer people that know, the better."

* * * *

The next email arrived one Wednesday afternoon after Bill had returned to Montana and while she was home alone. Rob was at work, just starting two days on duty.

A little stork told me you and your man have been busy. The more, the merrier.

Laura ran for the bathroom. She collapsed in front of the toilet, sick, sobbing. Twenty minutes later, she finally pulled herself together and called Det. Thomas. He wasn't in, but she left a voice mail and he called her back a few minutes later.

"He knows I'm pregnant. How can he know that?"

Thomas was quiet for a long moment. "Maybe he's someone close to you. We need to reinvestigate—"

"No. You ruled out everyone around me the first time. We know it wasn't Rob or Steve or Cody. It wasn't any of my friends. It damn sure wasn't my brother. This guy has *got* to be local."

Thomas went quiet again. "Laura, maybe it would be best if you left town for a while."

Rage washed through her. "No! I am *not* putting my life on hold again for this son of a bitch. He ran me off once, he's not doing it again. I want him to come after me once and for all so I can put a fucking bullet in his head!"

"You need to calm do—"

"Calm *down*? How *dare* you! You're not the one being stalked. You have no idea what I'm going through."

"No, you're absolutely right, I don't, but getting this upset isn't good for you or the baby."

She fell silent. He was right, of course, but she didn't want to admit it.

"Did you tell Rob yet?"

"He's at work. I don't want to worry him."

"You need to call him."

"No. There's nothing he can do."

"I'll get Hutchinson working on the latest email. Call Rob." He hung up.

She stared at the phone, trembling. She wanted this over with, wanted the bastard out of their life.

I can't even enjoy my pregnancy in peace.

Finally, she called him. She almost hoped it'd go to his voice mail, but he answered.

"What's up, baby girl?"

She broke down crying and it took her several tries to get the story out. "Calm down," he said. "I want you to pack. I'm going to call Sully."

When she tried to argue with him, he overruled her. "*Stop*," he said, taking Dom tone with her. "Are you listening to me?"

He didn't raise his voice. In fact, he lowered it, forcing her to listen. "Yes."

"Yes, what?"

"Yes, Sir."

"Good girl. Go pack. I'll call Sully. Then call Seth and have him come get you and drive you up to Sully's. You be ready to go when he gets there."

She didn't respond.

"Did you hear me?"

"Yes, Sir."

"Are you going to obey me?"

"Yes, Sir. But what about Doogie?" He weighed nearly a hundred pounds and still acted like a puppy.

"Let me worry about Doogie. I will call you back in five minutes, and you'd better be getting packed."

She wanted to break down crying again and knew she wouldn't—couldn't—disappoint him. "Yes, Sir."

"Good girl. Love you."

"Love you, too, Sir."

When he called her back five minutes later, she was already halfway packed and Sully had okayed her bringing Doogie with her to their house.

Two hours later, Seth was pulling his truck into Sully, Mac, and Clarisse's Tarpon Springs driveway.

Clarisse hurried down the steps first and engulfed Laura in a tearful hug as soon as she stepped from the truck.

"Hey, momma," Clarisse said as she laid her hand on Laura's tummy. "How you doing?"

"I've had better days."

Mac had made his way downstairs, with Sully behind him.

"Go on," Seth said. "We've got your bags." He grabbed Doogie's leash as the dog tried to lunge out of the cab and head for the bushes. "And I'll walk the moose."

"Thanks, Seth."

Clarisse hooked her arm through Laura's as Mac and Sully walked over to her.

"Hey, sweetie," Sully said.

"Hey." She burst into tears as the three of them gathered around her in a hug.

"It's okay," Clarisse softly said. A hard edge crept into her friend's voice. "You have your gun, right?"

Laura gave a tearful laugh. "Yeah. I'm afraid Sully and Sir would both spank me if I didn't."

"Might make me go a little switchy myself," Clarisse admitted. "You keep that on you, even here. Okay?"

"Yeah."

Seth rejoined them, a more subdued Doogie now walking on a slack lead. "Who gets this guy?"

Mac smiled and reached for the leash. "I think Bart's going to have his paws full trying to dominate this guy."

"Oh, my god," Laura said. "Please don't let Doogie chew any butt plugs!"

* * * *

Laura stayed with her friends for a week, spending time at the local gun range with Sully and improving both her aim and her confidence with her gun. When no more emails from the stalker arrived, she begged Rob to let her come home.

He finally relented and came to get her. He had three days off on rotation, and they spent it locked in the house, making love, curled in bed together, and watching TV.

Rob didn't want her to return to work, but finally gave in on that point, too. Laura tried to hide the worst of her morning sickness from everyone. It wasn't easy. She had to stay home until well past noon every day, usually when her stomach decided to behave.

As the weeks passed with no new emails from MedicineMan, there was still no sign of her missing journals. She'd scoured the laptop, Rob's computer, her desktop, and even Rob's personal laptop to no avail. They weren't on the shop computer, they weren't in Dropbox. Wherever she put them, they were well hid. Either she kept the file in some place she had yet to discover, or she'd deleted it by mistake.

It didn't seem plausible she'd stop journaling, but she finally had to let go of her need to find them. If she found them, she found them. It was consuming far too much of her energy.

Her pregnancy was four months along now, and while still on edge, MedicineMan's absence allowed her to resume some semblance of a normal routine. She was in the dive shop one Saturday afternoon when the boat returned from a dive.

Don Kern was listed as one of the passengers.

Shit. She hadn't checked the manifest.

When he spotted her he acted friendly but not creepy. Even better, he was holding a woman's hand. "Laura, this is my girlfriend, Tammy."

Whew. Apparently he'd found a happier hunting ground than the staff at Lemon Bay Dive. "Nice to meet you," Laura said with a genuine smile as she shook hands with the woman. "I hope we see a lot of you around here."

The woman beamed a radiant smile at Kern. "I hope so, too. This has been so much fun!"

Laura wasn't allowed to lift tanks. She couldn't dive. She couldn't work on regulators because of the risk of exposure to cleaning chemicals.

She couldn't do much, it felt like. In the office, she pulled her iPad from her purse. Rob and Steve both said she'd used it a lot…before. But she hadn't found much use for it other than reading the older journal files Bill had loaded on it for her. She didn't like browsing the Internet on it, no matter what Rob and Steve told her she'd done, because her laptop had a larger screen.

Sarah was in the middle of doing a replenishment order on the office computer and Laura didn't want to make her move. She sat at the other desk and, with the iPad and its little portable Bluetooth keyboard, she started working on her novel after using Dropbox to download the latest backup copy.

Sarah stepped out of the office to check inventory levels on a couple of things for the order.

Laura needed to look something up on the Internet, but still didn't want to disturb Sarah's order. She clicked on the pull-down of sites to find a quick link for Google and saw a list of other frequently visited websites.

She froze as she studied it. One of the listed links was a site called *www.classfriends.link*.

Why does that sound familiar?

She closed her eyes, feeling dizzy, and grabbed at the edge of the desk to steady her. This was maybe the second time she used the Internet on the iPad since the attack.

Since before.

She figured out how to access the browser history. Sure enough, the last time she'd accessed that site was the day before the attack.

Then she accidentally hit the Home button and the main screen appeared. One of those hunches hit her, the kind that recent experience told her was maybe more of a memory than a hunch. She swiped through the menu screens until she found what she was looking for.

An icon for the Evernote app.

With trembling fingers, she tapped it.

No wonder she'd never found the journals. She didn't find her journals on the computers because they weren't *on* the computers—they were stored here, on her iPad, via Evernote. She could have accessed them from anywhere if she'd had it installed on the other computers.

She closed her eyes and swore. The Evernote app *had* been on her phone, and early on she'd had Bill delete it and anything else she wasn't sure how to use.

Fuck. All this time there they were, waiting for her to find them.

She immediately exported everything into a document and sent it to her iPad so she could read it. She scanned ahead to the days before the attack, and other than a notation about signing up for the Classfriends site, there was nothing that would help.

Tear stung her eyes. She had been so sure, so *certain* that she'd find the answer there. Still nothing.

The final entry was at 1:14 p.m. the afternoon of the attack.

Doogie's getting snipped. I get to bring him home tomorrow morning. Poor guy, but he needs it. We should be getting our wedding invitations from the printer any day now. I can't wait! This is really happening. I've met Prince Charming. Well, my handsome Sir.

He's not an ugly toad, either.

I think I'm looking forward to the collaring even more than I am our wedding. And it's pointless to stay in the condo. I want to start moving all my stuff to the house. I'm going to surprise him with the news this weekend, over a candlelight dinner. I've got it all planned...

The memory returned. Not of the attack, but of writing that entry. How happy she'd been, making her shopping list, even the music she wanted to play on the stereo. Remembering how deeply in love she felt that afternoon.

And upset that, after all these months, there were still no more answers.

Steve entered the office and found Laura sobbing over the iPad. "Honey, what's wrong?"

She pointed to the device. "I found the missing journals. They don't tell me *shit*."

He turned her chair to face him. "Sweetheart, you knew it might not give you any information."

"I was so sure it would." Steve held her, let her cry against him. Sarah heard the commotion and walked in, closed the office door behind her, and sat with them.

"What's wrong?"

Steve told her. "Did it trigger any memories?" Sarah asked.

Laura finally sat up and shook her head. "Not of the attack. I thought it would. I thought for *sure* it would answer everything and I would know who did this to me."

The weather radio alarm sounded, blasting its warning tone and startling them, announcing a marine thunderstorm warning.

"Looks like the boat returned just in time," Steve said. "We'll have to cancel some charters this week if that latest tropical depression spins up our way."

* * * *

When Rob picked up Laura from the shop a little after four that afternoon, she told him what she'd found. He hugged her.

"It's okay, baby girl. We'll figure it out."

He wouldn't let her help with dinner, knowing she was emotionally worn out. She decided to explore the Classfriends site on her laptop. Maybe if nothing else she would remember something. The username and password combo was her usual, and she logged in. Her last recorded login date was the afternoon of the attack.

Nothing.

Something itched at her conscious, though. It was a feeling she hadn't had in weeks, like a buried memory wanted to come through. But it didn't feel like it was about the attack. And frankly, that's all she cared about at the moment was remembering who did it to her.

Rob didn't want to leave her, but he was scheduled to work a twelve-hour shift starting that evening. "I could call in or swap off."

"No, don't do that. I'll be okay. Really."

"You want me to call someone to come stay with you? Or I can take you over to Seth and Leah's."

She shook her head. "No. I'll be okay. I'll probably go to bed and watch TV until I fall asleep. You'll be home tomorrow night, right?"

"Hopefully. Depends on this storm." He stared at her. "You're sure you're okay?"

"I'm just…" She stared at the iPad, which she'd left on the coffee table. "I need to read through everything."

He cradled her face in his hands. "We've talked about this. You knew it might not be a magic pill. And you've got so much back."

"I know." She let him pull her close, holding her tightly. She couldn't take her eyes off the iPad. Somehow, she sensed it still might hold the answers.

If she could just figure it out.

* * * *

Thomas called her cell phone that evening.

"Two calls in a week?" she quipped. "To what do I owe the honor?"

"Are you at home?"

She didn't like his terse tone. "Yeah?"

"Doors locked?"

"You're freaking me out."

"I've dispatched a deputy to your house. He's already on the way."

She shivered and walked to the living room where she closed the curtains. "What's going on?"

"We discovered a woman's body late this afternoon down in Placida.

Not far from your shop."

"What?" She gripped the phone tighter.

"She was strangled and beaten pretty badly."

"What does that have to do with me?"

Laura knew. In her gut, she knew.

"Have you checked your email lately?"

She walked to the table where her laptop was set up and opened her email program.

Her blood chilled. Sure enough there was a message from MedicineMan.

Her spit dried up. "How did you know?" she hoarsely asked.

"He left a computer-printed note on the body. I can't tell you what it said because of the investigation. What does his email say?"

Her hand trembled as she clicked on the message.

Sorry I've been too busy to pay you any attention lately. Storm's around the corner, Laura. I'm ready to finish our business pretty soon. Here's a preview of coming attractions. ;)

Attached was a picture of a woman's body.

The face beaten beyond recognition.

She dropped the phone to the table and ran for the bathroom, barely making the toilet in time to puke her guts up. After she could walk, she drew the gun from her holster and returned to the living room. She heard Thomas screaming into the phone, and when she picked it up to talk to him, someone started pounding on her front door.

"I'm okay. I got sick. Sorry. There's someone at the door."

"Don't open it. Ask who they are."

She went to the front door. "Who is it?"

"Sheriff's Department. Are you okay, ma'am?"

She spoke into the phone. "He says he's a deputy."

"Can you see out the door?"

"Peephole."

"Ask for ID."

"He's in uniform."

"Ask, dammit!"

She called through the door. "Det. Thomas told me to ask for ID."

She watched as the deputy held up his ID to the peephole. In the driveway, she saw his marked cruiser. "He's got ID. And he's in a cruiser."

"I don't give a damn if he's in Santa's sleigh. Get his damn badge number."

"What's your badge number?"

The deputy read it to her, and a moment later, Thomas said, "He's legit, let him in."

She did. The deputy stepped inside and closed the door behind him. "Ma'am, would you mind putting that away?" He pointed to the 9mm she still gripped at her side.

Still stunned, she looked at the gun as if she'd never seen it before and returned it to her holster.

"Laura, let me speak to him," Thomas said.

She handed her phone to the deputy and tried to ignore the dangerous roll her stomach took. The deputy spoke to Thomas for a moment and turned to her. "Ma'am, where's your computer?"

Laura pointed to the laptop. "The message is still up." She walked into the bedroom so she couldn't hear him read it to Thomas. A moment later the deputy knocked on her bedroom door and she emerged.

"Here's your phone. They've already notified your husband. They've sent a car to pick him up from the firehouse."

"What did the note on the woman's body say?"

He shook his head. "You don't want to know. I couldn't tell you even if you did, because it's evidence."

Doogie quietly watched everything from the living room, and when she sat down on the couch he curled up next to her, his head in her lap. The deputy stood guard by the front door and twenty minutes later, another deputy brought Rob home.

He ran inside to her, hugged her. "Are you okay?"

She nodded. "Yeah. I guess."

Thomas wasn't far behind. "Hutchins tracked the email already. It was sent locally."

"What do you mean, locally?" Laura asked.

He looked at her. "The guy accessed the Internet through your shop's wireless modem. His computer ID was fudged, but he apparently wanted us to know where he connected at. You don't have it password protected, do you?"

She numbly shook her head. "I...I don't know. I never thought about it."

"Whoever he is, he's local. And he was either in your shop or parked outside, close enough to grab a signal and send the email."

"Meaning I might have seen him today," she numbly said.

He nodded. "Yeah. Meaning that."

* * * *

Stir-crazy didn't begin to describe Laura's state of mind. But when two weeks passed following the discovery of the woman's body with still no sign of an attack, Laura let her guard down, angry that she'd let herself be scared yet again.

It didn't help there was another tropical storm out in the Gulf headed their way.

Late Tuesday afternoon, Laura flipped the Open sign over, turned the showroom lights off, and locked the front door. She'd sent everyone else home a couple of hours earlier so they could take care of their storm preparations.

She felt tired and needed to go home, but frankly, she didn't want to return to an empty house. Well, Doogie was there because she didn't want to have to wrestle with keeping him from running out into the rain. She'd gone home and walked him at lunchtime before returning to the store.

Rob picked up on the third ring.

"Hi, baby girl."

"When do you think you'll be home, Sir?" she asked.

His tone of voice immediately changed to concerned. "Why? Is there a problem?"

"No." She looked out the window at the sky. The tropical storm was predicted to skirt to the south of them, but she still needed to double-check the boats' mooring lines and stow some stuff inside the cabins in case the wind picked up or the storm changed course. "I just don't want to go home yet."

"They have me on stand-by because of the storm. I can probably get away for a couple of hours. Do you want me to come home?"

"Could you? I'm at the shop right now. Meet me here, maybe we can grab a bite and you can follow me home?"

He paused. "What's going on, baby girl?"

"I think it's just the storm." She walked to the back door and glanced at the weather station. "The barometer's dropping a little already. I think it's got me on edge."

"Okay. I'll be there in about an hour. Gotta wait for Cal to get back from the store."

"I need to check the boats anyway."

She hung up, feeling better. She left her cell on the counter and went out the back door. The boats were secure but she liked to double-check. She clung to a piling and carefully climbed down into the larger cruiser, feeling for her keys in her pocket and finding them. The engine hatch was secured, and when she lifted the bilge access cover, the pump float was working and everything looked dry.

Good. It meant one less worry.

She replaced the cover then checked the ports and top hatch inside the cabin. Secured. She climbed out of the cabin hatchway and spied the hose and boat brushes on the dock. *Dang it.*

She sighed and struggled up to the dock, grabbed the brushes and dropped them onto the deck, then unhooked the hose. She'd stow them in the cabin instead of trying to wrestle them into the already crowded dock box.

Laura thought she heard a car pull into the lot at the front of the building, but then shrugged it off. *Probably someone at the real estate office across the street.*

She dropped the hose into the boat and was about to climb back in when she heard a car door shut. Sure it was nothing, but realizing she had to go to the bathroom, she returned to the shop and took care of business first. When she emerged from the back room she was startled by a dark figure standing by the counter.

"Hello, Laura." Don Kern.

"Jesus, you scared me!" Her heart pounded in her chest.

"I didn't mean to scare you."

"We're closed. What do you want?" she snapped as she walked past him and back outside. She didn't want to be rude but between the fright and the impending storm she was on her last nerve.

He followed her out to the dock and didn't offer to help when she climbed into the boat and opened the cabin hatch.

"I just had a couple of questions."

She turned her back to him to pick up the boat brushes from the deck and toss them into the cabin. "Sure, go ahead."

Laura heard the sound of his feet hitting the deck and felt the boat rock under his weight. Before she could turn, he shoved her into the cabin, leaping on her and pinning her to the floor.

She screamed but she couldn't reach behind her to get the gun. His knee dug into her back and he laughed.

"Oh, little momma's packing heat."

She felt him pull up her outer shirt and slide the gun from the holster. Then she froze as he pressed the muzzle against the back of her head.

"We have unfinished business, Laura."

She felt a blinding pain as her world went black.

Chapter Thirty-Seven

Laura came to in the cabin and found herself lying on her side on the bunk. She heard the diesel engines running, smoothly throbbing under the deck.

Her head hurt like a son of a bitch where he'd hit her, and when she tried to move she realized her hands and feet were bound. And there was duct tape over her mouth. At least her hands were taped in front of her. She was still fully dressed, so he hadn't raped her.

Yet.

She hoped the baby hadn't been hurt when she hit the floor.

The cabin hatch was closed. From the way the boat rocked she knew they were moving. Too fast for the long no-wake channel leading to the mouth of the bay, and the swells felt too big, too long, for the shallow channel.

They were in open water.

She managed to shift herself around so she could look out a starboard port. The gunmetal grey sky threatened with dark, heavy clouds building. She tried to see behind them but couldn't get a good enough vantage to see land.

Or else they were too far out.

With no sun, she couldn't use shadows to guess which direction they were heading, either.

Goddammit, what the fuck?

She started to struggle her way off the bunk and then realized her memory had fully returned.

All of it.

She *knew*.

Two days before the attack, she had signed up for the Classfriends site and filled out a profile. A message from the site arrived that very night from Don Kern.

She politely replied before deleting it.

And several more arrived the next day, until she finally set him to ignore.

And deleted all his messages, which explained why she hadn't seen them when she looked in the account.

Kern showed up at her apartment Friday night. She'd been aggravated by the knock on her door, and it was so stupid of her to open it in the first place when she spotted him through the peephole. She was going to tell him to leave or she'd call the police, but when she opened the door he shoved it, knocking her off balance as he rushed in and attacked her.

He kicked the door shut behind him and went after her. She'd screamed, clawed at him, ripping a few nails down to the quick in the process.

"I just want to talk to you, Laura," he'd said in a creepy voice, sounding very calm. "But you're such a bitch, you won't let me. So I won't let you talk to anyone else, either."

He'd hit her, beat her, and still she fought. She tried to get to the kitchen, where there was a knife on the counter from preparing dinner, and he slammed her into the wall. She knew she surprised him with the ferocity of her resistance. He wanted to tie her up and rape her before strangling her, he told her that. Then when she wouldn't stop fighting, he kept hitting her, finally getting the rope around her neck and strangling her…

Laura folded against the bunk.

How could I have been so fucking blind?

He'd wanted to get together with her and she'd politely declined, feeling a little creeped out by his enthusiasm and insistence. She'd made the mistake of putting the shop's website in her profile.

That's how he must have tracked her down.

Dammit!

MedicineMan.

She silently groaned, feeling terminally stupid. He'd baited her that day at lunch, told her what he did for a living and knew he was safe when she didn't react at all.

Shit. Of course, *that's* how he knew she was pregnant. He'd been at the doctor's office the day she found out. Probably overheard the receptionist asking her about Lamaze class information.

Now she wondered if he'd really just "happened" to drop by. The receptionist had said she hadn't been expecting him.

He'd likely followed her.

Wincing, she peeled the duct tape off her mouth, trying to stay quiet. And now her fear took over. He *was* going to kill her. He'd lied at lunch, knowing her memory was gone.

He had asked her out in college, and she'd refused him because she was dating someone else. The psych prof. Yes, that part was true.

She'd turned him down again after joining the Classfriends site when he asked her to go out through the private messages. She'd meant to tell Rob about it and kept forgetting, not thinking anything of it, used to turning down harmless FetLife creeps without a second thought.

In college, she'd paid little attention to Kern, too caught up in her relationship to even notice him, really.

Scanning the cabin, she spied a filet knife stowed in its scabbard, tucked into a cubby next to the small galley sink. Working with the rolling of the boat she made her way to it and managed to free it without stabbing herself.

Then she heard footsteps on the deck. She flopped back onto the bunk, turning her face away from the hatch, the knife clutched in her hands, and lay still.

She heard the cabin hatch open, then close again. He was likely checking to see if she was still out.

She wasn't sure he was gone until she heard his steps on the deck again. Sitting up, she held the knife handle between her knees and sawed through the tape. Once her feet were free she looked around for a weapon. She couldn't bring a knife to a gun fight—he'd simply shoot her.

She needed distance.

Unfortunately, the knife was her best—her *only* weapon. Then she had to grab the counter as the boat hit a hard swell and pounded into a deep trough, nearly throwing her off her feet.

Dumbass obviously doesn't know how to pilot a boat.

But a metallic rattle overhead drew her attention and she looked up.

Of course!

* * * *

Rob arrived at the shop and walked around back. "Laur?"

He went inside and found her cell phone on the counter. "Honey?" He stuck his head into the office, no sign of her. Then he realized what was wrong.

He ran to the back door and looked out again.

The cruiser was gone. "Shit."

He called 911 first, then Steve. Thomas showed up twenty minutes later while he was giving his statement to the responding deputies.

"How do you know something's wrong?" Thomas asked.

"She would never take the boat out in weather like this, for starters. And she was waiting for me. Plus there's a strange car in the parking lot."

Steve ran in. "What's wrong?"

Rob gave him the short version. "He's right," Steve said. "She wouldn't do that. Not willingly." He went behind the counter to the VHF radio, turned it on, and grabbed the mic.

"Lemon Dive One, Lemon Dive One, this is Lemon Dive Base, over." He let up on the button and they waited.

* * * *

Laura heard Steve on the radio from inside the cabin. Kern must have turned it on. There was a moment of silence before Steve repeated the hail.

"Lemon Dive One, Lemon Dive One, this is Lemon Dive Base. Laura, you out there? Over."

A relieved breath escaped her.

Thank god, at least they know I'm missing.

She heard the engines throttle back, idling. Kern thought she was still passed out, obviously. Then came the sound of him walking up to the bow, followed by the sound of him opening the front bow locker hatch and the rattle of anchor chain against the deck as he removed it.

Apparently he didn't know what the windlass was for. That was the spare anchor he'd tossed, the small one. In seas like this, it wouldn't hold, it would drag. It was mostly for back-up. They'd end up crossways to the waves with the wind blowing across it.

She shut down those thoughts as she made her hands race faster.

"Lemon Dive One, this is Base. Laura, if you don't answer, I'm calling Ft. Myers Beach. Over."

She knew he meant the Coast Guard station.

She heard the anchor hit the water and hurried her preparations, knowing she would only have one shot to do this. The speargun had a powerhead holder shaft affixed to the side. Fortunately, Steve kept a stash of .223 blanks in the cabin. Her hands trembled as she loaded the round into the powerhead and twisted it down, not yet arming it.

She examined the bands on the gun. One was a little dried out and cracked, but the other looked nearly new. She checked the spear and found it was secure.

She was out of practice, and it was harder to do on a pitching boat and with a baby belly, but she propped the gun butt against her thigh and managed to cock the band before she thumbed off the safety.

Then she armed the powerhead and backed into the alcove, wedged between the tiny galley on her right and the entry on her left, and waited.

Kern stumbled on his way back from the bow. She prayed for a splash but no such luck. He regained his footing and she followed his progress, heard him jump down from the gunwale to the deck. He paused long enough for her to wonder what he was doing before she heard him approach the hatchway.

She braced herself, holding the speargun ready. He wouldn't see her at first, would have to come down the steps before he could turn around to see her, and she could nail him.

The cabin door opened. He paused for a moment. "Okay, Laura, where are you? Playing hide-and-seek, are we?"

As expected, he stepped down. She let out a war whoop, jabbing him with the powerhead as she lunged. He screamed as it caught him in the back of the right thigh. She nearly dropped the speargun from the shock of the concussion but managed to hold onto it in the dim, crowded cabin.

He continued screaming in agony and dropped the gun to the cabin floor.

It went off. She heard the report but didn't know where the round hit. She realized she was still screaming, too—in rage. He fell on his back to the cabin floor, clutching his right thigh in his hands.

She fired the speargun for good measure. His screams turned into desperate, pained shrieks as the shaft pierced his abdomen.

"Go to hell, you son of a bitch!" The shaft end was still in the speargun and she yanked back, trying to free it, determined to hit him with the butt of the gun.

He wrapped his hands around the spear shaft, a gruesome tug of war going on between them. Every time she yanked the speargun, he writhed in agony, shrieking in pain. He was bleeding from his leg, and the wings on the shaft point pulled against his flesh as she yanked on it. She finally ripped the speargun free, the shaft still embedded in his gut, and he screamed again.

Kern was too busy with his own pain to fight back. Laura loaded and cocked a new shaft. The guns and shafts were normally securely stowed in the cabin's overhead compartment. She'd stripped the other guns of their extra shafts and had the shafts propped in the galley corner behind her.

He'll look like a goddamn porcupine when I'm finished with the son of a bitch.

An alarm went off in the cockpit, barely audible over Kern's inhuman screeching and finally grabbing her attention.

The bilge. She looked down and realized while Kern was still squirming, he was now splashing as well. Apparently the bullet—the hollow-point doing its job well—had breached the hull somewhere below the waterline.

"Shit!" She grabbed the spare shafts and scrambled up the steps through the open hatch, snagging a life vest from where they were stowed as she passed them.

Then the engines died.

Down in the cabin, Kern still screamed.

"*Shut up!*" she yelled down at him. "*Just fucking die already, asshole!*"

Laura slammed the cabin hatch shut behind her. There was the padlock on the dash, her keys still hanging from it. She grabbed the keys and shoved them into her pocket, then padlocked the hatch.

The mic swung from the radio in time with the pitching of the boat, and just behind it she spied the EPIRB beacon. She ripped it from its holder and flipped it upside down, activating it. Then she dropped it to the dash and prayed the signal was activated. She put on her Mae West and tightened the strap before grabbing the mic.

The boat was noticeably listing now, the bilge pumps unable to keep up with the water. As she tried, and failed, to start the engines, Kern still screamed from inside the cabin.

She gave that up as she realized she wouldn't be able to go up and cut the anchor loose in time, anyway. Laura knew from the rapid listing of the boat that she didn't have enough time to start the GPS and wait for it to get a fix on her position.

"Mayday, mayday, mayday. Coast Guard Station Ft. Myers Beach. This is the Lemon Dive One. I have activated my EPIRB. Rapidly taking on water."

She hoped the operator could understand her between her fear and the background scream of the bilge alarm. She was trying to remember protocol, stay calm, and failing.

"Mayday, mayday, mayday, Ft. Myers Beach. Lemon Dive one. Thirty-foot, white cabin cruiser. We are rapidly taking on water through a hull breach. I have an active EPIRB beacon, and I cannot fix my location by GPS. Over."

Laura closed her eyes and prayed and finally, through the static, she heard a woman's voice. *"Lemon Dive One, this is Coast Guard Station Ft. Myers Beach. Please stand by while we fix your EPIRB signal location. All traffic clear this channel immediately. Over."*

Laura clutched the mic and sobbed with relief.

Then she let out a shriek when the cabin hatch vibrated. Kern was up and moving and pissed off and apparently not dead yet. Not if he still had enough life left in him to hit the door.

"Ft. Myers, please hurry. There's two persons on board, but I've got him locked in the cabin. He's trying to kill me!"

* * * *

They heard her distress call. Steve grabbed the boat keys and bolted for the back door, Rob and Thomas on his heels. Thomas barked orders at the deputies as he ran.

At least she was alive.

Steve jumped into the other boat while Rob and Thomas untied the lines and cast off before jumping down to join him on the deck. It was two hours before dark and the seas were building. If they couldn't find her, they would lose her as the weather deteriorated and search choppers were grounded.

Thomas ordered Steve to ignore the no-wake signs and they flew down the channel through the deepening gloom toward the mouth of the bay.

"Rob, get the jackets," Steve ordered as he pointed with one hand at the cabin. "It's going to be rough out there." He opened the electronics compartment while steering with one hand and got the GPS started.

Rob dug three life vests out, taking the wheel for Steve while he donned his. The smaller boat didn't have as large a cabin as the cruiser, and with a narrower beam it wouldn't fair nearly as well in the rough seas.

But the twin outboards had at least three times the speed of the slow and steady diesels on the larger boat.

Over the radio, the Coast Guard operator broke in. *"Security, security, security. Hello all stations. This is the United States Coast Guard Station Ft. Myers Beach. We have a report of a vessel in immediate distress and taking on water with activated EPIRB beacon. The vessel is the Lemon Dive One, a thirty-foot white cabin cruiser, two persons on board. All vessels in the vicinity are asked to render assistance if possible…"*

The message repeated, giving the lat-long coordinates again.

Rob scribbled them down and punched them into the GPS, swearing while it took its time refreshing.

Finally, he was able to plot the course. "Four miles out."

Steve adjusted his heading and pushed the engines as hard as he dared in the deepening swells. They couldn't help Laura if they cracked the hull.

Thomas got on his radio and called in the coordinates to the sheriff's boat on stand-by. "And somebody call the Coast Guard and warn them about Kern. Tell them he's armed and dangerous and to be apprehended and taken into custody on suspicion of multiple counts of murder, as well as assault and attempted murder."

A man's voice broke through on the radio. *"Coast Guard Station Ft. Myers, this is the shrimper Pelican Bay. We are two miles north-northwest of that location, and proceeding to render assistance. Over."*

* * * *

Laura heard the exchange on the radio and screamed as Kern banged into the cabin hatch again. She keyed the mic and, ignoring protocol, yelled into it.

"Please, *hurry*. He's not dead yet. He's got a gun and he's trying to kill me!"

Despite her training she abandoned all attempts to remain calm. The deck was now awash. At this rate, with the seas as high as they were, they'd flounder in a few minutes. "You've got to hurry. *Please*."

She dropped the mic and yanked the life ring free from its Velcro straps holding it to the outside of the cabin wall. Then she pulled herself to her feet and stuck one foot through the ring to keep it in place on the deck. The EPIRB beacon now rolled back and forth on the dash as the anchor dragged and the wind took the boat and pushed it crossways to the swell. She grabbed the beacon and stuffed it down the front of her shirt, hoping the life vest would keep it in place.

Rob's voice came through the radio. "*Laura, honey, we're on our way. Stay calm. We've got the coordinates. We're coming.*"

The Coast Guard Operator broke in. "*Vessel, clear this channel immediately.*"

She grabbed the mic, beyond caring who heard her. "Sir, he's got my gun. I shot him with a powerhead, but he's got my gun. We're swamping."

"*Vessel Lemon Dive One, this is Coast Guard Station Ft. Myers Beach. Ma'am, stay calm. We have a rescue chopper en route and a commercial vessel is close by. Do you have a life jacket on? Over.*"

"You bet your *fucking ass* I do, Ft. Myers!"

It wasn't raining yet, but the wind was picking up and the temperature dropping, so it wouldn't be long.

She turned around and in the distance, the compass showed northwest, she spied vessel lights. Hopefully the shrimper. It was hard to tell from the brief glimpses she got before the boat dropped hard into each trough.

Laura keyed the mic again. "I think I see the shrimper."

She screamed at the loud bang. The cabin hatch exploded, a huge hole appearing in it. Kern stuck his arm through, blindly waving the gun. She dropped the mic and lunged with the speargun, impaling his wrist. She fired and yanked the speargun free from the shaft.

He dropped the gun and she reflexively grabbed it, tossing it overboard without thinking and mentally swearing at herself as it disappeared beneath the surface of the stormy Gulf.

Kern's voice roared over the sound of the wind, inhuman. *"I'm going to kill you, you fucking bitch!"* He flailed against the door, his other hand appearing as he tried to free himself but the shaft was long and kept him from twisting his arm.

That's when Laura felt the baby move. She slipped a hand under the life vest. Sure enough, she felt it again.

A sudden, unexpected calm descended over her. Laura dug another .223 round out of her pocket and fumbled it into the powerhead. She spun it down onto the shaft, arming it.

"No you're not, you bastard." She jabbed the speargun through the hole in the door and his scream nearly drowned out the sound of the report.

He stopped moving. She stepped back, trying not to stumble as the boat rolled again. She didn't look, didn't want to see. From the new angle of his arm through the door, he had to be dead. She must have caught him in the chest or head. Wherever it was, it was dead-on.

She dropped the speargun and grabbed the mic with one hand, the life ring with the other.

Her momentary calm quickly dispersed. "Ft. Myers Beach, this is Lemon Dive One. I'm swamping. I don't have much time. I've got the EPIRB beacon on me. Repeat, I have the EPIRB beacon on my person. Over."

"Lemon Dive One, this is Coast Guard Station Ft. Myers Beach. Roger. We have vessels and a rescue chopper en route to your location. Over."

"Roger, Ft. Myers. I have to go up to the bow. I won't be able to transmit. I'm sending up flares. Over." She turned up the volume on the radio and dropped the mic.

The water sloshing around in the stern had reached her ankles. The batteries, in a dry compartment in the dash, wouldn't last much longer. She didn't have a life raft on board, but the flare kit was stowed in the dash. She grabbed it and jammed it into her shirt, too. It was a tight fit between the life vest and the EPIRB beacon, but it was her only choice. With the life ring over one shoulder, she kicked off her sandals and carefully climbed onto the slippery gunwale, working her way up the pitching boat to the bow, gripping the wet handrails with all her strength. The cabin was higher, would keep her out of the water a few minutes longer.

There were definitely lights coming from the northwest, and now from the east, too. She pulled out the flare kit, trying to calm herself and not drop them or let them get wet. Her hands trembled from the shock and the stress and the cold. She was wet, soaked through from the spray.

Forcing herself to wait another minute to give them a chance to close in, she figured the wind direction and finally lifted her arms, closing her eyes as she fired the flare gun. Then she grabbed the cabin rail when the boat rolled again, barely keeping herself from sliding off the bow.

The flare swooped into the sky, exploding before finally fizzling out.

A moment later the radio came to life. "*Laura? Honey? We saw it. We're coming. Hang tight, honey—*"

"*Coast Guard Ft. Myers Beach, this is the Pelican Bay, we saw a flare. We're about a half mile from last reported location. Over.*"

Laura's teeth chattered. She couldn't tell what were tears and what was sea spray on her face. She forced herself to wait another twenty seconds, counting Mississippis as she did, before she sent up another flare.

The shrimper's lights were closing in, but her entire stern was submerged. The radio and bilge alarm died as the batteries went under. She had maybe a minute left before the boat sank.

The wind picked up, howling, and then the rain. She quickly fired her last two flares, including the test flare from the kit, and dropped the gun. All the while she prayed she didn't lose the EPIRB beacon, knowing if she did she'd die in the storm.

The deck pitched beneath her as a large wave finished the boat. It capsized, throwing her into the water. She nearly lost the life ring but managed to hold on to it somehow. With the hull still visible she swam for the boat while each swell tried to push her farther away.

She sobbed and took in a mouthful of salt water. Coughing, she flipped onto her back, clutching the life ring, and tried to control herself.

I can do this.

She had flotation, she had a life vest, she had the EPIRB, the water was relatively warm.

I am trained. Just float. Cough, swallow. Float and wait. Cough, swallow.

The baby kicked again.

What little calm she'd salvaged evaporated. Her baby! She had to stay with the boat!

She struggled to kick as another wave broke over her. She felt dizzy, coughing, struggling to breathe, and had just enough strength to flip onto her back again when she saw a bright, white light sweep over her.

No! She didn't want to die. *Not like this, please!*

She lost consciousness.

* * * *

Rob and Thomas held on for dear life, both soaked from spray. Steve's face grim, he pushed the boat as fast as he dared through the rough seas. In the distance they saw the shrimper light up, all its work lights blazing in the deepening gloom, its search spot sweeping the water.

They were less than a mile from the location when they heard the radio.

"*Coast Guard Station Ft. Myers Beach, this is the Pelican Bay. We've recovered one person from the water, they are unresponsive. Administering CPR now. Request instructions, over.*"

"*No!*" Rob pounded his fist on the dash. "No, goddammit, no!"

"Rob, we don't know if it's her," Thomas tried to reassure him when the Coast Guard came back on and gave instructions. Proceed on their course heading to meet with the rescue chopper. When the radio traffic paused, Steve grabbed the mic.

"Pelican Bay, this is Lemon Dive Two. We have visual contact and are proceeding to your location. We're less than a mile off your port bow. Did you recover a man or a woman? Over."

There was a pause during which Rob thought for sure his heart would stop.

"*Lemon Dive Two, this is Pelican Bay. I see you. We recovered a woman. Over.*"

Rob sobbed as his knees gave out and he collapsed to the deck.

Steve left him to Thomas. Between the boat and the radio and his own emotions, he had his hands full. "Roger, Pelican Bay. Please be advised she's four months pregnant. I have her husband with me, he's a paramedic. Over."

"Lemon Dive Two, roger that. Approach from my starboard aft, he can board from there, but it'll be rough. Standing by channel one-six. Over."

Steve looked to the north and saw the rescue chopper in the distance, racing in from Clearwater. They would drop a basket and a rescue swimmer. He nudged the throttles up, pushing the engines a little harder, trying to reach the shrimper first and silently praying.

Chapter Thirty-Eight

Laura's head hurt like hell. And her chest. It felt like someone had pounded on it. Her throat hurt, too, scratchy. She took a breath that set off a coughing fit, and it felt like she was choking on water. Someone rolled her over and she was aware of voices, what felt like a pitching deck beneath her...

* * * *

A loud roar filled her ears before the world shifted and dipped. She thought she heard Rob's voice, or was it Steve's? And then the world disappeared again...

* * * *

"*No!*" Laura sat bolt upright, screaming, thrashing, fighting. She had to get to the boat, she had to swim—

"Laura!" Rob gently shook her, his hands on her arms, his face in hers. "Honey, it's okay. You're safe."

The scream died on her lips and she stared at him, reaching for him. "Sir!"

He engulfed her in his arms as she cried, sobbing, relieved. "It's okay," he soothed her, burying his face in her hair. "You're okay, baby girl. You're safe."

"Where am I?"

* * * *

Rob's gut clenched. "You're at Bayfront. The chopper brought you to the Clearwater air station and they transported you here." But she knew him.

That was good, right?

"The boat—"

"It's gone. They'll send a recovery team after the storm clears."

"He's dead, Sir. I killed him. It was Don Kern." She cried, long and hard while he rocked her, holding her.

Rob breathed a sigh of relief. Apparently she remembered him. His not-so-secret fear, debilitating, sitting like a knife-riddled rock in his stomach, had been that she would wake up firmly in the clutches of the amnesia again.

"It's okay, honey. You're safe."

She looked terrified to ask. "The baby?" she finally whispered.

"She's fine."

"Oh, good—" She pulled back and stared at him. "She?"

Rob smiled. "Sorry. I know you wanted to be surprised. I didn't even think about it when they examined you. I was just so relieved that they said you're both—"

She kissed him, cutting off his words. "Thank you, Sir." She touched his face, as if trying to absorb his image. "What happened? I thought I was dead. I saw this bright light. I thought I was drowning."

Rob tried to stifle the laugh but didn't quite succeed. "It was the shrimper's searchlight."

They'd pulled up to the shrimper minutes before the chopper. Rob had enough time to scramble on board and examine her, trying to push his personal feelings aside and treat her like a critical patient and not let his emotions knock him back.

The shrimper crew had already cleared her airway and got her breathing again before he arrived, but she didn't regain consciousness. He couldn't go with the chopper, because it would have taken too long to load him, and was too dangerous with the rapidly deteriorating weather. Instead, he rode back to the shop with Steve and Thomas, who had a marked cruiser drive him all the way up to St. Petersburg, to Bayfront Hospital, with lights and sirens running.

"How long have I been here?" she asked.

"Just a few hours. They want to keep an eye on you, to watch for pneumonia. You swallowed a lot of water. They'll probably let you out in a day or two."

She nodded and lay back on the bed, closing her eyes, his hands clutched in hers. "But the baby—"

He nodded, kissing her hand and holding it, not letting go. "She's fine. Totally healthy. No problems."

* * * *

Laura covered her eyes. "I remember everything, Sir."

"I was afraid you might have amnesia again."

"No. I mean I have it all back." She finally looked at him. "I remember the attack, before. Everything." She reached up and stroked his cheek. "I remember *You*...Sir."

His eyes went wide as she nodded at him. The slow smile that lit his face filled her with love.

She told him what happened. "Then he came into the shop after I hung up with you. I was securing the boats, and he jumped me, knocked me out."

He looked down. "I'm sorry. If I'd been there—"

"No. Stop." She grabbed his hand. "Look at me, *Sir*, this is not your fault."

He stared at her. She could tell he wasn't convinced.

"Well, twice now this asshole nearly killed you because I wasn't there for you."

"He won't get a third try, Sir."

He brought her hands up to his lips and kissed them. "Are you really okay, baby girl?" he whispered.

She nodded, unable to hide her smile. "I am now."

There was a knock on the door and Rob turned. "Come in."

Thomas stuck his head in. "Is she awake?"

"Yes."

The detective entered. "How are you?"

"I remember everything. It was Don Kern the whole time."

Thomas nodded. "His car was parked at the shop. It was his girlfriend we found dead."

Laura felt ill. She remembered. The girl from the dive. Another victim. "Tammy Smith?"

A frown filled the detective's face. "How did you know? We just ID'd her an hour ago."

"She went out on a dive with him that Saturday morning. I was at the shop when the charter returned. He must have killed her that afternoon. Oh, god—"

Rob grabbed the wastebasket as Laura dry heaved, but she didn't vomit. He rang for a nurse, who came in and checked on her before leaving again to fetch the doctor.

Thomas was still there, had moved into the corner and now spoke. "I know it's a bad time to ask for a statement—"

"He's dead," she said flatly. "I shot him with a speargun. Multiple times. And a powerhead. Unless the cabin hatch gave way after it sank, he's still in there. If the powerhead didn't kill him by the time the boat sank, then he must have drowned."

He nodded. "Okay. When you're discharged, call me. I'll come take your statement."

Alone again, Rob looked at her. "It's over." He leaned in and kissed her forehead as he rested a hand on her stomach. "You're finally safe. Both of you."

"I feel like a different person."

"Well, that's understandable."

She shook her head. "No. I mean it. Like there's these two halves of me that are back together. I had some memories of before, but it was different. Like I was looking at things from an outside perspective without the context. Now I have all the original feelings and memories back, but there's this new part of me from the attack until now."

* * * *

Rob felt a chill run down his spine. He wasn't sure he liked where this conversation headed. "Is that good or bad?"

She met his eyes and smiled. "Don't worry, *Sir*. All of my parts love you."

He grinned. "You sure have a way of scaring me, you know that?"

"Gotta yank your chain, Fireman." She winked.

She *was* back. All of her. Even her voice sounded different. Or, depending on your point of view, she finally sounded normal again. Some might say it was from coughing up seawater, but even how she talked sounded different, not just her voice.

She sounded confident, assured. Her old self.

Rob's smile grew. "Gonna ring your bell, baby girl." He leaned in and kissed her again. "Glad to have you back."

She snuggled tightly against him, his shirt clutched in her fingers as if she was afraid he might leave her.

"I'm glad to be back, Sir."

Epilogue

Rob was prepared to help Laura through the nightmares he'd expected her to have. Surprisingly, she slept like a rock most nights, rarely waking unless she had to go to the bathroom. Which, as the baby grew, was frequently.

Having her memory back in full was a weird sensation for him. He'd gotten so used to the new Laura, so similar and yet different from his old Laura, that it was an odd adjustment going back.

The doctors assured them it likely wasn't the blow to the head so much as the emotional stress that brought back the memories. But it was a coinkydink, as Laura said. However it happened, they didn't care.

She noticed his discomfort. She was five months pregnant, and he was off for forty-eight hours on rotation. He had her feet propped in his lap, rubbing them, watching the original *Night of the Living Dead* with her. He wore shorts and a T-shirt.

She wore her leather collar, wrist and ankle cuffs, and her wedding ring.

And nothing else.

She cocked her head as she studied him.

"What?" he finally asked.

"You miss her a little, don't you?"

Rob stared at her. "Huh?"

Laura smiled. "The new me. You miss her."

"You're one person."

"I acted differently though. You and I both know it. I can see it all, looking back. I was a totally different person."

He shrugged. "I'm glad you're back to normal."

"Whatever *that* is."

He laughed. "Hey, baby girl, trust me when I say it doesn't matter how I have you, I do have you. That's all that matters to me."

She patted her stomach. "We have the proof of you having me right here, Sir."

He laughed. Old Laura shared her bawdy side with him, even though she acted professional at work. New Laura had been more reserved in that way. Tentative.

He'd missed her frequent laughter. "I didn't hear you complaining all the times I had you."

"Thank you, Sir, may I have another?" Their play had changed as her pregnancy progressed. He was afraid of inadvertently hurting her or the baby, so they'd downshifted to more sensual play, gentler.

And he was happy to do it.

Although he still gave her maintenance spankings, because it broke his heart to see the sadness in her eyes when he'd suggested giving up on those, too. Now, she stood and bent over the bed for those, without putting any pressure on her belly.

He was satisfied it wouldn't hurt the baby doing it like that, which had been his overwhelming concern.

He put her foot down and grabbed her arm, hauling her into his lap and kissing her. He caressed her belly. "You can have it all you want. Maybe I'll keep you barefoot and pregnant."

She wrapped her arms around his neck and nibbled his ear. "Might put a crimp in our sex life, too many kids running around. Maybe I'll take you to Doogie's vet."

He smiled. "You wouldn't do that to me, would you, baby girl?"

"No, I don't suppose I will." She snuggled against him, her head on his shoulder. New Laura hadn't been as much of a snuggler as Old Laura. That was one thing he was definitely glad was back to normal. They'd spent hours…before…wrapped together in front of the TV. Not that she had to be glued to him, but it was their personal thing.

And boy, how he'd missed it.

"I missed all of this," she admitted. "I didn't realize it then, Sir. I'm sorry." But she still wore the slightest of frowns.

He wrapped his arms tightly around her. "I'm sorry we didn't have the wedding you wanted."

"That's the least of my worries." She met his gaze and smiled. "Am I too heavy to carry to bed, Sir?"

He grinned. "I thought you'd never ask."

He carried her into the bedroom and gently lowered her to the bed. As he stood over her and stripped, he stared down into her loving gaze. So beautiful, and now her eyes were filled with nothing but peace.

No fear.

No worry.

Nothing but their future ahead of them.

Naked, he climbed onto the bed and kissed her before swinging around, positioning his cock over her open mouth. "Come as many times as you want, baby girl."

He laughed as she grabbed his ass and yanked him down on top of her, her soft moan vibrating through his cock as she happily began sucking his cock.

She spread her thighs wider when he dipped his head to her pussy. Clean-shaven, as ordered, he swiped his tongue down her clit and another, louder moan from her vibrated through him.

He struggled to hold back and get her over first. He'd loved doing this with her before she got pregnant, but even more now because she'd happily discovered she was hornier than ever.

And more sensitive than ever.

It only took him a minute to get the first orgasm out of her. Her fingers dug into his ass, almost painfully, as her back arched.

He inwardly smiled and redoubled his efforts. Two fingers easily slid into her wet cunt as he sucked and licked her clit. Before long, another round of loud, long moans, accompanied by her slick muscles squeezing his fingers inside her pussy, signaled he'd gotten her over again.

He waited until he knew he'd gotten four out of her and her entire body quivered beneath him before he took pity on her. Bracing himself with his arms to keep most his weight off her, he began rocking his hips, setting the tempo and letting her catch up and match his movements with her talented mouth.

"That's it," he encouraged, his eyes falling shut. "Just like that, baby girl. Suck your Master's cock."

A tiny moan escaped her. She loved it when he talked to her like that during sex. Something else he was so glad was back to normal.

"My good little cocksucker, aren't you? Yes, you are."

She undulated beneath him, her pace quickening, sucking harder, reaching between his legs to cup his sac and gently roll his balls along her palm.

That was all it took. He drove deep, Laura keeping up with him and skillfully deep-throating him, patiently waiting until he was ready to move before she dropped her head back to the bed with a happy sigh.

He laughed and turned around, pulling her into his arms. "Better, baby girl?"

She snuggled tightly against him, hooking a leg around his. "Always, Sir. You always make everything better."

* * * *

That Saturday night, Rob wouldn't tell her where they were going. But he'd picked out a plain black sundress for her to wear, and flat sandals.

She also suspected the duffel bag he'd tossed in the backseat held her leather cuffs and a leash.

Sure enough, they parked in front of Venture. When Rob shut the engine off, he turned to her.

"I know things are about to change for us in a big way in a couple of months. But I want to do this before that happens."

She nodded.

"We won't get a lot of chances to be here once the baby's born. Not at first. I wanted to do this now, while we can still—"

"Enjoy it, Sir?" She smiled.

He laughed. "Yes, my sweet baby girl."

He grabbed the bag and walked around to her side to help her out. She knew from the cars in the parking lot that most of their friends were already there. Sure enough, Loren had put her mad party skills to good use decorating the club.

Everyone applauded when they entered. Laura felt her face heat.

Tony called for quiet. "Now that the guests of honor have arrived, let's get started."

Someone had decorated a little archway. In front of it sat a pillow Laura recognized as one of Shayla's. Rob led her over to it and helped her kneel.

He turned and set the duffel bag on the floor and rummaged through it for a moment, but she didn't see what he had in his hand when he straightened.

She looked up at him, watching him as he spoke and so painfully in love with him she knew everything they'd gone through since the attack in March had been worth it.

Anything was worth going through to be with him.

To be *owned* by *Him*.

Rob looked at their friends, who gathered close. "You guys have been beyond wonderful all these months. We never could have made it through without your help and love and support. We ended up improvising our wedding, which we'd originally planned to do in front of you all after I formally collared her."

He looked down at her. "But better late than never." He smiled as a soft wave of laughter rolled through the audience.

He held up what he'd pulled from the bag, a velvet jewelry box.

She felt the lump in her throat and hoped she didn't start bawling in front of everyone.

He opened it. Inside lay a gold necklace with a heart-shaped locket. He took it out and stood in front of her.

"We've been through a lot lately. But I knew when I first met you how special you were. I was willing to wait as long as it took to not just make you my wife, but to make you my slave, if you wanted it.

"I consider myself damn lucky that I got a second chance with you, and even luckier that you picked me the second time around. No matter what you say next, you are my friend, my wife, my lover, my reason for being, my partner, and the soon-to-be mother of our child. Beyond all of that, and above all of it, I wanted to ask you in front of all our friends, will you please be my slave?"

She couldn't speak, but as the tears filled her eyes, she nodded hard enough to rattle her back teeth.

He smiled. "Is that a yes?"

"Yes, Sir!"

He knelt in front of her and fastened the necklace around her throat, touching the locket as he centered it against her flesh. "You have made me the happiest man in the world."

She threw her arms around him and kissed him as their friends cheered.

"I love you, Sir," she whispered.

He smiled, brushing her tears away with his thumbs. "I love you, too, baby girl. But I'm still going to bend you over a spanking horse and put five cane strokes across your ass tonight."

She let out a laugh. "Why?"

He grinned. "Because I want to."

THE END

WWW.TYMBERDALTON.COM

ABOUT THE AUTHOR

Tymber Dalton lives in the Tampa Bay region of Florida with her husband (aka "The World's Best Husband™") and too many pets. Not only is she active in the BDSM lifestyle, the two-time EPIC winner is also the bestselling author of nearly fifty books, such as *The Reluctant Dom*, *The Denim Dom*, *Cardinal's Rule*, the Love Slave for Two series, the Triple Trouble series, the Coffeeshop Coven series, the Good Will Ghost Hunting series, and many more.

She loves to hear from readers! Please feel free to drop by her website and sign up for her newsletter to keep abreast of the latest news, views, snarkage, and releases. (Don't forget to look up her writing alter egos Lesli Richardson, Tessa Monroe, and Macy Largo.)

www.tymberdalton.com
www.facebook.com/tymberdalton
www.twitter.com/TymberDalton

For all titles by Tymber Dalton, please visit
www.bookstrand.com/tymber-dalton

For titles by Tymber Dalton writing as
Lesli Richardson
www.bookstrand.com/lesli-richardson
Tessa Monroe
www.bookstrand.com/tessa-monroe
Macy Largo
www.bookstrand.com/macy-largo

Siren Publishing, Inc.
www.SirenPublishing.com

CPSIA information can be obtained
at www.ICGtesting.com
Printed in the USA
LVOW04s0222300116
472285LV00023BB/657/P